That

Loving Chris Henderson … at is there about him to love? … at's on a good day … but there was one achingly obvious fact that haunted my every thought, every minute of every day …

He sure could kiss.

As the countdown to the new millennium begins, there is one thing everyone agrees on: no one wants to be in Onslow for New Year's Eve.

So that can only mean one thing: road trip!

No longer the mousey, invisible, shy girl from years ago, Tammy Maskala is finally making up for all those lost summers. A new year with new friends, which astoundingly includes the bossy boy behind the bar, Chris Henderson.

She likes her new friends (at least most of them), so why does she secretly feel so out of place?

After chickening out on the trip, a last-minute change of heart sees Tammy racing to the Onslow Hotel, fearing she's missed her chance for a ride. The last thing she expected to meet was a less-than-happy Onslow Boy leaning against his black panel van.

Now the countdown begins to reach the others at Point Shank before the party is over and the new year has begun. Alone in a car with only the infuriating Chris Henderson, Tammy can't help but feel this is a disastrous start to what could have been a great adventure. But when the awkward road trip takes an unexpected turn, Tammy soon discovers that the way her traitorous heart feels about Chris is the biggest disaster of all.

Fogged up windows, moonlight swimming, bad karaoke and unearthed secrets; after this one summer nothing will ever be the same again.

That One Summer

C.J. Duggan

PUBLIC LIBRARIES OF SAGINAW

JAN 2 2 2015

BUTMAN-FISH BRANCH LIBRARY
1716 HANCOCK
SAGINAW, MI 48602

That One Summer
A Summer Series Novel, Book Three
Copyright © 2013 by C.J Duggan

Published by C.J Duggan
Australia, NSW
www.cjdugganbooks.com

First Kindle edition, published December 2013
All rights reserved.

This book is protected under the copyright laws of the United States of America. Any reproduction or other unauthorized use of the material or artwork herein is prohibited.

Disclaimer: The persons, places, things, and otherwise animate or inanimate objects mentioned in this novel are figments of the author's imagination. Any resemblance to anything or anyone living (or dead) is unintentional.

Edited by Sarah Billington|Billington Media
Copyedited by Anita Saunders
Proofreading by Sascha Craig, Lori Heaford, Frankie Rose

Cover Art by Keary Taylor Indie Designs
This ebook formatted by E.M. Tippetts Book Designs

Author Photograph © 2013 C.J Duggan

That One Summer is also available as a paperback at Amazon

Contact the author at cand.duu@gmail.com

PRAISE FOR
The Boys of Summer

Summer Lovin'

This book kept me up until the wee hours of the morning because I literally could not force myself to put it down – I just had to know what happened. Everything about *The Boys of Summer* absolutely blew me away.

Claire - Claire Reads

Best Contemporary Read of your Life

I cannot begin to describe the love I have for this book. *The Boys of Summer* is a story about self-discovery and first true love that will stay with you for a long time after you read it.

Hannah - A Girl in a Cafe

Fun, Flirty, Fantastic

All in all, if you're looking for a lovable and intense read, then this is for you. C.J Duggan has convinced me she belongs in the contemporary market and I cannot wait to read more from her.

Donna - Book Passion for Life

An Australian Gem

You won't regret buying this one; you'll totally fall in love with the story and all of the characters. C.J Duggan knows how to write a book you'll just be drawn into! I'm already waiting for the next one – impatiently, might I add! *The Boys of Summer* is an Australian gem!

Seirra - Dear, Restless Reader

Simply Perfect

Everything about *The Boys of Summer* was fantastic!!! C.J Duggan has written an amazing story and she was able to perfectly capture the Aussie summer, fun times with friends both new and old, and all the feelings of falling in love with the boy of your dreams. Bring on book two!!!

Tracey - YA Book Addict

Sweet, Intoxicating, Exciting

The Boys of Summer is a wonderful example of just how deliciously sexy, sweet and charming summer-fling books can be! A book that gives you goose bumps, makes you swoon over its incredibly handsome male cast, gets you hooked on the clever plot line and, ultimately, sends you out feeling all warm inside, satisfied and with a wide smile on your face.

Evie - Bookish

Also by C.J. Duggan
The Boys of Summer
An Endless Summer

Look out for
Someone Like You
Forever Summer
The Anita Bowman Diaries

www.cjdugganbooks.com

Dedicated to Jenny.
We met under the most extraordinary of circumstances,
that has now grown into the most extraordinary of friendships.

"Always remember to be happy because you never know who's falling in love with your smile."

\- Anon

Chapter One

Christmas night, 1999

Honestly! Whose idea was this anyway?

My hands slid along the hallway plaster, my only guide in the pitch blackness. One tentative foot in front of the other, I slowly skimmed along the carpet.

The only thing that pierced the silence was the faint calling from downstairs.

"87-cat-and-dog-88-cat-and-dog …"

Oh crap!

I shuffled along more urgently, my fingers scrabbling along the wall, hands searching faster. I was nowhere I wanted to be, that was for sure. Not that I knew where I was, exactly. Even in the long, dark hall I knew I was way too exposed.

I was too old for this.

My searching hands dipped into an alcove. Ah-ha! The feel of glossy moulded panels caused my pulse to race. Blindly, I fumbled at the new sensation under my fingertips, my heart skipping a beat when my palm brushed … a *handle?*

Eureka! A door.

"99-cat-and-dog-100 … Ready or not, here I come!"

Oh my God! Please open, please open.

Grabbing the handle, I wasn't sure what I feared the most – the door being locked or the sound of the handle twisting.

I braced my hand on the panel. Pushing inward, the door gave way but my relief was short-lived as it let out a painfully loud creak. I paused, frozen with the tension of possibly being discovered. Had I given myself away? I panicked as heavy footsteps sounded on the staircase, closing the distance. My eyes widened.

"One, two, Freddie's coming for you … Three, four, better lock your door." His voice sing-songed tauntingly up the stairs.

I threw caution to the wind and opened the door quickly, slipped through and shut it gently behind me with a click they probably could have heard in China. I winced at the sound and stood still.

Trying to control my breathing, I abandoned the door behind me, edging into the room; the all-consuming darkness was disorientating. I flailed my arms outward like a deranged zombie and stopped abruptly when my knees hit the edge of a … bed? My fingertips rested on the spongy surface, anchoring myself.

Yep, a bed, that's great. What now?

The footsteps made their way slowly down the hall and my mind raced in a panic-fuelled flurry.

The footsteps stopped outside the door. "Come out, come out, wherever you are!" the voice from the hall called.

My instinct was to dash back to the door, press myself up against it and prevent him from entering and catching me. But before I made the move, something grabbed my elbow, spinning me around. My shocked scream was quickly muffled by a hand that clasped across my mouth, the other hand pulling me close.

"Shhh," a voice breathed, so close that their breath parted my fringe.

With wide eyes and flared nostrils, my laboured breathing was the only thing that wasn't frozen. I tried to fight against the iron-like grip, but it only got me another "Shhh", and an aggravated one, at that. The silhouette in front of me tilted his head, listening to the sounds of the footsteps outside. They were so close, but it wasn't the *sound* that made me fear he was right outside the door. A flash of light danced momentarily under the door crack.

A torch? That was cheating!

I could feel the shudder of a suppressed laugh through his torso as I remained where he'd pinned me, pressed against the silhouette.

"Cheeky bastard," the voice whispered.

A whisper isn't the easiest way to identify a person in the dark. I reached up instinctively and gripped my fingers around his arm, trying to get him to remove his hand from my mouth. Before I could struggle further, he slowly moved his hand, but not before pressing his finger onto my lips as if accentuating the need for silence.

I wasn't an idiot.

The light had moved on from the door, and the footsteps receded down the hall. With the coast clear, I was about to lash out at the dark figure, but before I had the chance, I flinched as a hand unexpectedly clasped mine. I was yanked through the darkness – roughly yanked forward and manoeuvred into a new space. Hangers clanked and I squinted my eyes closed as clothing hit my face. Then the sliding panel of the closet shut behind me.

Behind us, I mean.

"We're in a wardrobe," the voice whispered.

No shit, Sherlock!

The stuffy interior gave a new meaning to blackness. In times like these I instinctively wanted to light a match, if I had one. Not that it was the greatest idea, surrounded by so much cotton in such a confined space. It would really give a whole new meaning to 'Murder in the Dark'.

Murder in the bloody Dark.

The silhouette was no longer a silhouette or a shadow; there was only blackness. I couldn't see a thing. The only knowledge I had of his presence was the heat that pressed against my arm in the confined space.

Unlike the dirty cheat Ringer who had somehow found himself a torch, all the better to hunt us down with in the not-so dark, I didn't have a source of light. On the one and only day that the Onslow Hotel was closed to the public we had all agreed to meet up for some late night Christmas drinks. After a full day spent with an annoying, loud, extended family and a belly full of Christmas food, it was a welcome refuge of sorts to hang out in the quiet bar. Until Amy's bright idea of: "Let's play Murder in the Dark."

My best friend, Amy, grew up here so I would often find myself perched at the Onslow bar after all the drunks had been herded, stumbling out the door. Ever since Amy had come home this summer and we had reconnected our friendship, I had found myself not just with my high school best friend back, but a whole new group of friends that came with her. For the first summer since, wow, I was sixteen, I was hanging with my best friend, and strangely enough 'the Onslow Boys'.

Huh, I was hanging out all right. That was when I realised that I was actually pressed up against an Onslow Boy right now.

But which one?

Alone in the dark with an Onslow Boy. Most girls' prayers would have been answered. The jury was still out for me.

Seeing as the annoyed whisperer had forbidden me to speak (even though it seemed he was obviously allowed to), I reached out and found his shoulder. I patted my way across his collarbone, neck, chin, cheek, lips – soft lips – nose … gently touching the contours of a freshly shaven face. Hmm … nice cheekbones. I momentarily wondered who it was, but as my fingers traced the creases deeply etched above his eyes, I knew instantly.

I smiled, dropping my hand.

"Hello, Chris!

Chapter Two

A blinding light pierced the darkness.

Chris squinted in the harsh light, his broody face lit by the luminous rays from his mobile screen. "How did you know it was me?"

I winced against the foreign light, pushing it away.

"It was easy. No one has a frown quite like you."

As if on cue his frown deepened, the phone highlighting his face like a nightmare. Of all the Onslow Boys to be trapped with it had to be the moody one.

"You know, that light would have been handy about five minutes ago," I said.

"Yeah, well, he would have found us for sure, then," he said, his attention fully focused on his screen as he thumbed through his messages. His serious expression was unchanged.

"Well, hiding in a wardrobe isn't exactly a genius plan."

His eyes flicked up. "Really?" he deadpanned.

I shrugged. "It's the first place I'd look."

Chris lowered his phone, the light still filling the small space. "I suppose you have a better idea, then?"

I straightened, suddenly feeling exposed by the light, and Chris's expectant, cold stare.

"Well … anywhere would be better than here."

With you.

Chris stared at me for an unnervingly long time; I kind of hoped the screen would flick off and plunge us both back into darkness again.

The only movement that had me believing that Chris wasn't cast of stone was the slight tilt to the corner of his mouth. He reached out and slid the door open.

"After you." He motioned with a sweep of his hand.

"Sorry?" My eyes widened.

"You think you have a better place; lead the way then."

Oh crap.

I lifted my chin and slid past him out through the opening while his mobile's screen was still lit and I could see where I was going.

It was short-lived, though. Just as I was about to get my bearings, the light shut off – or, more to the point, Chris had deliberately pocketed his phone.

Idiot.

I was back to square one, edging my way across the foreign space until my legs hit the edge of the bed. *Again.*

Okay, what now?

Just as my serious lack of a plan was about to be exposed, Chris tapped me on the shoulder.

"Shhh …"

What? I didn't say any… Uh-oh …

Footsteps thudded their way back down the hall. Before I had the chance to so much as panic, Chris pushed me to the carpet. I blindly followed Chris who was frantically sliding under the bed; he pulled me under next to him so fast I was surprised I didn't get a carpet burn.

My heart thundered against my ribcage and a new fear spiked inside me, pumping adrenalin through my body. My breathing was hard and frantic, but that had nothing to do with the footsteps outside.

It was seeming impossible not to breathe right in Chris's face.

Well … this was awkward.

I was so intimately wedged up next to Chris I could feel the press of his lips on my brow. His left arm was trapped under my body, his other hand rested on my shoulder blade. My palms were pressed against his chest; I could feel the erratic beat of his heart slamming violently against my hands.

I swallowed deeply. Now wasn't a good time, but hey, we were under a bloody bed. I was sure my whisper wouldn't be heard outside.

"Chris? Do you think you could move over a bit?" I whispered into his neck.

He breathed out loudly. "I can't."

"Why?"

His fingers touched my lip again, probably necessary, but nevertheless infuriating.

"I WILL FIND YOU. IT'S ONLY A MATTER OF TIME," Ringer shouted, his steps echoing as he jogged down the hall. The torch beam flashed on the floor outside as he passed. Chris's body physically sagged with relief.

"Good ol' Ringer, he isn't the sharpest tool in the shed," Chris chuckled.

I shook my head in disbelief. "Hasn't he found *anyone*? How is that possible? Not even with a torch?"

"I think we'll be safe here for a bit," said Chris.

"Don't be so sure," I mused.

"Why?"

"Under a bed, Chris? I mean, really?"

"Oh for … What is it now?"

"It's the second worst hiding spot you could think of."

Chris shifted, but all it did was draw him closer. "I didn't see you find any place better."

"You didn't exactly give me a chance."

Chris scoffed. I could feel him flex his hand under my collarbone; no doubt my weight on top of his arm was cutting off his circulation. My body lay flush against him, my chest pressed up against his. I could feel every breath, every pulse, every beat of him. I cleared my throat.

"Um … Are you sure you can't move over?" I asked.

"*Yes.*"

"Why?"

"Because there's a saxophone case digging into my spine."

"Saxophone case? How can you possibly tell?"

Chris's shoulders shifted in awkward shrug. "We're in my room."

Chapter Three

Oh …

Okay, so I didn't know what to say to that exactly. It wasn't every night of my life that I found myself pressed up intimately against an Onslow Boy, in the dark, in his bedroom, in his bed. Well, okay … under his bed. Still, it did make for interesting conversation.

So what did you get up to on the weekend, Tammy? Oh not much, just front spooning with the local publican of the Onslow Hotel.

Maybe I wouldn't say that. To a lot of people, Amy's dad was still the publican! He'd just recently sold the pub to his daughter's boyfriend, Sean, and her cousin Chris (on paper, they officially took over in the New Year), but still, after decades of Eric Henderson being at the helm, it might take people a fair while to get their head around the change. Yes, I most definitely wouldn't mention that, especially seeing his daughter Amy was my best friend. Gross. That would be disturbing on so many levels.

The building was eerily silent now; there was no sound from outside the room. No sound *at all.* My neck was beginning to ache from the awkward position I was trapped in, pressed up against Chris, holding my head off the ground. Maybe now that Ringer had disappeared into the night to murder the others I could relax.

But if I did that, I would be resting my head on Chris, and that would be weird. On the other hand, we couldn't really get much closer than we were now. And this was all his bright idea, anyway.

I tried not to think about it as I let my rigid posture melt against his. My head rested against his shoulder and I found instant relief. I could feel Chris's muscles tighten as I relaxed against him. I could tell he was looking down at me, his scowl probably deepening as I settled in for the night. Oh well … what else was new?

I sighed. "I don't think Ringer is very good at this game."

Chris scoffed. "Ringer couldn't find his way out of a brown paper bag." I felt his body shift, almost as if relaxing too … but not quite.

"So … a saxophone, huh?" I said.

"Yeah. Year Seven band. I wasn't very good." He said it as if it was an embarrassing confession.

Ha! Chris Henderson not good at something? Mr Perfectionist, 'you do it my way or the highway', control freak.

Not likely.

"I find that hard to believe." I yawned, closing my eyes. Mmm, Chris's shoulder was actually quite comfy.

"Hard to believe what?"

My eyes snapped open.

Oh crap, had I actually said that out loud?

"Oh, I just meant that …" I was saved by the creak of the door opening. This time it was my hand that instinctively flew to cover Chris's mouth. Covering his warm, soft lips I was momentarily distracted by the foreign sensation of it, until the torchlight danced around the edges beyond the bed. Chris's hand slowly clasped my wrist, pulling it away from his mouth. Instead of remaining still like I thought he would now that we were under threat, he drew me closer. His hand splayed along my shoulder blades, protectively pushing me into his chest. My face snuggled into the alcove of his neck; I could smell the remnants of his musky cologne and couldn't help but smile. In all of my mum's romance novels a man always smelled like sandalwood and pine. I thought that was just in trashy novels, but as I breathed in, Chris really *did* smell like that; he smelled divine.

Oh God, now was not the time to be thinking of Mills and Boon. I knew why Chris drew me near; my back was at risk of being exposed by the searching torch beam should it skim past. I leaned further into him, away from the edge of the bed. If the saxophone wasn't digging into him before it sure would be now. I bet he was glad he never took up the tuba.

Wait a minute … Why was it so quiet? Where was Ringer's cliché horror movie commentary? I waited for shadows to dance around the dark room, but they didn't. The torchlight had gone. Holy crap, while I'd been too busy thinking about romance novels and tubas … where had Ringer gone?

I lifted my head from Chris's shoulder. He was so still, as if he was wondering the same thing. I wish I knew Morse code; I could have tapped out the question on Chris's chest.

Where was Ring …

"BWAHAHAHAHA …"

A hand latched onto my leg and dragged me out of my hiding spot only far enough until my ankles were exposed. I let out a blood-curdling scream, right in Chris's face.

"Ringer! Let go, you …!"

"Are you ticklish, Maskala?" Ringer asked, threatening to take my shoe off.

I kicked out against him. "Don't you dare!"

He let go of my foot, there was a click and the room flooded with light. I scurried my way from underneath the bed, Ringer standing by the doorframe hunched over in fits of hysteria.

"Oh yeah, laugh it up." I army crawled out from under the bed, struggling to find my footing. "I wouldn't be so smug if I were you, it took you long enough to find us."

Ringer's eyes lit up. "Us?" His smile soon faded as Chris crawled out after me, a look of surprise lining his face as his eyes flicked between the two of us.

"Oh … *I see.*" He wiggled his eyebrows.

I burned crimson; I wanted to tell him not to look at us like that, that it wasn't what it looked like, but I was cut off by Chris.

"Of course you bloody see; where did you get the torch, you cheat?" He brushed imaginary dust off his jeans. He didn't seem the least bit embarrassed by Ringer's smug expression.

"Hey, there's nothing in the rule book that says you can't have a visual aid," Ringer defended.

"What rule book?" Chris's younger brother Adam appeared in the doorway, his best friend Ellie standing next to him with her arms wrapped around her body.

"You took bloody long enough." She glowered at Ringer.

Ringer held up his hands in surrender. "Hey, I looked, I really did, but I couldn't find you anywhere."

"Well, next time, try checking the cool room," Ellie said, rubbing vigorously at her bare arms. Maybe there *were* worse places to hide than in a wardrobe or under the bed.

Adam puffed out his chest. "See, I told you it was a good spot to hide."

Ellie rolled her eyes, something she did often around Adam. "You're right, why would he think anyone would be stupid enough to hide in there?" She turned to us, as if seeing us for the first time. "So where were you guys hiding?"

All eyes focused expectantly on me and Chris. I tried to think of something to say that didn't sound so lame as hiding under a bed, but there was no sugar-coating it.

Just as I was about to openly confess our location, Chris beat me to it.

"Oh, Ringer found us in bed together," he said, brushing past me with a parting wink.

My mouth dropped open. "No, he didn't," I insisted, quickly following him out into the hall to avoid their knowing smirks.

"You may be ashamed of our love, Tammy, but sooner or later we must declare it to the world," Chris called over his shoulder as he headed down the hall.

Stunned, I paused in the hallway. "H-he's only joking," I stammered, turning back in time to see him head down the stairs.

Adam's smile broadened. "Of course he is, and that's the most interesting thing of all."

I spun back around to face him. "Why?"

They were all looking at me. Ellie glanced at Adam and then Ringer, a huge grin spreading across her face. "Because Chris doesn't joke … ever."

Ringer elbowed Ellie. "Must be love."

"Oh, shut up!" I scoffed, before marching down the hall and leaving their sniggering behind.

Yep! I was way too old for this.

Chapter Four

Now was my chance.

A chance to escape before Amy appeared from hiding and bullied me, as usual, to stay longer, drink more, and play Cupid with any red-blooded male within a ten-kilometre radius. It was her thing. And Chris was most definitely within a ten-kilometre radius.

I noted, relieved, that the Three Stooges didn't follow; instead, they headed to Adam's room. I tiptoed across the landing, ready to turn onto the staircase.

"Hold it right there, Maskala!"

I paused mid-step; at first I thought I was being paranoid, that maybe I had conjured up Amy's voice in my head. I looked around, confused when I didn't see anybody, worried that I was losing it.

"And where do you think you're off to?"

I was losing it. The voice trailed down from above me, like some heavenly being. My head darted to where I thought it was coming from and, sure enough, I was met with a familiar, beaming smile.

The manhole cover had been shifted to the side and Amy's face peered down at me from beyond.

"Boo!" She grinned. With expert ease, one leg appeared from

the opening, then the other. She climbed out, lowering herself by swinging like a monkey, something she had obviously done a hundred times before. She dropped onto her feet with an 'ooph' before straightening and dusting her hands.

"I have never lost a game of Murder in the Dark yet," she said triumphantly.

I shook my head. "A misspent childhood," I said as I picked a cobweb from her hair.

"That's what I said." Sean dropped to the floor after her, making a much louder thud with his six-foot-three frame. He still managed it with the agility of a jungle cat; it would almost have been graceful if it wasn't for the over-obsessive, paranoid brushing off of imaginary creepy crawlies and cobwebs. He shuddered.

"Next time we hide in the cool room," he declared.

Amy rolled her eyes. "That's the worst hiding place you could ever think of."

"You could always hide under a bed," I added.

Amy scoffed. "No one would be stupid enough to hide under a bed; you might as well have a neon arrow pointing to you."

My smile faded as I cleared my throat. "Anyway, I better get going, I have to …"

"Go for a run in the morning," Amy said in a robotic, bored voice as she looked at me. "I know."

I smiled coyly. Was I really so predictable?

It was my morning ritual to go for a good run; my body craved the outlet, having my muscles burn and my adrenalin soar with the crisp, fresh morning air. Most people thought I was mad, but in a lot of ways it was my sanity; it calmed my overactive imagination. I didn't expect anyone to understand, I sure knew Amy didn't.

"Off you go then, GI Jane, I'll see you at twelve."

My brows lowered in confusion.

Twelve? Twelve?

"You are still coming?" Sean asked.

My eyes glazed over; I bit my lip and tried for the life of me to remember what the hell was happening at twelve.

"Hello?" Amy laughed. "Sleepy Sunday Session at the lake house."

"Oh," I said, "riiiighhhht. Of course . . . TWELVE." I nodded.

Amy looked at me side on as if contemplating something, that maybe I had lost my mind for forgetting such a momentous occasion.

Truth be known, I was still getting used to the sudden change in my social life. Since Amy had returned to Onslow from being away all these years, I had suddenly been plunged into a new scene with new acquaintances and situations that I still didn't exactly know how to deal with. It seemed I was part of 'the gang', since I was involved in every drinking session, lunch, dinner, lake excursion, party and ritual Sunday sessions at Sean's lake house. It was nice to be included, to be around people that were funny and friendly.

Then why was it that I felt like I didn't belong? Amy had been my best friend until she was shipped off to boarding school after we'd snuck out together late one night. It sounds a little extreme, but considering what happened that night it really hadn't been.

My parents had been mad too, but they wouldn't have dreamed of sending me away, not that they had the money. Now she was back in Onslow we had picked up our friendship where we'd left it, but now that she had Sean too, I couldn't help but feel like a third wheel sometimes. I knew they tried their best to include me in everything and they liked having me around, but they often drifted off into knowing smiles and glazed, mushy looks that made me want to sidestep away. But who could blame them? It was the honeymoon period and they were crazy about each other. Who was I to rain on their parade?

A flash of light flickered across our faces, momentarily blinding us.

"There you are!" sing-songed Ringer. "Where were you two love birds nesting?"

Amy cut me a dark look, a light shake of her head as if warning me not to say a word.

"We were up in the ceiling," Sean said proudly.

Amy closed her eyes and breathed deeply as if counting silently to stem her anger; all she could manage was a whack to Sean's arm.

"What?" he asked, surprised. "What was that for?"

"Cut it out, you two," Adam said from the stairs in his best mock stern voice, as if imitating his Uncle Eric. Ellie, as usual, was not far behind.

"Hey, guess what?" Adam said, leaning on the stair bannister. "Chris made a joke."

Amy's eyes narrowed in confusion. "Chris doesn't do jokes."

"Chris doesn't so much as smirk, let alone joke," Ellie agreed. "It was the equivalent of unearthing a volcanic ash-ravaged village after centuries of …"

"It's not that rare," said Sean.

"I don't know, it's pretty rare," said Amy.

Sean smirked, rubbing the whiskers on his jaw line, throwing a cheeky grin toward Ringer. "We've seen it before."

Ringer grinned and nodded. "Yep! The one and only time you'll see Chris happy is when he's getting some; am I right or am I right?" He held up his hand to Sean.

Sean just looked at him. "Mate, I'm not high fiving you."

I couldn't help but laugh. I loved the way the Onslow Boys would rough-house and trash-talk each other. I looked at Ellie and Adam expectantly, to exchange our own amused smiles, but when my eyes met inquisitive stares from Ellie, Adam and now Ringer …

Coldness swept over me.

"You don't say?" mused Ellie, staring at me.

Wait, surely they didn't think …

My eyes widened with horror. Their curious gazes and smirks made heat flood to my cheeks.

"GOODNIGHT!" I said too loudly as I brushed past a confused Amy and Sean and headed down the stairs, quickstepping through the restaurant, dodging a Christmas tree, and into the bar. Chris was propped up on the bar watching TV. I couldn't even look him in the eye as I rushed past, clasping at the front door handle and tugging violently, almost jarring my arms as the door refused to give. I fumbled at the deadbolt, attempting to lift and tug, but it was stuck.

Come on, come on, come on!

I felt the press of Chris next to me as he moved to unbolt the door from the bottom, then the top with expert ease.

"I'll do it, just calm down. You okay?" he asked, the usual serious gaze back in place.

I scoffed, pushing my hair behind my ear. "Next time do me a favour – hide in the bloody ceiling."

Chapter Five

There was one thing that was for certain: no one wanted to be in Onslow for New Year.

"I would sooner die than be here at the stroke of midnight," said Ellie as she smeared a palmful of tanning oil over her shoulder.

"Turn!" called Amy.

Without missing a beat, Ellie, Tess, Amy and I turned from our backs onto our stomachs like synchronised rotisserie chickens, at least according to the boys.

Resting our chins on our forearms, our view changed from the shiny lake stretching toward a long deck that led up to Sean's lake house. The deck was the perfect sunbaking platform; sure, it was hard as a rock, but there was no chance of sand in the belly button so that was a definite plus.

I straightened my towel and repositioned myself as best I could to notice that my view had altered since our last rotation. I lifted my sunnies to spy a figure sitting at the outdoor table near the barbecue. Elbows resting on the tabletop, leaning over an open binder, chewing on the end of his pen, scowling intently at the page, was Chris.

He wore his practically trademark Levi jeans and black T; it didn't scream summer attire, but then nothing about him ever did.

if talking to himself, shaking his head
vily marked something on his page. Any
d jokester from last night was clearly long

ost times I saw him, sporting the same serious
was always working a shift behind the Onslow
ba... clock, hanging with his boys. My gaze shifted toward th... again where Sean and Toby stood, shirtless, in the distance at the end of the jetty, wrestling with tangled fishing line and arguing over whose fault it was. Ringer and Stan were fishing on the opposite side, casting each other dubious looks as they suffered through the long-standing tradition of Sean and Toby's alpha male dance with one another.

I suppose I should have been relieved; during my warm-up before my run that morning I had suffered more than one moment of dread at the thought of meeting up with everyone at twelve. In fact, like usual, I had psyched myself up into a state, to be prepared for taunts about what Chris and I had gotten 'up to' last night that had caused Chris to crack a smile. I had even gone so far as to take a deep, steadying breath as I walked down the steep incline of Sean's driveway, preparing for the array of questions that would surely follow. Even though there was nothing to tell (like, seriously, *nothing*), it didn't matter. I had always hated confrontation and it seemed like that would never change.

So when I arrived at Sean's place and was met by nothing more than cheerful hellos and earnest smiles, it became perfectly clear: I didn't know these people at all. No wonder I always felt so out of place.

"Tammy." My attention snapped back to the frying corpse beside me. "You're blocking my sun," said Amy.

"Oh, sorry." I moved to lie back down on my stomach, fidgeting to get comfy. Resting my chin on my arms again, I sighed a long, deep, contented sigh, shutting my eyes and letting the heat of the sun's rays warm my skin. My peace was soon disturbed by a none-too-subtle elbow knocking into mine. I peered to my left just in time to catch Amy wink at me with a cheeky grin.

"Oh, I don't know, Ellie, what's wrong with counting down the New Year in the beer garden?" Amy asked in all seriousness.

Ellie's head bobbed up, her white-rimmed sunnies masking the dark, searing stare that no doubt bore into Amy.

"Are you serious?" Ellie hitched herself up onto her elbows. "It's 1999, Amy, we're counting down into *the new* millennium, a new century! As if I'm going to spend another year sitting in the beer garden of the Onslow Hotel … No offence."

Amy shrugged. "None taken."

"Isn't the world supposed to end, anyway?" asked Tess in a sleepy, mumbled voice.

"Exactly!" Ellie straightened. "And I'll be damned if I am going to spend my last moments on this earth at a Blue Light disco singing 'Auld Lang Syne' with my parents."

"It won't be like that," Amy piped up. "Do you honestly think Sean would let it be like that? That I would?"

I knew Ellie had meant 'no offence', she had even said it herself, but I could tell by the incredulous tone in Amy's voice that she was getting a bit shitty that Ellie was depicting the Onslow so negatively.

I mean, if the choice was death over spending time there, then yeah, I could see why one would be pretty insulted by that.

On paper, the weeks leading up to and beyond Christmas looked like they had been pretty turbulent for Amy and her family. They had sold the Onslow Hotel, but in reality it wasn't as if anything much had changed; even though the Onslow sported a new sign on the front verandah boasting 'Under New Management'.

It had been a huge relief for everyone that Sean and Chris had bought the hotel and not one of the city types with bulldozers on standby.

Well, it was a relief for *almost* everyone. I spied Chris rip a page out of his folder and screw it up.

Closing my eyes, I attempted to zone out of Amy and Ellie's bickering, pressing my forehead against my arms, hoping that if I kept out of it I would soon just melt into the deck and avoid the drama. Whatever they chose for New Year's was fine with me.

It had seemed like a perfect plan and I was just starting to doze off in the warm sun when Amy elbowed me again, completely jolting me from my Zen-like state.

"Amy!" I glowered, rubbing my ribcage.

"Did you know about this?" Amy's voice was high and squeaky, which always meant trouble.

"Know about what?" I asked, mystified by her heated question. What had I missed?

Amy tilted her sunnies back and twisted herself to sit and face toward the jetty, glaring over at the boys.

"RIGHT!" she said before launching herself to her bare feet and stomping along the deck toward the long jetty where the Onslow Boys sat fishing.

"Uh-oh …" Ellie sing-songed.

"I thought she knew; I thought everyone knew," Tess added quickly, biting her lip, worry lines etched in her brow.

"Knew what?" I asked, watching Amy close the distance between her and Sean.

What the hell had I missed?

"Amy was under the impression there was going to be some grand New Year extravaganza at the hotel this year," Ellie said.

"And then I just asked if we should wait until the boys got back from their camping trip." Tess grimaced.

"Camping trip?" I asked.

"Yeah, the camping trip Amy obviously had no idea about." Ellie sat up, crossing her legs. "You too, it seems? The New Year's Eve boy bonding expedition they've planned." Ellie shrugged. "Adam mentioned it. They go into the bush, chant and share feelings and stuff."

"Not exactly," a voice said from above.

The three of us swivelled around and found a silhouette towering over us, blocking the sun.

Chris.

"Please don't smash my illusion of what you boys actually get up to," smirked Ellie. "Adam paints quite the vivid picture."

"I bet he does," Chris said, staring off at Amy and the boys in the distance. The three of us followed his gaze to see Sean who, smiling upon Amy's approach, was now not quite so happy.

Amy stood in her lime green bikini, her hands on her hips whenever they weren't furiously flailing around.

Sean held his hands up as if asking a silent question, something that seemed to infuriate her even more.

Their body language said it all.

Toby, Ringer and Stan shifted awkwardly, throwing each other wide-eyed grimaces, no doubt wishing they could be anywhere else in that moment.

"Trouble in paradise?" called an approaching voice. Adam walked through the back bi-fold doors onto the deck, cracking a can of Coke and taking a fizzy sip. He stopped beside Chris. Adam hip and shouldered his brother, causing his drink to fizz over and spill onto the deck.

Chris eyed his younger brother much like he did everyone, as if he was a bug under a microscope that needed to be stepped on. The two Henderson brothers stood side by side, Chris swiping Adam's Coke can out of his hand with a gentle shove to his shoulder before taking his own sip.

"Help yourself," said Adam good-naturedly. "I backwash anyway."

Chris choked mid-sip, working into a coughing fit, rasping insults toward his brother. Adam beamed like he'd just been showered in compliments.

"You're a bloody dickhead," rasped Chris. He worked to pour the remnants of the can out, the brown fizzy stream dribbling and disappearing between the cracks of the decking.

"Watch it, Boss Man, Sean will use you as a mop when he sees that on his deck," laughed Adam.

Chris flicked the excess drops from the can before crushing it in his hand.

"Somehow," Chris said, frowning toward the jetty, "I think Sean has bigger fish to fry."

And that's when we heard the scream.

Chapter Six

There was a loud splash and I couldn't be sure who had hit the water first.

Toby, Ringer and Stan were hunched over in hysterics as Amy and Sean flailed and splashed about in the water. Their bent-at-the-knees, tears-in-the-eyes laughter made me doubt it had been entirely an accident.

Ellie, Tess and I scrambled to our feet and followed Chris and Adam over to the jetty. We didn't know whether to laugh or offer support as one hand then another appeared from beyond the decking, splaying themselves on the surface, anchoring themselves into place.

"I swear to God, Sean Murphy, you're a dead man!" panted Amy as she struggled to hoist herself onto the deck.

Sean clamped his two large hands onto the jetty boards and pulled himself out of the water with ease.

"*You* pushed *me*!" He laughed.

"And you pulled me in!" Amy shouted, as she tried to claw her way onto the platform, rather unsuccessfully. Now on deck, pooling water at his feet, Sean offered her a hand.

"Don't touch me!" Amy slapped his hand away.

"Aw, come on, Amy, I'll take you bloody camping."

"Whaaat?" groaned Chris.

Sean ignored him; instead, he was trying not to appear amused as Amy hooked her heel on the edge of the pier and awkwardly tried to pull herself up with very little success.

"Don't bother," she bit out. "I don't want to go anywhere with you."

Amy always did have a stubborn streak.

"Yes, you do," Sean said. He bent, grabbed her firmly by her arms and ignored her slapping at him as he pulled her up and out of the water as if she weighed nothing. He set her down on her feet, which was all the better for her to glare up at him.

The glare was lost on Sean. His mischievous eyes twinkled as he looked down on Amy. Absolutely no one could doubt he loved her, that he was fully consumed by her, when he looked at her like that. It made my heart unexpectedly pang with jealousy. No one had ever looked at me like that.

"I'll take you camping," he repeated in all seriousness.

The boys sure stopped laughing then.

"Sure we will," added Adam. "You can cook us meals and keep the camp tended to while we do men's business."

That earned Adam a jettyful of murderous stares, none deeper or more intimidating than Chris's.

Just as I was about to tease him on behalf of the sisterhood for being so angered, he spoke.

"They're not coming."

"Excuse me?" Amy's murderous attention turned from Adam to Chris.

"Here we go," sighed Ellie.

"You heard me." Chris unapologetically locked eyes with Amy, as if the subject was somehow non-negotiable.

This was a mistake, a big mistake.

Amy crossed her arms. "I don't believe this. So, what? No girls allowed? Is that what you're saying?"

Adam slapped Chris on the shoulder and said, "It's been nice knowing you, buddy," before he sidestepped away.

Now everybody's attention was fully focused on Chris.

Sean scratched the back of his neck, grimacing. He turned to me. "What you think, Tam? You've been pretty quiet."

I flinched at the question.

Oh God, leave me out of it …

Now, much to my horror, all eyes shifted to *me*.

So much for avoiding confrontation.

"Oh … um …" I fidgeted under their scrutiny. "Well … I don't know." My eyes locked briefly with Chris's. They were burning into me like laser beams, his folded arms an open scowl of distaste that made me feel like he just wanted me to get on with it. It made me fluster even more. "Well, we could just, um …"*Oh God, help!* "We could always take a vote?"

Take a vote? Seriously? I inwardly cringed; I needed to just shut up.

Chris scoffed at my answer, plunging his hands into his pockets. He looked over the group.

"What? You can't be serious," he said.

My eyes darted over the others who all looked as if what I had said made perfect sense. *Surely not.* Sean laughed, squeezing my shoulders as he moved behind me.

"Nice one, Tam!" Sean beamed. "We shall take a vote. All those in favour of the ladies coming with us for our New Year's camping extravaganza, raise your hands."

Sean led the way, holding his hand straight up in the air, followed by a rather smug-looking Amy. Tess, Toby and Ellie also raised their hands to the sky, followed by Ringer and Stan. Adam raised his hand, smiling at Chris, clearly taking immense joy in the outcome.

"Those against?" Sean called, causing everyone to plunge their arms down comically fast.

Chris never moved. Not once. In fact, he was so still that if it wasn't for the deep sigh emanating from him, I would have sworn he had turned to stone.

"Well, what do you know – a fucking landslide," Chris bit out.

"Sorry, mate, the people have spoken," Sean said, hooking his arm around Amy and leading her toward the lake house, leaving a trail of water behind them.

"Better make room for our make-up bags, Chrissy babes," crooned Ellie as she walked past Chris, following them to the house.

Toby guided Tess to follow, offering Chris an amused shrug.

"Well, show's over. Come on lads, better check those fishing rods; I fancy smoking a kipper for breakfast." Adam slapped Stan on the back.

"You don't know much about fishing, do you, mate?" quipped Stan.

I smiled, watching the boys make their way back toward the jetty, exchanging trash talk as they went. But then I realised I was now alone with Chris and his angry eyes. He didn't need to say a word for me to know he thought I was solely to blame for ruining his New Year's plans, as if my bright idea had backed him into a corner. Maybe it had? So, in true Tammy Maskala fashion, I did what I liked to do best. I smiled apologetically and brushed past him, refusing to meet his eyes as I made a beeline toward the house for a speedy escape. Even in my hasty departure, call it paranoia, I guess, I couldn't help but feel Chris's eyes burning a hole in the back of my head.

Chapter Seven

Opening the door to my one-bedroom flat, I threw the keys on the little table by the door.

Peeling off the strap of my knapsack, I pinched the bridge of my nose with a sigh, praying that what lurked at the front of my brain was not the beginning of a migraine. I'd been an idiot – too much sun and not enough fluids. A migraine was a reasonable punishment, really.

Even though the sun was now dipping in the sky, taking the edge off the scorching heat, my flat was still painfully warm. I flicked the cooler switch on and it chugged to life. I pulled the curtains closed, shielding my eyes from the blinding, late evening sun. If nothing else, I would have to shower the tanning oil off of me before bed. I had to manage that much before I slunk into a world of pain. I slumped onto the soft couch and shook it from my thoughts.

No, Tammy Maskala! Stop it. It's positive, positive, positive, remember?

Positivity: my new mantra. I'd try to use it before the New Year so at least, by the turn of the new century, looking on the bright side would be second nature.

A niggling piece of me doubted my chances.

I rubbed at my throbbing temples; I could be as positive as

I liked, but that wouldn't have any effect on the onslaught of a migraine in its first stages. There was no amount of positive thinking that would keep that at bay. If anything, the less thinking I did the better, which was fine by me – the less I thought about the murderous look Chris Henderson had given me the happier I would be.

I had voiced my unease with Amy.

"Tammy, please," she had said. "Have you ever seen the way he treats *me*?"

I suppose, but I wasn't like Amy. She was so sure of herself; whatever room she walked into she dominated. She could play pool, skull a beer, hell, she could even arm wrestle each of the Onslow Boys. They were her friends, not mine, so when one of them gives me a dirty look, unlike Amy, I'm not about to tell them where to go.

I had to think, though. I had to think of an excuse to get out of this New Year's camping trip. Talks had begun as soon as we entered the lake house that afternoon. It seemed settled, a non-negotiable trip up the coast to the Port Shank Music festival to count down the New Year. That was the plan, a plan that had somehow automatically included me. Chris had sulked his way into the house, perching quietly on a stool at the counter as everyone talked excitedly around him. The two of us seemed like the most unenthused of the group. Maybe I should have bloody voted against it.

Thinking was overrated. My head throbbed with pain.

With a whimper, I dragged my feet across the carpet and up the hall to the bathroom to two crucial things: a cool, clean shower and a medicine cabinet with my painkillers.

Wow. My life rocked.

I knew the drill. After my shower I shuffled to bed and darkness, and tried not to move, just let sleep take me over before the pain, before the blinding nausea I hoped I could beat. And it might just have worked. The pounding in my temple was nothing to do with pain; it was owing to the incessant ringing of my phone instead. It jolted me awake, momentarily disorientating me until I recognised the continuous, shrill rings. I scrounged for the only source of light at my fingertips as I pulled my digital clock radio into view.

Whoa!

It was ten o'clock at night; I had been asleep for four hours. I patted my bed for the phone, wondering who would be calling me at this hour. I had my answer the instant I accepted the call. Pounding music bled through the receiver.

"TUESDAY!" Amy shouted.

Half asleep, I waited. I figured she was probably talking to a customer.

"Tammy? Are you there?"

"I'm here." I yawned.

"Oh my God, are you in bed? Already?"

"I had a migraine."

"Riiight," Amy drawled, as if she wasn't entirely buying my story.

"Tuesday," she repeated.

"What about it?"

"That's when we leave. For the New Year's trip."

My heart pounded in my chest. *So soon?*

My mind went blank and I couldn't speak. I was in shock at the urgency, but of course it was urgent. New Year's Eve was Friday; yeah, of course we had to leave sooner rather than later.

"Tammy, you *are* coming." Amy's voice sounded dark.

"Oh well … I …"

"Tammy, if you don't come, I'm going to be really pissed," she said.

"I just think that maybe it's turned into more of a couples' thing."

"A couples' thing?" Amy repeated, as if she could hardly believe what I'd just said.

"Well, you know, you and Sean, Tess and Toby, Stan's bringing his new girlfriend. And, well, Adam and Ellie have each other to hang with, and Chris and Ringer can do their fishing things."

In other words I had gone from the usual third wheel to a spare tyre; I really didn't want to be the awkward tag-along.

"It is sooo not a couples' thing. Remember, this was originally a boy bonding expedition that we happen to be gatecrashing. If anything, it will be more of a chance for us girls to kick back while the men go hunt and gather for us."

"You sound just like Adam." I laughed.

"Ugh, kill me now," Amy said. "So that's it. You're coming and we leave Tuesday. We'll discuss the finer details later, plus something else you might find *very* interesting."

"Now hang on a sec, I didn't say … What would I find interesting?"

"Oh, just a certain something a certain someone said about you."

"What?" I croaked. *What had they been saying about me?*

"I might have overheard a certain Onslow Boy talking about you, that's all."

Onslow Boy?

"What? When? Who?" I stammered.

"See you Tuesday!"

Chapter Eight

Tuesday gave us one day – ONE day.

What the hell do you take camping, anyway? I had no idea; as far as nature was concerned I liked to run through it and around it, not live in it. Sleeping with ants and snakes and God knows what else was *not* my thing.

I had to think of an excuse.

I invited the girls to lunch at the Bake House Café in town to learn more about what exactly was going on for Tuesday. It also gave me a chance to invite Amy half an hour early before Ellie and Tess arrived, to grill her about who had been talking about me and exactly what they had said.

Maybe Chris had been slagging me off to his mates, but by the tone of her smug voice I doubted it was anything like that. I really hoped it wasn't, but then again at least I would have a good excuse for not wanting to go.

I heard the ding of the bell above the café door and expected to see Amy's beaming grin as she scanned the tables, looking for me. I straightened expectantly with an inviting smile, only for it to drop clean off my face when Chris appeared instead.

SHIT.

I slid under the table, my spine making an infuriatingly large fart-like sound against the linoleum seat as I disappeared out of view. What was I doing? Oh God, I hoped he hadn't seen me. How was I going to explain this?

"Ah, young Chris! Good to see you, how's things?" called Norm the baker from out the back.

I grimaced under the tablecloth.

Just go, just hurry up and go.

"Yeah, good thanks, Norm."

Legs walked on the other side of the table, along the line of cabinets as he no doubt looked over the baked goods. I dared not even breathe.

They chatted about their businesses, about the Onslow. Chris seemed in no hurry to order.

My legs ached and my neck cramped, hunched over under the table; apparently it was time to chat. It was odd, hearing Chris talk to Norm. I didn't think I had ever heard Chris string together so many sentences before, and come to think of it, not only was he speaking, but he sounded … normal. Lighthearted, almost.

It was unsettling.

"What are the specials today, Norm?" There was a bang as Chris slapped the counter.

Just grab a bloody pie and go.

"Oh, now hang on a second, young fella, Betty left the list here somewhere."

I sighed, hearing Norm rummage through papers.

He rummaged.

Rummaged.

Rummaged some more.

"Ah, here it is!"

HALLELUJAH!

As Norm rattled off a painstakingly long list of specials, I couldn't help but check my watch every five seconds, ever aware that Amy would be rocking up at any minute and I would be busted. My skin prickled with embarrassment. Why did I think myself so smart as to organise a meeting half an hour before the norm? If

I had just said twelve thirty I could have avoided this altogether.

"Sounds good! I'll go for the number seven, thanks, Norm."

Finally!

"Excellent choice! Eat in or take away?"

"Eat in, thanks."

I cringed and closed my eyes. *Nooooooooooo* … This could not be happening.

There was no crawling my way out of this one.

Literally, there wasn't, because I had thought about it, but there was no way I could get out of this without being caught doing so.

The Bake House was a long, gallery-style set-up, booths on one side of the wall and cabinets and service area on the other. Depending on where he chose to sit… If he sat toward the door, his back to my table, I might have stood a chance.

I tried to slow my breathing, to not move even an inch as I listened to the direction of his footsteps. Mercifully they headed in the direction I had hoped they would, away from me and toward the door.

I was going to be okay, I could get out of this with relatively minimal damage to my ego.

"Is this today's paper, Norm?" Chris called out.

"Sure is, help yourself," Norm's voice called from out the back.

I heard the rustling of a newspaper in the distance, followed by footsteps closing in toward my direction.

Oh no-no-no-no …

He was walking this way, all right. His unmistakable Levi denim-clad legs swaggered into view, so painfully close I could reach out and touch them, maybe even trip him. I momentarily entertained the thought before brushing it from my mind.

My heart drummed so fiercely I could swear Norm would have heard it out back. My mouth went dry as I watched every single footstep make its agonising way toward …

He was going to sit at my booth!

This could not be happening, this could not be happening.

Try and explain this, Tammy, when Amy rocks up and you're nestled under Chris's table.

I edged myself as best I could out of touching distance, my eyes widening as the seat dipped under Chris's weight.

His kneecap was barely inches away from my forehead.

This was not okay.

I heard him casually cough as he turned the pages of the newspaper.

"Onslow skate park opening to mark the New Year," he read aloud. "Outdoor cinema a raving success."

Was he serious?

"Locals fight to save historic gum tree … School wins local funding bid … Girl trapped under Bake House dining table."

My head snapped up so quickly I headbutted Chris's knee.

"Ahh …" I clasped my head where it hurt.

Chris slid out of the booth and lifted the skirt of the tablecloth to look at me.

Was he seriously laughing at me?

"Are you okay?"

"I'm fine!" I snapped. Trying to gain some form of composure, I clawed at the seat with one hand, trying to slide out from underneath as I nursed my eye socket.

Chris moved to the side and offered me his hand. I would have slapped him away, but I really did need the help; I had been crouching in such an awkward position my legs were numb and refused to work.

"Easy now, don't hurt yourself."

Ha! Too late for that.

I managed myself into a seated position once again, Chris standing before me. I couldn't bring myself to look at him – for one, I couldn't stand to see his smug smirk and two, I only had one functioning eye.

"Christ, are you okay, Tammy?"

I winced, rubbing my eye. "I think so."

"Don't do that, here let me look." Chris pulled my hand away. "Look at me."

I slowly managed to lift my eyes to him and to my surprise he didn't look smug at all. His brow was furrowed in concern as his fingertips gently pressed around my eye.

He whistled. "Looks like you're going to have one hell of a shiner."

"From your knee? Perfect!" I grimaced.

"Hey, Norm, do you have any ice?" Chris called out.

"Oh no, Chris, don't. I'm fine," I pleaded. But it fell on deaf ears as Chris worked on securing some ice cubes in a cloth Norm organised for him.

"What happened?" Norm asked, the look of alarm spread across his face.

"It's all right, Norm, no one's going to sue you," Chris half laughed as he sat next to me, holding the ice-cold package to my face. Chris continued to pacify Norm. He seemed more shaken than I was. Apparently his wife, Betty, didn't leave him in charge very often and if anything happened on his watch it wouldn't be worth his life.

A broad smile spread across Chris's face. "It's all right; it will be our little secret," he said as he winked at me.

I grabbed the cloth from Chris's grasp, unnerved by his kindness, by the lightness of his mood and the transformation of his smile, a smile that lit his entire face. I must have been staring at him, a deep frown etched across my face as if I were sitting next to a stranger.

In a way, I kind of was.

"Tammy, are you all right?" His smile melted into a grim line, as if unnerved by my catatonic stares.

If anything was going to give me a migraine, an old-fashioned knee to the head would do it.

I cleared my throat, scooting away on my seat. "I'm fine … Thanks."

Taking the hint, Chris climbed out of the booth, watching me with uncertainty.

"You sure?" he said as he sat down opposite me.

"I'll live."

If embarrassment wouldn't kill me first.

Chris opened his mouth to speak when the chime above the front door sounded and Amy entered. Her smile dropped with surprise when she laid eyes on us and her brows furrowed in confusion.

"Jesus, Chris. What. Did. You. Do?"

Chapter Nine

"It was an accident!" I said quickly.

Amy's attention broke slowly away from Chris to me.

"What happened?" she asked.

Oh crap. It was enough that Chris must have worked out that I had hidden under a table to avoid him, but did I really have to say it out loud?

I hadn't been prepared for questions; there was no easy way to explain this, especially with Chris's dark-set eyes burning into me.

I ran into a door? Slipped on a tile? Got kneed in the face by your cousin? The latter, the fact, sounded the least believable and by far the hardest to explain. Still, the truth would set you free, right?

"I uh …"

"She got hit in the head with a salt and pepper shaker," Chris blurted out.

Huh?

"What?" Amy's frown deepened.

"Yeah, well, she asked for me to pass the salt and I … uh … overshot the mark."

"Jesus, Chris!" Amy exclaimed. "What were you thinking?

You're not hanging with the Onslow Boys now; Tam's not going to catch it like Sean would, you're such a Neanderthal."

Amy plonked down in the seat next to Chris and punched him in the shoulder. "I hope you said you were sorry."

Chris's brows rose as he looked at me. I could tell he was trying not to smile.

"Of course I said I was sorry; even fetched ice for her face."

"So you bloody should." Amy shook her head and rolled her eyes at me. "Boys!"

I smiled a small smile. I felt kind of bad that she was giving Chris such a hard time. For a split second I had actually believed that I was hit in the face by a salt shaker.

"Let me look," Amy prompted, leaning forward.

"Oh it's nothing, really."

I tried to slap Amy's hands away, but there was no use. Once Amy had something in her head she would not let go.

I heard Amy gasp as she removed the ice-filled tea towel from my eye.

"Whoa, you're going to have a ripper of a black eye."

Awesome.

Norm appeared from the kitchen and set a cup of coffee in front of me. "Here you go, Miss Maskala."

"Oh … I didn't …"

"No, that's all right, it's on the house. If there is anything else you need you just sing out. Just rest up and take it easy."

Oh, now this was getting too much.

"Thanks, Norm." I smiled weakly.

I wanted to slink down in my seat, to hide under the table in mortification, but that was what had got me into trouble in the first place.

Norm returned a minute later, plonking down Chris's number-seven special order in front of him. Amy and I stared at his plate.

Chris straightened in his seat, his eyes aglow with hunger. He readily grabbed his knife and butter sachet when he glanced up and paused. His eyes shifted from me to Amy and back.

"What?"

"Really?" I asked. "Banana bread?"

"What's wrong with that?" Chris asked warily.

"Nothing, I guess, I just assumed a number seven would have been a steak, or a greasy fry-up of bacon and eggs or something." My lips twitched, fighting not to smirk at his dainty serving of toasted banana bread.

"Yeah," Amy said with a laugh. "Man food."

"It's got walnuts in it," Chris defended.

"Whoa. That's hardcore." I grinned.

Chris ignored us and instead opened his sachet in a huff, slapping the butter onto his bread.

Norm came back with a pen and notebook.

"Now, was there anything you wanted, young Amy?" he asked, writing the date on his pad.

"Oh, I don't know." She turned to Chris. "What do you say, Angela Lansbury? Do you want to share a pot of tea with me?"

Chris dropped his knife with a sigh. "Norm, can I have this for takeaway?" He pushed his plate away.

"Aw come on, don't be like that." Amy leaned her head on his shoulder.

Chris nudged her. "Get off me or I'll throw a salt shaker at you, too."

Amy mock gasped. "Hey, Norm, might pay for you to confiscate your salt and pepper shakers just in case they fall into the wrong hands."

"Salt and pepper shakers?" He looked up from his notepad, troubled.

"Yeah, just to lower the injury rate." Amy winked at me.

Norm scratched his head in deep thought. "But we don't have any salt and pepper shakers, only individual sachets."

Oh SHIT!

My eyes widened as big as saucers, flicking to Chris who had closed his eyes in a moment of dread.

The confusion spread from Norm to Amy.

"But you said that …"

The door chime sounded. "Ugh, I'm starving!" said Ellie.

"You're always starving," Tess said, as they pushed their way through the front door.

I braced myself for the onslaught of 'What happened to you?' questions. How were we going to explain it this time?

"Chris," Ellie said, surprised. "What are you doing here? Oooh, banana bread, yum!"

"Here, have it." Chris pushed the plate toward Ellie. "I've lost my appetite."

"It has butter on it already, but no salt," Amy said, her eyes shifting between us knowingly.

Ellie plonked down in the soft leather booth next to me. "Gross. Why would I need salt?"

Amy shrugged. "Stranger things have happened."

Norm coughed. "I'll, uh, leave you all a minute to decide."

Chris shifted uncomfortably in his seat, checking his watch. "I better get back; here, Tess, have my seat."

Amy slid out of the booth, letting Chris out. He stood, grabbed his wallet from his back pocket, thumbed out a twenty and chucked it on the table.

"Keep the change, Norm," he called.

Norm poked his head into the café from the kitchen. "Thanks, mate, see you next time."

Chris shifted his attention back to our table.

"So you ladies are still coming camping, I take it?"

"You betcha," Ellie said through a mouthful of banana bread.

The corner of Chris's mouth curved upwards. "You do realise there are no power points in the base of the gum trees to plug your hairdryers into."

Amy rolled her eyes with annoyance. "Shut up!"

"As if we're that naïve, Chris," scoffed Tess.

As for me, I made an instant mental note.

Don't. Pack. A. Hairdryer.

"Just so you know." He shrugged. "Seeyas."

Our eyes locked briefly before he nodded goodbye and left, the sound of the door chiming and slamming shut.

I looked back at the girls, each one staring at me. I was suddenly aware that I had been left to a pack of wolves. I could almost hear the cogs of speculation turning in Amy's head as she tried to unravel the mystery between me, Chris and the salt shaker in the bakery.

It sounded like some demented version of Cluedo.

I grabbed a menu. "Let's order, shall we?" They were all quiet for a moment, taking my cue to peruse the menus. I started to relax, just a little, thinking that maybe I had escaped the questions altogether.

"Oh my God!" Tess gasped. "Tammy – what happened to your eye?"

Ugh. Kill me now.

Chapter Ten

I had a tendency to hide things, even from the people closest to me in my life, just like I had hidden my slightly puffed-up, bruised eye.

I tried to squeeze out the crusty contents of a thousand-year-old foundation tube I found in the bottom of my bathroom drawer. A testament to how long it had been since I had worn make-up. I wasn't sure mixing it with water had helped much, but I kind of knew that my parents wouldn't even notice and I had never been so thankful for their diverted attention.

"Well, I think it's wonderful!"

Of course she did; my mum thought everything was wonderful. I followed her into the crowded garage, skimming sideways to dodge old light fixtures, fishing rods and bicycle pumps, a pile of retro seventies tiles, a dust-covered cabinet housing bolts and a whipper snipper cord. I accidentally banged into a box of home brew bottles – they tipped sideways but I mercifully caught the box before glass shattered on the floor and I juggled them back into place on top of the old ride-on mower.

My mum had somehow navigated her way through the space with expert ease, like she had done a million times before. I followed the track she had worn in the second-hand carpet on the concrete floor. I sighed, shaking my head as I always did whenever I saw this place. My dad had a garage sale addiction and was always in search of the next treasure. You would often find him sitting on the verandah in his second-hand bottle-green corduroy chair, scouring the *Trading Post*. There was one thing Mum and I both agreed on: the chair was hideous.

"Well, I *don't* think it's wonderful," I said. "I don't want to go on a New Year's couples' retreat."

"Hmm," Mum said as she struggled to unlock the door at the end of the shed. I couldn't help but smile. Mum always kept the end room (her office) locked like Fort Knox, as if anyone would want to steal the treasures that lay within.

The garage filled with light as Mum got the door open and manoeuvred her way into her self-confessed 'woman cave'. It hadn't been without a fight that Dad had agreed to sacrifice prime square footage for Mum's office. It gave him less room for storing his crap.

I followed Mum into her office – or rather workshop, really. Inside housed shelf after shelf of handcrafted, unique pieces of Nina Maskala pottery. It was unique all right – no two ashtrays were the same. And there were lots and *lots* of ashtrays. It seemed that Mum had moved on from such humble ashtray beginnings and since branched out into vases, fruit bowls and …

Oh my God, what was that?

My mum followed my eye line.

"Do you like it?" She beamed, picking up her piece with pride.

I swallowed deeply. Whatever it was, it was hideous. "W-what is it?"

"It's my new thing I'm working on; it's a flower."

That's a flower?

"What do you think?"

Oh, dear Lord. How did I tell my mum that her flower looked like a vagina?

"I'm going to make a whole bouquet of them!"

A bouquet of vaginas.

"I thought I could make up baskets and bouquets and donate them to the local nursing home."

"What does Dad think of them?" I eyed the flower sceptically.

"Oh, I gave up showing him my work ages ago; he would only ever grunt a reply."

"Well, I definitely think you should seek his approval."

"Yes." She tilted her head and admired her handiwork. "They are rather beautiful."

Mum placed the flower back onto the mantel and turned to me, her eyes meeting mine, and for the first time today I felt like I had her full attention.

"Go!" she exclaimed, raising her brows. "Honey, you need to take a break. Make the most of your break from uni and just go have fun with your friends."

It wasn't that simple. Of course, I didn't explain the sole reason for not wanting to go.

Yeah, perhaps I would be a third wheel.

Sure, I didn't fancy being confronted by the endless array of questions from Amy, the ones I knew I couldn't avoid forever.

The last thing I wanted was to go into the embarrassing details. With Chris at the bakery until Ellie and Tess showed up, I'd missed my chance to find out which Onslow Boy had said what about me, so my brilliant plan? I had ended lunch early with the 'I've got a headache' excuse so I wouldn't get grilled by Amy. Yep! I used the old 'I have a headache' excuse, a new low. Mind you, since I was holding an ice pack to my face it was extra believable.

But I couldn't tell my mum any of those reasons.

Aside from my own personal anxieties about going on the trip, any excuse would seem lame; they all sure sounded lame to me.

As if on cue, I was startled by my mobile buzzing and vibrating in my pocket. The screen flashed *Amy*. Biting my lip and staring at the screen, I winced as I was about to do something I had never done before, especially to Amy.

I pushed the mute button, silencing the phone.

It was official, I was a shitty friend. No, even worse.

I was a coward.

My mum's shoulders sagged as she read the look on my face.

"You're really not going, are you?" Mum said with a sigh.

I shook my head, cementing the decision and pocketing my phone again. I would tell Amy tonight, once I had psyched myself up a bit, worked out what to say. So that was it: I was not going. I'd made up my mind. I waited for the onset of relief to flood me, but instead I couldn't help but wonder. If this was what I really wanted then why did I feel so miserable?

Chapter Eleven

Okay, so I didn't expect that.

I hung up the phone, feeling quite mystified with the conversation that had just gone down. I had psyched myself up in order to have the 'I'm not going' speech ready for Amy. I had even thought of multiple comebacks and reasonings in my defence. I had taken in a deep breath, sat down on my bed and prepared myself for what was to come, so when Amy had said, "Okay," I had fallen into surprised silence.

Okay?

And it wasn't even a short, sharp okay, or a 'pfft whatever' okay. It was a chirpy, upbeat 'no worries, maybe next time' okay. I didn't know what to say to that.

"If you change your mind, we leave at lunchtime tomorrow. I better go, I have a million things to do. If I don't see you tomorrow then I'll just see you next year. Next millennium!" Amy laughed before hanging up the phone.

Not only had I not expected that in a million years, I was not prepared for how utterly shit it made me feel. I straightened my spine. Yep, I had made the right decision. It really was no big loss. I wasn't going and Amy was obviously happy and preoccupied by the big trip anyway. It would be a good chance for her to get away and spend some time with Sean; she wouldn't want to spend the trip babysitting me anyway.

It seemed I had seriously over-thought my own importance to the expedition.

Good. What a relief; I was officially off the hook, good news indeed. I eyed the handwritten notes I had made in point form, all the reasons for not going, the list I had apparently not needed anyway. I flipped over the paper, my lips pinching into a smile as I recalled how yesterday, before leaving early from my 'headache', Tess had handed out stapled A4 sheets of an itinerary she had worked on. Apparently she had quizzed Toby on the details and customised it into a schedule that we could all follow. She had even gone so far as to make a list of travel essentials and recommendations. Tess was truly adorable, if not a little neurotic. A rather endearing fact, really, and I could totally relate. Aside from the long-forgotten foundation tube in my bathroom drawer, my little flat was organised on an OCD level of standards. It kind of had to be – my life didn't allow for anything less. Aside from my part-time job as a personal trainer I was studying full-time for my Bachelor in biomedicine. I needed to be organised, especially since I had a new social agenda that meant every spare minute was spent with Amy and the Onslow gang. Well, *had* been with. Now it seemed I would have a couple of days all to myself, more time to …

Well, to work on scrapbooking my trip to China like I had always wanted to, to re-categorise my CD collection, rework a new fitness track for the new clients that would inevitably start up a fitness regime in the New Year. It was always a busy time for personal trainers, the start of a new year. New Year's weight-loss resolutions ruled. But until then, I could even go down to the Onlsow for a quiet drink if I wanted to, knowing that Chris wouldn't be there to serve and stare daggers at me. Yep! I had so many projects I could take care of – repainting the laundry, cleaning out my wardrobe … Lots to do.

I paused for a moment. New Year's Eve … Oh God, I had

visions – visions of me sitting wedged in between my parents on their sofa, watching Mum's favourite movie, *The King and I*, for the millionth time. A coldness swept over me – so many hours to fill over the next few days.

No, Tammy! Positive, positive, positive!

I sat bolt upright in bed, clutching at my heart, breathing heavily. I was twisted in my sheets, a light sheen of perspiration across my skin. My eyes blinked at the whirring of the ceiling fan as I gathered my bearings.

Oh, thank God, it was just a dream.

I closed my eyes and breathed in deeply, burrowing my head in my hands. *Just a dream*, I repeated over and over. *Just a dream, just a dream, just a dream.*

I had dreamed that Mum had roped me in to making bouquets of clay vaginas over the holidays. Hundreds and hundreds of them – they filled Mum's woman cave to the ceiling, vaginas towering over, threatening to topple and bury me forever. Actually it wasn't a dream; it was a nightmare, and potentially my fate for the next week if I didn't escape Onslow.

It was ten a.m., a massive sleep-in by my standards. No doubt I was mentally exhausted from the day before, if not suffering a mild concussion from being kneed in the face. After having fallen asleep reading Tess's itinerary over and over, I had awoken with a new attitude. Scrapbooking and painting the laundryroom was not a positive way to enter the new millennium.

Peeling the sheets back, I dived out of bed and grabbed my phone on the way to the bathroom. I rang Amy's mobile but it went straight to message bank.

"Hey, Amy, it's me. I changed my mind. I'm coming; I'm definitely coming, so wait for me, okay? See you soon."

I ended the call, smiling at my new-found feeling of excitement. This was going to be great – a road trip! A better chance to hang out with fun people and escape Onslow. What had I been so afraid of? Ellie was right – the thought of staying in Onslow was horrific; I would sooner be a third wheel.

If nothing else, the journey would prove to be a spectacular one. The boys had planned to take the route up the Queen's Highway, through the ranges and along the remote coast. Apparently it was one of the most picturesque highways in Australia, or so it said on the itinerary.

Shoving clothes and my make-up bag into my green Esprit beach bag, I was grateful now that it was a lunchtime start; I was going to need every spare minute and still I felt like I wasn't ready.

I ticked off the list methodically:

Sunscreen
Lip balm
Leave in conditioner

I laughed, wondering if the Onslow Boys' list read the same.

Any personal medication needed

Oh crap! My migraine tablets, way to go, Tess! Pedantic people were often picked on, but you could never accuse them of being unprepared. Highly organised people would always have the last laugh. I circled the sentence as a reminder to grab them before ticking off other key items.

My pen hovered on the sheet.

Sleeping bag? Bugger!

Chapter Twelve

My mum was officially a saint.

After a mini-freakout and blind panic over all the things I didn't have from the list, I had rung Mum, jabbering away like a lunatic as I watched the clock count down before my eyes. I had tried Amy again but she was obviously busy sorting out her own list. I left another frantic message.

"Wait for me, I am coming!"

Mum, sensing the urgency, arrived in record time. She carried two armfuls of goods from the Land Rover as I shut and locked the door behind me.

"Leave them, Mum, there's no time! I'm going to be late."

Mum let the contents of her arms spill back onto the back seat. "I guess that means you need a lift?" Mum curved her brow in good humour.

I pecked Mum on the cheek. "Would you?"

Mum shook her head. "Hop in."

The wheels screeched as we turned the corner crazy fast. It wasn't because of the time limitations – Mum always drove like that. You always knew when Mum was nearly home; you could hear her turning up our street and roaring into the driveway.

Dad always shook his head. "She is going to go straight

through that bloody garage one day," he'd say.

It was our own personal joke.

Accompanying Mum's horrendous driving was Mum's horrendous music. Barry Manilow blared out of the speakers. Any time we stopped at the traffic lights, I would slink down in my seat and pray no one noticed me, although Mum did draw attention our way, slapping the steering wheel and singing at the top of her lungs:

"*At the Copa, Copacabana*
Music and passion were always the fashion
At the Copa ... they fell in love!"

Ugh, seriously, take me away from this place.

The light took a painfully long time to turn green, but when it did Mum slammed her foot onto the accelerator as she bore through town like Steve McQueen on the streets of San Francisco. She flew up Coronary Hill and made a large sweep into the drive. I instinctively turned down the music.

"Thanks, Mum. You're a lifesaver." I hopped out of the car, working to open the back door to retrieve my things. I had never been so happy for Dad's garage sale obsession – everything I needed to complete my list had been found in the garage.

"Did you want to have a look and check if what I grabbed is all right?" Mum called from her seat.

I slammed the passenger door, shouldering my cargo and dragging the big duffle bag from Mum along the stone drive.

"No, it's okay; it will be fine. Thanks heaps."

Mum smiled. "I knew you would change your mind, I read it all over your face yesterday."

What? Surely not. Yesterday I had been displaying my most resilient 'I am so not going' look. And I'd meant it, too.

"Don't look so puzzled, Tam, I can read you like a book. Go have fun with your friends and stop stressing for once."

"I don't stress." I lifted my chin.

Mum shook her head, as if not believing a single word. Not that I could blame her, I didn't believe them myself.

Mum started up the engine. "Behave yourself, especially with those Onslow Boys in tow." Mum winked.

"Mum!" I looked around in horror.

"I mean it, Tammy – condoms were the one thing I couldn't find in the garage."

"Oh my God! I'm going!" I blanched, juggling my baggage and wanting to get far away from my mother's awkward jokes. Not that they were entirely jokes.

"I'll see you next year," she called, before pulling into gear and circling out of the drive, Barry Manilow's 'Mandy' following her down the hill.

I waved, watching the dust settle in the drive. Could she be any more mortifying? Luckily no one had come outside to witness it.

I continued to drag the duffle bag Mum had packed with travelling essentials toward the hotel verandah. Bloody hell, what had she packed, a freaking toaster and kettle? This thing weighed a ton. All of a sudden I wished I could take a moment to examine the contents of the bag; with Mum in control, God only knows what else she'd thrown in there. Her openness and honesty seriously creeped me out sometimes. You would never catch Amy's mum talking like that. Not in a million years. And as if conjuring her into existence, I heard Claire Henderson's voice.

"Hello, Tamara." She always called me that. "I hope you had a nice Christmas."

Claire Henderson sat comfortably in a white Adirondack chair on the verandah of the Onslow Hotel, wearing white capri pants and halter, her thick, ash blonde hair in a high ponytail, her eyes shaded by Chanel sunglasses, her perfectly manicured hand holding an iced tumbler with clear liquid. No doubt her infamous lunchtime G and T.

"Hello, Mrs Henderson," I groaned. Backing up toward the hotel, pulling my bag up the steps …

Thump-thump-thump.

Clearly out of breath by the time I got to the verandah, it

was of no surprise that Claire Henderson hadn't budged from her shady recline; Claire Henderson didn't do 'help'.

She lifted her sunnies to spy my bags as I let them fall by my feet.

"And what have you got there?" she asked.

I fought to catch my breath, placing my hands on my hips. "Camping gear," I managed to breathe out, stretching my aching back.

Claire's confused blue eyes snapped up. "Camping gear?" she asked.

"For the road trip," I said.

If Claire Henderson didn't have a face full of Botox, she would have probably been frowning at me right then, but seeing as she was unable to do that, I had to take the blank stare instead. Maybe Amy hadn't told her about it. It *had* happened kind of quickly, I suppose.

"The New Year's road trip," I repeated.

"Oh, honey, I don't know how to tell you this." Claire Henderson sat up straight.

"Tell me what?" I asked.

"Sweetie, they've already gone."

Chapter Thirteen

This morning?

"But I'm sure the itinerary said twelve …" I fumbled the papers out of my pocket, my eyes ticking side to side until I found it clear as day: 'Meet at the Onslow at twelve.'

"See?" I all but shoved the paper into Claire's face.

"Yes, well, apparently the boys wanted an earlier start; I would have thought Amy might have mentioned it."

"Well, I wasn't going to go, but then I left her a message this morning letting her know I was coming."

"And she never got back to you?"

I shook my head, folding up the itinerary and tucking it back into my pocket.

Claire sighed. "She was running around like a headless chicken this morning, squawking orders at everyone. The new time threw everyone off, maybe she forgot to check her messages?" Claire said soothingly.

"Yeah, maybe," I said, although we both knew when it came to Amy and her new beloved Nokia phone, she was rarely parted from it and checking it every five minutes. There was no way she would have not received my several messages.

A pit formed in my stomach. Maybe Amy hadn't wanted me

to go? Maybe she was punishing me; after all, I was the one that had ignored her phone calls. She might have been mad at me for not telling her what really happened at the Bake House. I would have left me behind too.

I looked over my pile of camping gear.

Well, this was awkward.

"Oh, leave that there, Tamara. Come inside and I'll get you a drink."

I sidestepped away from my gear, not really wanting a drink. Instead, I just wanted to call up Mum and get her to take me away from here. I could lock myself away, scrapbook and paint my laundry like I had originally planned. I swallowed down the tears that threatened to bubble to the service. My best friend didn't want me around.

I followed Claire as she pushed against the main door. Eric Henderson was perched at the bar, talking to Max, one of the barmen, who was restocking the fridge.

Both sets of eyes turned expectantly toward Claire and me, confusion dawning across Eric's face the same way it had with Claire.

"Don't ask," Claire said; maybe I looked more upset than I realised.

Eric held up both hands as if silently stating, 'I'm not saying a word.'

"Max, can you please get Tamara a drink – anything she wants, our shout." Claire squeezed me reassuringly on the shoulder before motioning me to sit at the bar. Even though they weren't the owners anymore, not much had changed; they were still living in their apartment upstairs until they found a place to buy. Sean had made it perfectly clear that there was no rush. They spent most of their time living in their town house in the city anyway, except for occasions like now when they agreed to hold the fort for what would be Sean and Chris's last chance to get away before they officially took over. My heart sank; they would be well and truly winding their way through the picturesque scenery of the Perry

Ranges by now, all laughing and joking, full of excitement. I didn't want a drink; I just wanted to call for a ride home.

"Can you excuse me for a minute? I just have to make a call." I smiled weakly, sliding off the stool and making my way outside, pulling my mobile out of my pocket. Looking at the blank screen was a painful reminder that there were no messages from Amy, not a one.

I phoned my parents number, hoping that Mum had made it back in time to pick up. I mentally calculated her speed and the distance – yep, Barry Manilow would have sung her home well and truly by now. On the fourth ring, Mum's voice answered.

"What did you forget?" she asked.

"Can you come pick me up, please?"

"Pick you up? Why?"

Hot tears burned under my lids; I didn't want to have to tell her. I felt like a complete idiot standing here next to my things on my own. No doubt Claire was relaying to Eric and Max what had happened; it was just so embarrassing. The sooner I could get away from here, the better.

"They left without me." I bit my lip, trying not to get emotional.

So when Mum laughed hysterically down the phone, it snapped me momentarily out of my misery and into confused anger.

"You think that's funny?" I scoffed.

"Oh, honey, I think it's hilarious."

Wow! I knew my parents often lacked a sensitivity chip, but this was downright mean. What a way to kick a person when they were down.

Mum contained herself as best she could before speaking. "I suppose it's time to come clean," she said. "Promise you won't get mad?"

"What are you talking about?" I exclaimed.

"Well, call me a traitor, but I may or may not have called Amy after you left last night."

"What?"

"Okay, so I did. I gave her the heads up that you were going to call her to tell her you weren't coming."

"WHAT?"

"Oh, Tam, I saw it all over your face; I knew you didn't mean it. I just wanted to tell Amy not to be too harsh on you, that you would most likely change your mind by morning. I know my daughter, honey."

My mouth gaped in horror, at the utter betrayal by my own mother, by my own friend. It all made sense now; Amy was so light and easy-going on the phone at my news, I should have known.

"And I was right, you did change your mind," Mum said.

"So what?!" I scowled at the phone, furious. "What difference does it make? They've still gone. You could have given Amy all the heads up you like; I left her enough messages but she still left without me. Your little theory is seriously flawed, Mother."

"Yes, I know they left this morning," Mum said.

I threw my arms up in despair. "Yeah, well, seems like everyone is in the know except me."

"Relax, Tammy, Amy didn't want me to stress you out by the early departure, she didn't want you to change your mind again, which, knowing you, you probably would have."

I scoffed. She was probably right but I would NEVER admit that.

"Yeah, well, that's brilliant because you may not have realised this, Mother, but I am actually stranded here with no ride now," I ranted. "So can you please come and pick me up?"

She sighed. "Tammy, you have a ride."

"Oh, do I? Really?" I asked sarcastically, staring out at the near-empty car park. "How interesting. And who, supposedly, am I riding off into the sunset with, huh?"

"That would be me," a voice said from behind.

Chapter Fourteen

I squealed, spinning around so fast, startled by the unexpected voice.

Chris?

"What are you doing here?" I clutched a hand to my heart.

"You ready?" he asked unenthusiastically, eyeing my pile of goods before frowning back at me. "We're only going for a few days, you know. You've packed enough for an Amazonian jungle expedition."

"I … I like to be prepared," I stammered. And this, well, this I was definitely not prepared for.

Chris sighed. "I'll get the car." He made his way toward the steps before pausing. My heart still pounded fiercely when he turned to look back up at me, a small twitch curving his lips. "You might want to finish your phone call."

Oh shit, the phone!

"H-hello, Mum, are you there?"

"As I was saying … You have a ride and by the sounds of it you just found that out for yourself."

"Chris Henderson," I whispered into the phone.

"Apparently he wasn't leaving till later anyway, so it worked out all right. Besides, Amy said it would give you two a chance to sort out your stories, whatever that means?"

I knew exactly what it meant. It was Amy's way of punishing me, of punishing Chris. I had read it all over his glowering expression. For someone who didn't want girls on the trip in the first place, being stuck in a car the whole trip with me would be his worst nightmare.

Well, join the club.

"I'm not going," I said.

"Tammy, don't be like that," Mum chastised.

"Like what? This is like unravelling a Miss Marple murder mystery, there are so many twists and turns."

"Just go catch up with your friends and relax."

"I am so over this." I shook my head, tears of frustration threatening to spill over.

"Tammy, you are going to have to learn to just relax. Your friends are expecting you and I think it was nice of Chris to agree to take you."

The thought of the awkward hours stranded in a car with him made me want to leave my things behind and hide. Under a bed. Though that would be the first place he would look.

The sound of a thundering V8 engine neared and suddenly all thoughts of escape seemed hopeless.

"I better go, my ride is here," I said, my words dripping with sarcasm. "Say hi to Amy for me next time you chat to her,"

"Try to remember to have fun, love. Remember your mantra: positive, positive, positive."

"Goodbye, *Mother*." I ended the phone call.

Pfft … Positive, positive, positive.

I would have to desperately dig deep to find any trace of positive energy in me, and just as I thought I might grasp onto some small fibre of it, my eyes landed on my ride.

What. The. Hell.

"So what do you think?" Chris stood with his elbow leaning

casually on the open door of his jet black panel van. He looked up at me expectantly. "Pretty sweet ride, huh?"

"If you're a serial killer," I said, cautiously descending the steps.

Chris's head snapped around with surprise, his eyes almost as dark as the van itself. He slammed the car door and folded his arms, glowering at me as I approached.

"I'll have you know, Toby and I have spent the better part of six months fixing this old girl up."

I wrinkled my nose. "Really?"

"It's got a 308 and a four barrel carby."

"Why, it could be grease lightning," I smirked.

I didn't think a death stare could vary in so many ways, but Chris had mastered a variety of pissed-off stares like no other. The one he was now casting me was a whole new level of anger.

Oops.

I cleared my throat and looked away, suddenly super aware that the last thing I should do was alienate my ride, but then the thought did occur to me: did I want to be trapped in a car with Chris Henderson for three days? Three long, insufferable days – could I subject myself to any more death stares, sneers, scoffs and deep sighs? Maybe I would be doing myself a favour if I gave him good reason to leave me behind. Before I fully acclimated to the idea, my attention was snapped back to the present and the duffle bag that landed at my feet.

I frowned toward the verandah where Chris had moved and was readying himself to turf my other bag down.

"Hey! Watch it," I snapped. "You might break something." It was a possibility, though I didn't know exactly what. Maybe Mum had slipped in a crockery set? Who could honestly guess?

"Let me guess," Chris said with a smirk as he slung my beach bag over his shoulder and trotted down the steps. "Hairdryer?" He threw a cocky smile and grazed my shoulder as he passed, heading for the van. My eyes burned into his back as he opened the double doors to chuck in my bag. He turned to me expectantly, his hand out for me to pass him the duffle. I snatched it up, trying not to let the strain of its weight show as I lugged it over and carefully placed it into the back. I attempted to, anyway. With a rather inelegant lack of grace, I hitched it up onto my knee, trying to be all cool and casual, as if I was totally in control …

I so wasn't.

Chris plucked it from me as if the bag weighed nothing and turfed it into the back.

"Careful!"

"Relax, it landed on the mattress."

Mattress?

I peered into the back. Sure enough, a mattress lined the whole floor up to the front bucket seats. The windows were blacked out and the inside walls were lined with black carpet. Oh, ick. All it needed was some leopard-print cushions and a disco ball.

It would seem that black was a common theme throughout Chris's van, and the colour matched his mood.

Chris slammed the back shut. Viewing time was over.

I half expected him to say, "Let's get this show on the road," or "We're burning daylight," but instead I got a rather lacklustre, "Get in."

Yep! Three long days.

Chapter Fifteen

Claire and Eric waved us goodbye in a pearly white-smiled send-off.

Claire looked utterly relieved that Chris was giving me a lift. He'd saved the day.

"See! All's well that ends well." She smiled as she hugged me goodbye.

Disappointment must have been etched in every crease of my face when I thought I had been left behind; I wondered what expression Claire and Eric read in my face now? I could only imagine my attempt at a good-humoured smile was coming across as nothing more than a pained grimace at best.

I opened Chris's car door and slid into the passenger seat, the leather sticking to my skin in the heat. I dipped my sun visor to shield my eyes from the bright sun glare. The sun's rays reflected off the newly polished dashboard that still smelled like Armor All spray. It was sickly sweet and smelt brand new.

Chris slid behind the steering wheel beside me, flicked down his visor and a pair of sunnies fell into his lap. He scooped them up and quickly put them on. That was a bonus, I thought. I wouldn't be able to see his guaranteed eye-rolls and those death stares. The engine roared to life as Chris fired up the black beast and my senses were assaulted with the growl of the engine and Bruce Springsteen mid-chorus, singing 'Brilliant Disguise' through the speakers.

Normal people would apologise and turn down the volume. Normal people would say something, anything at all, before shifting the steering column into gear. But not Chris. Instead, he placed his arm on the back of my headrest as he craned backward, reversing out, before shifting gear and pulling us away from the Onslow drive.

Most people would offer a cheery double honk to Claire and Eric as they waved from the verandah, but not Chris. He lifted one finger from the wheel in a half-hearted wave as we sped away.

It was so like him; everything was understated. I guess I was amazed that he had managed to string together a handful of sentences at all in order to communicate anything. We sat in silence. I couldn't believe I was going to spend three whole days cooped up in this car with him. It was going to be the longest three days of my life.

Surprisingly, after a little while he did start talking. It was about his car, but it could have been worse. And he did seem rather animated about it. I tucked that knowledge away for emergency conversation material in the hours of awkward silences that were sure to come.

I was actually relieved that Bruce Springsteen filled what would have been an otherwise unbearable silence. I peered at him out of the corner of my eye. He'd propped his arm on the ledge of the open window and his black hair fluttered in the breeze. He was usually so staunch and straight, unmoving, but now he seemed ... well ... kind of relaxed.

He turned his head every now and then to view the passing lake scenery; he tapped on the steering wheel and whistled lightly to the chorus of a song; he pulled at his safety belt as he straightened in his seat a bit. Was this an insight into a whole other, chilled-out side to Chris, I wondered?

He slouched down and seemed to melt into the leather of his seat a bit. It was the first time I had seen his shoulders relax, as if the more distance we put between us and the Onslow the more comfortable and clear-headed he became.

Interesting.

Chris leaned forward to lower the music, but it was too late now; there was a ringing in my ears.

He had nice hands, tanned by the sun, tidy fingernails; he could totally be a hand model with hands like those. If you were going to notice Chris and like him, his hands would probably be the first thing that would draw you to him, seeing as his face was always an intimidating scowl. It wasn't the first time I had noticed his hands – there had been countless times he had served me a drink at the bar, or handed me change and I had noticed how nice they were. The second thing I noticed about Chris (if I was noticing things) was his shoulders. They were so square, so symmetrical; he looked like he was a swimmer. He had great posture, even when he stood behind the bar between customers, with his arms folded – his stance was straight, proud, expectant. Yep! Your eyes would trail from those hands to those shoulders and usually be met with a piercing flick of the deep brown eyes that would cause you to quickly look away, or caused *me* to, anyway.

He had been pretty intimidating in the beginning, but as time wore on I just found him downright rude, no matter how lovely his hands and shoulders may be.

"What are you staring at?" Chris's voice pulled me out of my thoughts.

Oh crap! Was I staring?

I snapped my head away to look out of the window. "Nothing."

"They're not that white, are they?" he said.

My attention moved from the window to Chris again with a confused frown.

"Sorry?"

His head tilted downward as he shifted his leg a little to expose … a kneecap.

I smiled. "You're wearing shorts?"

"You don't have to sound so surprised." He lowered his leg.

"I don't think I've seen you in shorts before." My eyes trailed over his tan cargos; it seemed that in line with nice hands and shoulders, Chris had nice legs. *Okay, best not to stare*, I thought. But then something grabbed my attention.

"You have impressively tanned legs for someone who lives in Levi's," I mused. "You don't sun-bake in a pair of budgie smugglers on the weekends, do you?" That would just be too much.

Chris burst out laughing, so loud and abruptly it caused me to flinch at the unexpectedness of it. Laughter from Chris was as rare as seeing him in shorts.

"Budgie smugglers?" he asked.

"Yeah, you know, Speedos, Y-fronts,"

"I know what they are, Tammy, and the answer is *no*, no I don't do that." He grinned, concentrating on the road.

I took a moment to study Chris, not out of the corner of my eye this time but to unapologetically study him. I wanted to fully absorb the rarity of his smile, of his good humour, because let's face it, it would probably be the first and last time I saw it.

I curved my brow. "So exceptionally tanned legs but no weekends spent in budgie smugglers, eh? Curiouser and curiouser," I smirked.

Chris coughed. His face flexed back into those familiar stern lines as he straightened in his seat. "Tamara?"

I cocked my head. "Yes, Christopher?"

His lips twitched as he fought not to smile. "Stop staring at me."

And as quickly as the moment had come it was gone again. He controlled his smile and settled back into his regular serious, no-nonsense Chris.

"I can't help it," I said, reluctantly shifting my gaze back out to the road. "It's so very fascinating."

"What, my legs?" He shifted, as if checking them out.

I didn't answer; I relaxed in my seat, resting my head on the seatbelt strap.

Nope, it wasn't his legs that were fascinating. It was his smile.

Chapter Sixteen

It had been a rather animated start.

One I'd hoped would be a bit of an ice-breaker, but it did little to fully thaw his icy exterior. An hour and a half into the journey we were cruising through the winding terrain of the Perry Ranges in stone-cold silence – well, aside from Bruce Springsteen on repeat who now felt like a close and personal friend of mine. He was the buffer that saved me from feeling *completely* uncomfortable. If I had been travelling with any other Onslow Boy, there would have been free-flowing conversation, constant chatter and incessant flirting, not that I revelled in such things. Flirting to me was so very alien I didn't quite know how to do it. And with the Onslow Boys there was always a shameful amount of flirting.

Maybe this was the best outcome. I didn't wholly feel a part of the Onslow gang; I struggled at witticisms or keeping up with the banter of in-jokes and shared memories I knew nothing about. I was usually just a bystander, smiling in good humour or laughing politely at things I didn't really understand. Amy was so comfortable and boisterous with these guys, nothing worried or fazed her. Mum's words echoed through my consciousness. 'Just try to relax, Tammy.'

I scoffed at the thought. *Relax?* I didn't know the meaning of the word – my mind was a constant churning of worry. The only peace I really afforded myself was when I went for my runs and worked on my fitness circuits. Any other time my mind would race at a million miles an hour, never at peace. It hadn't taken my doctor long to pinpoint that my migraines were brought on by stress, that with a combination of full-time study and my fitness job I was running myself thin. He advised me that something had to give. Pretty amusing, really – it didn't matter how physically healthy and fit my body had become, my mind was still as frazzled as ever. Maybe a few days of sitting in contemplative silence with Chris would do me good, keep me occupied in a different sense. A welcome distraction from reality, from working out, studying. Just me (and Chris) and the road to a new year – hell, a new century. This might actually be good for me. I squared my shoulders.

Positive, positive, positive.

"So why did you hide from me at the Bake House?" Chris asked.

Oh crap!

I didn't know where to look. Especially now, as Chris flicked his sunnies up onto his head and glanced at me expectantly. The canopy of towering gum trees flickered shadows across his face as the afternoon sun battled to pierce through the dense bushland lining the road.

"Oh, I was just joking around." I gave a quick laugh, wiping a crease from my lap.

"You were avoiding me," he pressed, his tone serious.

"I wasn't avoiding you," I said, squirming under his scrutiny. A bubble of unease surfaced in my chest, but then a thought popped into my head. I looked pointedly at him. "Why would I do that?"

Ha! Ball's back in your court. Maybe it would make him have a think as to why anyone might want to avoid him; he wasn't exactly a ray of sunshine and considering the last time we interacted he had given me such a penetrating death stare … Have a think about *that,* Mr Henderson.

I watched his reaction – there was no evidence of him even

taking in the question, as if he wasn't even giving what I had said a second thought.

He shrugged. "You tell me," he said matter-of-factly, as if he wasn't even particularly invested in the answer.

Unease turned into anger. Was he so blind to himself? Did he have no real sense of why I would perhaps want to go to such lengths to avoid him? His nonchalant attitude made me feel like a bit of a weirdo, as if I just did random weird things all the time. I expected him to shrug, roll his eyes and say, "Chicks."

I narrowed my eyes at him. Maybe it was time I did him a favour. "I hid because, frankly, at that moment you were the last person on Earth that I wanted to see."

Chris's brows rose. "Really?" he said, a mixture of amusement and intrigue lining his face.

I crossed my arms. "Just because your friends put up with you doesn't mean I have to. If the choice is to be subjected to your pissy-pants attitude or hide under a table, well I clearly choose the latter."

"Pissy-pants attitude?" He glowered.

I leaned closer. "Believe me, that's sugar-coating it." I looked back out of the window, conversation over.

A long silence settled between us. An immense sense of satisfaction swelled in my chest, a feeling of pride, I guess, from staring down the beast and telling him what for. Maybe honesty really was the best policy.

I snuck a glance at him, scowling at the road ahead. Then again, considering we weren't anywhere near our destination, this was going to be one hell of a road trip.

Nevertheless, I still felt empowered, until, of course, my attention was caught by the chuckle coming from beside me. That smile was back. Chris rubbed his jaw line in humoured wonder as he glanced at me.

"Not bad for someone who doesn't like confrontation," he mused.

My brows narrowed. I had never told him that, I had never

admitted that to anyone; it was my own Achilles heel and something I would never voice out loud. I shifted uneasily.

"And what makes you think I can't handle confrontation?" I lifted my chin in defiance. "I can handle it just fine."

Chris tilted his head incredulously. "Tam … you hid under a table."

Oh, right.

I didn't know what was more infuriating – the fact that he was so obviously right or that he had called me Tam. It sounded so foreign on his tongue, so strangely intimate. Usually any of the boys would playfully call me Tammy, Tamara or Tim-Tam. Sean and Amy would occasionally call me Tam, but no one else and *especially* not Chris.

It was unsettling.

I closed my eyes and rubbed at my temples, a dull ache slowly surfacing in its old, familiar way. I rubbed the back of my neck. I needed to relax – the last thing I needed was a migraine. My best form of avoidance of Chris was to stare out of the window, but the constant whirring and flashing of scenery going by was a sure-fire way to induce an instant migraine. My eyes needed to focus on nothing; I just needed to be still and silent. Luckily, Bruce had remained turned down and was really only acting as croony background music. I swallowed deeply, trying not to fear the worst.

I shifted in my seat, making myself more comfortable.

"What's going on?" Chris said. "Will you stop fidgeting?"

At this point I really couldn't care what Chris thought. Fine, I would sit still for a while and hope that maybe I was being paranoid, that perhaps I had just been worked up from the chaos of the morning and the pent-up frustration. Maybe I was dehydrated. If I sat still with my eyes closed, maybe I could rein this thing back in.

"You okay?" Chris's voice pierced the darkness.

"Hmm," I said. "Fine."

I breathed in deeply, wishing I had paid more attention to the meditation techniques I was taught when I was a teenager. For now I would try for stillness, for silence. That could work – just breathe, relax. Shut off my thoughts and let go.

I concentrated on my breathing and not the thunder of the engine. I could feel my shoulders sagging and my body melting into the leather bucket seat as I calmed my mind and my body into believing everything would be okay. And just as I was about to breathe a sigh of relief, my eyes blinked open.

I sat up straight in a panic. "STOP THE CAR!"

Chapter Seventeen

Oh no-no-no-no-no …

As soon as Chris had jolted the car to a violent stop on the gravelly side of the road, I unbuckled myself and almost kneed him in the face as I scurried over the back of the seat like an uncoordinated spider.

Hmmmph. I landed fair on my back; bless the mattress for breaking my awkward dismount.

"What the hell, Tam? What happened? What are you doing?" Chris asked as he swivelled in his seat to watch me. I crawled over the mattress to my Esprit bag, unzipped it and dumped the contents out onto the mattress.

No-no-no-no-no …

I scrambled through my belongings, fearing the worst. Surely I couldn't be so stupid? I stilled. Leaning back on my heels I delved into the pocket of my shorts and retrieved Tess's list. I unravelled it and sure enough there it was, boldly circled, the only thing not ticked off the list.

Any personal medication needed.

My heart sank. In all the chaos of searching for bloody sleeping bags and other essentials I had organised through Mum, I had completely forgotten to pack the most important thing of all:

my migraine medication. My heart pumped and a light sheen of perspiration made the nape of my neck sticky, or was that just the onset of sickness? Oh God, I was in trouble.

A blinding streak of light assaulted me. I shielded my eyes against the offending rays. Chris stood before me, holding open the back door to the panel van.

"What did you forget?" He sighed. Ha! Now he just sounded like my mother.

I held up my hands, slapping them on my thighs in defeat; I shook my head. Hot tears welled in my eyes as my traitorous chin began to tremble.

I tried to scoop up my belongings in between horrid sniffling sounds that came involuntarily out of me, as now did the water works, gushing tears from my eyes.

Just *perfect!*

A hand snaked gently around my wrist.

A perfect hand.

"What's the matter?" Chris's voice was soft. "What can I do to help?"

I looked up at his face. The hard lines had melted into something that looked like … concern? I pulled my hand away.

"I just forgot something really important," I said, trying to keep it together.

Chris's brows rose in alarm. "Oh … right." He straightened and the gentle hand let go of my wrist. Shoving his hands in his back pockets, he attempted to look casual, but he looked anything but. "Well, we might be able to find a petrol station or something up the road to find what you need."

I shoved my belongings back into my bag, pausing only to meet Chris's eyes in confusion.

"What I need?"

He cleared his throat. "Um, yeah … You know."

I raised my brows in silent question.

He sighed in agitation. "Where you can get … girl stuff," he whispered the last words, as if someone might overhear him on the side of a highway in the middle of nowhere.

It took a moment for the penny to drop and I broke into a weak smile. "Ooooh, I see." I nodded. "Chris, I don't need a tampon." I had great joy in watching him squirm at the sound of that word.

"Oh, right. Okay. Well … good." He moved, refusing to look at me as he slammed the door on my smirk, coating me in soothing darkness again. At least his moment of unease had momentarily snapped me out of my despair.

I placed my bag aside, took a deep breath and climbed back over the seat again. Chris waited until I had settled in before he opened the driver's door and slid in beside me. He gripped the steering wheel and looked ahead as silence settled over us; this time there was no Bruce to mask it.

I sighed, pushing my fingers back through my hair, gathering the tendrils at the base of my neck. "I forgot my pain medication."

The infamous crease pinched between Chris's eyes and I knew what he was thinking: 'Is that all?'

"Oh, right," he said as he clicked his seatbelt into place. "Well, we can always pick up some Panadol at the next servo."

I shook my head. "I wish that would work. I get really bad migraines, like *really* bad. My vision goes and I get nauseous and the pain …" I broke off. I didn't want the tears to come again. That would just make it worse.

"How often do you get them?" Chris asked.

"Usually about once a fortnight, lately more frequently," I said.

"Do you know what causes it?"

Stress.

I shrugged. "Just prone to them; I guess I'm just lucky like that."

"Are you getting one now?" His eyes studied me like I was a bug under a microscope.

I bit my lip. "I really hope not." My voice shook. Truth be known, I had become so reliant on having my painkillers at hand come an attack, and I was at least able to shut myself away in the comfort and darkness of my own home and manage myself through the pain. But not like this, stuck in a van in the middle of bushland with a moody, silent boy who probably thought I was just being a drama queen.

Chris's knuckles brushed against my arm, snapping me out of my thoughts. "Here," he said, holding out his sunglasses. "Put these on."

My gaze lifted from the sunglasses to his face as the corner of his mouth pinched into a smile.

I grabbed them from him, my fingers brushing his. "Thanks," I said.

Chris cleared his throat as he placed his hand on the steering wheel and he started up the engine again. "Well, let's get this show on the road."

I tried not to laugh and slid on his sunnies.

Normal suited Chris.

We had been travelling for an hour, maybe two? I couldn't be sure. All I knew was a storm was brewing and as black clouds rolled in, so did the familiar migraine pain. There was no denying it now, this was definitely a migraine.

Tears burned my eyes – what once had been worry of potentially being far away from home without my medication had now become a bone-jarring reality. I'd never thought that such a beautiful, picturesque trip through the wide open spaces and leafy ranges could feel so claustrophobic.

As the panel van hummed forward through sweeping turns and bends, it only reinforced how completely out of my comfort zone I was. I could almost feel the colour drain from my face as my skin became clammy and spots danced across my vision, forcing me to keep my eyes shut tight behind the sunglasses. I guess I turned out to be the perfect travel partner for Chris – there was no small talk from me, I was all about silence. I left him alone and he left me alone. I just wanted to crawl into a hole and block out the whirring of the engine, the motion of the car sweeping around bends, which only heightened my nausea. I tried desperately not to think about vomiting or passing out, but the more I thought the more miserable I became.

At some point I must have drifted off, awakened only by a feathery touch to my cheek.

"Tam?"

The car was still, the world was silent, save for the odd bird call in the distance. I stirred gently, not wanting to move in case I was thrust into the pain that spiralled its way through my head in excruciating pulses with every movement.

I felt a palm cup my forehead, then my cheek.

"You're burning up."

That was the last I heard before feeling my passenger door fly open and a voice near my face spoke gently.

"Tam, we've stopped at a rest area. There are toilets here if you want to freshen up."

My bladder agreed that that was an excellent idea, the only thing that could possibly have made me move.

"That a girl. Come on, I'll help you." A hand clasped onto my arm, strength for me to lean on, to help me stand. I eased myself out of the car and clutched at my temples. Squinting through blurred vision, I could see a hexagon-shaped concrete block in the distance that housed the public toilets back off the road amid the bushland. It was like a beacon to me as I broke from Chris's hold and headed slowly over.

"You all right?" he asked, following closely behind. It was kind of reassuring to think that if I stumbled he would break my fall. I waved him off, managing nothing more than caveman-like grunts as I shuffled toward the toilet block. The last thing I needed was for Chris Henderson to help me to the toilet. I stumbled forward, determined to force myself through the door, out of his sight. Then I could crumble.

"Whoa!" Hands grabbed my shoulders and steered me to the

left. “Not that one.”

Oh, right, maybe I did need his help.

Thankfully, the toilet block was cool and dark inside. I managed to do what I needed without passing out and waking up in a compromising position. It’s amazing how determined you can be even on the edge of delirium. Mind you, I didn’t get a chance to fall into mindlessness with Chris calling out every minute, asking if I was okay. I didn’t know which of us was more frightened of me hitting the women’s toilet floor, him or me?

I splashed cool water onto my face and the back of my neck and squinted at my cloudy reflection in the rest room mirror. I didn’t need a whole lot of light to know I was as white as a ghost, my eyes bloodshot, my hair in disarray.

I was an absolute train wreck, but right now, I couldn’t care less. I had to get out of there, the churning of my nausea made only worse by the dank surroundings of the toilet block. I edged my way outside and spotted Chris pacing then jerk to a halt when he saw me.

Chapter Eighteen

Was I dreaming?

There was no noise, no thumping V8 engine, no Bruce. Nothing but silence – beautiful, underrated silence. Something cool pressed against my forehead; a soft sensation smoothed over my head. The movement was hypnotic, back and forth, sweeping and dividing the tendrils of my hair. I snuggled deeper into the dream. My cheek felt warm, in stark contrast to the cool feeling on my forehead. This was a strange dream, one that I didn't want to wake from. I felt safe, rested; no pain reached me here. I wanted to stay forever. The stroking motion through my hair stopped.

No, don't stop. I squirmed. Something touched my shoulder blade, a delicate squeeze.

"Tammy?"

No, no, I wasn't ready.

"Tam?"

There was that name again.

The cold compress swept away from my brow and ran a delicious cool trail along my cheek and around to the nape of my neck, causing my eyelids to flutter open.

"Tammy, you better drink something, you need to keep your fluids up." The squeeze to my shoulder turned into a series of gentle taps.

I squinted and blinked, trying to focus on a light glow in the distance. I groaned and rubbed my face before stretching one arm up to the heavens, expecting my bones to crack and pop. I savoured the sweet, sated feeling of unravelling from sleep, but most of all basking in my blissful new reality: no pain. It was over. As I stretched, the back of my hand whacked against something.

"Jesus, Tammy, watch it!" A strong hand grabbed my wrist. "You nearly took out my eye."

I lifted my head a little and looked around me. My head was resting on a thigh? I sat bolt upright and my head slammed against something hard.

"Faaaaar … Tammy!" I swivelled around, clutching the back of my head to see Chris gripping his jaw, his face contorted in badly disguised surprise and pain.

"Bloody hell, you just got rid of one migraine." Chris winced as he worked his jaw to check it wasn't broken.

I bit my lip. "I'm sorry, you just startled me."

Startled was an understatement. I took in the darkened surrounds lit only by some crude camping glow wand or something wedged in the corner. My knees dipped into the spongy mattress. We were in the back of the panel van. My eyes settled on Chris who sat with his elbows resting on his knees, looking pissed off as he continued to rub his jaw. This was definitely not a dream.

"W-what time is it?" I asked, looking past him through the windscreen. It was completely dark.

"After eight."

"EIGHT?"

"You were out cold." Chris shrugged. "Must have needed it."

Wow, eight. I was out cold, all right. The last thing I remembered was coming out of the toilet block, and then nothing. Nothing until I felt the coldness on my forehead. I spotted a face washer near Chris's foot. I smiled. I thought I had been dreaming, but with that and the smooth, rhythmic feeling of fingers running soothingly through my hair, it seemed I definitely hadn't been. And the warmth against my cheek was Chris's thigh? I swallowed deeply. I could feel my face flame and was thankful for the dim lighting. My eyes slowly lifted to look at Chris.

"Thanks," I said.

Chris's brows lifted in surprise. "Wow. This is not the normal reaction when girls wake up in the back of a panel van."

I cocked my brow. "Oh? Been many, have there?"

Chris stretched out his arms, folding them behind his head as a boyish grin lined his face. "Hundreds."

"Lots of damsels in distress?"

"I'm actually thinking of painting a red cross on the side of the van."

"Sounds lucrative; you should charge by the hour," I said, throwing the wash cloth up at him. He caught it with impressive reflexes.

I took a moment to study this playful side of Chris, taking in the lines of his face, the jagged folds of his hair that were ruffled in a casual messy, cool way. He wasn't beautiful like Toby, cute like Stan or oozing charisma and raw sex like Sean did. He was something else entirely. As much as I hated to admit it, he was the epitome of handsome – silver-screen good looks, smouldering, broody, he was an utter enigma.

But who was the real Chris?

I secretly wondered which other girls he may have had here in the back of his panel van in the past. I tried to pinpoint any of the girls that strutted around the Onslow like a conveyer belt of sex, ripe for the picking. I hadn't really been into the pub scene until getting back in touch with Amy recently, but still, even I could recognise the whispers and doe-eyed looks girls gave him as they held out their hands to Chris at the bar for their change. It was somewhat amusing – Chris didn't even give them the time of day, but that didn't stop them from trying. Maybe that was a part of the attraction?

I couldn't exactly guess who may have caught his attention, I couldn't even imagine who he may have invited into the van, or up the stairs to his bedroom, or into the beer gar …

I stilled.

"You all right?" Chris shifted with unease.

My eyes snapped up to lock with his. I quickly looked away again, my mind racing at a hundred miles an hour. My cheeks burned as my memory flashed back to a time – the only time – I had seen Chris with a girl, something I had completely forgotten until now.

"Yeah. Nothing. I'm fine."

It wasn't an unusual state of affairs for Amy and me to sneak out. To us, our parents were utter killjoys when it came to anything beyond ten p.m., which basically left an entire social scene out of reach, locked beyond our front doors, unexplored. At fifteen, it was an injustice of gargantuan proportions. More so for Amy whose older cousins, Chris and Adam, taunted her nightly by coming and going as they pleased. They were a little older, sure, but the big difference was that they were boys. Such double standards.

On one warm summer night, Amy and I had planned to pull off the ultimate deception and sneak out for Todd Macki's eighteenth. Word on the grapevine was that it was going to be epic. Pretty much every teen in town was going to gatecrash; we simply had to go. The plan was for me to sneak out and ride across town to the Onslow, hiding my bike behind a bush in the beer garden. Amy would 'accidentally' leave the fairy lights on in the beer garden and I would tiptoe through, having not broken a leg in the dark. The dim lights were a much-welcome sight as I fumbled my way up the back staircase to the top landing near the back door of the second storey. The plan was that I would wait there until precisely five past twelve at which time I would tap our secret knock on the back door panel to signal that I had arrived and the coast was clear.

I prided myself in being a masterful creature of the night that could slide along the edges of blackness with the elegance of a jungle cat. In reality, I was just smart enough to remove my jangly bracelets and wear my sensible (quiet) Converse sneakers to trek to our meeting point.

Wrapping my arms around my legs, I settled in to wait on the landing and glanced at my watch: eleven forty-five, early as usual.

I sighed. *Always better to be early*, I thought, as my gaze traced the star-lined sky, my lips tilting into a devilish grin. My parents would be livid if they knew my whereabouts right now.

Impatient and bored, I had felt bold, brimming with confidence and self-assurance.

Maybe Amy was (by some miracle) running early. There was no point in us both waiting around, twiddling our thumbs for the next twenty minutes when we could be at the party of the decade. I sat up and my fist hovered over the back door, ready to make contact when laughter floated up from below.

My eyes had widened, heart had pounded and I'd dived onto the platform. My palms connected with the wooden landing and I'd squeezed my eyes shut, praying no one could see me. The laughter dipped into conspiratorial whispers as footsteps continued down below. I opened my eyes, listening intently to the movements. A gap in the decked landing let in a faint slither of a subtle glow from the fairy lights beneath. I squinted, fixing my eye slowly to the gap, searching out the people whose voices lingered in the shadows under the stairs.

Even through the tiny crack it didn't take me long to find them. Broad, square shoulders were bathed in the subtle glow of the lights in the small space under the stairs. I had gasped and pressed my face into the slatted wood as the shadows moved beneath. A small hand slid along his shoulder, gripping the fabric with such force I thought it might tear. He pressed her back against the post, her fair skin illuminated white in the light as she gasped at the unexpectedness of it. She affixed her hungry stare on him as he lowered his mouth to hers. My eyes widened as the heated scene played out before me. I couldn't turn away. I had never felt more scandalous than at that moment in my life. At fifteen I had never seen or experienced anything like it. Excitement twisted in my stomach seeing her gasp as he trailed his mouth down her neck. I bit my lip as I watched his fingers slide slowly, wickedly against the girl's collarbone, only to hook the strap of her top and peel it slowly downward, revealing a small, milky white breast. An unexpected feeling shot through me at the sight of his thumb teasing the pebble-like bud as he kissed her once more, and my, *how* he kissed her. I felt the pang of jealousy – never had I ever been so wanted, so desired. I imagined for a moment that I was that girl in the dark, that I was the one who was pressed up against the beam, as he slowly lowered his head to trail kisses along my exposed skin. The girl arched her back, her neck twisted in exquisite madness, her fingers folded through the dark tendrils of his hair. Her breath had hitched as his tongue slid teasingly along her nipple.

"Chris!" she gasped, the word carrying its way up the stairs.

I flinched backward and kicked a pot plant off the landing. I covered my face to stop from screaming as I heard the plant shatter below. Before I could worry that it might have landed on anyone, the back light to the beer garden flooded the space. I scrambled backward, out of sight. It seemed I wasn't the only one concerned with being discovered – hearing the muffled giggles beneath me as they scurried out of the space. I leaned forward and peeked over the ledge just enough to see Chris running out of the side exit of the beer garden, leading the girl by the hand as they fought to catch their breath from laughing. He looked back at her with a boyish grin, as if he would follow her to the ends of the Earth, as he pulled her through the gate and into the darkness beyond.

I sat back, plastered against the bricks of the hotel, my breath laboured, my cheeks aflame from all I had seen.

I could only hope that I would remain undiscovered. The back light switched off again and I had shaken my head, trying to clear the fog. I eyed my watch in the gloom: one minute past twelve. I had exactly four minutes to gather myself and try to forget what I had just witnessed.

Chapter Nineteen

I had never told a soul about that night.

In fact, I had forgotten all about it. How was that possible? I must have felt so intensely wicked and mortified about my secret spying that I had blocked it out of my mind altogether, until now, as I thought back to Chris's fingers stroking my hair, entirely innocent, simply to comfort a sleeping girl.

Heat still flooded my cheeks at all the confused emotions fifteen-year-old Tammy had felt on that night. It also cemented the knowledge that Chris may have been distant, moody and mysterious, but he sure knew how to treat a girl.

I had no doubt that he had had his fair share, under the beer garden steps, in his room, in this van. I couldn't bring myself to look at him, suddenly annoyed at the feelings that twisted in my stomach, at the thought of him having girls in there, anywhere. It was the same feeling I'd got that night, a sharp unexpected jolt of jealousy. It was pathetic. Stupid.

Jealous over Chris Henderson? I don't think so.

"Are you okay? You look kind of flushed." Chris's voice snapped me from my lurid thoughts.

"I'm fine!" I said too quickly. "Migraine's gone, I'm good to go." I crawled toward the front seat.

"Where are you going?" Chris asked.

I paused mid-climb, looking back at him expectantly. "Oh, um, I'm okay to keep going."

Chris twirled the face washer casually around his finger. "I thought we might set up camp here for the night; we're nowhere near any fine eatery or civilisation, but the toilet block is here, which is something I guess."

My heart pounded as I lowered my leg and slid down to sit on the mattress beside him. "But the itinerary said we would stop in Calhoon first night; isn't that where the others would be expecting us?"

Chris shrugged. "We've lost too much time with the late start and the unplanned stopover." He eyed me expectantly. "Besides, we're in pretty thick roo country and I don't fancy busting up my windscreen by ploughing into one."

No. I didn't want that either.

"Best make camp here."

My heart sank; I had grand visions of catching up with the others, setting up tents and swags together, even perhaps us girls persuading the boys to stay in a hotel, although I didn't much like our chances. At best it would be an established camping ground with hot showers – the height of luxury. Instead, no thanks to me, we were hours and hours behind the others, stuck in the middle of nowhere in the back of a panel van.

"You hungry?" Chris grabbed a shopping bag and rustled around inside it. "It's not exactly Michelin Star cooking, but Melba rustled me up a batch of salad rolls and a pack of Anzac biscuits. Aw sa-weet!" he cried. "The old girl has chucked in some frozen Primas, God love her." Chris pulled out the drinks, beaming like he was a kid at Christmas. He chucked one over to me that I juggled into catching.

I eyed the juice box sceptically, a grin pinching at the corner of my mouth. Amy had often complained that Chris was Melba's favourite. This might just work out in my favour. I couldn't help but speculate that Melba hadn't packed lunch for Adam or Amy.

Interesting, I thought.

Amy being the only girl and Adam being the charismatic charmer, it surprised me that Chris was the favourite.

"Thanks," I said, watching Chris set aside his precious goods. He lined them up straight like soldiers and set the bag aside.

"It probably wouldn't hurt for you to take it easy, anyway," he said. "We can get your medication when we hit Calhoon tomorrow." He passed me a salad roll.

"It's a nice idea," I said, "but there is one small problem."

"What's that?" Chris asked through a mouthful of roll.

"They're prescription meds." I sighed.

He swallowed. "Bugger."

"Yep." I picked at my soggy bread roll.

"Drink!" Chris's voice sounded firm. "You need to keep your fluids up," he insisted.

"Forever the barman," I mused.

"Keeping people hydrated is my profession," he said, breaking the plastic straw of his Prima and shoving it into the fruit box. I couldn't help but smile at him; Chris, the serious, no-nonsense publican, sipping from a Prima like a boy in a schoolyard. He looked so unguarded, so innocent, and then my mind flashed back to his taunting mouth in the beer garden that night. Looks were deceiving. He wasn't as much of a puzzle as people believed. He was just understated – unlike the other Onslow Boys he was private and didn't wear his emotions on his sleeve. No; instead, he lurked in shadows and drove black panel vans with the windows blacked out. What was that saying? It's the quiet ones you have to worry about? Great! And I was stuck with him tonight.

Not feeling hungry, I wrapped the remainder of my roll back up and placed it aside. "I might freshen up a bit before I call it a night," I said. "Do you need help to set anything up?"

The gurgling sounds of the straw sucking up the last remnants of juice answered me, before Chris crushed the packet with satisfaction. "Nope! It's okay, I'll set up camp."

Relieved, I grabbed my toiletries before he changed his mind and roped me into setting up some complicated camping apparatus.

I struggled with the latch of the back door, jiggling and twisting, even going so far as to put my shoulder into it, which got me nowhere, either.

I struggled with the stupid thing until I felt the press of Chris lean against my shoulder and place his hand over mine.

"Not like that." His words breathed out near my cheek. "Like this." He twisted and lifted the handle with ease, freeing the lock and pushing it open, mercifully giving me room to move from the heat of his torso.

"Thanks," I said too quickly, as I gathered my things and moved toward the toilet block. Fumbling my goods, flustered, I dropped bits and pieces along the way.

Please don't be watching. Please don't be watching …

I managed to steal a glance back toward the car before going into the Ladies' toilets. My eyes briefly locked with his amused ones as Chris sat casually on the edge of the van, a crooked grin curving his lips.

Bugger.

Chapter Twenty

I took my time cleansing, scrubbing, toning and moisturising.

It was as close to a shower as I was going to get. I changed into my nightwear and pulled my hair up into a high ponytail and out of my face. Even though I had slept a good portion of the day away, I was bone tired, and suddenly grateful that Chris had made the call to stop for the evening even if we were a good six hours behind schedule. Driving on into the night and reaching Calhoon at four in the morning wouldn't put us in good stead for the next day's leg – driving tired was not only dangerous for Chris, but getting overtired was another migraine trigger for me. No, I needed a good night's rest. So I took my time, allowing Chris to set up tent and get changed himself while I busied myself brushing my teeth.

I didn't know exactly what warranted camping attire, but Tess's list recommended flannelette PJs as the coastal roads can be chilly of a night, even in summer. I knew we weren't that far into the journey, or maybe it was the fluoro lighting in the toilet block that flickered with a disco of bugs buzzing above my head, but the night was still stifling, the air thick and warm. As I stood in my white and navy striped PJs, the only nightwear I had packed, I stretched out the collar and fanned myself. I'd probably be grateful for it as the air cooled and I settled in the tent for the night, but not yet I wasn't. I packed all my gear back into my toiletry bag. Chris had had enough time to set up. I zipped up my toiletry bag and made my way outside.

I paused. A frown etched my brow as I neared the van, following the dull light and soft music that filtered out of the open back door. I spotted Chris perched on the end of the mattress, his foot hitched up on the tow bar. He was relaxed, whistling along to the tune.

He straightened and sat up when he saw me approaching.

"Feel better?" he asked.

I kept walking, peering around the other side of the van, bewildered. I did a full circle around it, checking in all directions.

"Where's the tent?"

Chris pushed his hands in his pockets, a perplexed line creasing his brow. "What tent?"

My pulse spiked in anxiety. "The sleeping tent?" I envisioned a large, multi-winged tent that could house a family of five, with even a shady verandah part to sit in outside on deckchairs. Like the one on the front of camping shop catalogues, that kind of tent.

"Oh." Chris cocked an amused brow and scratched the back of his neck. "Ya see, the thing is …" He tapped on the mattress beneath him. "I don't do tents."

I squared my shoulders, a grave look on my face. "That's not camping," I said coolly.

Chris smiled, reaching in to grab his bag. "You'll thank me in the morning." He winked, shouldered his backpack and headed for the toilet block.

Okay, no sweat. We would just sleep in the back of the van. The very confined, claustrophobic van.

It appeared that in my absence Chris had been busy – he had placed all the baggage aside (well, most of it was mine; he was a light traveller, so it would seem) and set the mattress up with fresh black sheets and a navy plaid doona. To top it off there were two lumpy pillows that looked like they had seen better days. The bed was made army-style immaculate, crisp and taut; you could really bounce a coin off it. I was impressed, but not surprised. If Chris did something it was always with military precision. I knew Chris's goofball of a younger brother was in the army but maybe they had gotten it wrong? Maybe Adam and his lighthearted wit and people skills needed to be behind the bar and Chris needed to be shipped off to the South Pacific or wherever they go to these days?

I stood with my hands on my hips eyeing our sleeping quarters, the very *cosy* quarters that Chris had no doubt planned on sleeping in alone until I had crashed the party. No worries, we were both adults here, no problem. I had my sleeping bag. I grabbed for it, unclasping the pull string and dumping out the – whoa! Hot pink roll. Okay. I could work with this. In one flick, I uncurled the sleeping bag and pulled it apart, revealing a …

"Oh my God," I said aloud. I looked on in horror at the giant caricature of Punky Brewster with two thumbs up. Dad and his bloody impulse purchases at garage sales. Sure, this would have been handy, and no doubt I would have loved it … when I was five! Knowing Dad, it had probably been buried in the garage for the past fifteen years. A very delayed discovery indeed.

I am not sleeping in this. I could only imagine how amusing the Onslow Boys would find it. I quickly gathered it back up, rolling it and shoving it back into its cover, cursing and punching it in with all my might.

Why doesn't anything go back in the way it comes out?

I heard Chris's footsteps crunching on the gravel as he approached the car, rounding the back of the van with a towel slung over his shoulder.

I eyed his damp hair with interest. "Did you have a bath in the sink?"

"Just a freshen-up." He brushed past me and chucked his bag in the back.

Wow, he smelt good, like he was ready for a night on the town. He had even changed his T-shirt with a new black one. I fought not to smile as I envisioned his wardrobe in his room filled with nothing but identical black T-shirts all hanging in a line. I guessed I should really know that; I mean, I had been in his closet only a few days ago. Not that I had paid much attention … to the clothes.

"Aren't you hot?" Chris's voice snapped me from my thoughts.

"Excuse me?"

"What's with the flannies?" Chris's eyes looked me over with guarded amusement. There was nothing I hated more than the up-and-down look; the kind you got when walking into the Onslow on a Friday night. Except this was not a look of appreciation. He was looking at me like I was an idiot.

Damn Tess's list.

"I thought it might get cool on the coastal road." I adjusted my top.

"Well, we've got a ways to go before we find out, so if I were you I'd get changed; there's no A/C in this hotel." Chris leaned in, grabbing a pillow and shoving it under his arm.

I opened my mouth to say that I didn't have anything else to wear, when I paused and watched him make his way to the front passenger door. He hopped in the front of the car with his pillow.

"W-what are you doing?" I asked, climbing into the van and crawling toward the front. I rested my elbows on the back of the bucket seat where Chris was making himself at home, punching his pillow and shuffling himself into a recline.

"What's it look like? We've a big day tomorrow – early start." He lay with one arm behind his head, his body partially skew-whiff. He looked really uncomfortable.

"You can't sleep there!" I insisted. "You have hardly any room."

"It's all good; I've crashed on worse couches." He sighed, closing his eyes.

I stared down at him for a long moment. I didn't know

whether to be flattered by the gentlemanly gesture or annoyed that he found the mere thought of sleeping next to me so offensive.

"You're being ridiculous," I said. "There's plenty of room for both of us on the mattress."

Kind of.

"We can even sleep top to toe if you want?" I suggested.

Chris laughed. "At the risk of kneeing you in the head again, I think not. Go to sleep, Tam."

I took a moment's pause as if waiting for him to speak again, but it was obvious that the topic was closed. Fine, I thought, let him suffer from leg cramps and a bad night's sleep; it was his problem, not mine.

I pulled the back doors shut and fixed myself on top of the doona.

What was his problem, anyway? He didn't have to act like he might catch something off me. Heaven forbid he'd get girl germs.

I nestled onto the mattress, trying not to focus on the fact that he was lying just near my head, divided only by a seat.

"Goodnight, Chris," I said.

A deep sigh emanated from the darkness.

"Goodnight." The sound of his body shifting on the leather seat screeched as he tried to manoeuvre into a more comfortable position. I bit my lip; he must have been so uncomfortable.

I shook the thought from my mind. I couldn't let myself worry about Chris and his comfort, because I had my own to worry about.

Stupid flannelette pyjamas!

Chapter Twenty-One

It was still dark when we hit the road.

I didn't exactly know if it's just what you do when you're on a camping trip (get an early start) or if he was just trying to make up for lost ground. My guess was that Chris had had the worst night's sleep possible and was awake, anyway. I tried not to take so much pleasure in it, so refrained from bursting out into an 'I told you so' dance. Plus, it was too early for that stuff.

We had a six-hour drive to Calhoon ahead of us. The idea of it made me want to cry. It also meant that the others would no doubt have moved on to the next point by the time we reached it.

All I wanted was a shower – a long, hot shower.

"I don't suppose Melba packed breakfast by any chance?" I looked at Chris behind the wheel. He was sporting some serious bed hair.

"No," was his clipped response.

Geez, sorry I asked.

Having forgone my morning run, my foot bounced up and down in the footwell. I tapped out a beat on my knees. I felt completely restless. Considering we were in the middle of nowhere, running in remote wilderness probably wasn't a good idea. I guess, if anything, if anyone *had* stumbled across us, we were the dodgy-looking ones in our black serial-killer van. I smiled to myself – I wondered how many a poor passer-by last night had avoided the rest stop, having seen our dodgy car parked there. I sure would have kept going.

"So, if it's not Grease Lightning, what do you call it, then?" I asked.

"It doesn't have a name." He looked at me like it was the most ridiculous question he'd ever heard.

"Every car has a name," I said. "Black Betty? The Beast? She needs a name."

"She?"

"Of course, all cars are girls," I said. "So, really? No name?"

"Well …" Chris paused, as if changing his mind about what he'd been going to say.

"'Well, what?" I straightened in my seat, intrigued.

"The boys have a name for it." He fought not to smile.

Uh-oh.

"What?"

Chris glanced out of the window, a smile broadening across his face. "You don't want to know."

Oh, now I did!

I went to press further but he promptly changed the subject.

"There's a petrol station and cafe about fifty kilometres from here, we can stop there for some breakfast."

Food? God, yes!

I wanted to clap my hands together and squeal at the thought. Though a lot of girls had phobias of eating in front of boys, I was not one of them; I loved my food. I was a constant source of hatred and envy owing to my fast metabolism, but truth be known, I worked my butt off – quite literally. Fitness was everything to me; though sometimes my diet did lack the certain balance that you'd think a personal trainer should have. A New Year's resolution, for sure. Like the rest of the world, I planned to eat healthier. I kind of felt like a hypocrite being a personal trainer some days, telling mums and businessmen what to do when I didn't necessarily do it myself. I needed to be hypnotised or something. No Monte Carlo biscuits in between meals!

"I don't know what kind of selection they have," Chris added. "Probably just your typical potato cake and Chico Roll from the bain-marie." He almost looked apologetic.

I wanted to laugh – people always assumed that I was a muesli and yoghurt girl based on my athletic nature. Ha! Perhaps I could get away with it after all. Live a lie until I was caught scoffing down a chocolate Chokito for afternoon snacks. Let Chris think I was healthy on the inside, I thought.

I switched my mobile on. I had kept it turned off in an effort to save its battery.

"Don't bother, there's no reception up here," Chris said.

"Well, I guess I can't be completely mad at Amy, then," I said, mainly to myself.

"Why would you be mad at Amy?" Chris asked. It seemed like he was genuinely interested.

I sighed. "My mum and Amy conspired against me in a way to get me on this trip."

"You weren't going to go?" he asked, surprised.

"I seriously didn't think I was, but apparently – and this is the most infuriating part – my mum can read me like a book. It's pretty frustrating when someone knows what you're going to do before you even make the decision to do it."

Chris frowned. "I don't get it; how did they conspire against you?"

"I told my mum I wasn't going and it took me all afternoon to pluck up the courage to tell Amy. And when I did call her she was suspiciously okay about me not going."

"Well, that doesn't sound like Amy at all," Chris agreed.

"I know! It should have been a massive red flag. Apparently my mum had rung her to tell her I was coming and to expect a phone call."

He laughed. "Ah-ha!"

"Yeah, the plot thickens. Amy didn't want Mum to tell me

about the departure time being brought forward in case I really did freak out and didn't want to go. So how did you get roped into it, anyway?"

"I wasn't going to leave until today, do a nonstop drive to Point Shank, have the alleged time of my life and then head back. But when Amy came and begged me to go early because I had to bring you, well, the plan changed somewhat."

I cringed, embarrassed. "Sorry."

Chris shrugged. "I was coming anyway."

"So what tactic did she use against you?" I asked. "Guilt? Blackmail? Torture?"

Chris smiled. "I shall never reveal my weaknesses."

"Did she promise you banana bread?" I teased.

Chris burst out laughing. "That's it. You know my weakness."

"Hmm," I said with a sly smile. "Handy to know."

A silence fell between us, but it wasn't awkward; it was light, easy, comfortable.

"Thanks for bringing me, Chris. I mean, for waiting, or leaving early. Or whatever you call it, thanks." I looked at his profile until he glanced my way, his brown eyes meeting mine for a moment before returning to the road.

"It's nothing." He shrugged.

I smiled and looked back out of the window.

It wasn't nothing.

I hummed a happy tune as I forked another helping of pancake into my mouth, swinging my fork from side to side as if I was conducting an orchestra. I was in heaven – blueberry pancake heaven. I looked up to see Chris perusing his newspaper in silent study.

"What are you looking at?" I asked with a mouthful of batter.

He shook his head as he lifted his paper with a shuffle. "Nothing."

To think I used to be intimidated by those eyes. Now I had

managed to spend some time around them I must be getting used to the varying degrees of his stares. There was the 'I'm so bored right now' deadpan, or the 'I wish you would just shut up right now' stare-down, and there was the 'Kill me now' look that was usually followed by a sigh of frustration. I munched thoughtfully on my breakfast, amusing myself no end with profiling Chris. Of course, there were other looks too. Like the humour that flooded his eyes when he laughed – not that that happened often. Or the look of concern that had been etched on his face when he watched me make my way to the toilets yesterday when I was unwell. Those moments made me uncomfortable; they were glimpses of something so foreign I didn't know how to react to them. Bitter, moody and silent Chris I could handle, but anything else had me stumped. Luckily they were fleeting moments.

A double beep sounded from somewhere, making me jump.

"And hello reception!" Chris announced as he delved into his pocket and grabbed his phone, flicking through the screen.

"There's service here?" I grabbed for my own.

"Yep!"

I turned it on, waiting for any magical ding. And sure enough, one-two-three-four chimes went off.

"Someone's popular," Chris said without taking his eyes from his message.

The first was a missed call alert from my mum, probably wondering if I was okay or if she was forgiven. The first text message said as much.

Gello sweety, hop youtt hsving fun, ring me when u can. Lobve mum.

Yep, that was Mum all right. At least she got a couple of words right.

There was one missed call from, hello-hello: Amy Henderson. Followed by a message.

I am so-so sorry, please don't be mad. I was totally freaked out that we had to leave early and when your mum called I was worried that she was wrong that you wouldn't change your mind and come. Aunty Claire said you guys had left and I am SO HAPPY, yay for Chris!! Even though I totally had to blackmail him. Can't wait to see you. Travel safe and see you soon!!! Xxx

My shoulders slumped. How could I possibly stay mad at her, or Mum for that matter? As I re-read the message, one thing bothered me.

I totally had to blackmail him. I knew I had joked about it, but something kind of bothered me that she'd had to resort to such extreme measures to force him to take me, and what could she possibly have over him, anyway?

"Any news?" Chris's voice snapped my attention away from my screen.

"Oh, just from Mum and Amy. You?"

"They've left Calhoon, but have decided to stop over for the night and camp at Evoka Springs. It's only a few hours past Calhoon. They said they would wait for us to catch up."

My eyes brightened. "They're going to wait?"

"Yep!" Chris finished texting back and hit send. "We should get there about three this arvo if we have a good run."

"Oh, we will. No migraines here!" I saluted.

"All right, well, we'll get some food and drinks for the road and keep going then." He paused, looking down at my plate. "After you've finished your pancakes, of course."

I grinned like a Cheshire cat. "Of course!" I picked up my fork and continued to eat and hum with much enthusiasm. When a day started with pancakes it was destined to be a good one.

Chapter Twenty- Two

I prided myself in being a pretty patient person, really. But this was ridiculous.

So much for having a good run and getting to our destination by three. I glowered across the road to where Chris paced in front of the Black Cat Cafe (that, incidentally, *did* serve the best pancakes ever). I sighed, flicked off my shoes and placed my bare feet on the dash as I watched him laugh and pick at the peeling paint of a fence post as he talked animatedly.

It was his third call that ranged from serious and business-like to upbeat, chatty laughter. I wondered who he could be chatting to – or, more importantly, who was putting that smile on his face. He did know about the Black Cat Cafe and the landscape of this trip pretty well. Maybe he had made the voyage a few times before with the boys. Or maybe he had a mistress at every port or petrol station. Maybe he was hooking up a booty call for when we got to Calhoon – a widowed cougar with fire-engine red lipstick and manufactured curls.

If we ever *did* get to Calhoon.

I eyed the flashing charge button on my mobile and figured I had some time to kill. I dialled Amy's number and she answered on the second ring.

"Tammmyyyyyy!" she squealed down the phone, so loud I had to hold it away from my ear.

"I've changed my mind, I'm not coming," I said dryly.

"You better bloody be!" she shouted.

"Relax," I said. "It's just a joke. Wouldn't miss it for the world."

"We're leaving Calhoon about lunchtime, but we'll wait at Evoka Springs for you guys."

"EVOKA SPRINGS, BABY!" someone shouted in the receiver.

"Piss off, Ringer," Amy snapped

"Someone's excited." I laughed.

"You wait until you get up here; it's so beautiful, you are going to bow down before me and thank me for getting Chris to bring you."

"Yes, about that …" I glanced out of the passenger door. Chris was still on the phone. "How did that come about?"

"Well, *as usual*, he was being his normal whinging, whiny self. 'I'm coming, I'm not coming, I'm going, I'm staying'. Actually, kind of sounds like you."

"Shut up!"

"Anyway, after he had a moan about leaving early I told him to quit his shit, he could come later if he absolutely had to, and that it actually worked out pretty well because you would be rocking up at twelve."

"I'm sure he was thrilled about that," I mused.

"Oh no, don't tell me he's being a dick?" Amy asked.

"No, no, he's all right. I just wondered what on earth could *make* Chris Henderson do anything."

"Oh, it was easy. Blackmail."

I laughed out loud. "Ah, yes." My stomach churned. What was I anxious about? "Must have been something pretty good," I said, trying for a lighthearted 'I don't really care that much' tone.

"Well, yeah, *hello*," Amy said, like it was the most obvious thing in the world, and that I should automatically know what she was referring to.

I, of course, had no idea and my silence must have told her as much.

"Oh. My. God. That's right, at the Bake House; I didn't get a chance to tell you, did I? You left early."

My mind searched back to that day and I suddenly remembered the whole reason why I had planned to meet Amy early. It was to quiz her about her cryptic message about what a certain Onslow Boy had said about me. My heart pounded against my ribcage and my mouth went dry.

"So? So what about it?" I said quickly, my eyes widening as I spotted Chris looking both ways before crossing the road toward the car.

"I can't believe I forgot to tell you."

"Told me what?" I all but shouted as Chris walked in front of our car.

"That I overheard—"

Beep-beep.

My phone went flat.

"Noooooooo!" I screamed at the blank screen in frustration. Chris paused at the driver's door before leaning in the open window and looking cautiously at my phone, then me.

"Something wrong?"

I threw my dead phone on the dash in a huff, running my fingers through my hair. *Nope, nothing I can't find out … in six hours!* Six long, painful hours. Hours of speculation.

Wait a minute.

I sat up. "Can I use your phone?"

"Sorry." Chris slid behind the wheel and slammed the door. "Mine's as flat as a tack."

Of course it bloody was, Mr Have-a-chat.

Of all the times for him to actually find his voice and want to have a nice long chinwag, it had to be now?

He revved the engine and I sat, broodily staring off into space. What had Amy overheard? Who had been talking and could she have used it against Chris as blackmail? Was he the one talking about me? Was it good? Bad? Or was someone confiding in him? And why did any of it matter so much?

Chris ejected his Bruce Springsteen tape and reached for the glovebox. "Here, pick a tape. You can program the next leg of the journey."

Chris nodded his head toward the stash. I took my feet off the dash and tentatively grabbed for a couple of cassettes. I read the cover of the first one and grinned from ear to ear.

"No way!"

Chris eyed me with interest.

I couldn't get the tape out of the cover quick enough.

I slotted it into the player; I turned the volume up. 'Rhiannon' flowed out of the speakers.

Chris smiled. "Nice choice."

"Are you serious? I love Fleetwood Mac."

"They're one of my all-time favourites," he agreed.

The next several hours seemed kind of manageable – maybe music really did soothe the savage beast?

We rolled into Calhoon after lunch, a pretty little town with elm tree-lined streets and old Victorian charm. A nice little tourist attraction not too far away from the coast and Evoka Springs. The engine rumbled as we turned down the main street, with Fleetwood Mac's 'Tusk' blaring from the sound system, echoing conspicuously down the quiet street.

"Just going to make a quick stop," Chris said. I jumped, startled by his voice. It had been a couple of hours since he'd last talked, in typical Chris style. He pulled into a car space and nodded toward the shops. "There's a shop there if you want to grab a cold drink or anything. Back in a minute." Before I could respond, Chris had dashed across the road and walked down the street. I yawned. It was somewhat unnerving that I was getting used to all his little Chris-isms.

I stepped out of the car, stretching my arms to the sky,

groaning as I heard my bones click and pop from sitting down for so long. I stepped up onto the kerb to stretch my legs for a bit. I didn't want to wander too far from the car, as Mr Genius had taken the car keys with him and, nice town or not, the last thing I wanted was for the van to be hijacked.

Not that anyone would want it.

Still, my Punky Brewster sleeping bag was in there and to lose that really *would* be a tragedy.

I perused the window display of the local real estate agent, daydreaming over all the in-ground pools and water views that were selling for a fortune. How lucky people were that could afford a place like that, I thought. I wondered if they knew it.

Tourists probably stopped off in Onslow and looked at our real estate and thought the same thing. How lucky we were to live in Onslow. And here we were fleeing from it, cringing at the very thought of being stuck there for New Year's Eve. I wondered if anyone from Calhoon had fled and headed for Onslow to count in the New Year. I grabbed a fresh bottle of water from the shop next door and headed back to the car. I sat in the passenger seat with the door open, sunning my legs, and eyed my watch with annoyance.

Come on, Chris!

I was itching to get to Evoka Springs, to hang out with the others, catch up with the girls, grill Amy over the thing she hadn't gotten a chance to tell me.

I drummed my fingers impatiently on the dash, watching the slow tick of the dashboard clock. Ten minutes had gone by. I let out a frustrated sigh. My legs were getting hot, getting that tingling that starts to happen when you're on the verge of burning. I lifted my feet into the footwell and slammed the car door.

I closed my eyes and took in a deep breath. "*Men*," I sighed.

"What about them?"

I yelped, jumping at the unexpected voice and at Chris's head poking in the open window of the passenger door.

"Jesus, Chris!" I slapped his shoulder and clutched at my

heart. "You scared me to death; don't do that."

He chuckled as he made his way back to the driver's side.

"Sorry about that," he said as he got back into the car. "Here, consider this a peace offering." He threw a yellow package in my lap.

"What's this?" I eyed it sceptically, as if half expecting it to explode in my lap.

Chris put his seatbelt on. "Open it and see."

I looked from the package to him and back again with guarded uncertainty. I tried to tear away the sticky tape that held the parcel shut. Chris watched on with silent amusement.

I peered into the bag and stilled. My eyes widened as I looked back at Chris. He was now openly grinning.

"Are you kidding me?" I exclaimed. "When …? How …?" I stammered inelegantly as I dumped the contents of the bag onto my lap.

My migraine medication spilled out.

"I called your mum this morning and asked if she could get the Onslow chemist to fax a copy of your painkiller prescription through to Calhoon so you could get it filled."

I stared at the bottle in awe. "That's what you were doing this morning? All those phone calls?"

"It took a few. Your mum, the Calhoon chemist for their fax number, the Onslow chemist to give them the details … They were all pretty helpful. Seems like it's pretty important stuff you got there."

My eyes watered with relief at having my pills with me. But most of all, my heart swelled with gratitude. He'd been so thoughtful. I lifted my gaze to meet his, unapologetically, tears and all.

"This is amazing … Thank you," I whispered, my voice threatening to break.

I thought Chris might have been embarrassed by my girly display of emotion, that he would have shrugged it off the way he usually did, or maybe just done what he did best and stayed silent.

Instead, he looked right back at me. His gaze ticked across my face in silent study, before a crooked line pinched in the corner of his mouth.

"Most girls get sentimental about flowers," he teased.

I sniffed, wiping my eyes, and gave a small laugh. "Not this girl. Food and meds keep me happy."

"Well, you're easy to please, then."

I could feel his eyes still on me as I placed the bottle back into the bag.

"Get me to a phone charger and I'm all yours," I joked.

Chris's good humour was replaced with awkward surprise.

Oh God, what did I just say? I wanted the ground to open up. *Why couldn't I just learn to seriously shut up!*

Chris cleared his throat and adjusted his side mirror.

"Well, in that case …" He started up the car and threw me a cheeky grin. "Let's get you charged, then."

Chapter Twenty-Three

"Taaaaammyyyy!"

I was all but knocked over by a fierce, bone-crushing bear hug as Amy collided into me at a run.

"You made it!" she squealed, dragging me around in circles as though we were playing Ring a Ring o' Roses.

Sean stood next to Chris, watching.

"How come you never act like that when we reunite?" Chris asked Sean in blank-faced seriousness.

Sean slapped Chris on his shoulder. "Don't worry, mate, I assure you there's a song in my heart."

Amy dragged me down a sloping dirt track. "Come check out our camping spot, it's wicked."

I couldn't help but laugh and throw the boys a worried look as she led me away, linking her arm with mine.

"Boy, am I glad you guys are here," she said.

"Miss me that much, did you?" I joked.

But Amy's serious expression never faltered. "Let's just say I'm hoping some fresh company melts the ice, so to speak."

Before I could ask what that meant exactly, I heard distant cries.

"Tammy!" Ellie shouted from her deckchair, alerting Tess and Adam to our approach.

Adam stared pointedly at his naked wrist. "You're late!"

"Better late than never." Tess beamed as she hugged me. "Good trip?"

"*Yeah, right*," Adam scoffed. "The poor girl was subjected to Chris for two days, can't you see how incredibly fragile she is?"

"Well, best take a seat, Oh Fragile One." Ellie hopped up, offering me her seat.

I obliged. "Where is everyone?" I looked around the convoy of vehicles parked on an angle like a wind break. Gear and tents were all set up.

"Toby, Ringer, Stan and Belinda have gone down to the river to go fishing," Ellie said unenthusiastically.

"Belinda?" I asked. *Who was Belinda?* "Is that Stan's new girlfriend?"

"Sure is, isn't she, Ellie?" Adam grinned and nudged Ellie with his foot.

Ellie grimaced. "She hates me!"

"What? Why?"

"Probably because I'm his ex," she said. "But even if I wasn't – trust me, she and I are like water and oil. We do not mix."

"That's brilliant, Ellie; it perplexes me why you even needed to copy my science homework when you have such insightful knowledge about liquid components," Adam teased.

She glowered. "I'll turn your nose into a liquid component if you're not careful."

Adam cat-called, holding his hands up in surrender. "Easy, now."

I leaned toward Amy to whisper, "Is this the ice that needs thawing?"

Amy cringed. "I wish."

I followed her eye line toward Tess. She sat on the nearby log; her eyes may have been watching her two best friends, but she looked a million miles away.

I threw a questioning look to Amy.

She sighed. "I'll tell you later."

After the initial hysteria of our arrival, I managed to take in the beauty of the bushland surroundings. I sat in one of the camping chairs, enjoying the cool breeze. It was so quiet. Soothing. It was hard to believe that we were on our way to the coast when we were so thickly enclosed by trees.

Adam said that once we broke out of the ranges in the next leg, it would literally be like turning a corner and bam, the ocean would be right there in front of us. I couldn't wait. Time spent *not* jammed into a car, another bend, yet another hour. Although I relished being out in the open at the campsite, I couldn't help but find myself glancing up the track to the panel van where Chris and Sean stood, peering under the bonnet. Catching up on men's business, no doubt. A familiar voice called from behind, shattering my focus.

"NO WAY! He brought the SHAGGIN' WAGON!" Ringer called.

I spun around. "The what?"

A shirtless Ringer strode up the track with a fishing rod slung over his shoulder. Behind him trailed Stan, Toby and a petite girl with a pixie haircut.

Ringer passed me, admiring the van. "The Shaggin' Wagon; that's what it's called," he laughed.

"THAT'S what you call it?" I asked Ringer in horror, standing up from my chair.

Ringer shrugged, dumping his fishing gear in the back of Sean's ute. "The mattress is a bit of a red flag, don't you think?"

"Shut up, Ringer," warned Chris as he approached from the track. He gave Ringer a shove as he joined our group.

Ringer shoved him right back. "How many miles has she clocked up now, you old stud?"

The macho rough-housing escalated, scuffing up dust as Ringer trapped Chris in a headlock.

Ellie sighed. "Yep, the gang is back together."

Ignoring the caveman display (and seriously wanting to forget the only reason the van could possibly have that name), I turned back to the group.

"You must be Belinda?" I smiled, reaching out to offer a hand to the unfamiliar girl.

"Hey." She smiled coyly and took my hand. "Tammy, right?"

"That's me," I said.

Belinda's eyes sparkled with a warmth that made me instantly like her. She was such a delicate thing, she only came up to Stan's shoulder, with jet black cropped hair and alabaster skin that would no doubt burn easily in the sun. She was pretty much the exact opposite to Ellie's blonde, bouncy self.

"We were just about to give Tammy a tour of the campsite," beamed Ellie.

Belinda's sparkling, friendly eyes dimmed as they flicked toward Ellie, as if the sun had gone behind a cloud. "Oh, okay, cool." She nodded.

Yep, Ellie might have well been right about Belinda's lack of love for her, but in true Ellie style she just met Belinda's tension with a pearly white smile, as if she hadn't noticed anything out of the ordinary.

Tess linked her arm through mine. "Welcome to paradise." She led me away from the settling dust and dirty looks.

Toby took the lead toward the camp ground. "That's Tess's and my home." He pointed to an army green, two-man tent.

"Yeah, they're just the plebs outside the city walls," added Adam.

Passing another dome-like tent, Toby continued. "Bell and Stan's humble abode." He grazed his hand along the side of the red canvas.

"And mission control, here is Adam, Ellie and Ringer's chateau." We came to a multi-roomed tent with an awning and fold-out table and chairs, with long life milk, stacked baked beans and a box with Cruskits and Vegemite, amongst other things, spread out on the table.

"I am so glad you're here," Ellie said. "You can bunk in with us."

"Yeah, this is where all the hot, single people stay." Ringer propped his elbow on Adam's shoulder and raised his eyebrows in a 'hubba-hubba' motion.

Stan shook his head. "Ignore him."

"Yeah, we do," added Belinda with a cheeky grin.

I scanned the grounds where they had made themselves at home – everything was spick and span and in such well-aligned order. My body seemed to relax somewhat. The neat campsite really spoke to the OCD in me. I wondered if the boys were usually so well organised, or whether it was something to do with Tess's organisational skills that had influenced the group.

I turned to Amy. "Where are you and Sean camping?"

Amy folded her arms. "We've been voted off the island."

I blinked at her, confused. "Sorry?"

"Honeymoon section is that-a-way." Adam pointed to the woods.

"Fine by us." Sean threw Amy a knowing smirk that caused her to blush and look away.

"Ugh, seriously, you two, quit it," Ringer said, wrinkling his nose in distaste.

"Ah, someday, Ringer." Sean slung his arm around Ringer's shoulders and looked up whimsically to the sky. "Someday, you too will be shunned from the group over the love of a woman."

Ringer shucked Sean's arm off. "I would sooner … drive the Shaggin' Wagon." Ringer sneered as if the very idea was so unsavoury.

Chris's eyes darkened. "I'll pretend you didn't just say that, young Ringo."

"Uh-oh, mate, anything but the car." Adam's eyes darted from Ringer to Chris and back in mock horror.

"Mate, it's a bucket of rust; you're kidding yourself," Ringer argued.

"You seem to forget that I found him that bucket of rust," Toby said.

"You know what I mean – you're dreaming if you think you're going to pick up any chick in that car." Ringer laughed.

"He picked up me."

All heads snapped toward me.

I shrugged, playing it cool. "I think the van is hot."

Literally. I nearly died of heat exhaustion last night.

Toby broke into a slow grin as he took in Ringer's troubled expression.

"Really?" Ringer asked.

"Oh yeah," I said taking a step forward. "The shiny black paint … The spongy … soft …mattress … The purr of the engine vibrating through your body." I stood right next to him, whispering in his ear. "So. Hot."

I was so close I could hear Ringer swallow deeply. His Adam's apple bobbled up and down and he cleared his throat as he stepped back a little, away from me, not knowing where to look or what to say.

Ha. I couldn't help but giggle as I turned to catch the bemused faces of the group.

"Wow," breathed Adam. "There is something so insanely hot about a woman defending a car."

Everyone burst out into startled laughter. All except Chris, who just looked at me with those intense brown eyes and a crooked grin on his face.

Ringer puffed out his chest. "So, uh, Chris … do you think I could borrow your car next weekend?"

Chris paused. "Let me think about it."

"Really?" Ringer's brows rose in surprise.

"No," Chris said short and sharp, unfolding his arms and leaving the group. He brushed past me sideways, his hand gently squeezing mine as if to say 'thanks'. It happened so quickly I thought I might have imagined it. All the same, it made my stomach twist in excitement at the unexpectedness of it.

"Aw, come on, Chris, you know I was only kidding." Ringer followed him, his thongs crunching down the track as he pleaded his case.

Toby watched on as the two walked across the camp clearing. "The only way Ringer is going to get near that car is if Chris runs him over in it."

Stan laughed as he slung his arm around Bell and started toward the makeshift kitchen.

"Well, the night is young," said Stan.

Chapter Twenty-Four

"What is that?" I asked, though I knew the answer.

I was no expert on camping paraphernalia, that was for certain, but my heart skipped a beat when I spotted something unmistakably familiar in the campsite.

Adam followed my eye line. "It's a solar shower," he said, as if it was the most obvious thing in the world.

The canvas bag was hanging from a tree not too far away from the camping kitchen, on full display; there was no privacy screen, just a bag dangling from a makeshift rope, the showerhead dripping onto the muddy earth where people had used it before. Right now it seemed like the most beautiful thing I had ever seen.

"Do you want one?" Amy asked. "It's not very warm, but it does the job."

My eyes lit up. "I would do anything for a shower."

Sean's brows rose. "Anything? Did you hear that, Chris? She'll do anything." A wicked smile plastered across his face as he waited for Chris's reaction.

The reaction never came. Chris ignored him and disappeared inside the large canvas tent.

It was my cue to leave, avoiding Sean's gleaming eyes. I didn't have time to take the bait. I was on a mission.

The walk back down the track to the campsite seemed a lot longer in thongs and a bright, floral bikini. I slung my towel over my shoulder and pulled my ponytail loose, the second most amazing feeling in the world. The first would no doubt be the shower I was headed for.

I was almost giddy with excitement – having spent last night in my flannelette PJs in the back of the van had felt like the equivalent to wrapping myself in cling wrap and sleeping in a sauna.

I couldn't wait for this.

"Don't take too long," Ellie called from her camping chair. "We're heading into town."

My heart sank a little. "We are?" The last thing I really wanted to do was get back into the car.

Amy took my towel and hung it on a tree branch. "Yep, us girls thought we would do some shopping," Amy chirped as she handed me a bar of soap. "Plus," she said under her breath, "we wanted to get Tess away for a while." My eyes instinctively moved to Tess who was intently reading a book in the shade.

Was something going on with Tess? No doubt Amy would tell me when she could. I thought that this was the whole idea of the road trip, to get away for a while, but apparently some of us needed to get away from the getaway.

"Come on, tell the truth," said Adam. "Now say why you're really going into town."

Amy cut Adam a dark look that did little to intimidate him.

Ellie straightened. "Well, you needn't think I'm going out in my cut-offs and singlet top."

"Going out?" I questioned.

"Uh, yeah, apparently there's a great little pub in Evoka," said Amy. "We thought we might head down there tonight."

"Bloody hell, is that why you're going to town? To buy an outfit?" Sean laughed.

"*No.*" Amy glowered. "We just thought we'd get some

supplies, seeing as we were in such a rush to leave, thanks to you boys wanting to leave so bloody early."

"The early worm gets the fish," Sean said.

Amy scoffed. "I haven't even seen your fishing rod in the water yet."

Sean wrapped his arms around Amy and nuzzled her neck. "That's because I've had better things to do."

There was a collective groan. "Get a room, you two," said Adam.

I wrestled with the showerhead. "How does this thing …" and before I could finish my sentence a stream of cold water hit me in the face. I spluttered and gasped at the unexpected icy cold that ran down my skin.

"Oh-my-gosh, oh-my-gosh," I breathed out as I vigorously rubbed soap over my shoulders and stomach, thinking that maybe the friction would warm my skin, or just to get washed as quickly as possible. I whimpered through the motion.

I wiped the water out of my eyes, only sensing that someone was standing near at the exact moment that they reached over my head and twisted the nozzle. The freezing water blasted hard and fast all over me and I gasped in shock again.

I heard a chuckle. "Warm enough?"

I blinked through the droplets of water to see Chris standing next to me. That had me gasping for a completely new reason.

He was wearing nothing more than a pair of footy shorts. I took in the ripped lines of his biceps, and his impressive broad shoulders that narrowed in toward his waist. I took in his tanned, smooth skin that shone in the afternoon sun.

Chris usually worked inside, or stood glowering by the sidelines on any one of our gatherings. I had never seen him so *exposed* before, and boy was he exposed.

Dribbles of water ran down his arms as they worked, adjusting the stream some more. The clear rivulets splayed down his chest and rolled down his toned, taut stomach. I wanted to reach out and follow their line with my finger.

Wait, what? I snapped my thoughts away from following the descending crystal beads.

A cold shower right now was actually exactly what I needed.

"Hang on a sec," Chris said as he trotted back to the camp kitchen, disappearing behind the canvas flap. He returned with a full water jug.

"Here's something I prepared earlier," he smirked. "Tilt your head back."

Without hesitation I did as I was told. He trickled a deliciously warm stream of water over my head, washing the suds from my drenched tendrils of hair.

I closed my eyes, forcing myself not to groan with pleasure at such a welcome sensation as he slowly, almost teasingly, dribbled the stream over me. All too quickly it was over and the cool stream from the showerhead overtook any feeling of warmth Chris had thoughtfully afforded.

I smiled brightly at him. "Thanks."

I almost felt the same heated warmth from Chris's coffee-coloured eyes as he stared down at me. It was the first time I had held his stare, and it didn't hold anything other than kindness.

My stomach fluttered with butterflies.

"Do … do you want me to leave it running?" I stammered.

Chris broke into a smile, the tooth-exposing kind, as he eyed the showerhead. "Sure."

I nodded like a zombie, passing him the rose-scented cake of soap, his fingers brushing mine.

"Thanks."

"That's okay," I said. I reached for my towel in a daze and stepped aside as Chris moved forward to take my place.

Shivering I wrapped the towel around me before looking up and pausing. Everyone was sitting and standing around the campsite, watching with such deep-set, if not amused, interest.

Geez. All they needed were some 3-D glasses and a bucket of popcorn.

I blushed crimson; in those mere moments under the water I

had completely forgotten we had an audience, that our exchanges were not just limited to us and us alone anymore, that we were part of a group – a smug, staring group.

I wrapped the towel tightly around my body, pushing the soaked tendrils of hair over my shoulder. Amy came over with an extra towel for my hair, her brow curved with interest. I braced myself for the insinuating comments that might come as she handed me the towel.

She folded her arms and looked at me as I rubbed my hair vigorously.

"Wow," she whispered. "If this is how you two behave in public, I don't want to even know …"

"I'm going to get dressed!" I piped up before marching up the track toward the panel van, my thongs squelching with every step as I dared not make eye contact with anyone.

As far as showers went, that was definitely the most mortifying one I had ever had.

"Come on, let's go! Let's go!" Amy called as she wound down the window.

With my hair still wet, I jogged toward Sean's Toyota twin cab ute where Amy sat behind the wheel. I opened up the passenger door and climbed inside. Ellie, Tess and Belinda sat in the back, all buckled up for the expedition.

"I can't believe Sean is letting you take his car," said Ellie. "It must be love."

Amy was too busy adjusting her seat to reply. "Bloody legs like a spider," she muttered under her breath. She pulled her seat forward so she could touch the pedals.

"Who has legs like a spider?" A set of tanned elbows rested on the open driver's window, startling us all.

"Bloody hell, Sean!" Amy slapped at him.

Sean flashed his pearly whites. "What time will you be back?"

"Never you mind," called Ellie. "This is women's business."

Sean grimaced. "You're going to talk about feelings and crap, aren't you?"

Amy smirked. "Most definitely."

"Well, in that case," he said, pecking her on the forehead, "take your time."

Amy rolled up the window before starting the car.

"Dare you to drop a big wheelie," I joked.

"No way!" she said. "It wouldn't be worth my life." Instead, she settled for a polite double toot, waved goodbye, and pulled out onto the road.

Chapter Twenty- Five

So we didn't exactly launch immediately into talking about our feelings.

But by the glimpses I caught in the back seat through the rear-view mirror, maybe we needed to.

Ellie looked bored, Tess looked sad and Belinda looked like she would rather be anywhere else.

I cleared my throat. "So! What's our first port of call?" I said in my best upbeat voice.

"I don't think there's a lot to choose from in Evoka, but it's the closest thing we have at our disposal," grimaced Amy.

"I know what is in Evoka," sighed Tess. "Hippy shops with wind chimes, stress balls and crocheted beanies."

"How do you know?" asked Belinda.

"My mum dragged me to the Mother's Day market here one year. Not a lot to choose from." Tess shrugged as if she didn't particularly care, though.

"If the only dress shop in town is limited to tie-dyed products I will be so annoyed," said Ellie.

"Surely it won't matter. I doubt the Evoka pub is black tie," I said reassuringly.

Ellie examined the end of her blonde ponytail for split ends.

"It's only the second day and I am already bored out of my mind."

"Well, don't you dare say that in front of the boys." Amy flicked a warning look in the rear-view. "The last thing I need is Chris saying, 'I told you so.'"

I wanted to defend Chris's honour, I don't know why, to say that I didn't think he would say that, but then I thought better of it.

It was twenty minutes down a winding dirt road before we hit the smooth bitumen that led into town. The first sign of civilisation was passing a shack set back off the road among thick bushland.

Amy started laughing hysterically.

"What's so funny?" I asked, glancing at the others. They looked just as perplexed by the outburst as I felt.

Amy fought to contain herself. "Did you see that place back there?"

"What about it?" asked Belinda.

"That's the pub." Amy slapped the steering wheel.

"Whaaaat?" groaned Ellie.

"Definitely not black tie," added Tess.

I glanced back, seeing nothing but a line of bitumen as we sped forward. "Did the sign really say 'Villa Co-Co'?"

"Better grab ourselves some tie-dye, ladies," Amy continued to laugh.

Ellie shook her head. "I would sooner die."

Evoka was a blink-and-you'll-miss-it kind of town; it housed a small local supermarket, post office, pub, butcher and a one-stop tourist shop with said hippy incense and scented oils, woven baskets and postcards. After seeing the 'Villa Co-Co' pub, we reached an unspoken agreement that finding an outfit for a night out seemed less important than it had before. Instead, we opted for some peaceful roaming around the tree-lined streets. Regardless of its humble setting, Evoka was a beautiful place and the last stop before the towns that dotted the coast along the way toward Point Shank.

We pushed our way through the front door to the tourist shop, assaulted immediately by the powerful fumes from the incense that burned on the counter. The shop was cluttered with an array of interesting artefacts, from bejewelled elephant statues to wind chimes and dream catchers; you had to really look amongst the collection in order to take it all in.

I sidestepped between two tables piled high with tea towels and gem stones, and took extra care as I manoeuvred my way through the small space. I spotted a cardboard sign on the counter that stated in permanent black texta: 'You break. You buy.' I tucked in my elbows. I really didn't want to be stuck with buying a dragon sculpture holding a crystal ball or something equally hideous. And a broken one, at that. My gaze skimmed along the cluttered shelves as I edged my way toward the back of the store.

I was open to the idea of finding a souvenir for my parents, perhaps, and paused at a stand that housed guardian angel pendants. I tilted my head to read the scripture on the little cards and froze.

The hair on the back of my neck rose at the low growling from behind me. A deep, guttural growl that taunted me, practically dared me to move. My eyes widened as I caught the reflection in one of the outlandish gold-plated mirrors on the wall of the most massive dog peering at me through the beaded curtain from out back. I locked eyes with the beast and realised I had made a big mistake. It flinched back and barked an ear-piercing bark.

I screamed.

The others raced around the corner and paused, seeing me pressed up against the wall on tippy toes.

"Aww, look at the puppy," Ellie crooned.

"Puppy?" I squealed. "It's a bloody monster."

"It's a Saint Bernard." Amy waved me off like I was being overdramatic. As she edged closer to the bead curtain she held her hand out tentatively for the beast to sniff it.

"Hello, beautiful, what's your name?" she cooed.

The giant stepped forward and sniffed the air, before flinching back and barking incessantly.

"Aww, it's okay, we won't hurt you," Amy said over the noise.

"WINSTON! NO!" a woman cried. She parted the beaded curtain and pulled on the dog's collar, edging him into the back room. "Go on, you know you're not allowed in here." She groaned as she pushed the resisting eighty-odd-kilo beast away.

The woman closed the door behind her, muffling the outraged barks from behind. Breathless, she smoothed over her frizzy, salt and pepper hair as she smiled at us with coffee-stained teeth.

"Can I help you?" she asked brightly. Aside from us disturbing Winston, she seemed utterly delighted to see us.

"Um, we were just looking, thanks. Sorry to frighten your dog," I said.

"Oh, not at all." Her bangles jingled as she waved off my sentence as if it were nothing. "He likes to think he's a guard dog, but he's nothing but a giant teddy bear. Are you ladies passing through?"

"We're camping near here; we thought we would just pop into town to do some shopping." I smiled.

"We were kind of looking for a clothing store," Belinda added. Ellie cut her a dark look as if to be quiet, which Belinda ignored. "We were wanting to go out tonight, but we didn't really pack anything suitable."

"Going out?" the lady asked. "In Evoka?"

I wanted Belinda to shut up, too. Somehow handing out all our personal information didn't sit right with me; it was the kind of scene you would see in a horror movie. You know, where there's a group of campers that stop off at a gas station and tell the innocent-enough shop man exactly what they were doing and where they were going, only to be picked off one by one in the dead of night by a masked, chainsaw-wielding psychopath. I glanced around to see any sort of apparel in the shop.

"Villa Co-Co, is it?" asked Tess. "That's the pub, right?"

The lady's eyes suddenly lit. "Of course! Villa Co-Co … What fun!"

"Really?" I asked sceptically.

"Oh yes, Peter and Jan have just come back from Bali and they throw one hell of a party." She walked around from behind the counter, her long velvet skirt swooshing along the floorboards. "Follow me, ladies," she sing-songed as she walked toward the back of the shop.

We all looked at each other, uncertain exactly what to do, when Ellie shrugged and made the first move after her.

In a tentative line, we manoeuvred our way to the back of the shop, where the lady unravelled a plastic sheet off a clothes rack and wheeled it out from the corner.

"If you're going out, you're going to have to look the part," she said.

Amy smirked as she folded her arms. "It's not black tie, by any chance?"

The lady looked puzzled at the question. "Yes, you're not from around here, are you?"

"No. No we are not," I agreed.

After being pointed in the direction of a changing room, we took turns in flicking through the clothes of the woman's hidden stash, giggling over the eclectic array of fashion.

"Oh my God, is she for real?" whispered Amy as she held up a bat-winged '80s power suit.

"I think it's hilarious," added Belinda as she pressed an electric blue Lycra dress against herself.

"Hey, can I have a look at that?" asked Ellie as she took it from Belinda. "You know, if you took the shoulder pads out of this, it wouldn't be so bad …" she mused.

Amy disappeared into the changing room, which was really just a curtained corner. "Villa Co-Co won't know what hit it," she called.

"You're not seriously contemplating wearing any of this?" I whispered to the curtain.

"Why not?" laughed Tess as she tried on a 1920s-style hat. "It would be worth it just to see the looks on the boys' faces."

Amy poked her head out from the curtain. "YES! We should totally pick something for tonight."

Bangles and tinkering china approached. "Ladies, I have made you some Devonshire tea. We have a lovely courtyard in the back. You can talk over your outfit decisions."

"Um, I think I love Evoka," Ellie said, draping her dress over her shoulder and following the lady out of the back French door.

"Ta-da!" Amy flung back the curtain, sporting a leopard-print miniskirt and a black lace spaghetti strap top. She actually looked really good, and my heart sank a little as I eyed what was left on the rack.

"I love it!" beamed Tess.

"I can't wait to see Sean's face," Amy said as she adjusted the straps.

"Wow, we are really doing this, aren't we?" I asked.

"Yep. It's all or nothing," said Belinda.

Taking on board their expectant looks, I sighed and went back searching through the rack. It was all well and good to rock up at the local pub tonight having made some questionable fashion choices, but something deeper niggled inside my mind. It was more than being the centre of attention, or looking like a fool in front of the girls; I didn't care about that. But I didn't want to look a fool in front of the boys.

In front of Chris.

Chapter Twenty-Six

Belinda was kind enough to wait for me as I used the changing room.

Although, in reality, I really didn't need or want her to. I would have been perfectly happy if she had just gone out to the courtyard with the others while I stayed behind the curtain and stared miserably at my reflection.

"I don't know about this," I said, biting my lip.

"Come on, show me," Belinda called.

"I just don't think …"

"Tammy, now."

I sighed deeply. "Okay."

I peeled the curtain back and stepped out from the alcove, facing another full-length mirror next to where Belinda sat on a stool.

I turned, trying to look at myself from all angles, only to be stilled by Belinda's wolf whistle.

"That is hot!" she said.

"I look like a belly dancer." I pulled down my midriff top that exposed my belly. The long, flowing white skirt pulled around my legs with a shimmering gold embossed pattern etched across the layers. The white was a stark contrast against my tanned skin.

"A *hot* belly dancer," Belinda added.

I knew she was just being nice; I didn't really know her so what else was she supposed to say? You look like a dog?

"Ringer said you had a bangin' body." Belinda folded her arms.

"What?" I turned, wide-eyed.

She shrugged. "I asked him what you looked like, and he was very accurate in his description. Come to think of it, very *detailed*." She tilted her head in deep thought.

I turned back toward the mirror. I wondered if that was the conversation Amy had overheard? I still had to clear up what she had blackmailed Chris with. If that was it, I felt a little disappointed and I didn't want to admit the reason why. Somehow I had convinced myself that maybe Chris had said something about me. I shook the idea from my mind – who had I been kidding? He would have been the last person to say anything at all, let alone about me.

I sighed. "I am sure Villa Co-Co is the party capital of Evoka, but I think I'll pass." Stepping back into the change room, I was suddenly overwhelmed by a deep-seated misery. Sometimes I wished I could just let go, just stress less and enjoy myself like the others, but I was always plagued with doubt, with worry. Afraid of not fitting in, which was ironic as I sabotaged every chance of fitting in by constantly stepping aside from everyone.

Belinda was still waiting for me as I stepped back out and placed my outfit back onto the rack. She offered me a small smile. "That's okay, I won't dress up either. It was a silly idea."

"Belinda, you don't have to …"

"No, it's okay," she said as she slid off her stool. "I'm not a sheep; I don't follow others just because they're doing it."

Maybe she was just trying to make me feel better?

Somehow, I didn't think so. It turned out, I kind of liked Belinda. I liked her quiet strength and understated presence.

"Come on, I may very well need your back-up while I break it to the others," I said, making our way toward the courtyard.

"I wouldn't be too worried – how many fights break out over

Devonshire tea? None, I'm guessing; it's just not civilised."

"I hope you're right," I said with a laugh.

I was relieved the others bought their outfits anyway, even though they decided that maybe Evoka wasn't exactly the right place to try them out. They vowed that they would wear them out somewhere, though.

"It's a shame, really," said Amy, heaving her bags along as we walked toward the car. "That's actually the first time I've seen Tess laugh in a while; I think the silly fashion parade was a good distraction for her."

I glanced back at the others trailing several metres behind us; I felt a pang of guilt surge within me. "Now I feel bad that we're not dressing up."

"Huh? Oh, no, don't be silly, it's going to take more than stepping out in fancy dress to cheer up Tess long term," Amy said.

"What's going on? Is Tess okay?" I pressed, taking the moment to find out once and for all the mystery behind Tess's sad eyes.

"I hope so, I hope this trip gets better for her than it started, but I think she is at a bit of a loss as to what to do, and none of us really know what to say to her."

Do about what? What didn't I know? I remained silent, hoping Amy would continue.

"It's Toby," she said. "He's been really distant of late, we've all noticed it. And the first night we camped they must have had a humdinger of a fight in the car because they weren't even speaking to each other when they arrived and I could tell Tess had been crying."

"Well, all couples fight," I said. *Yeah, like I was some expert.*

"Not Tess and Toby. Not like this. I would have shrugged it off as well, but I can see it too. Like how he sat by the fire most of the night, just staring into the flames. He's so distant, so not himself."

"Does Sean know anything?" I asked.

Amy sighed. "He says he's going to have a talk to him, pull him aside and see what's going on."

I nodded. "Maybe some time alone together will be good for them; you know, Toby and Tess."

We approached the car. Amy slung her bags in the back of the ute, glancing at the others' approach. "I hope so," she said, "because I really don't like where this is headed."

"Where's that?" I asked quickly.

"The one other time I saw Toby distant and agitated like this."

"When was that?"

"The last time he broke up with his girlfriend."

"Those little shits!" cried Ellie.

We slowed down as we made our way past the Villa Co-Co hotel, only to see Ringer's car parked out the front.

"I can't believe they went without us! I bet they've been there all afternoon." Ellie glowered out of her window.

"Should we go in?" I asked, wondering if Amy would slow down and do a U-turn. Instead, her brows narrowed and she pumped the accelerator.

"Pfft. Let them have their macho boy bonding."

Amy stared at the road with an evil grin.

I cocked my brow and glanced into the back for support. "Amy, you scare me when you look like this."

"Let's just say, we have a full tank of fuel, and I happen to know there is late night shopping in Calhoon."

Ellie gasped. "You're not seriously thinking of trekking back to Calhoon?"

"Well, ladies, if we're going to make a fashionably late entrance, we might as well do it in style."

I bit my lip, a thrill spiking in my stomach as I turned to see the same manic look in the others' eyes. Amy glanced in her rear-view mirror, no doubt seeing the elated smile across Tess's face.

Amy turned to me. "What do you think?"

Without hesitation, this time I decided for once to be a sheep. This time I'd follow the crowd, and I'd jump in with both feet.

"Let's do it!"

Chapter Twenty-Seven

It was dark by the time we returned to the campsite.

We sort of expected to find a note with 'gone pubbing' left for our convenience, but instead we found Stan reclining in his fishing chair with a stubby, staring into space. His entire face lit up when he saw us approach.

"Hey," he said, standing up quickly. "What took you so long?"

"Just a side-trip shopping adventure," said Ellie as she held up her bags with glee. She turned to Tess. "Come on, we'll get ready in the big tent."

Tess cringed. "I have never gotten ready in a tent before."

"That makes both of us," Ellie said. She held the canvas partition back for Tess.

I turned to smile at Bell and Stan, but they were too busy reacquainting themselves with one another with doe-eyed looks.

And that's my cue to exit.

I took my bags to the van, my second home these days. Amy headed toward the woods. "Meet back at the car in fifteen!" she called back.

Ellie's head poked out through the canvas. "Fifteen minutes? Are you serious?"

"Fifteen minutes," Amy repeated.

Oh-crap-oh-crap-oh-crap.

I ran as best I could up the slanted dirt track toward the van. The others may have never gotten ready in a tent before, but *I* had never gotten ready in the back of a *panel van* before.

This was going to be interesting.

I made my way around the back, juggling my baggage to reach for the back handle, praying that Chris hadn't locked the car. As the magical click sounded and I pulled the door open I was flooded with relief. I threw my shopping bags in the back and hopped inside, ensuring to leave the door slightly ajar so the interior light stayed on. Light was a necessity when applying mascara. Unlike the gypsy skirt in Evoka, in a cute little shop in Calhoon I had managed to find a fitted, white summer dress with vintage lace embroidery. It was so delicate, so light and feminine and cost an absolute fortune from one of those indie clothes designers. Still, I had fallen in love with it and felt like I wanted to walk into the Villa Co-Co and see Chris from across the bar, and I wanted for once to stride into a space with absolute confidence, offer a coy smile perhaps as I locked eyes with him. I had run through all the scenarios as I'd looked over my outfit in the changing room. And then, of course, I had snapped out of my daydream.

Why was I so intent on making a good impression on Chris?

I didn't know where my head was at lately, and it didn't help that I had seen a different side to Chris the last couple of days: a caring side, a lighthearted side. But why wouldn't he be? He's on holidays and we were all relaxed (well, aside from Toby and Tess – that was a worry). I was sure it wouldn't take long for Chris to seep back into his old, grumblebum ways, especially around his friends.

And then I had another scenario go through my mind: me entering the Villa Co-Co and being completely ignored by him while he drank with the boys. It was a possibility – just because we were forced to travel together and he had done a few nice things didn't mean he thought of me any differently.

I blinked a couple of times, snapping out of my thoughts. I had to hurry up; I had done nothing more than lay out my dress and accessories as I sat back on my heels, obsessing about stupid 'what if?' scenarios.

I had too much to do in too little time, and too little space, so it would seem. I balanced awkwardly on the spongy mattress as I undressed and slipped on my new under things. I had really gone all out, going so far as to buy some new perfume, which I sprayed liberally over my half-dressed body. I smiled to myself as I sprayed it on the mattress as well. Won't that have the next girl Chris brings back here guessing. I stilled, a familiar pang of jealousy twisted in my stomach.

I didn't want there to be another girl.

Right! Enough of that, time to get a wriggle on – quite literally, as the best way to get this thing on was to step into my new dress. Leaving the lip glossing and moisturising till the very last minute, my hair and face could happen on the way to the pub. I tried my best to stay upright but the spongy floor underfoot was making it somewhat of a challenge. I swayed from side to side like a drunken sailor, trying to manage one foot through the opening of the dress. I bent over so as not to hit my head on the ceiling and braced one hand against the van wall to steady myself. I tentatively stepped in the dress, and started to shimmy the dress up with my free arm. I was on the home stretch as I managed to pull the tight-fitting dress over my hips. I released the wall to use both hands.

Almost done.

And with those famous last words, the back door to the van flung open and I was blinded by a harsh light.

I screamed and covered my bra as I fell over, squeezing my eyes shut, as if by some kind of miracle it would make me disappear.

"Don't look at me! Don't look at me!" I yelled. Worrying less that it could be an axe-wielding maniac breaking into the van than simply someone seeing me in my underwear.

"It's a little late for that," said an unmistakable voice.

My eyes snapped open to find Chris casually leaning in the open doorway of the panel van, torch in hand.

"Don't you knock?" I yelled, trying for angry and less mortified as my arms wrapped around my white lace bra.

"I was actually more worried that the interior light was left on – a flat battery in the morning would not be ideal," he said in all seriousness, as if seeing me half naked in front of him was the least of his worries.

That idea actually made me *more* uncomfortable. He didn't even look me over with any type of male appreciation. Sure, I had wanted to make a good impression, but this certainly wasn't how I had planned to go about it.

"What are you doing back here anyway?" I asked, annoyed as I turned my back on him to finish hitching my dress up over my shoulders.

"Just seeing what was taking so long, but then we had to remind ourselves that it was probably taking you all four hours to put your make-up on."

"Ha! Well that's … where … you're … wrong," I said, struggling to reach around behind me to the back of my dress to zip it up.

Oh crap!

Chris sighed. "Come here."

I turned, wide-eyed. "W-what?"

"Come here," he repeated, trying to stop his lips from twitching as he turned the torch off and set it aside.

I swallowed deeply and tentatively stepped forward. He held out his hand, to help me out of the van. I took it, almost feeling an electric current pulse from his skin as it touched mine. Goosebumps formed on my flesh that had little to do with the warm summer night, or the fact that the back of my dress was open, exposing me in a new way. He helped me down from the van, guiding me to the ground. He was bathed in a rich yellow glow from the interior light. For the first time I actually took in the fresh, clean lines of his navy polo shirt, and his dark Levi's were back. His jagged, jet black hair was dry from his shower earlier and my mouth involuntarily pinched into a smile as I realised he was freshly shaven.

"You sure it didn't take *you* four hours to get ready?" I mused.

A familiar pinch formed between his brows as he circled his finger in the air. "Turn around."

I did as he asked, still clasping my hands to my front to hold my dress in place. He pulled the fabric together and gently manoeuvred the zip upward. He paused only to gather my hair and slide it over my shoulder so he could pull the zip all the way up. I managed to glance back at him, taking in the dramatic lines etched on his face in concentration. He had edged the zip all the way up and my new dress tightened over my body the way it should.

"Thanks," I said, and went to move, but his hand stopped me.

"Hang on a sec, there's a button thingy here."

I could feel him fumbling with the fabric at the nape of my neck, struggling to slot through the button. I could feel his breath on the back of my neck, more so when a deep sigh of frustration blew out as he struggled to master the button loop.

"Having trouble?"

"It won't defeat me," he said through gritted teeth.

I smirked, holding my hair to the side and stretching my neck out so he could work on the infuriating, delicate button.

After a long moment and a few curses under his breath he said, "There! You're good to go."

"Thanks," I sighed, adjusting my dress. I spun around. "What do you think?" I mentally slapped myself as soon as the words fell out. Chris was not my BFF or one of the girls, what did I expect him to say?

So when he said, "Nice," it shouldn't really have felt like he was knifing me in the heart.

Nice … Nice? A cup of tea was nice.

"Wow, thanks, you really know how to make a girl feel special," I said coolly, reaching for my clutch, concentrating on packing the things I needed for a night out on the town. Lipstick, compact, money, ID. I shoved each piece in my bag with irritated force.

I turned expectantly to him and was startled by the fact that he had moved next to the panel van door. I grabbed the other, pulling to shut it, but he stopped me. He caught the door and my eyes met his.

"What did you want me say?" He stared down at me with a quizzical narrowing of his brows.

Beautiful, stunning, gorgeous, let's forget about the others.

I blinked, trying to compose myself. It was just a simple question.

I let go of the door, leaving him to shut them. "I don't want you to say anything," I said lowly, turning to make my way down the track to meet the others.

Chapter Twenty-Eight

I was met by a rather sheepish-looking Bell and Stan.

I paused. "Bell, you're not dressed?"

Belinda smiled coyly, taking in her cut-off jean shorts and T-shirt. "Oh yeah, um, if it's all the same I think we might just stay here." She looked at Stan beside her.

"Oh, a romantic night in, then?" I teased.

Stan sighed. "Not exactly."

Before he could explain, we heard, "HEADS!" A football hurtled through the darkness, and we quickly ducked.

Ringer jogged into view, laughing. "Sorry," he said, before he scooped the ball up near Stan.

Ringer pushed in between Bell and Stan, slinking his arms around their shoulders. "We're going to have so much fun. Anyone up for charades?"

I cringed, thinking that the dodgy-looking Villa Co-Co sounded far more appealing. "Where's Amy?" I asked, looking for Sean's car.

"Oh, um, she said she would meet you there." Belinda winced.

"What?" My head snapped around.

"She said you could catch a lift back with Chris."

Oh did she now?

"You're going to need two cars to bring back the drunken hordes anyway," Stan added.

I heard Chris's footsteps from behind. "You ready?" he asked unenthusiastically as he stood beside me.

Wait until I catch up with my traitorous friends.

"Lead the way." I smiled sweetly.

Chris turned to Ringer who was busy handballing the footy to himself. "You sure you're not coming?"

"And suffer through Sean and Toby having a deep and meaningful?" He shuddered. "I think not."

My interest piqued. Maybe Sean was actually taking the opportunity to have a heart to heart with Toby; maybe it would help and Tess and he would be all right. I really hoped so.

I did as best as I could to keep up with Chris's long, determined strides.

"We're in Ringer's car," he called over his shoulder as he made his way toward the large, canary yellow Ford.

I expected many things from Chris, but one of them wasn't opening the door for me. It stopped me in my tracks.

His elbow rested on the door frame, his brows rising expectantly. "Something wrong?"

"Uh … no, not all," I said, quickly moving to slide into my seat. The door closed after me as Chris sauntered around the front of the car toward the driver's side.

Ha! Who said chivalry was dead?

I worked to quickly apply some gloss onto my lips in the dark, patting the strawberry flavour on my bottom lip and pressing them together. In the mad rush I had had little chance to do anything else. I self-consciously ran my fingers through my hair before Chris opened the door and slid in next to me. Beyond the strawberry scented lip gloss, Chris's sharp, musky aftershave filled the cabin.

Aftershave on a fishing trip? Interesting.

"So Villa Co-Co, huh? Sounds like a very happening kind of place," I mused.

Chris started the car, flashing a grin.

"I'll let you be the judge of that."

Villa Co-Co was a single-storey weatherboard hotel with a large verandah out the front. It sat back in the leafy confines of a blue gravelled drive that led off the main road. Blue, red and yellow party lights flashed along the entire length of the verandah roof. The only tropical clue bearing support to its name were the fish fern and bird's nest palms housed in multi-coloured pot plants dotted around the entrance.

I closed the passenger door. "I don't think we're in Kansas anymore, Toto."

What struck me was the distance we had to park away; the makeshift car park on the abandoned dirt lot beside the hotel was absolutely packed with cars. One car was being pressed up against by a couple with wandering hands and thrusting tongues as we walked past. I quickened my steps to catch up to Chris.

"There weren't that many cars here before." I clasped my arms around myself, warily eyeing the figures that loomed near the entrance of the hotel.

"Must be the full moon that drives people out," Chris said, looking up at the large illuminated disc in the sky.

I gulped, looking at the eerie face smirking down at me from above. "Yeah, brings out all the crazies, you mean."

Chris stopped and I ran into his back with a yelp. There was a devilish glint in his eyes as he smiled, slow and wicked. "You have no idea."

Before I could question him, he laced his fingers with mine in a firm grip and led the way inside.

Chris pushed his way through the front door and music assaulted my senses. I winced at the sound and the smell of cigarettes. It was as if all the oxygen had been sucked out of the room, and for that matter the lighting too. It was so dark inside it seemed like we were in a nightclub, minus the sticky drink-stained carpet. Rose Tattoo's 'Bad Boy For Love' screamed from the speakers. I involuntarily stepped closer to Chris, squeezing his hand tight, just to make sure he didn't let go. This was one crowd I really didn't want to get lost in. Unlike the subtle warm lighting that lit the open, airy Onslow Hotel, this place was small, dark and loud, and crammed with bodies ranging from the soiled work clothes of the toothless local timber cutter to the rowdy local in a grass-stained cricketing outfit shouting for shots at the bar. A group of girls chewed speculatively on their cocktail straws as they looked Chris up and down. Their eyes dimmed as they landed on me. And that wasn't even what dominated the entire bar space – lining the bar was a sea of leather-clad, tattooed, hairy bikers. All we needed was a drunken sailor and a go-go dancer and it would truly complete the picture. Chris smiled down at me as if he were revelling in my unease.

"Want a drink?" he shouted, smiling wickedly as he dragged me nearer the bar.

"No! No." I dug in my heels. "I mean shouldn't we find the others first?"

Safety in numbers, right?

I could only imagine what the others were thinking of this place; they were probably in a corner somewhere, looking on with the same wide-eyed horror that I was. The sooner I located them, the sooner we could all link arms and make an escape back to the cars and the campsite.

No wonder Ringer had returned – that should have been a red flag right there.

My gaze swooped around the dark, crowded space, hoping that one of the flashing party lights would flash onto a familiar face. And it did.

"Oh. My. God."

Chris followed my eye line to fix on what had me so stunned.

"Is that Ellie?" I asked. "She's dancing in a cage."

"Are you honestly surprised?" laughed Chris as he started to lead me through the crowd, drinks forgotten.

"Uh, you mean am I surprised at Ellie or the fact that there is a human-sized cage in the bar?"

Go-go dancer – check.

"Fair point," he said. He manoeuvred us through the crowd with expert ease and guided me toward a booth near the back of the pub. It sat next to a stage that had band equipment set up on it. The name scrawled across the drum kit read 'Spank the Monkey'. I could only hope that it was their night off.

Sean, Toby and Adam sat at the table completely unaware of our approach until Chris slammed his hand on the table, causing their heads to comically spin around and their hands to grab for their beers.

"Look what I found," Chris announced, tilting his head toward me. "She was chatting up some bikers at the bar; thought I better intervene." He guided me toward a seat.

"How about you go dance in a cage somewhere?" I smiled sweetly as I sat down.

"Oh no you don't," Adam piped up. "Ellie has five more minutes."

"So there's a time limit, is there?" I asked.

"There is when there's a bet on," Adam grinned.

"A bet?" Chris asked. He sat next to me so I shifted a little on the bench seat. There wasn't much room; I felt him pressed right next to me, his body heat elevating my own.

I was somewhat distracted when Toby spoke.

"Adam bet Ellie she wouldn't have the guts to dance in the cage for ten minutes."

I couldn't help but laugh. "It's Ellie, of course she's going to take the bet."

"Exactly." Adam beamed. "Best bet I ever lost."

We all tilted our heads toward the cage where Ellie was imprisoned.

"With a friend like you …" I shook my head, trying not to find it so funny.

Adam finished the last of his beer. "I better go and see how she's doing; do you think she would find it funny if I tried to slip a fiver in the cage?"

"I think you might get kicked in the face," I said with a laugh.

"Now that I would pay to see," said Sean.

Adam flipped us the bird, picked up his empty beer glass and disappeared into the crowd.

I wondered where the other girls were but I didn't need to wonder for too long. An ear-piercing scream was so shrill it could be heard over even the loudest of music.

"Tammy!" Amy screeched as she dragged Tess through the masses, pushing people out of the way to reach our table. "You made it!"

"No thanks to you," I glowered.

"Oh, don't be like that." She waved off my words.

"You know you are going to give me serious abandonment issues if you keep leaving me behind," I said.

"Not to worry, Chris will always be there to give you a lift," Amy said with an obnoxious wink-wink. Oh my God, she was such a dork, I half expected her wink to come with a nudge-nudge. And the fact that she had done it in front of everyone, I could feel myself blanch. I had thought that her leaving me behind to ride with Chris was some form of punishment. It appeared not. She raised her brows in a 'hubba-hubba' kind of way and looked between me and Chris. Oh my God! Was she seriously trying to play Cupid? My insides twisted.

"How much have you had to drink?" Sean mused suspiciously.

"Not much." Amy shrugged, swaying on her feet.

Tess held up six fingers behind Amy's back. Not that that told us much: six shots or six pints? Whatever it added up to, it was six of something too many.

"You always were a two-pot screamer," said Chris.

Amy's eyes cut Chris an acidic look. "At least I know how to have fun," she snapped.

"Tammy, come dance, this place has the BEST music," she said, leaning over Chris and grabbing my hand. Amy's tunnel vision as she strode away, regardless of who or what was between her and the dance floor, made my moving past Chris jerky and awkward. I tried not to decapitate him as Amy pulled at my arm.

"Sorry," I whispered as I almost fell on top of him when trying to get to my feet. Tess took my other hand.

"Just go with it." She laughed as we were dragged through the crowd to what I guessed was a dance floor.

Go with it? I thought. *As if I had any other choice.*

Chapter Twenty- Nine

I didn't know how Ellie managed to dance ten minutes in a cage, but she did.

Ten minutes on the dance floor and I was looking for an exit. It wasn't that I was unfit; I mean, I ran marathons for fun. But this was a different kind of marathon. No fresh air, no natural light, and no fluids for hydration. My enthusiasm was fading fast.

I bumped into a couple dry-humping next to me who were certainly getting rehydrated with each other's fluids. I cringed and danced away. By now Ellie was free from her cage and getting swung around the dance floor by Adam with their famous version of dancing. Kind of like … If Kate Bush and Mick Jagger had a love child, it would dance like Adam and Ellie.

I was doing my best nonchalant sidestep away, when one of my favourite songs started. I turned to point at Amy, who was already pointing at me, and we squealed with excitement at each other as the Eurythmics' 'When Tomorrow Comes' blared from the speakers.

I was filled with renewed energy all of a sudden and transported to my youth as Amy and I started to dance and sing all the lyrics to a song we knew off by heart. It didn't matter that we were in a dive of a hotel, surrounded by seedy strangers – at that moment it was just Amy and me on the dance floor. It was as though we were at a school social or at the blue light disco at the back of the Onslow, bullying the DJ to play our favourite songs.

It was just us, two best friends having a good time, until I felt the slide of a hand along my lower back. I spun around in surprise and collided with a chest; I looked up and my eyes locked with Chris's.

"Do you want a drink?" he asked, leaning toward my ear, his breath tickling my skin.

Momentarily dazed, I nodded yes. His hand left my waist and he peeled off toward the bar. My heart pounded – having realised it was Chris vying for my attention, even after the jolt of excitement had shot through me, as quickly as it had come the disappointment soon followed as he left.

What had I expected, for him to take my hand and lead me onto the dance floor like Patrick Swayze? Chris didn't do dancing; he did staring sullenly from the side, or trash-talking about guy stuff with the guys. I was an idiot to think anything else.

"What was that about?" yelled Amy, dancing in front of me.

I shrugged. "Nothing."

"That look on your face doesn't say nothing," Amy said. "What did he say?"

"He just asked if I wanted a drink."

"Ugh! Forever the barman." Amy rolled her eyes.

I couldn't help but think she was right; it was always as if he was on duty, as if he couldn't just relax and be himself, whoever that was. I thought I had seen glimpses of it in the car, but that's all it was, a taunting flash of someone else that never stayed around.

"What's going on?" Tess intervened, trying to catch her breath as she took a moment from tearing up the dance floor.

"Oh, Chris is getting Tammy a drink," Amy said.

"Nice of him to ask me, I'm dying here," Tess said, fanning herself.

"Where's Toby?" I asked. It was an innocent enough question, but when the light dimmed in her expression I regretted it immediately.

"He went back to the campsite," Tess said.

"Oh." It's all I could manage; this was definitely not normal Tess and Toby behaviour. Any talk Sean must have had with him – if he had – obviously hadn't helped.

I felt kind of stupid about the pang of disappointment I had over being asked if I wanted a drink. Seriously. If that was my biggest issue …

An ice-cold sensation pressed against my back and I gasped and jumped away, spinning around to see a devilish gleam in Chris's eyes.

"Here you go," he said, passing me a raspberry Vodka Cruiser.

I took it from him. "Thanks … I guess."

He just grinned and walked back to the table where Sean sat.

"Ugh! Seriously, when are you two just going to get it on already?" said Amy.

A flushed Ellie leaned her elbow on Tess's shoulder and wiped sweat from her brow.

"Sorry?" I asked, trying not to choke on my drink.

"Why don't the two of you just do it already?" she repeated.

I laughed nervously, hoping it didn't sound forced. "How much have you had to drink tonight?" I asked.

Ellie straightened. "I'm as sober as a judge."

"A cage-dancing judge," I mused, sipping on my Cruiser, hoping that the subject would be changed, and fast.

"What are we talking about?" Adam appeared next to Ellie, passing her a beer.

"NOTHING!" I said a bit too quickly, casting the others a dark, warning stare.

They ignored it.

"Be warned, Adam, you might not have the stomach for this," said Amy.

"The stomach for what?" asked Adam, his eyes widened in expectant excitement as if what we were discussing could possibly be gory or disturbing.

I had to get out of there; I needed air and plenty of it. I had to break away from their knowing looks. The *last* thing I wanted was for them to confide in Adam, Chris's brother. I knew he was kind of one of the girls, being Tess's and Ellie's best friend and all, but still. At the end of the day, he was Chris's younger brother. I could only imagine that this kind of knowledge would be used as hours and hours of torture against Chris.

"I'll be right back, I just have to get some air," I announced quickly, before dodging my way through the crowd. I hit the front door, pushed it open and ran out to grab the wooden rail. I took a deep breath; the clean air was glorious – it was as if I could get drunk on the stuff. Instead, I eyed my bottle of vodka, still in my hand. I stared at it for a long moment; well, if I was going to be drunk it might as well be on the real stuff. I tipped the bottle back and sculled the bottle until my eyes watered.

"Whoa, easy there," Adam's voice spoke from behind me.

I lowered the bottle again, catching my breath and coughing.

"You know, drinking alone is pretty sad," he said, leaning against the railing.

"I don't think you could ever be alone at Villa Co-Co," I said.

"Ah, yes, I dare say each and every one of us will take a little piece of Villa Co-Co away with us." Adam dreamily looked off into the distance.

"Hopefully not alcohol poisoning," I added.

"Yeah, well, that's Amy's department, maybe Ellie's, and if the night pans out right it's sure as hell going to be Tess's problem."

"How is Tess?" I asked and immediately thought I probably shouldn't have.

Adam sipped thoughtfully on his stubby, the same darkness casting over him as it had Tess. "She doesn't say too much to me, probably because she knows that I'll lose my shit. But put it this way – by the end of this trip, Toby and I will be having words and I won't be pussyfooting around like Sean does."

Adam spoke each word as if it was a dark promise; it chilled me to the bone. "What's he done, anyway? What is wrong with Toby?" I asked. "Seems like no one knows. Maybe that should be the question that's being asked."

Adam shrugged. "That's the problem, no one knows, I don't even think Toby knows or if he does he's not saying, but my loyalty is to Tess not him, and if he doesn't man up and talk to her soon then I'm not going to just stand by and watch him hurt her."

I grimaced. "I know it's hard, but try to think about what Tess wants, what she needs in a friend right now."

Adam sighed. "I knew you'd be all logical and reassuring and shit."

I smiled. "Sorry about that."

"Ah, that's all right." He straightened. "Do you want me to give you some reassurance?"

"Um, okay …"

Adam leaned closer to me. "I won't tell anyone."

Chapter Thirty

I looked at Adam, thoroughly bewildered.

My mind raced with questions, but I didn't get to ask even one of them as the door behind us opened and music flooded onto the verandah.

"Oi, your women are looking for you." Chris stood in the open doorway, glowering at his younger brother.

"Ha! Only because they're too tight to buy their own drinks." Adam grinned. He peeled himself off the railing and made his way to the open door. "I was going to take Tammy back to the campsite; she has a bit of a headache …"

I did? What was he on about?

Adam continued. "Do you think …?"

"I'll take her," Chris snapped, never taking his broody expression off me.

I couldn't take my dumbfounded eyes off Adam.

Headache?

"Thanks, bro!" Adam tapped Chris on the shoulder, stepping back through the door. He winked at me and mimed that his lips were locked and he had thrown away the key.

My breath hitched; is that what he had meant? That he wouldn't say something to Chris? What? That I liked him? I guess

I should have been relieved, but the last thing I needed (aside from Amy playing matchmaker) was for Adam to none too subtly try to hook me up with his brother.

His broody, fuming, scary-looking brother who stood in front of me.

He stalked over to me, took the bottle from my hand and threw it in the nearby bin. "Let's go."

"But I haven't …"

"Now!" he growled over his shoulder as if the point was completely non-negotiable.

Geez, what did I do?

I hurried after him, stumbling in my footwear, the stupid over-strappy, blister-inducing heels that Ellie had convinced me to buy.

"Chris." I stopped to take off one shoe, then the other. "Wait."

Either he hadn't heard or he just chose to ignore me as he stalked off into the car park.

Ugh. What a bloody child.

I thought maybe removing my shoes would help me move faster, but as I winced and hopped on the sharp gravel it kind of had the opposite effect.

"Ooh-ah-ooh-ah—ah." I limped my way across the never-ending stretch, my anger building with each painful step.

Just. You. Wait. Chris Henderson.

Chris had reached the car long before me. He had flung the passenger door open and was glowering at me, waiting for my arrival.

There was the Chris I knew.

"Get in." He pointed.

Pain being the least of my worries now, I stormed the final couple of metres and threw one shoe in the car then the other. I slammed the car door shut and pushed Chris against it.

"Don't you dare speak to me like that!" I yelled. "I'm not one of your lackeys, you can't boss me around like that, and what's with the freakin' attitude?"

"Have you taken one of your tablets?" he snapped.

"What?"

"I'm guessing you're one of two kinds of stupid," Chris said.

What the hell?

"One, you haven't taken your medication to stop your migraine or two, you have *and* you've been drinking. Either way it makes me want to throttle you."

My mouth gaped open. I was completely taken aback by every offensive rant that came from his mouth, before I thought about it.

"Chris!"

"You're right, I can't tell you what to do, but have enough sense to realise that your actions affect other people."

"Are you going to let me explain?"

"You know, Tammy, I'm not always going to be around to give you a ride and if you think …"

"For fuck's sake, CHRIS, I DONT HAVE A FUCKING HEADACHE!" My scream echoed through the car park so loud I wouldn't have been surprised if the music had stopped and the entire population of Villa Co-Co had heard.

Chris's brows rose in confusion. "Then, why did you say—"

"*I* didn't say. I never said. *Adam* was the one who told you I had a headache, *Adam* was the one that suggested you take me home, *Adam* was—"

"But why would he do that?" Chris asked, confusion etching his brows.

"My God!" I tugged at my hair in frustration then put my hands on my hips. "I'm guessing *you're* one of two kinds of stupid. One, you're blind or two, ignorant. Or both. Either way it makes me want to throttle *you*."

Chris's mouth pinched at the corner. "What's with the freakin' attitude?" he said.

Touché.

I sighed. "Why do you think they left for the camping trip early and blackmailed *you* to stay back and drive me? Why did they leave for Villa Co-Co without me and have *you* take me? Why suggest I have a headache so *you* can whisk me away into the night?"

Chris crossed his arms over his chest, his expression unmoving and unreadable as he waited for me to spell it out.

He was really going to make me do it.

I buried my face in my hands.

God give me strength.

I looked him dead in the eye. Best to get it out of the way – now that Adam knew, there would be no peace, anyway. "Because they're playing matchmaker." I waved my hand, motioning between us. "With you and me."

I braced myself for Chris to laugh, or openly grimace, or maybe blush, but he did none of those things. I waited. I tilted my chin up a little; I wasn't going to cave with embarrassment. I was going to stand my ground.

The only thing that thawed my resolve was when Chris broke into a brilliant white smile.

"What?"

Chris leaned against the car, his smile growing wider and wider as his devilish eyes watched my troubled expression.

"What's so funny?"

Chris hooked his hands behind his head, looking like the cat that got the cream. I couldn't help but break into a smile myself; this unexpected reaction was contagious.

"What are you thinking?" I said.

Chris looked me dead in the eye. "Let's give them what they want."

Chapter Thirty-One

My smile evaporated from my face in shock.

"W-what?" I swallowed.

"They are so obviously bored with their own petty existences."

"Yeah," I said. "I guess?"

Chris pushed off the car, moving to stand before me, the same devilish twinkle in his eye. "Well, let's give them something to talk about." He inched closer to me.

"What are you suggesting?"

"You might have to call on your academy award-winning acting skills."

"Go on."

"Here's an idea," he said. "We pretend that we're having a summer fling, but we don't admit anything. We act kind of cuddly but flat-out deny anything's going on. What do you think? They'll drive each other wild speculating. It will kill them. Plus, it'll stop them from playing Cupid if they think it's already happened."

My grin matched Chris's. "Sounds pretty devious."

"No more than they are."

True.

"So you in?" He held his hand out to me. I looked at it for a long moment before giving it a firm, business-like shake.

"I'm in." I paused, thinking. "So how do we start this masterful plan of deception?"

"First we'll have to plant the seed," Chris said as he opened the car door for me.

"Oh? And what's that going to be?" I asked with interest.

"The person with the biggest mouth."

When we arrived back at the campsite we found Ringer throwing Maltesers in the air and trying to catch them with his mouth. Having witnessed one roll from his lips onto the ground only to be picked up and placed back into the packet, we both respectfully declined his offer when he passed it our way.

"You guys weren't gone long," Ringer said with a mouth full of chocolate.

"No, I had a headache," I said, trying not to look at Chris.

"Yeah, well, Villa Co-Co isn't the place to nurse a headache," said Ringer.

"Where's Romeo and Juliet?" asked Chris as he propped himself on a nearby esky.

"You know young lovers." Ringer grinned, nodding toward their tent.

"What's Toby's excuse, then?" The words fell out of my mouth before I could stop them.

Both boys looked at me, unable to answer, because, unlike everyone else, Toby was a complete enigma.

"Anyway, I'm going to turn in for the night. Better rest this head of mine. Night, boys."

"Night, Tammy," said Ringer.

"Night," Chris said, trying not to smile.

I tentatively walked toward the path, my strappy heels dangling from my hand. I winced with every sharp stick or piece of bark that dug into my feet. It must have looked like I was doing the walk of shame, the infamous ungodly-hour stumblings of a girl with messed-up hair and raccoon eyes. I smiled to myself, lost in my thoughts before a new thought entered my mind.

I was heading toward the van.

I stilled. Was I sleeping in the van tonight? I mean, that's where all my stuff was, but would that be weird? Sleeping in Chris's van and not the tent. I bit my lip and looked back down the track. I couldn't go back, that would be awkward. My mind raced at a million miles an hour, conflicted by what to do.

"Night, Tammy." I jumped, startled when a voice pierced the darkness.

I muffled my cry with my hands.

A rich chuckle emanated from the dark like a nightmare, until a light flicked on.

"Sorry, I didn't mean to scare you," Toby said, trying not to laugh as he stood from his camping chair.

I clutched at my heart. "Jesus, Toby, you nearly copped a shoe in the face."

I had walked straight past Toby and Tess's tent and hadn't even realised. The treetop canopy above us cast deep shadows eerily all over the camping ground; not even the light of the full moon could penetrate in some places. Toby's torch shone at my feet.

"Why aren't you wearing them?"

I held up my heels. "Hiking boots they are not."

Toby nodded. "I don't know much about women's shoes, but I'm guessing you're right."

"The blisters on my feet think so too."

An awkward silence fell between us, and just as I was about to say goodnight and continue my awkward, painful trek up the track toward the van, Toby spoke.

"Hang on a sec," he said. He shucked off his shoes and handed them out to me. "They're about ten sizes too big, but I assure you I haven't any foot diseases; they will be definitely more comfortable than those."

I stared at Toby's sneakers, taken aback by the kindness. Of late I had heard nothing but the whispered speculation about Toby and Tess and how Toby was being a jerk. I hadn't thought much of it, and, to be honest, I didn't really know him. I hadn't talked to Toby much outside of the group setting.

He shook the shoes. "Go on, take them."

I so badly wanted to ask him what was wrong between him and Tess, why he was shutting down. I wanted him to tell me that everything would be all right, that they would be all right because, let's face it, we all believed if Toby and Tess couldn't work it out, no one could. I took his Converse shoes.

"Thanks," I said, taking them and placing them on the ground and slipping my feet inside. They were comically huge but compared to the sticks and sharp gravel they were like walking on clouds.

Toby smiled, looking at my feet. "There you go," he said.

It was the first real smile I had seen from Toby in a long while. Although I was so desperate to ask, I didn't dare. He wasn't really my friend anyway, and he had probably gotten enough grilling from his real mates asking him what the matter was.

If they didn't know, he sure wasn't going to tell me.

But then all of a sudden he did.

"Do you ever feel like you have so much to say, but you just don't know how to say it?" he asked out of the blue.

I stilled, almost forgetting to breathe as I took in his words. Toby was talking, and he was talking to me. I didn't move, afraid I'd spook him.

I kept it simple. "I feel like that all the time."

His eyes flicked up to meet mine, as if he was trying to gauge if I was serious. Toby sighed and pushed his hands deep into his pockets. "Every time I go to speak, or try to confess …"

I inwardly cringed. Confess wasn't a good word; it implied that he had done something wrong. My heart thundered in my chest.

"Sometimes," I said, "you just need to say it, no matter how it sounds. Some things are better out in the open. Better said than left unsaid."

God that sounded confusing; did that even make any sense?

Toby nodded like he completely understood.

"You'll know when the time's right to talk about it. Whatever it is you need to talk about." I tried to sound soothing, but I was worried I wasn't being any help at all.

"Yeah, I will," Toby said, lost in his own musings. And then just like that he snapped out of his deep thoughts. "Well, be careful walking in those shoes – they might be more comfortable but they might not be much easier."

"Oh yeah," I said, blinking, refocusing. "Thanks, though, you're a lifesaver."

"Night, Tammy."

"Night."

I turned to shuffle my way up the slanted gravel track. My mum had always taught me never to judge anyone unless you walked a mile in their shoes; I just had never expected to be walking in Toby Morrison's, literally.

I punched my pillow for the millionth time, trying to get comfortable. It was impossible, considering it was partly the crappy pillow's fault, but mostly it was because I was lying in the dark, on the mattress, still in my dress.

In the back of the van, I had struggled and fallen, nearly dislocated my shoulder trying to undo the back of my dress. If I'd had access to a pair of scissors I would have had no qualms about shredding the bloody thing into a million pieces.

Frustrated, I had crumpled to the mattress, giving up, trying to think of the silken fabric as soft against my skin instead of the reality of its scratchy lace edgings. I would never have had this problem if I had bought the bloody hippy dress from Evoka.

Where the bloody hell was Chris?

Probably planting the seed like he had planned, sitting with Ringer at the campsite, although me crashing in the van tonight was no doubt going to be a topic of conversation.

A wicked smile lit my face. I could always call out from the van. "OH, CHRIS! I NEED YOU TO TAKE MY CLOTHES OFF!"

I giggled to myself; I was so funny. Wouldn't they just love that? It would not be the most subtle of planted seeds. I thought it was probably better to just try to sleep instead before I did do something stupid. Little did I know that as far as doing stupid things was concerned, Chris was going to take the whole freakin' cake!

Chapter Thirty-Two

I hadn't even realised I had fallen asleep until two things happened:

The door to the van opened and I was hit in the face with a piece of plastic.

"Sorry," Chris laughed.

I hitched myself up onto my elbows and winced against the van's bright interior light. "What was that?" I croaked, looking around me for the flying missile.

"Trust me, you don't want to know."

Well, NOW I did!

I sat up, stretching my arms to the roof as I continued to look around the mattress.

Chris climbed into the van, leaving the door ajar, and rummaged through his bag.

"Uh, you know how we were going to plant the seed, subtly?" he said.

I lifted the bedding, still searching for the mystery missile. "Hmm," I managed, blinking to wake myself up.

He cringed. "Well, I might not have been quite subtle enough."

"What are you talking abo—" I froze, my eyes fixing to the very *thing* that had hit me in the face. I scooped it up and turned it in my hand, as if studying a wondrous object. My eyes flicked up in horror to see Chris almost bracing himself for me to lose my shit.

"Are you serious? A condom?"

Chris ran his hand through his hair. "I know, I know."

"THIS is NOT subtle," I said.

"Well, I didn't ask for it," Chris defended.

"So what? You just stumbled onto this on your trek home?" I asked in wonder, trying not to think how I had come about wearing another person's shoes.

"Honest to God, I didn't even get the chance to plant the seed with Ringer, we were too busy talking about other stuff and I thought, well, maybe the fact you were sleeping in my van might be subtle enough anyway, and just as I was calling it a night he stopped me, went into his wallet and chucked *that* at me. And then I chucked it at you."

Chris was rattling on in a blind panic, as if what he was saying was so far-fetched I might not believe him and was about to call him on it.

It was curious to see the usually cool, calm, collected Chris fumble over his words.

I started laughing and threw myself back on the mattress. A wry, relieved smile broke across his face.

"I'm glad you think it's funny," he said, throwing the blanket over my head, muffling my laughter.

I peeled off the cover, hitched myself up onto my elbows and watched as Chris stood outside the open end of the van and brushed his teeth.

"What did you say when he gave it to you?"

"Whert curld I serh?" he asked with a mouth full of foam before he shoved the brush back into his mouth.

"You should have reminded him I had a headache."

Chris choked on some toothpaste as he fought not to laugh.

I buried my head in my hands. "Oh my God, Chris. We're living a lie."

I lifted my head only to face a wall of exposed abs as Chris stood outside the van, peeling his top off. I quickly looked away, nuzzling down in my bedding and turned onto my side. A moment after Chris had rinsed his mouth out, the back of the van dipped under his weight as he once again rummaged around in his bag. I heard him as he shucked off his shoes and undid the belt and zip of his pants before shutting the back door and plunging us both into darkness.

All of a sudden, the van felt claustrophobic, far too small for the both of us. I held my breath, bracing myself until Chris climbed over the seat and made himself comfortable in the front.

But he didn't. Instead, he lay down next to me. My eyes widened. He puffed up his pillow and shimmied himself into a little spot, his arm pressing against me as he made himself comfortable.

"You got enough room?" he asked.

"Yep, plenty," I lied.

Chris was so close I could feel the heat from his skin; I could hear every intake of breath he made.

I lay frozen in an awkward twisted position, afraid to move. It was like being trapped under the bed playing Murder in the Dark all over again, except this time I didn't have to fear Ringer – well, not until the morning and this time it would be for a whole other reason.

Oh my God, Ringer thinks we're having sex! Which means by morning everyone will think we've done it and they'll all be looking at us with 'they have just totally *had sex' eyes.*

I sighed.

"What's wrong?" Chris asked.

"Oh nothing, this bloody thing itches," I said, which wasn't a total untruth. I clawed at my dress.

Chris hitched himself onto his side. "Are you still wearing your dress?" he asked, laughing.

"Pfft, no!"

Chris reached out, carefully sliding his hand up my arm to my shoulder, feeling the delicate lace of the material. "Yeah, you are. Why?"

I lifted my chin. "Because it's actually quite comfy."

"When it's not itching?" he repeated.

"Yeah, well aside from that."

"You can't get it off," Chris spoke in such a way that I could completely imagine him grinning, thinking it so hilarious that I couldn't get out of my own clothes. "Did you even try?"

"Of course I tried," I snapped.

"Whoa, okay, I see it's a touchy subject," he said as he pulled himself up to a sitting position. For a moment I thought he was actually offended and was making a move toward the front seat.

"W-where are you going?" I sat bolt upright.

Chris paused. "Nowhere. Turn around." His voice was low.

"Chris, it's fine, I was nearly asleep. I can just …"

"Does everything have to be a bloody debate with you?"

My mouth gaped. "No."

"Then turn around."

This time I did as he asked.

No biggie. He's done this before; it's the same as before. Except the zipper is going down instead of up, and he's half dressed, and in the dark, in the back of the Shaggin' Wagon with a condom floating around somewhere. Yep! No big deal whatsoever.

Chris gently swept my hair to the side, his fingertips lightly grazing along the back of my neck. It was just as he had done earlier in the evening, but somehow the dark heightened my senses; I could feel his breath on the back of my neck; I could hear him swallow deeply as his fingers gently worked on the buttoned clasp at the top. Just like he had struggled before to do it up, he was having trouble undoing it. He shifted closer; I could feel his leg press into my tail bone. I could hear my own laboured breath that seemed so painfully loud, but it was nothing compared to the thunderous beating of my heart that was practically deafening to my ears.

I bit my lip – a part of me wanted him to hurry up, but an even bigger part of me wanted him to take his time.

"Got it." His words were low and close to my ear.

He then, with an agonisingly slow and steady hand, peeled the zipper downward. It was as if he was unravelling me. I pressed my lips together, closing my eyes, as I briefly imagined that this wasn't just about a clumsy girl wanting to get out of an itchy dress, but it was because he wanted to undo my dress. Because it was Chris and me, in the back of his van. Because I was a girl he had seen from across the room, a girl he had walked with and guided through the dark, a girl he didn't have to pretend he was sleeping with to play a joke on his friends.

I almost gasped at the maddening sensation of Chris's thumb as it accidently grazed my bare back. I leaned back a little, hoping that more would come of it, but as quickly as it had been there it was gone, until I felt the press of his lips resting on my shoulder.

It was utterly distracting until his beautiful hands slid over my bare shoulders, pushing the fabric of my dress so that it fell forward. I grabbed the material, lightly brushing my fingers against his as I pulled the material down toward my waist. Chris's breathing quickened and he watched me, motionless for a long moment, almost as if he was contemplating what to do next.

I turned my head, my cheek so near his; even in the dark I could sense his lips were close. If he didn't know where to go from here, *I* sure did. Just as I was about to make the next step, an easy one, by closing the distance between us, he took the next bold move.

"Goodnight!"

He shifted back, lay down and rolled over, facing away from me.

I stared at his back in stunned silence, half naked and bitterly disappointed.

Chapter Thirty-Three

After that, sleep did not naturally follow.

Instead, I lay there in my bra and undies, staring up at the ceiling, wondering what it was exactly he had found so repulsive about me. I had worked myself into such an over-exhausted state of worthlessness and frustration. The worst thing was I knew Chris wasn't asleep either; you could always tell by a person's breathing if they were asleep or not. Sleep was full of deep, relaxed breaths, and there was nothing relaxed about Chris. He lay with his back to me, probably wondering how he would possibly face me in the morning. Well, I would make it easy for him, I thought.

As soon as the first slither of sunlight even threatened to lighten the sky, as quietly as I could I rummaged through my bag to find my running gear: my Lycra three-quarter pants, sports bra, my ankle socks and runners. With my water bottle, I wrapped it all up, deciding I could get dressed outside the van; it wasn't like anyone would be up at this hour, anyway.

I slowly unclicked the door and slid out. I glanced back at Chris's apparently sleeping body. A pulse of anger shot through me as I remembered how humiliated I had felt last night. I wished I had just slept in the bloody tent. I slid out the back of the van and gently closed the door before quickly getting dressed and jogging along the walking track.

I had thought that running might clear my head; that it would be a welcome return to feel my muscles cry and my lungs burn as I pushed myself to stride longer, run faster. I would run until either I vomited or could push through it, but as I collapsed against a tree, sweat dribbling down my back, my cheeks flushed with heat, there was nothing clear about my mind at all.

I was still haunted by his touch. Had I imagined his laboured breath? The way he had gently caressed my skin? I could almost still feel the burn of his lips on my shoulder.

I trudged back up the path. Up ahead I could see the gang hovering around the makeshift kitchen, heating up baked beans on the campfire as the billy boiled.

My face flamed with embarrassment. Ringer had probably blabbed about the condom he had so thoughtfully gifted Chris and me. I slowed my pace as I headed back toward the campsite. *Let Chris face them first.*

I saw him before he saw me.

Standing shirtless by the makeshift kitchen, spooning a mouthful of Nutri-Grain, he was listening intently to Sean who sat on a folded out camping chair holding a captive audience. So captive, a dribble of milk slid down Chris's chin, which he wiped away with the back of his hand.

God, how could such a thing be so sexy? I needed to have an ice-cold solar shower.

I was grateful for Sean holding the spotlight; it made my approach from the track of less interest than I had anticipated. I received only distracted glances and half-hearted waves from the enthralled group that surrounded Sean. The only person who didn't seem so enthralled was Chris, whose deep brown gaze locked with mine briefly before I quickly looked away, sliding into the spare space next to Bell.

"What's going on?" I whispered.

Bell grinned, munching thoughtfully on a toast finger. "Sean was just retelling a gripping tale of love and loss," she said with a giggle.

"But mostly loss," added Stan quietly out of the side of his mouth. He and Bell exchanged looks and caught a case of the giggles.

Sean's eyes darkened. "It's not funny."

"No, it's not," added Chris as he sat beside Adam on the opposite side of the table. "It's bloody hilarious."

"Okay, what have I missed?" I looked around the snickering group.

Toby stretched his arms toward the sky before linking them behind his head, a mischievous glint in his eyes. "Sean thought he'd try to get all chummy with the owners of Villa Co-Co."

"I would call it more like flirting." Amy crossed her arms, a smirk curving her mouth.

"True. There was some shameless flirting going on," Toby agreed.

"Get stuffed, she was old enough to be my mother," piped up Sean.

"Which makes it all the more disturbing," mused Amy.

"Anyway, I don't know if you saw Jan? The Madame of Villa Co-Co?" Toby asked me.

I tried to cast my memory back; I hadn't really been there that long. I did remember a short, dumpy, overtanned lady with spikey, peroxide hair swanning around the place in a kaftan and fake acrylic claws. For the briefest of moments I had entertained the notion that she looked like a human-sized pineapple. Could she be …

"Oh my God, the Pineapple?"

They all burst into the loudest, most hysterical laughter, none laughing louder than Adam who banged the table with his hand and grabbed his stomach.

"That's her." Toby pointed at Sean. "The Pineapple!"

The only person not laughing was Sean. He sat rubbing the stubble of his chin with a wry smile. "All right, all right, get on with it, Tobias, you're enjoying this way too much."

Toby tried to regain his composure as he wiped his eyes. Tess sat next to him, catching her own breath as she waited with glee for him to continue. They both seemed normal and relaxed. I hoped this was a good sign.

Toby cleared his throat. "Anyway, the Pineapple."

Ringer snorted.

"Shhh." Ellie elbowed him.

"So, I'm not sure how it happened exactly but the Pineapple honed in on the great almighty Sean; she must know a businessman when she sees one, who knows? They were talking about business and hotels and all the stuff that would make you want to take a cyanide pill, it was so utterly boring." Toby groaned.

"Except for you, Chris, you would have loved it," Amy pointed out.

"Sounds riveting," Chris deadpanned.

"Anyway, as the night wore on, I think her top got lower so the cleavage got bigger and bigger."

"There was a lot of cleavage," grimaced Tess.

"And with each shift of her low-cut top, her hand would motion the barman for another jug of beer."

"So the Pineapple had big jugs?" I asked Sean, trying not to laugh.

He shook his head. "Massive."

"There were jugs everywhere," Toby exclaimed, holding his hands up with dramatic flair. "Anytime Sean finished another jug, she would be like, 'Let me get this one, let me get this one.'"

"Where were you, Amy?" I asked.

"Rolling my eyes next to him."

"We learned about how she and her husband have just returned from Bali because they import furniture, and how they want to open up a restaurant over there, all really fascinating stuff, and we thought, you know, these people are quite switched on really. But we sort of really didn't realise how switched on and business savvy they were until it was closing time," said Toby.

By now my elbows were on the table; I had fully leaned forward, just like the others had been before.

"What happened at closing time?" I bit my lip.

"The Pineapple disappeared and a waitress slipped Sean a folded piece of paper with a smile."

Before I could ask if the Pineapple's phone number was on it, Sean sighed. "A hundred and seventy-eight bucks."

"What?"

"Mate, you ruined my punchline!" Toby slapped the table, annoyed.

I must have looked confused until Chris spoke. "The Pineapple was running a bar tab the whole time."

I tilted my head in sympathy, but Amy continued to shake her head.

"Some savvy businessman you are," she scoffed.

I patted Sean on the shoulder. "Never mind, you weren't to know she was a rotten pineapple," I said, trying not to laugh.

I stood to make my way for some brekky, making a conscious effort to not make eye contact with Chris. If there was one thing I could sympathise with Sean about, it was that you couldn't always judge a book by its cover. That I knew for sure.

Chapter Thirty-Four

"I wouldn't bother with that if I were you."

Ringer's voice snapped me from my daydream as I stood beside the solar shower with my cup of tea, mentally psyching myself up to have a shower and then get changed.

I turned to where he was busy packing up chairs.

"I have to," I said.

There were just no two ways about it; I had to wash off the sweat from my run, I had to feel human if I was going to sit in the van with Chris again for hours and hours. Something I was *not* looking forward to.

"Just do what the rest of us are gonna do." Ringer groaned as he lifted a twenty-litre esky onto the back of the ute's tray.

I looked expectantly at him.

He rolled his eyes. "Tammy, where are we?"

I looked around.

Um, nowhere?

"We're at Evoka Springs." He said it as if it were the most obvious thing in the world.

"Yeah, so?"

"So do you know why people stop here?"

"Gemstone elephant statues?" I said, taking a sip of my tea.

"Evoka SPRINGS, baby!" Ringer pointed behind me. "See down that track, where Sean and Amy's love nest is?"

"Hmm."

"Well, about three hundred metres beyond that is a giant watering hole."

"Heated springs?" My eyes lit up. "Why didn't you guys tell me yesterday?" I shuddered at the memory of the icy water.

"Uh, not heated exactly – actually, it's just like a big river – but the water is warm as."

Oh, okay, so that sounded better than an ice-cold shower. And I didn't fancy my chances of Chris offering to pour warm water on me again. If anything, Chris seemed more likely to pour ice-cold water on heated situations.

I tipped the dregs out of my cup. "Are you going down?" I asked.

"We all are! Better get your swimmers on." He shrugged. "Or not, doesn't worry me." Ringer winked and flashed a cheeky grin.

I jogged up the path, feeling all the expected excitement of not wanting to get left behind as I rushed to change into my swimmers. The last thing I hoped to see was Chris coming down the track in the opposite direction, dressed in nothing but his black footy shorts with a towel slung over his shoulder.

God, he looked good.

I snapped my thoughts from such perviness. Besides, I was still mad at him from last night, wasn't I? Oh no, was I starting to turn into an Amy clone? Holding a grudge and being dramatic? I really didn't want to be like that; besides, what was his crime, not finding me irresistible?

No, I didn't want to be that girl. So, in the true spirit of *positive, positive, positive*, I met Chris's guarded eyes with a bright smile.

"Going for a tub?" I called, making my way toward him.

Don't look at his shoulders; don't linger on his pecs; eyes up front and centre!

He held up a cake of soap with a smirk.

"I hope that is environmentally friendly?"

His face seemed to relax a little; the guard came down. "Absolutely," he said with a grin. "The fish are going to smell like roses."

He had the most beautiful smile. How had I missed it before? Maybe because it was so rare, but when he smiled in front of me it was utterly transforming; Chris was like the sun appearing from behind the clouds.

I wanted to get to know him, the real him. I didn't want to dismiss him in petty anger because he didn't make a move last night; I wanted to find out what pushed his buttons, what made him tick. I had seriously contemplated getting a lift with Adam and Ellie or Stan and Belinda rather than spend another day with Chris in the van, but I never entertained the thought for long. I had grown quite fond of the van.

Of Chris.

"So, has Ringer mentioned anything to you?"

My eyes blinked at his question. Oh God, that's right, last night's gift from Ringer.

"Oh, um, no, actually. I was kind of expecting the worst. You?"

Chris shook his head. "Not yet. Give it time, he'll strike when we least expect it."

"It's like Murder in the Dark all over again."

"So what's our plan of attack today, then?" Chris asked, toeing a circle in the dirt.

"As in?"

"Operation Summer Fling?" He looked at me, a glint of amusement twinkling in his eyes.

My heart skipped a beat. Was he serious? After the way last night had ended I had thought maybe it was just a joke, but did he still want to go through with it?

"You mean, plant more seeds?" I asked, afraid to hope.

He shrugged, squinting up at the sky. "Keep 'em guessing, I reckon."

My stomach twisted in excitement. "Okay, I'm really not an expert at this or anything."

"Would you like me to lead the way?" Chris asked, sporting a cheeky grin.

I blushed. "You might have to; you seem to be naturally more devious than I am."

His brows rose in surprise. "Oh, really?"

"Well, hiding in cupboards, under beds, making secretive calls to local chemists …"

Chris nodded as I spoke. "I am pretty sneaky."

"*So* sneaky," I agreed. "So the problem is, how will I know how to react to you when I have to?"

All humour faded from Chris's eyes as he looked into mine. There was nothing but smooth calmness in his expression, no aggressive lines etched above his brow. He looked so much younger than usual. I wanted to look away but I couldn't; his gaze pinned me into place. A slow, crooked smile pinched the corner of his mouth.

"Oh, trust me, you'll know," he said, and just as I thought he had robbed me of all breath, he slid past me on the walking track and continued on his way toward the campsite.

The stillness of the tranquil surrounds were disturbed by the Tarzan-like hollers injected into the air every time one of the boys launched themselves at a run at the long rope from the embankment. They flew through the air and plunged into the water of the Evoka Springs.

It was Chris's turn to take the rope. His biceps pulled into taut, moulded curves that stretched just as impressively as his back muscles when he reached and pulled for the rope. Wearing Chris's sunnies, my eyes secretly gazed at the line along his ribcage as he inhaled a deep breath before launching himself into the air. My breath hitched when he flung into a backward somersault, plunging feet first into the murky water. I straightened from my recline, lifting the sunnies from my eyes and holding my breath until his head poked up out of the water with that famous hair flick boys do. As soon as he broke the surface everyone cheered. They had good reason to; it had been impressive. I just melted back on my towel in relief, placing Chris's oversized man sunnies back on.

As tradition had it, Bell, Tess, Ellie, Amy and I were all lying, sun-baking on our towels, watching the alpha males trying to outdo each other with testosterone-fuelled antics. After we had gone for a dip, washing our bodies and hair with flowery-scented soap, we lounged on our towels, refreshed and sunkissed.

While the others chatted about the things they missed, like hairdryers and running hot water, I lay silently, propped up on my elbows, watching Chris's body slowly appear out of the water. It was as if a movie was playing out in slow motion before my eyes – he ran his hands back through his hair as the excess water dribbled down his tanned skin. We hadn't said two words to each other since we had all congregated by the river over an hour ago, so although I knew he planned on planting a seed of intrigue, I guess he hadn't meant he would necessarily do it anytime soon. Heck, if at all. But as he made his way up onto the bank his eyes locked onto me, he winked, and strode toward me.

Oh-crap-oh-crap-oh-crap …

I shifted myself into a seated position, not knowing what that wink meant until he came over. Chris stood above me, shaking the excess water off his hair, causing me to flinch and scream.

"Chris, doooon't!"

He collapsed onto my towel beside me, laughing.

"You're an idiot," Amy glowered, wiping off wayward droplets from her shoulders.

He ignored her; even turning his back on me so he could watch as Adam took the rope.

So what, that was it? Was that his idea of planting the seed? Seriously? Share my towel? Prop himself here after some tomfoolery and get dry?

That was something any of the Onslow Boys would do on a regular basis. I didn't know if the wink had meant he was going to try something to arouse suspicion or not, but my lips twitched in silent amusement. Two could play at this game.

I shifted onto my knees. "You look tense, Chris," I said, placing my hands on his shoulders to balance myself. I could feel the flex of his muscle twitch under my unexpected touch.

To his credit (apart from that), he didn't bat an eyelid. "Yeah, I must have slept funny," he replied, kinking his head from side to side.

I scooted closer, kneading at the base of his neck. Chris stretched his head forward, involuntarily groaning as I pressed my thumbs into the muscle.

"There?" I asked.

"Mmm-hmm," was his only response as he brought his head forward, shutting his eyes.

I didn't dare look to my left where Amy was no doubt watching with distaste, and I didn't want to bring my eyes forward to possibly lock eyes with a smug Onslow Boy.

I knew that if I made any kind of connection I would be brought undone; I wasn't a very good liar.

I worked my thumbs into Chris's taut back muscles that were so incredibly tight and knotted. And then I thought about how tense he was all the time, in his job, in his life. Why *wouldn't* he be all knotted up like a pretzel?

Being a bit of a fitness freak, I was not unaccustomed to sports massages – if anything, it was one of my addictions in life, so I was pretty well versed in using an array of techniques to get the blood flow into tissue. I bit my lip, concentrating on the vast landscape of Chris's back. His skin was so soft, so flawless under my touch. I was mesmerised by every hypnotic circle I pushed into his flesh. Chris's eyes were still shut and only the odd sound of pleasure escaped him.

"I'm not hurting you, am I?" I whispered in his ear.

"No, it's good, don't stop," he mumbled sleepily.

A twist of pleasure knotted in my stomach as I gently raked my fingertips down his spine, causing him to shiver.

I smiled. "Chris Henderson, are you ticklish?"

"Don't even try it."

"How very interesting …" I raked my fingers tauntingly upward.

"Tammy," he warned.

My little public display would certainly have everyone speculating by now. I slowly ran my fingers toward his ribcage.

But I was stopped by a blood-chilling scream from the water.

Chapter Thirty-Five

My stomach plummeted to the ground.

Chris moved like lightning – he was up and off my towel before I'd even blinked. He powered his legs along the ground as he entered the water, the river turning into a mesh of churned foam as Chris, Sean, Stan, Toby and Adam converged toward Ringer. I hadn't even noticed him swing into the lake.

I stood, my hands bracing my cheeks as everything played out like a horror movie. Chris and Sean dragged Ringer out of the murky water. It was turning pink around them.

That's when I saw the blood.

"Get a towel!" Sean yelled as we all moved out of their way.

"What happened?" cried a tearful Ellie.

Ringer's jaw was clenched as he manoeuvred himself onto a nearby log before Adam skidded along the sand with a clean towel ready for his foot, which was flowing with blood.

"Jesus, mate." Adam cringed as the blood stained the towel immediately.

"I stepped on a bloody bottle neck or something," Ringer hissed through gritted teeth.

Chris crouched beside Ringer, popping a bottle of water with his teeth. "Sorry, mate, this might sting but I've got to clean the wound, make sure there's nothing in it."

Ringer nodded. He was white as a ghost and looked a bit woozy, propped up only by Sean's steely grip on his shoulders.

I didn't like the look in Chris's eyes; they read that what he was about to do was going to hurt him more than it would hurt Ringer. I doubted entirely if that was true, but he poured water over the wound anyway. Ringer tensed and Ellie grabbed his hand.

"It's going to be all right, Ringo," she comforted him, looking wide-eyed at the emerging wound as Chris's water cleared the sand away and revealed just how bad the cut was.

It was deep.

Adam looked away. "Tess, can't you do something? You're a doctor."

Tess's eyes widened in alarm. "I'm a pharmacist," she emphasised. "It's a bit different."

"Well, what about you, Ellie? You're a nurse," Adam said in a panic.

"A *dental* nurse." She shook her head. "Ask Tammy, she's the biomedical genius." She pointed at me.

I was about as qualified in such things as anyone else, but before Adam accosted Toby's mechanical skills, I pointed out the obvious.

"It's going to need stitches. We need to wrap it in something clean and apply pressure, a T-shirt will do. We have to stop the bleeding until we get back to camp to the first aid kit."

"We'll have to go to emergency in Calhoon and get it seen to," Stan said.

"Well, we'll pack up the site and wait for you to get back. Whether we have to stay another night or go back, we will," added Sean.

"Hello, I'm right here, you know."

We all looked at Ringer.

"Sorry, mate." Sean grinned.

"Come on, get me to the bloody hospital."

The four hundred metres back to the campsite seemed to take an eternity, probably more so for Sean who carried Ringer on his back. We wasted little time in applying a bandage and propping him up across the back seat of Stan's car.

"We'll wait for you here," Toby said through the open window.

"Don't you bloody dare," Ringer called from the back seat.

"Mate, we're not leaving without you," Toby glowered.

"If you don't go, you won't make it to Point Shank in time for New Year's and I'm already ruining these guys' lives." Ringer nodded toward Stan and Bell and winced.

"Hey, we volunteered," Bell said sternly to him.

Sean rested his arms on the windowsill fixing his earnest gaze on Ringer. "Stop being a tool, Ringo. We're not leaving without you."

Ringer's eyes were full of pain, but utter sincerity. "Go," he said.

"Get fucked! We're staying," said Sean.

"We'll call you from the hospital," said Stan as Bell climbed into the passenger seat beside him.

"We'll be here."

Stan shook his head. "At least hit the coast today, settle in Portland, if anywhere. We'll see what then." Stan fired up the engine.

We all stepped away from the car as Stan backed out and reversed around. An immense sadness filled the atmosphere as Ringer pressed his hand against the window then waved goodbye. We all smiled and waved him along, calling out well wishes and that we'd see him soon. And just as the car disappeared through the bush scrub, the frantic rush of panic from moments before and the shock of what had happened fell upon us in stony silence.

I stared off into the distance, feeling numb and worried for Ringer. Even though I knew he would be okay, taking Ringer, Stan and Bell from the group changed everything. Just as I was about to let the reality wash over me, I felt a hand pull at my elbow. It tugged me around and before my glassy eyes could register what was happening, Chris had pulled me into a fierce embrace. His arms enveloped me in such warmth, such strength that I melted against his bare skin. My cheek burned against his chest as I wrapped my arms tightly around him. His hand smoothed over my hair just like it had that time when my consciousness had danced between wake and sleep in the van that night.

It could have been his way of stirring speculation amongst the others, but something in his embrace told me it wasn't about that; it wasn't about making a show for anyone else, it was that part of Chris, the kind, seldom-exposed Chris that had come out to comfort me, to support me yet again. I never wanted any other Chris to steal him away again. But just as easily as the emotion had come, it slid away into a stony grave as he peeled his arms from me.

"I better help pack up," he said, clearing his throat.

"Sure," I said, hoping I wasn't blushing. "I'll start packing the van."

Chris paused, his dark brown eyes studying me for a long moment. "Do you still want to travel in the van?" he asked.

Would it be weird that I did? Or was the deal for Chris to drop me off with the others so I could catch a ride with Amy and Sean the rest of the way? Was he finally able to offload me and get rid of the annoying girl he'd had to pick up because his cousin had blackmailed him? I suddenly felt really stupid, shifting awkwardly under his gaze.

"Um, is that okay?"

Chris's expression never faltered as he shrugged. "If you want."

I did want.

But wow. He didn't have to act so enthusiastic about it. He was so hard to read. Although I don't know what I had expected – for him to crumble to his knees and beg me to go with him? No, I didn't expect that, but, hey, I hadn't expected the hug either.

I nodded. "All right, I'll start packing the van, then."

Yep! No biggie, travelling alone with Chris. That's what I told myself over and over again as I headed toward the van. Then why was it my heart wanted to leap out of my chest?

It didn't take me long to get everything secured and packed in the back of the van. I shut the door with a sigh, thinking to make myself more useful with the bigger pack-up of the campsite.

I peeled the tent flap back to help Amy pack up the last of the food.

I smiled, handing over the half-used carton of long life milk when something triggered in me. A long-forgotten conversation stemming back to my flat mobile phone.

Blackmail.

"Oh my God," I laughed.

"What?" Amy stilled.

"It's been such a crazy couple of days, I can't believe we still haven't finished our conversation from days ago."

Amy's brows narrowed and she looked at me like she had no idea what I was talking about.

I looked around to ensure we were alone in the tent; I kind of felt a bit stupid bringing it up again. Still, we were going to be separated for probably another whole day of travel and I really did want to find out what was so juicy that she could blackmail Chris about. Maybe I could use it to my advantage.

"What you used to blackmail Chris with, you never got a chance to tell me."

Amazement spread across her face. "I can't believe we haven't finished that conversation – what has become of us?"

"I know," I laughed.

"I'm sorry, my head's been all over the place lately. Just when I thought this trip would be about relaxing I've been nothing but stressed."

"Everything's all right, though? With you and Sean?"

"Oh God, yes, amazing, good. No, I just meant the whole Toby–Tess saga, Bell not liking Ellie, no hot showers and now Ringer. Don't say anything to Sean, though, I'm acting like I love every minute of this hellish trip."

I couldn't help but feel that somehow I had gotten the better end of the deal; following on later with Chris, it had kind of kept us away from all the group's drama.

Amy gathered up a box. "Help me with these boxes to the car and we'll finish this conversation once and for all."

Chapter Thirty-Six

Why did I feel so nervous?

As if carrying boxes of breakfast goods to the car was the equivalent to walking Death Row? Maybe I didn't actually want to know the answer anymore. What if what Amy had to say would make me think differently about Chris, about the Chris I had come to know these last couple of days? I felt sick.

Amy slid the box along the back tray. I handed her my box and she did the same. She turned to me with a speculative look in her eyes.

"What is going on between you and Chris, anyway?"

Oh no! I didn't want to have *this* conversation. Amy had that juicy 'tell me more' look in her eye, but the truthful answer was incredibly dull. Besides, that would defeat the purpose of our devious faux flirtations. Chris's faux flirtations, anyway.

"No way, I'm not stalling this conversation again," I said, pointing the finger at her.

She shrugged. "Fair enough, but I'm guessing you already know it."

"Know what?" I screamed to the sky. This conversation was so hyped up in my head it was destined to be anticlimactic.

"Well, I was lingering in the bar one late night lock-in… I pretty much just left the boys to their own devices and was cleaning up in the main bar when a certain conversation emerged that piqued my interest."

I curved my brow. "About?"

"You!" Amy smiled broadly.

My heart thundered so fast in my chest I thought it might explode.

"So naturally I pretend I'm not listening and start stocking the fridge," Amy says with pride.

I am frozen on her every word: frozen solid, afraid to move in case she stops talking or we are interrupted.

"So I heard your name and who should be singing your praises but none other than *Ringer*." Amy accentuated his name with excitement.

My shoulders slumped. I had kind of expected it all along. Ringer speaking highly of me wasn't exactly a secret, he openly flirted with me any chance he got, but he flirted with everyone. It was his calling card, more so now that Sean was shacked up with Amy.

Amy continued. "So he's talking about how fit you are and how banging your body is and he can't believe you're single and all that, and then the conversation changed and they were talking about some random that he hooked up with the weekend before, and I swear those boys are the worst gossips I've ever met."

Yep. Definitely anticlimactic. I tried not to seem overly disappointed as I smiled politely.

"Anyway, I don't remember what piqued my interest again – maybe it was because they were paying Chris out about something, I always like to see that – but I think they were questioning his bachelor status and running off a list of names of people he rated. They were throwing names at him left, right and centre. Sharnie Maynard, Ellie Parker, Julie Hooper, Laura Pegg – he was just shaking his head, not answering – you know, giving his best Chris Henderson stony death stare – but then something interesting happened."

"What happened?"

"Sean mentioned your name and his face completely changed."

I started breathing quickly, my chest rising and falling rapidly. I refused to take my eyes from Amy, I didn't dare ask what she meant but I didn't need to as she leaned in closer to me.

"It was like a light switch went on. Sean said 'Tammy Maskala' and his eyes lit up; it was all they needed to give him absolute hell about you for the rest of the night. It was like they had discovered this massive secret about him."

"What did he do?" I breathed out.

Amy laughed. "After he went bright red? He tried to kick them all out, threatened to cut off the beer supply and bar them for life. But you know what?"

I shook my head.

"He never denied it. Not once." Amy beamed smugly.

"So that's what you blackmailed him about?" I whispered.

"I said if he didn't pick you up and give you a lift I would tell you everything I overheard that night about him having the hots for you."

I blanched. "You didn't!"

Amy puffed out her chest. "I did."

Amy then moved on to how utterly amazed she was at how shocked I seemed considering the way we had been acting with each other. The shower, us sneaking off early last night, the shoulder massage ... There was no mention of the condom, thank God. Amy revelled in it all. But I was still digesting what between us had been real and what was fiction.

"It's so obvious you two are into each other, and I would usually be all about the details, but Chris is my cousin so it's kind of gross." Amy grimaced as if she were torn between wanting to know and never, ever wanting to know.

"Well, I'll spare you, because, in all honesty, nothing has happened."

"Sure-sure," Amy said as she sauntered back toward the tent.

"It's true," I called after her.

Amy shook her head. "You are the worst liar." She laughed and disappeared through the canvas flap.

I stood in the middle of the clearing, confounded by my new-found knowledge.

Chris *actually* liked me. It wasn't all a prank. Then why hadn't he made a move on me last night? I'd sure given him the opportunity. He hadn't even looked me over in the way a male appreciates a woman with my lacey white dress last night; in fact, I think his word was 'nice', not exactly high praise. He was happy to pretend to be into me for the boys' benefit, but if he really did like me, why was he holding back?

Oh crap, I don't know.

All I knew was, I was afraid to hope, but desperate to know. Amy's story was interesting, but having spent the last two days with Chris it had done nothing but conflict my emotions. With every flash of tenderness from him there was an equal display of broodiness.

I sighed. I wondered what the next leg of the road trip would bring. If there was one thing that was for sure, I was going to push some Chris Henderson buttons and in order to do that I might just have to play my own little game.

Chapter Thirty-Seven

Knowledge is power, right?

Then why was it that I didn't feel the least bit powerful? Amy's words played over and over in my mind, and as I analytically turned every one of them over in my head, by the time I had readied myself to get into the van, I had all but convinced myself that Amy must have gotten it wrong.

Seriously, it was just a look. Big deal, so his 'look' changed.

Hardly an admission of undying love. So what if he hadn't denied the taunts? Chris wasn't the sort of person to bow down to pressure – well, unless he was blackmailed by a pesky younger cousin.

A line pinched between my brows, a mirror image to Chris's as I approached him from the track. I doubted his troubled look was a product of overzealous obsessing about feelings, though. No. Instead, his troubled eyes flicked up to me.

"Are these yours?" he asked, holding a pair of size ten men's navy Converse shoes. His gaze shifted from them to my petite size six feet and back to these mysterious objects. He turned them over in his hands, inspecting them as if they were a newly discovered ancient relic.

Oh crap! Toby's shoes.

"Ah, no. Actually I better return them."

I reached for the shoes but Chris lifted them out of my reach.

He cocked his brow. "Bring men's shoes home often, do you?"

I sighed. "Yes, I am quite the kleptomaniac with a foot fetish. You better guard your Italian leather loafers with your life," I quipped.

A spark of amusement glinted in his eyes, but the frown remained. "I don't own Italian leather loafers."

"Really?" I questioned. "You don't rock them out with white knee-high socks?"

The corner of Chris's mouth pinched. "No, but I'll look into it."

I reached for them again but he was faster than me, lifting them even higher. If I had been his younger brother I imagined his next move would have been to place his hand on my forehead and, pushing me back, laugh as I wildly swung arms. Luckily, he didn't go that far.

"Hmm, interesting," he said mainly to himself as he held one shoe up to the sun, inspecting it.

I placed my hands on my hips. "You can talk. I may have confiscated a pair of shoes on my travels, but let's not forget what you brought back last night, Christopher Condom!"

Just as my words spilled out, proudly thinking myself quite the word player, the sound of a branch snapped from behind me. My eyes widened; I could almost feel a cold shiver run down my spine as I turned and had my worst fears confirmed.

Adam stood at the edge of the track, arms crossed casually across his chest, grinning from ear to ear as if enjoying the show.

"Sorry to interrupt," he said. The bright, devilish white flash of teeth was almost blinding as he looked from Chris to me.

Did I really just call him Christopher Condom?

I wanted to die.

Of all the people to overhear *that* particular conversation, it had to be his little brother Adam. I could almost see the speculative cogs turning in his head as he filed Christopher Condom into the 'remember for all eternity and use against Chris' file.

I didn't have to look at Chris to know he would be scowling. I didn't want to know if it was directed at me or Adam.

"What do you want?" Chris bit out.

Plunging his hands into his pockets. "Hey, I'm just the messenger; Sean said it's time to go."

Taking advantage of the moment of distraction, I grabbed the shoes out of Chris's hands.

"I best return these, then," I said. I looked straight ahead, not daring to meet either pair of their eyes as I moved past Adam and made my way down the track.

Mortified!

Seeing only the indented bark chips and scuffed-up dirt as any remnants of Toby and Tess's campsite, I made my way toward Toby's lone blue Ford ute, thinking if neither was around I could just slip the shoes in the back of the tray. I was about to veer off the track and cut through the scrub to make my way to the clearing where his car was parked under a towering gum. Skimming my way through the branches, working to push myself through the thicket, I stopped when I heard raised voices beyond the scrubby barrier.

Not wanting to do an Adam and stumble into a private conversation, my eyes darted around for a quick, silent escape.

But as the heated conversation escalated, the last thing I wanted was to be discovered, so I had little choice but to crouch behind a bush and ride out the storm.

My heart pounded; I tried to keep still, slow my breaths and not think about the uncomfortable position I had settled myself into. I was soon snapped out of my worry for comfort when I heard what sounded like Toby's voice.

He was yelling. Pleading with someone. Oh no, had I stumbled across him and Tess fighting? I had thought everything looked okay at breakfast. At least, they were sitting next to one another.

And Toby had seemed in good spirits – everyone was.

But clearly not now.

I clenched the shoes to my chest like a life vessel, saddened by the conversation I couldn't quite make out. I was glad. I didn't *want* to hear it.

Then, of course, as if the Gods were conspiring against me, the voices grew louder. They shifted closer to me, so close I could make out the outlines of bodies through the bushes as I crouched lower so as not to be discovered. I held my breath.

A slender, blonde figure stormed away, pausing only when Toby snared her elbow.

"Ellie, wait!"

Ellie?

Ellie spun around, her eyes glassy and wild. "You have to tell her!"

Toby's hand dropped from her; he seemed broken, exhausted. "I can't."

"It's driving her crazy, the way you're acting. She's not stupid, she knows something is going on."

Toby's eyes were downcast. He slowly shook his head as he mulled over Ellie's words. "It would ruin everything," he said.

Ellie wiped away a stray tear.

"Hey, come on." Toby stepped closer and rubbed her shoulder. "You're supposed to be happy, not sad."

She sniffed and smiled weakly. "I am. I am happy. I just can't wait for it to be over."

My stomach churned. Whatever was going on, it didn't sound good.

Toby sighed, pulling her into a hug. "Not much longer."

What. The. Fuck?

I couldn't witness any more.

I had been holding my breath for so long I was in serious trouble of passing out. I felt nauseated, bewildered, horrified, angry.

I mean, seriously. What the fuck?

I edged away from them, scrambled to my feet and stormed in the opposite direction. I was so mad at what I had heard I didn't care if they heard me. Let them bloody hear me. I burst through bushes, crunching a determined line back up the track, my heart pounding, my mind racing, anger bubbling under the surface of my skin before the last defeated emotion slammed into me and my stomach plummeted. I stopped, bent over, hands on my knees as I caught my breath.

Poor Tess. Poor, sweet Tess.

I squeezed my eyes shut, hoping against hope that what I had witnessed was just a dream, that I would wake up any minute, or maybe even that I'd simply misinterpreted what they'd been saying. Maybe I was on the wrong track entirely.

But as I opened my eyes, blinking and focusing on the pair of shoes I still held in my hand, grasped so tightly my knuckles were white, I didn't think I was. Anger gave way to sadness. I knew I probably shouldn't have jumped to conclusions – hell, only moments before Adam had walked into my own conversation and probably come to his own inaccurate conclusions.

I tried to soothe myself that maybe what I had overheard hadn't been wildly inappropriate, that Toby's distance couldn't be so disturbing. If this was a glimpse of the new century to come then I wanted no part of it.

Not. For.

I threw one of Toby's shoes.

A. Single.

Then I threw the other one.

Minute.

They both ricocheted off the same gum tree and disappeared in the thick scrub. It afforded me a moment of satisfaction, but it didn't last for long. I continued my heavy-footed stride up the track. So determined was I to leave the memory behind me I didn't even see Adam until my shoulder bumped into his as he walked in the opposite direction.

Startled and shunted out of my troubled thoughts, I snapped, "Watch out."

Adam steadied me with his hand. "Sorry," he half laughed. "Whoa, woman on a mission. Don't worry, we won't leave without you."

I scoffed. "Since when has that ever been a problem?" My words dripped with sarcasm.

Adam tilted his head as he studied me. In moments when Adam was serious (which weren't very often), you could really see the resemblance between him and Chris; the familiarity of his focus almost caused me to melt from my defensive stance.

"Are you all right?" he asked, genuinely concerned.

I wanted to blurt out what I had just seen and heard; I wanted to scream it from the treetops so Adam could tell me not to be ridiculous and that I was overreacting. I wanted desperately to be pacified, assured that everything was going to be okay.

Instead, I said, "I'm fine." I broke my gaze from his sexy, Chris-like eyes.

As I moved past him he caught my arm. "Hey, Tammy. Don't let my brother upset you. I know he can be a dick sometimes but you know what he's like." He shrugged.

What was he talking about?

I tugged my arm free as something primal peaked inside me. I had been in a hell of a mood this afternoon but something in Adam's words that had been meant to comfort rubbed me the wrong way.

This was so not about Chris. But if it had been … I shook my head. "You don't know him at all. None of you do, you only see what you want to see. You think just because people seem good and pure on the outside that it means they're good people? Sometimes people need to stop with the wisecracks and smart-arse innuendos and have a proper look at the person inside, because as it stands, if I had to choose between being stranded with any of you lot or Chris, believe me, I would rather be stranded with him, a hundred percent."

And just as I was about to lift my chin and stride away like a bad-arse, someone cleared their throat from behind me.

Chapter Thirty-Eight

Not again.

Adam nervously rubbed the back of his neck and openly cringed. I didn't need to guess too hard who was behind me.

Chris displayed a perfect poker face, as if he hadn't just overheard my mad rant about him.

"Ready to go?" he asked.

I nodded, staring at the dirt as I turned coyly back to Adam.

"Bye," I said quietly, like a chastised child.

I was so embarrassed. Adam's mouth had gaped several times during my impressive spiel. I had thought he was trying to butt in, to defend himself and the group from my rage, but thinking about it now, he was probably trying to warn me of the captive audience behind me, the audience I now brushed past on my way toward the van.

This had not been an ideal start to the day. I mean, seriously, it's not like we were all hanging out in a maze, accidentally turning a blind corner and happening upon heated *private* conversations. We were camping, for goodness sake. Even if Chris had overheard my character appraisal of him, I couldn't have been gladder to get into his black panel van and get some distance from everyone else for a while.

Maybe Ringer, Stan and Bell were the lucky ones, away from all the drama, the drama that was no doubt going to get a whole lot worse.

Mercifully, Chris didn't mention a thing. He simply slid in behind the wheel and fidgeted himself into comfort, inspected the side mirror, selected a cassette and adjusted the volume. He oversaw every action meticulously, like a pilot ticking off his protocols in the cockpit of his aeroplane. I had become accustomed to his little ritualistic tics over these last few days – the familiarity comforted me, and Lord knows I needed to be comforted. Chris pulled into gear and edged us away from what had been our temporary home and I let the sweet sound of Bruce crooning out of the speaker soothe me away from my troubled thoughts.

We pulled behind a line of cars at the mouth of the track that led out of the grounds and spilled off onto the main road. Sean's suntanned arm rested on the open window of his twin cab at the front of the queue, Amy by his side with her legs on the dash.

"Next stop, Portland," he shouted out of his window, saluting his brow and turning onto the main road.

Adam followed next in Ringer's bright canary yellow Ford, Ellie readjusting her ponytail in the rear-view without a care in the world. They edged out, followed by Toby's blue ute idling directly before us. My eyes burned into the back of them, my mouth agape as I saw Toby flash a smile at Tess, saying something that made her laugh. So light, so normal as if the only person carrying the weight of impending doom was me.

The burden was heavy, lodged in my chest. I swallowed it down as I slid Chris's sunglasses over my eyes.

Soon it was our turn and we pulled onto the main road and fell into place behind the conga line of cars winding their way toward the coast, a step closer to Point Shank.

I can't exactly say I was uncharacteristically quiet; I wasn't a chatterbox to begin with, nor a social butterfly. That was probably the one thing Chris appreciated about me, how I was perfectly content with silence, so he didn't mind me being his plus one. But there is silence and there is *silence*, and my silence this time was electric and generated a swirl of tension between us.

A part of me wanted to tell Chris what I had heard between Toby and Ellie. These were his friends, he had a right to know. Maybe he'd tell me what to do. Did I do anything? Did I confront Toby? Tell Tess? Accost Ellie? Or did I mind my own business and stay out of it entirely? My leg jiggled up and down as I mulled it over. It was a nervous habit – it always bounced like that when I was anxious – and apparently it was very annoying, or so Chris said as he reached over and clamped his hand on my knee.

My whole body stilled. The feel of Chris's hand on my bare leg burned my skin and wiped my memory clean of all my thoughts and troubles. Anytime we came into contact, no matter how big or small, my body reacted in the most disturbing of ways.

"Stop it," he said, moving his hand away and leaving a warm impression on my skin. I almost wanted to start moving my leg just so he would reach over and touch me again. I crossed my arms and bit down on my thumbnail, concentrating fiercely on not jiggling my leg.

"He'll be all right, you know." Chris's words broke me away from my thoughts, my eyes shielding their confusion behind his sunnies.

When I didn't answer he continued, "Ringer – he'll only need a few stitches. Trust me, I've seen him banged up worse over the years."

Oh God. Ringer. I'd forgotten all about him.

I inwardly cringed, feeling even worse. *Poor Ringer, poor Tess. Who else could I pity?*

"You weren't even thinking about Ringer, were you?" Chris asked, glancing at me and back at the road.

I chewed on my lip. "No," I admitted, hating how guilty I sounded when I said it.

Chris sighed. "You're not worrying about my bonehead

brother, are you? I threatened him with grievous bodily harm if he goes stirring."

My mouth involuntarily curved upward. I could totally imagine Chris had done exactly that.

"Although, thinking about it," he continued, "probably a bit harsh considering."

"Considering what?" I asked.

"Well, we are kind of provoking them to talk about us, so we can't exactly get mad if they do."

"True. Still, you don't want to be known as 'Christopher Condom' to your mates, do you? You know how a nickname can stick."

Chris laughed. "I'm guilty of handing out a few myself."

"Oh? Like what?"

Chris winced. "You know Alan Pasternack?"

My smile fell from my face. "You didn't."

"I did."

I didn't know whether to openly gasp or be impressed. Alan Pasternack was a year below Chris at school and had been famously known for being the paper delivery boy whose mates bet him one hundred dollars to cut his hair into a mullet. He never saw the hundred dollars and the mullet stuck around a bit too long. But more famously than that, Alan got a nickname: Pastel-Knacker. It was both cringeworthy and highly amusing and all of a sudden I saw the Onslow Boy in Chris, in the devious, boyish grin he flashed.

It was kind of hot.

I controlled my urge to smile and looked out of the window as I said, "Kids can be so cruel."

"Well, I imagine there isn't much word play on a name like Tamara Maskala."

I thought back to a less happy time. "I think the worst I got in school was Tamara Mascara."

"Not the most imaginative lot," Chris mused. A service station loomed on the horizon and Chris flicked the indicator on. "Better top up," he said, veering off the main road toward the mustard and off-white service station.

"Mmm," I responded, my mind miles away, this time not haunted by the present but by the past.

Chris pulled into the servo, unclipped his belt and slid out.

"Did you want anything?"

I shook my head.

Minutes passed, but it could have been hours for all I knew as I stared off into nowhere, shucking off my shoes and hugging my legs so as not to jig them while lost in my thoughts.

A burst of warm air flooded through the front seat as Chris opened his door and slid back inside, juggling an armful of drinks and chips: two of everything.

He rustled through his goods. "Chewy?" He held out a Juicy Fruit packet. I smiled, held out my hand and he flicked two white parcels onto my palm.

"Thanks," I said, popping both into my mouth. I chewed my gum and watched Chris's profile as he took a long swig on a bottle of creamy soda. I was thankful that he didn't press me for my thoughts, demand to know what was wrong. He wasn't that guy.

It seemed I was more guarded than I realised, although I should have known, seeing as how I kept my guard up even with Amy, my best friend. It wasn't normal to keep things bottled up, was it? Keeping things to yourself, keeping secrets? Look at Toby and the colossal mistake he was making by not speaking up. Not that I had such a burden of my own, still not thinking Chris would really care to know. I decided against my better judgement to voice my thoughts.

I grabbed my knees tighter and parked my gum in my cheek so I could talk without chewing. "When I was in Year Seven, I remember all the boys compiled a list."

Chris lowered his drink, looking at me as if surprised his quiet companion was suddenly speaking. Or surprised I was out of the blue talking about when I was in Year Seven. Or both.

He shifted in his seat, facing me to listen.

"It was a list of the perfect dream girl; if they could take traits from each girl in our group, what would it be? So they chose

Melinda Smart's legs, Fiona Martin's face, Amy Henderson's body, Carla McKay's hair ... something of each girl in our group. They even chose hands, eyes, personality."

"Sounds like Frankenstein's bride," mused Chris.

I laughed. "Yeah, pretty much."

"So what part were you sacrificing?" Chris asked, screwing the lid back on his drink and placing it aside.

I stared at my knees. "They didn't want anything from me." I shrugged. "Not even my brain."

I said it so matter-of-factly I didn't expect for Chris's good humour to slide away, for his eyes to narrow. I wasn't looking for pity; it was just what had been on my mind.

The mind is funny how it can flow like a stream; wash from one subject to the next. Tammy Mascara wasn't even all that bad; it certainly wasn't my worst memory. Being the frizzy-haired, shy girl in school hadn't been easy. I hadn't fit in then and I didn't now, but that was okay. Even though many of my personal traits remained the same, I was happy to say I wasn't that shy girl anymore. I had worked hard to ensure that.

Chris opened and closed his hand on the steering wheel, focusing on the motion, deep in thought.

"Yeah, boys do things like that," he said quietly. "In fact, I probably would have done the same thing if I'd been there."

What was he saying? That he wouldn't have picked any part of me as his dream girl, either? Something panged inside me, a raw emotion that bubbled to the surface and pooled into a toxic slick.

It was an honest admission. I just hadn't expected my heart to sink so much.

"Mine would have been a bit different, though," he said, his brow furrowing, concentrating on the flex of his hands as they clasped the steering wheel. Clench and relax, clench and relax. Perhaps this was his leg jiggling equivalent. I was considering reaching out to stop it in a moment; I smiled a small, secret smile at the thought.

His hands slid over the wheel, his beautiful hands.

"Oh, and what would have made yours so different?" I half laughed, hoping it didn't sound too forced.

His hand stilled. Gripping the top of the wheel, he sat straight back in his seat.

"Because if I'd had to choose perfect, I would have just chosen you."

He had said it so clearly. Matter-of-fact. So certain, and now his eyes were on me, deep and burning as if a fist had wrapped around my heart and squeezed it to a stop.

I swallowed deeply, looking at him, waiting for him to break into laughter, to say 'just kidding' and start the car up and be back on our way.

But he didn't.

"I would choose your legs even when they're jigging and driving me to distraction. I'd choose your face because it creases into something so amazing when you find something funny (which, incidentally, isn't often enough for my liking).

"I'd choose the way your cheeks go red whenever you're embarrassed, just like they are now.

"I'd choose the fact that you're smart, kind and funny and you don't even know it." His eyes ticked over my face in a long, silent study. "It's a pretty big list, but yeah. I'd choose everything about you."

My chin trembled like I was a small child.

"Well, you obviously don't remember the frizzy-haired girl from school, because I assure you if you did—"

"I remember," he said, cutting me off. "I remember the knock-kneed, shy girl who used to drink raspberry lemonade in the restaurant and openly swoon at Sean Murphy every time he came into your vicinity."

I cringed. Yep, he remembered me.

Chris smiled. "You're not as invisible as you think."

Chapter Thirty-Nine

There was nothing like the blast of a car horn to pour ice water over a moment.

Sean pulled in behind us, honking his horn in a series of annoying rhythms.

"Way to go, lead foot!" he shouted out of the window.

The whole way from Evoka Springs, Chris had overtaken every car until he'd had an open road in front of him. It had earned him some jeering, lewd hand gestures and aggravated toots along the way from Sean, Adam and Toby, but Chris had just coolly saluted and flattened the accelerator pedal to the floor.

As I checked my flushed cheeks in the rear-view mirror, a yellow car appeared in the reflection as Ellie and Adam pulled in next. Seeing them brought me back to reality. They pulled into a parking bay. Toby and Tess wouldn't be far away.

"It's not my fault you drive like an old woman," Chris called back.

As he went to open the car door I grabbed his arm.

"Do we have to go with the others?" I said.

Chris's gaze dropped to where my hand rested. I quickly drew it away, my mind whirring over how best to explain my outburst.

From the look on his face, Chris was wondering the same thing.

Please don't ask me why. I didn't want to face Toby and Ellie. I honestly didn't know what I'd say to them if I did.

He silently appraised me as if I were some puzzle that had to be solved. I braced myself for the questions to begin, so when he did nothing more than open his car door and slide out of the seat, I didn't know how to feel about that. Had I angered him by wanting to ditch his friends? I guessed that was essentially what I was asking.

"An old woman? On behalf of old women everywhere, I resent that," Sean said incredulously as he ambled over to Chris.

"You try lugging all this gear weighing me down – the ute's half full of Amy's beauty products."

"I heard that," called Amy from Sean's ute.

Chris leaned his elbows on the open door of the van. "You going to wait at Portland for the verdict on Ringer?"

"Yeah, I'll call Stan when we get there," said Sean.

Chris nodded sombrely. "Okay. We might push on past Portland, catch up with you at Point Shank." He said it so casually, like it was no big deal, but Sean's eyes immediately darted toward me, then back to Chris.

He flashed a less-than-subtle cheesy grin. "I see," Sean mused.

"What's going on?" Adam sidled up with a bucket of hot chips and a Coke under his arm.

"We're getting ditched," said Sean.

"Get stuffed." Chris half laughed before slinking back into the driver's seat, shutting his door. "I won't be sorry to leave your ugly mugs behind," he quipped, starting up the car. Sean leaned his arms on the open window.

"How do you put up with him, Tammy?" Sean asked.

I eyed Chris. "Oh, you know, he kind of grows on you."

"Yeah, like a fungus," added Adam.

Chris gave him the finger while revving the engine, as if the purring growls were some kind of threat.

"All right then, you know where we plan to meet up?" Sean changed the subject.

"I know the place," said Chris.

"Remember?" Sean held a finger up to his lips miming, 'Not a word."

What was that all about?

Chris nodded, as if whatever this secret was would be taken to the grave.

I thought I was the only one burdened with a secret, but the boys didn't look burdened – they looked smug. And there was nothing more frustrating than a smug Onslow Boy.

There was no use even asking – they no doubt had some stupid boy code that wasn't going to be broken.

"You're right to go?" Chris asked.

"Yes!" I straightened.

Let's get the bloody hell out of here before Toby arrives.

Chris's brows rose, taken aback by my enthusiasm.

"All right then." He pulled into gear. "See you fellas at Point Shank."

"Keep the home fire burning for us till we get there," Sean said with a wink.

Chris sounded his horn and sped off, leaving the others as nothing more than small dotted figures in our rear-view mirror. I knew what would be happening; they would all be gathering around asking Sean what that was all about. There would be some sarcastic comments made and speculation would run high.

Amy might have even been a bit pissed off that I hadn't spoken to her before leaving. It had all happened so fast I hadn't eve had a chance to think about it.

When the question had tumbled out of my mouth, the last thing I had honestly expected was for Chris to agree and leave the others behind. At best, we had one more night together on the road before we reached Point Shank.

My stomach churned and I didn't know if it was relief or dread that filled me at the thought of reaching our destination so soon. The others may assume it was some secret lovers' tryst, but, in truth, I just couldn't face the group. Couldn't stomach seeing the unhappiness in Tess's eyes. I had to tell her what I'd heard, I knew I did. It was the most confrontational thing I would force myself to do and I felt sick to my stomach just thinking about it. Something needed to be done, I just didn't know if I would do it before or after the New Year. I had exactly one more night to figure it out.

I expected Chris to ask why I had wanted to leave the others behind. But he didn't. His stony silence was a welcome refuge; maybe he had simply wanted some peace and quiet too.

But there was this thing wedged between us now, this unspoken elephant in the room. I couldn't believe the others had interrupted us at that exact moment between us, leaving so much unsaid. He had mentioned things that made my stomach twist, but now as I glanced at his profile I saw nothing but the Chris of old, the shut-down, intimidating businessman, though I was well over being intimidated by him. If anything, he was just damn frustrating; his mood transformed within seconds and I just never knew what I was going to get.

I placed the sunnies on top of my head, and turned to look at him – really look at him. "Why are you always so serious?" I asked.

Chris scowled as if on cue, something I found more amusing these days. "What do you mean?" he asked. He rolled one shoulder, guarded. Annoyed.

I watched him intently. "You're not like the other guys."

Chris breathed out a laugh. "Well, I'll take that as a compliment."

I didn't answer.

Chris's humour dissolved. "I have my own brain and I use it. I'm not a sheep. I don't just follow anyone."

"Yeah, but sometimes it's about just joining in and having a laugh," I said.

"So in other words you want me to be a stereotypical Onslow Boy?"

Did I? Did I want him to be a larrikin? Flirty and bubbly, loud and occasionally obnoxious?

That wasn't Chris.

Chris stared intently at the road. "To be honest, I really don't care what people think. If a group of girls made a list of the perfect Onslow Boy, do you really think they would want any part of me?" he said with a smirk. "Ninety percent of the time I'm the only sober person, the buzz kill, the responsible one coaxing girls down from tabletops, breaking up fights, cleaning up vomit, calling last drinks, being designated driver."

"Why's it always you, though?"

"Someone's got to do it. If they're going to be idiots, I just want to make sure they're being safe idiots."

And just like that I saw the real Chris. Responsible, hardworking, always looking out for others, and not giving a damn what it took.

I realised I didn't have to try so hard to work out what made Chris tick – it boiled down to 'what you see is what you get'.

My heart swelled; I was overcome with attraction for the boy by my side. He didn't think himself an Onslow Boy? Oh, he was an Onslow Boy, all right. He was the glue that held the ship together. The group would not function without him, and most alarmingly of all, I knew I couldn't function without him, and it both thrilled and scared me to death.

I decided I would tell Chris about Toby, seek his advice; *but not yet.*

For now I had something else that needed to be said. "Don't you dare change for anyone, Chris Henderson."

You're perfect.

Just as I had thought, Chris didn't take compliments well. He shifted in his seat and glanced uncomfortably out of the window.

He laughed nervously. "Does this mean I make the list?"

"Yeah, you're okay, I guess," I teased, trying not to think of his perfect hands, kissable lips, and shoulders that I wanted to dig my nails into.

I swallowed. Yeah, best not to think about it.

He curved his brow at me. "Just okay?"

"Well, all right then, how about NICE." Ha! There's a word for you.

Chris's smile faltered a little. I could just see his brain ticking through memories and landing on having called my evening attire 'nice' just last night.

Now he understood how gutting it was.

"You know that nice for me means 'absolutely beautiful', right?" he asked.

What?

I crossed my arms. "No, I didn't know that."

Chris smiled. "Well, now you do."

Chapter Forty

We wound our way through the last of the bushy canopy. As we grew nearer to Portland, the real sign of change was the ochre-coloured rock formations that intermittently sliced their way through the green landscape. Mercifully, it was on Chris's side of the car in which the scenery plunged into a sheer drop with only a flimsy white railing in front of it that didn't look like it could prevent a tricycle from plummeting over the edge, let alone a souped-up panel van. I would personally have preferred a six-foot-high lead fence.

My skin felt sticky against the leather seat and I didn't know if it was owing entirely to the warm afternoon sun beating down on us through the windshield, or the fear of death that made my stomach reel every blind corner we took.

I thought better of it than to make conversation with Chris as he drove; I wanted his full attention on the road. I had even turned down the music a little so he could give the drive his full concentration. Beside me and my white-knuckled terror, Chris seemed really relaxed, elbow propped up on the windowsill, the warm breeze riffling through his black hair. Every so often he casually admired the beauty of the countryside, not in the least bit affected by the drop directly beside him.

I wanted to scream, "Eyes on the bloody road!" but as quickly as he looked away from the road he looked right back again.

The only words Chris had spoken during our commute through the hills were, "Not long now."

I didn't know entirely what that meant. Not long now until we arrived somewhere? Not long now and we would plummet to our deaths?

Considering he had announced that it wasn't long over an hour ago, I was very underwhelmed thus far.

But just as I thought I couldn't stand rocketing around the windy, steep hillsides any longer and would put my head into the recovery position between my knees, he said, "Tammy, look!"

Suddenly all my anguish seeped away, replaced by a bright, beaming smile. As out of nowhere we had turned a corner and bam! The ocean was right there. It was like a magic trick, as if Mother Nature had tucked away this little piece of heaven in the corner of the world, as though she had wanted to surprise us or reward us for surviving the road of death.

I'd take it. The long stretch of blue-green water surged into a delicious foamy mass against the rocks below. Now I found myself not afraid, but instead leaning over toward Chris to peer down the rocky incline.

Even though we grew up with Lake Onslow on our doorstep and were constantly in danger of being waterlogged most of our lives, there was always this mystique and wonder about the ocean. It always managed to take my breath away, especially when it appeared from nowhere.

"We're about twenty-five kilometres from Portland, so we're making good time."

"Are we stopping in Portland?" I asked, confused.

Chris dipped his sun visor against the blinding sun. "No, we'll push on through."

I felt pangs of regret as we drove in one side and out the

other of the huge coastal town of Portland. It stretched along a vast promenade opposite a white sandy beach that was swarming with bikini-clad and shirtless tourists. People were everywhere: strolling, shopping or dining in the endless line of quirky cafes that dotted along the promenade.

Our jet black panel van roared as we made our way down the main street; it seemed so out of place in this bright, sparkling coastal town.

I could only imagine the others setting up camp here for the night, walking these streets after the evening sun had kissed the horizon. I kind of envied them. It was a far cry from the nothing that was Evoka, that was for sure. I wondered if it was too late to change our mind, to stay here and soak up the bustling atmosphere. But as we rolled farther on, down a strip of man-placed palm trees, we drove by the 'You are now leaving Portland' sign and my shoulders involuntarily sagged.

I felt like when I was a kid and my parents had just driven passed a McDonald's without stopping for a Happy Meal – the disappointment was palpable.

"Don't worry," Chris laughed, as if amused by my childlike wistfulness. "I know a better place than Portland."

I straightened with interest. "Really?"

"If you're keen, it's about five hours from here but if we crash there tonight, Point Shank is only three hours beyond that."

My heart plummeted.

Another five hours' driving today?

"Okay," I said, trying not to sound too miserable.

"It's pretty busy in town, but there's a place just up the road that serves the best fish and chips in the southern hemisphere. You want to stop?"

Poor Chris, it was like he was trying to placate my disappointment by littering the journey with little treasures so as to make it more bearable.

He had been so good. Without even questioning why, adding to all the other ways he had looked out for me, he had agreed to break away from the others. He had helped me when I'd had the migraine, he had hunted down my prescription and medication, he'd helped me into my dress, *helped me out of it ...*

I slammed the lid closed on that memory, of the embarrassing way I had tilted my head to the side, begging for him to make a move, and he had. In the opposite direction.

Yeah, best not to think about that. The remnants of that night still burned with shame, even after Amy had told me of her discovery of just how much he liked me; even after he had given me quite possibly the best compliment of my life earlier on today.

Because if I'd had to choose perfect, I would have just chosen you.

My heart may have threatened to break through the wall of my chest at the time, but now I just felt ... nothing. Because I knew it wasn't for real. If I had learned nothing else these last few days, it was that Chris wasn't really in charge of his own emotions. He was a fever one minute and Antarctica the next. He seemed to struggle on any level of personal connection; the only thing he seemed to do was Band-Aid a feeling, say things that would make me feel better, like now.

Chris eased the car toward a car park. I looked at the restaurant we were pulling into ...

"Does that say 'The Love Shack'?"

Chris cut off the engine and we looked up at a one-storey weatherboard cafe with bi-fold doors that opened onto a small deck with a huge red sign flashing 'The Love Shack' at us in neon.

The lobster on the sign was bending his claw into a thumbs up.

I raised my brows at Chris.

"Hey, I said they had great fish and chips, not that they would feature in *House & Garden* magazine."

"Uh, no. That would require taste," I half laughed.

"Well, I assure you the taste is there, it's just all in the food and trust me – that's all that matters."

He opened his door.

I slid out from my side, not taking my eyes from the hideous, flashing sign. If someone had told me that I was going to enter The Love Shack with Chris Henderson, I would have laughed – laughed like I was right now.

"Cut it out," warned Chris, trying to act like it wasn't funny.

I imitated the thumbs-up lobster and laughed even more.

Chris just shook his head and walked on without me.

Chapter Forty-One

Oh crap! Chris was looking at me.

He was looking at me with a smug 'I told you so' glint in his eyes as he licked the excess dribble of lemon off his salty fingers.

He sat across from me with the stretch of blue ocean at his back; it seemed so inappropriate that I was glowering at such a beautiful boy in such a beautiful place. It took all of my willpower not to glance at his lips as he pressed them together, savouring the tangy flavour.

I was still chewing thoughtfully on the most amazing piece of flake I had ever tasted in my life. I had known it would be the second I'd placed the lightly battered white flesh on my tongue.

Damn it!

"So?" Chris asked, a devilish curve teasing the corner of his mouth.

I snagged a chip out of my basket with a casual shrug. "It's all right," I lied.

Chris laughed at me and pressed his back against his cane chair. He stretched his arms into the air and linked them behind his head as his bright, toothy smile spread across his face.

"Just all right, huh?"

Attempting not to smile was impossible, I was such a terrible liar. I scrunched up my face and avoided those deep, knowing eyes. "Yeah, if you like that whole insanely delicious flavour thing, it's all right, I guess."

"Ha! I knew it." Chris slammed his hand on the tabletop, the vibration causing the salt shaker to tip on its side.

We both reached for it and grabbed it at the same time. Chris's hand rested on mine. My eyes flicked up to his face, which was now no longer lined with the lighthearted humour from a moment before. I went to move my hand away but his fingers were clasped over mine. He gave them a light squeeze.

He spoke lowly. "Careful, you know how dangerous these can be."

It took me a moment to remember. The last time we had sat alone opposite each other was when I had hidden from him under the table at the Bake House.

Not my proudest moment. Heat flooded my cheeks at the mortifying memory of that day. It also didn't help that I was more than a little aware of Chris's scorching hot skin resting on mine. I moved to sit the salt shaker upright. Chris slid his hand away, his gaze still pinning me to my seat. I brushed the excess salt off the table, trying to act casual. I could feel Chris's eyes watching my every movement.

Stop staring. Change the subject.

I cleared my throat, dusting the salty granules from my hands. "So where are we stopping tonight?"

Chris's eyes lit up as he tipped back on his chair. "Oh, just a little place I know," he said with a wolfish grin.

I cast him a dubious look. "How incredibly cryptic of you."

"It's hard to explain; you'll see in five hours' time." He dunked his chip in a blob of tomato sauce.

Five. Long. Hours.

Upon dusk, we veered off the main road down a side track. Finally.

My temple had been pressed against the window for the last few kilometres and I straightened up and looked around. The headlight highlighted a wooden sign with words I didn't catch as we sped by. The sudden turn made my heart leap with excitement. We had been driving in one long, straight line for hours having left the beauty and the wonder of the coast disappointingly behind. No longer dancing along its edges, we had headed inland only to be faced with flat, uninspiring country that made me wish we were winding through the hills again … almost.

I didn't know how Chris was doing it, hours upon hours of endless driving. I noticed him stretch his neck, or roll his shoulders in fatigue sometimes. I had even offered to take over for a bit, but that had just earned me a wry smile and a polite decline.

Probably some kind of territorial thing. Whatever; fine by me. I had dozed fitfully along the way, trying anything to kill some time. Of course, it didn't help that the only real reprieve from the heat had been our open windows. I didn't know if Chris wanted to conserve petrol or prevent his car from overheating or what other reason there was for not using the air con.

The last of the sun was melting down for the day, cooling the air and bringing with it a reprieve from its scorching rays, which was something, at least. The others were no doubt long settled in near the beach around Portland somewhere, setting up camp, catching up with one another, looking after Ringer.

My mind flashed back to this morning to Toby and Ellie. I pinched the bridge of my nose – I didn't want to think about them right now. This morning seemed like a lifetime ago and I kind of wanted to keep it that way. I moved to massage my temples and let out a weary sigh.

"We're nearly there," said Chris.

I stretched in my seat, wondering where 'there' was. I envisioned a glorious big bathroom with heated showers, maybe a hut with a king-sized bed. Instead, Chris veered off into an open, sandy clearing and slowed the van to a complete stop. He turned off the engine and drummed his steering wheel in excitement.

"We're here." He grinned, flinging his door open and sliding out.

I glanced around, examining where *here* was exactly. And just as I had suspected, *here* looked like nowhere. No toilet block, no showers, no public barbecue or picnic tables. Nothing.

Chris had said he would take me somewhere better than Portland. Having remembered the thriving cafes, glistening sand and stretching ocean, I grabbed at the open window and stared tentatively into the fading light.

Absolutely nothing.

Chris stood near my door, stretching his arms toward the stars with an almighty groan. His T-shirt lifted and exposed a flash of ripped muscle. All of a sudden I didn't feel so dismal about our situation. Still, I would have liked some answers. I unclicked the passenger door and pushed it open. My legs felt like jelly, my circulation obviously cut off from below my waist.

"Where are we?" I winced.

"Shh …" Chris held up his hand. "Do you hear that?"

I stilled, listening intently. What was I listening for?

"I don't hear anything," I whispered.

"Listen," he snapped.

I was in no mood to play Murder in the Dark, I Spy or Listen to the freakin Noise. I just wanted to have a shower, a long, hot sho—

I froze. I *did* hear something: a low, unmistakable rumble. I wondered how I could possibly not have heard it to begin with. My eyes widened as my gaze locked onto Chris. He smiled wide and bright.

"Change into your swimmers," he said, doubling back toward the car.

I didn't question, I just moved, quickly rustling through my gear and ducking on the opposite side of the van from where Chris was also changing. I had gone from fatigue to heart-pounding excitement. Adrenalin pumped through my veins as I tried to guess at what lurked beyond the fading light.

I secured my bikini string on my hip as I walked around the van and collided with Chris, his head entrapped inside his T-shirt as he tried to pull it over his head.

"Watch it," his muffled voice said.

I tried not to laugh; it was a position I had been trapped in many times in a women's changing room.

I stepped forward, gathered the fabric and pulled upward. "Hold still," I laughed.

I didn't actually do much, as Chris managed to yank it off his head, his hair all ruffled and standing on end, which caused me to laugh even more.

"Don't laugh, I could have died." He scowled.

I shook my head. "Honestly, how old are you?"

He didn't answer, he just looked at me, his eyes darting at my attire, and then quickly back to my face. It was so fleeting, but there was no mistaking the meaning in his eyes.

It was the look I had hoped for last night in my new dress. Instead, I found it here, standing before him in my turquoise bikini. I concentrated on keeping my own gaze nice and high, away from his black footy shorts and the wall of bare taut, tanned skin just begging me to look. I would not give him the satisfaction.

"That sound better be a running shower," I said.

Chris chucked his T-shirt inside the open window of the van. "Even better." He tilted his head and started toward some bushes along the perimeter.

I called after him, "So, what, I'm supposed to just follow after you, am I?"

Chris shrugged. "Or you could stay here, by yourself."

I glanced around. Hmm, alone, scantily clad in the quickly fading light … I had seen enough horror movies where Jamie Lee Curtis screamed her way through some trying times. Yeah, not gonna happen.

"Chris, wait up."

Chapter Forty-Two

A fence? We were climbing over a fence.

Or, rather, what once was a fence and was now just a low lying wire string that had seen better days. Still, the barrier was a universal statement for keeping people out and away from something forbidden, something private, or in this case, something breathtaking.

My feet sank into the sandy embankment as I cautiously followed Chris down the steep dune. As I stepped carefully toward the horizon, I watched as the sunlight bled into the expansive, deep blue sea, but our obvious main focus was what Chris was striding for.

Closer than the sunlight glistening off the ocean was a man-made ocean pool, a barrier built up with concrete and sandstone, creating a calm expanse of water that contrasted with the rhythmic crests and swells beyond it as the ocean pummelled its edges.

The wind and sea spray tickled at our skin in the darkness, lit only by a line of towering, wrought iron street lamps. Just two were lit; all the others were dark. Damaged, smashed by bored delinquents, no doubt.

But they weren't here now. The beach was deserted.

"Are we allowed to be here?" I asked, struggling to find purchase in the sand.

"Which answer would you be happy with?" asked Chris.

"Uh, the law-abiding one."

"Then, yes, absolutely we're allowed to be here."

A sense of foreboding chilled my blood as Chris led me up the grassy track. The grass was long and wild, only partly trampled down, which suggested it wasn't well used.

"Is this safe?" I asked, hating the shaky sound to my voice. My bare arms were speckled with goosebumps and I tried to rub them away. I wasn't cold in the balmy December breeze, but nervous with the worry that what we were doing was wrong, that what we were about to do was forbidden.

Chris turned his amused focus on me as he walked backward through the grass. "So many questions!" he said with a laugh, before spinning around to concentrate on his steps.

I wanted to ask how he knew about this place, but clamped my mouth closed, thinking better of it.

No more questions. Stop being a wimp and just go with it.

I swallowed down any reservations I had and decided to enjoy my surrounds. We were no longer cooped up in the car, we were alone, just the two of us without the others and their drama, and tomorrow we would finally reach Point Shank. The others may have been settling in at Portland, even going out for tea and the clubs maybe, but Chris was right; he had taken me somewhere better than that. He had brought me to a secluded slice of paradise, even though we were probably trespassing. I quickened my pace to walk beside him, our arms brushing with every unsteady step we formed in the sand.

"Just answer me this, then."

"Mmm?"

"There isn't going to be any police tape or chalked outline of a body up here, is there? That's not the reason no one's here?"

Chris laughed. "I hope not – that would be a serious buzz killer."

And the icing on top of a long day, I thought.

My stomach twisted with excitement as we reached the railing that linked the way down toward roughened concrete steps, part of the sweeping barricade that surrounded the pool. On top, the whole perimeter of the concrete fortress was divided with steel poles with a single chain linking them together – not much of a barrier between the seeming protection of the man-made water hole and the entire ocean beyond.

Unlike me, Chris didn't seem nervous at all. As he walked along the wide edge of the pool he seemed comfortable, right at home. For some unknown reason I followed him exactly, stepping in his footsteps as if we were walking in a minefield. Why on earth wasn't this place swarming with tourists? The air was still thick and warm and the full moon rose in the sky, adding to the minimal, eerie light the two lonely lamps cast over half the pool. No amount of lighting or lack thereof would make it less uninviting, though. Unlike the ocean, it was free of seaweed and creatures of the deep … or was it? What if a shark had catapulted on a wave over the ledge? Or an octopus had wanted a sea change (so to speak)? I'd watched the Discovery channel; I had seen it happen.

I chewed on my lip thoughtfully, ready to plant myself on a concrete step and sit this adventure out.

Chris sighed. "The tide cuts off the main access from the beach, see?" He pointed toward a rocky, harsh landscape. "That's why no one's here. Plus there's a bigger pool over in Breckon Beach. That one's patrolled and popular with late night swimmers. This place would have been the go back in the '80s maybe; now it's mainly used by athletes who want to do laps without having to worry about hairy-backed men in Speedos and screaming kids."

"But we're here; I mean, we made the effort to come here, so why don't others?"

Chris ran his fingers along the chain-linked pole with a casual shrug. "Maybe they do. Maybe late night lovers come skinny dipping here at midnight … Who knows?" He stepped toward me, his hand skimming over the chain.

"You mean there might be an Onslow Boys equivalent on their way here right now? The Breckon Beach Boys?" I said, looking back to where we had walked from.

"Christ, I hope not," Chris laughed. "I'm kind of enjoying the serenity."

Yeah, the serenity littered with my thousand paranoia-infused questions. Lighten the hell up, Tammy!

I turned back around and flinched. Chris was standing close, really close, leaning on the railing with amusement.

"Guess we better not muck around then." Even in the night-time shadows I could tell that amusement lined his face; I could tell simply by the way the words had fallen off his tongue. They were tauntingly suggestive. If he thought it was funny to make me squirm under his penetrating stare, well, I wouldn't give him the satisfaction.

I lifted my chin. "Keep dreaming, Henderson. I'm not skinny dipping," I said proudly. "I don't care how secluded this place is."

The light of the moon illuminated the brilliant flash of Chris's toothy smile. "More's the pity," he said. "To be honest, I'll be amazed if you even get in." He walked right up to the edge of the pool.

"Why wouldn't I?" I said quickly.

Chris stretched his arms to the sky. "You just don't strike me as a girl who gets out of her comfort zone much."

Comfort zone?

My entire summer had been spent out of my comfort zone. This whole trip had been massively out of my comfort zone. But I had done it. Against all my better instincts, here I was. I had even been prepared to potentially do something last night with Chris that was completely out of character. I had wanted him to kiss me – everything in my body language had screamed as much at him. He would have to have been blind not to have understood that much last night, but he had known. Of course he had. Why else would he have spun around so fast other than to avoid me?

I felt not so much the burning of humiliation rising in me, but more the burning of anger.

He didn't know anything about me. So what if I didn't want

to go skinny dipping? Just because I had some safety-related questions over the creepy, poorly lit, abandoned pool, I was a girl who never pushed the boundaries? That never went against the grain?

Fuck you, Chris Henderson.

My brows narrowed and all of a sudden I hoped that I was illuminated well enough that he'd see just how angry his statement had made me.

I pushed past Chris, my feet slapping angrily against the cool, wet concrete as I glanced out toward the massive pool.

"You don't have to, you know," Chris said, looking uncomfortable. "I just thought that it was kind of a cool place to bring you after a long trip."

Oh, now he was trying to be nice and supportive?

Underneath the glow of the pool light, I stood close enough to count all the different shades of brown in his eyes, eyes that ticked across my face as if trying to solve the mysteries of the universe through me. Then they lit up, as if at that very moment he had realised what my determined, serious gaze meant.

"Tammy, wait …"

It was too late. In an act of defiance, as he reached out toward me, without a second thought I dived into the water.

Chapter Forty-Three

I had been so proud, so confident.

Until I hit the water.

Not only was the pool filled with salty ocean water, I wasn't entirely convinced that the water hadn't made a direct line from an Antarctic iceberg itself. The ice-cold water sliced against my skin.

I broke through the surface, gasping with the shock of it. The freezing assault on my body that had not long ago been clammy and warm from the trek through the dunes now stung in bitter pain. But my next gasp had nothing to do with the paralysing sensation of the water.

I was met with a far bigger problem.

Oh my God! Where was my bikini top?

My feet found purchase on the bottom of the pool, allowing me the balance to be able to cover my breasts with one arm while clawing frantically through the impossibly dark water with the other. At least, I hoped it was impossibly dark.

Shit, shit, shit, shit, shit …

"Looking for something?"

My eyes locked onto him, still standing on the pool ledge, the perfect viewpoint. My brows narrowed. Chris held up a scrap of material. Corded, turquoise strings with two triangles that dangled from his hand, dancing in the summer breeze.

This couldn't be happening.

"I feel like I'm living in a *Carry On* movie," Chris joked before clearing his throat and forcing himself to be serious. "Look, I was just trying to stop you from diving in, but, um, I kind of only stopped part of you." He swung the bikini top around his finger, averting his eyes from me.

I had never been so glad of dodgy lighting.

Chris braced himself for some kind of homicidal rant about my top, but, truth be told, as my body slowly acclimated to the freezing water, it felt good floating, my weight suspended and soothed from the stiffness, aches and pains of the day's travel. As the water cradled me, carried me, it swept all my cares away with it.

"What are you standing there for?" I called. "You look like a coat hanger, get in already."

Chris's eyebrows lifted in surprise.

"What's wrong? Cold water out of your comfort zone?" I jabbed.

Chris took a deep, chest-expanding breath. I couldn't tell if it was to psych himself up or if he was praying for patience.

"Well, here," he held up my top. "You want me to chuck you this?"

Maybe it was the calming sway of the water that lapped at my skin, or the protection of shadows, the feeling of the open air and summer breeze that rippled across the water's surface. Maybe plunging into the murky depths of the unknown had made me reborn?

I didn't know, but what I did know was that I felt free, and I liked it. I liked it a lot.

"Keep it!" I yelled, working quickly to edge my bikini bottoms down. I slid them from my legs and scrunched them into a ball. "Here," I called, and I threw them toward Chris. He caught them in shock and held them up, his brow curving.

I just smiled and removed my arm from my chest, unaware if he could even see me. But I didn't care. I kicked myself away from the ledge, deeper into the shadows.

Chris had moved closer to the lamp light; for a moment I thought he was walking away, again reaching the edge and backing off, backing away from me.

Panic spiked inside me. What had I done? Maybe I'd misread it; maybe he didn't want to get into the water with me, after all. Had what I had done in a bold, wild moment repelled him so much that he didn't want to swim at all now?

In the depths of the shadows I watched him warily, watching intently as he made his way toward the railing and worked on tying the strings of my bikini together and looping my bottoms onto the steel pole as if for safekeeping. Under the light, I caught the bemused smile and the slight shake of his head that I'm sure I wasn't meant to see. He moved toward the edge of the pool and his eyes landed on me. I hunched my shoulders under the water. Even under the protective cover of darkness Chris's eyes locked onto mine easily enough. So easily, and so readily, his smouldering, dark eyes burned directly into my soul.

I didn't feel protected by the shadows anymore – if anything, I felt like I was under a giant spotlight.

All my bold confidence gushed out of me, poured into a locked box I couldn't begin to unlock again. I felt nervous. I was so exposed.

Chris's mouth broke into a wolfish grin. "So much for not skinny dipping," he said, popping the top button of his black footy shorts.

My breath hitched as he unzipped the fly, causing the shorts to loosen a little. I quickly looked away. I was completely out of my depth.

Chris didn't dive; instead I heard the padded steps of his feet followed by an almighty splash. Water sprayed over my head and back.

His head broke the surface, gasping in a breath of horror.

"Holy shit, it's fucking freezing!" He flailed around much like I had as the shockwaves ripped through him.

I laughed, completely unsympathetic to his suffering.

"It's beautiful," I said with a sigh.

"Please tell me it gets better?" he asked, his voice filled with tremors.

"It does," I said. "Put your shoulders under. It's worse if you don't."

Chris lowered his broad, bare shoulders and my stomach twisted with regret at having given him such advice. Still, his beautiful face was visible, looking at me like he was going to say something but hadn't made up his mind whether to release the words.

I wanted to hear them. "What?" I asked.

Chris shook his head, fighting against the smile that tried to break through his lips.

"Nothing."

"You were going to say something."

"Was I?" he asked with interest.

"Yeah, I could tell. What were you going to say?"

Chris dipped his head under the water for a second and smoothed his hair back off his face; he looked like he was modelling for Dolce & Gabbana, he was so breathtaking by moonlight. Although we were in a large, almost Olympic-sized pool, and we were metres apart, I couldn't help but be acutely aware of how completely naked we were in it. My heart raced with nerves as Chris swam toward me and latched onto the concrete edge in the shadows.

I swallowed, trying not to seem uncomfortable by his sudden nearness, by the fact that he was so close I could feel his breath near my shoulder.

Alarmingly, it wasn't embarrassment, or wanting to edge away that made me feel uncomfortable. I wasn't either of those things. It was a whole other sensation that spiked in the pit of my stomach that made me breathe quickly and have trouble keeping my thoughts focused and gazing above the waterline.

It was the same way I had felt last night when Chris had

helped me undress in the dark van.

I inwardly scoffed. *Yeah, and that turned out so well. Christ, Tammy, get a grip of your hormones, you sex-starved maniac.*

Starved? Yeah, that was kind of an understatement; it had been a while, a long while actually. And now there was a naked Onslow Boy next to me. No wonder I felt a little unsettled! Okay, *really* unsettled.

I tried to keep cool, to look calm and casual, just like he appeared to be. Obviously my naked presence didn't have the same effect on him. That knowledge would help me stop from doing anything foolish like I had last night.

"So? You were going to say?" I tried to keep the conversation flowing, distract myself from his nearness. His *nakedness.*

Serves me right – I got into this, now I had to suffer the consequences.

Chris stood up on the pool floor, exposing his broad shoulders as the water lapped below his ribcage. I remained hovering with my shoulders under the water; I didn't have the luxury of standing.

Chris rubbed his jaw line, laughing.

"What?"

"I wasn't going to say it," he said.

"Say what? What were you thinking?" I pressed.

Chris lowered his shoulders in the water again, never moving his gaze from me as the humour in his eyes disappeared.

"I was thinking, alone in the dark with a naked, beautiful girl. This is soooo much better than Portland." He grinned.

A shiver ran down my spine and I knew it had nothing to do with the chill of the water. My heart slammed against the wall of my chest and my stomach twisted with the sheer thrill of Chris's confession.

Beautiful girl. Did he really think I was beautiful?

He was grinning like a fool, so maybe he was just joking.

"Are you sorry you left the others?" I asked, then inwardly slapped myself. Why had I just asked that? Some things I really didn't want to know the answer to, and I had the feeling that was one of them.

Chris's brows knitted together in deep thought, but he still didn't break eye contact, studying me. There was no smile, no cheeky glint of humour. It had all melted away, replaced by the stony exterior of the Chris of old. I literally braced my bare back against the concrete wall, the rough edges digging into my skin.

"Seriously, you want to know?" he asked.

After a second, I nodded involuntarily. I didn't want to know. I didn't want him to say, 'We should have stayed in Portland,' or 'I wish the others were here right now, it would be so much more fun,' or 'Are you kidding? Of course I wish we were with the others - being stuck here with you is a nightmare.'

I was snapped out of my thoughts as Chris glided through the water, and edged closer to me and my naked body. He stopped so close I dared not even move. If I did, I would brush against his bare skin and might not be able to fake the fact that it wouldn't mean anything to me.

"You really want to know?" His voice was husky and serious.

I swallowed, wishing I could just slink away into the depth of the dark water and disappear.

Escape.

But then he said, "Tammy, there is no place else I would rather be than right here, right now, with you."

Before I could take in the weight of his words, Chris edged closer, slow but deliberate.

Placing his hands on either side of me, caging me in against the pool wall, his body that sheltered me from the breeze that rolled in off the ocean was now replaced by his breath, warm and welcome on my skin. He was so close, but not touching.

I wondered if maybe it was a test: a test of wills, of who would break first. I desperately wanted to reach out to him, to bring my shaking hands up and slide them over his shoulders, to press skin to skin, drawing him near and crushing against him, like the stirrings of waves slamming against the rocks.

Chris was like a rock, a boulder hovering over me, barricading me in, his heated eyes ticking tauntingly over mine. If this was a test of wills, I forced every weakness in me to stand firm, defiant. I had made the first move last night and been rejected.

Not again.

Don't move, Tammy, don't look at his eyes – focus. Ignore the curve of his bow-shaped mouth. Christ, it looked so kissable. Try not to think about that, try not to think about the flex of his muscles so near your face, try not to think about … oh God.

I swallowed as his leg brushed against mine, the sensation too raw, so unexpected I forced myself not to reach out and pull him toward me. As if reading the moment of weakness on my face, Chris smirked.

Cocky bastard.

He could torture me if he must, but I would not fold. No way, no how, not again. As I was about to run through the same chant in my head, over and over again to cement my stance, I suddenly didn't need to.

Chris folded first.

Chapter Forty-Four

I had expected him to pull away.

It had never occurred to me that he would close the distance between us. I had been so distracted, busy battling my own desires, controlling my urges, that I didn't notice until it was happening.

The heated look of need in his eyes made my heart stop. His gaze dipped to my lips.

I wasn't a girl being led into the dark Onslow Hotel beer garden. No, this was better. Much, much better.

I closed my eyes, waiting for him to tell me this was a mistake, waiting for him to stop. Instead, his fingers skimmed along the dip of my spine causing me to suck in a breath. My eyes flung open, locking with Chris's wicked gaze just before his mouth descended slowly onto mine. His kiss was achingly tender, brushing against my lips, capturing the breath he drew out of me, then a gasp as his body pressed against mine. My back grazed against the rough, concrete wall but the pain slicing into my skin was the furthest thing from my racing thoughts as I felt Chris's desire push against my stomach. I lifted my hands to slide over his slick shoulders just like I had fantasised. I opened my mouth to him, his hot tongue teasing mine like I had hoped it would. What had begun as a slow, soft exploration turned into frantic, deep, burning need as Chris kissed me hard. Tasting the salt from the ocean on his lush mouth, it was as if all our reservations were swept away. My arms circled around his neck, drawing him closer, pressing skin against skin with no apology. There was no room for pleasantries, just deep-seeded desire as Chris fisted my hair, tilting my head for better access to my mouth.

He broke away from his drugging kisses, his lips hovering close. "Is this what you want?" Chris breathed into my mouth.

He grabbed my leg and hooked it around his waist. I gasped as he pressed against me.

This was what I wanted, *he* was what I wanted – of this I was certain, even if just for one night.

I wanted Chris in every way.

I bit my lip, answering his question by skimming my hand along his shoulder, down his chest, over his stomach and dipping below the water.

Even in the shadows I could see his face transform – his eyes fluttered closed and he breathed out a long, shuddery breath across my neck. He wrapped his hand around mine, guiding me up and down below the water.

This was madness. Our intensity for one another, the way our mouths found each other as if we fitted together so perfectly there was no question what was going to happen.

"Tammy, look at me," Chris said, his voice raspy.

I lifted my eyes, almost shy, despite the way my hand slid across the most intimate part of him. He swallowed hard, stilling my movements.

"Are you sure?"

My lids were heavy and my body shivered against every sensation, against the slide of Chris's palm over my belly as he brushed the backs of his fingers over my breast.

"Yes," I breathed.

"Because if you want, I'll stop," he whispered, cupping my breast and kissing my neck.

Like hell I wanted him to stop.

I hooked my other leg around his waist, leaving nothing to his imagination. He claimed my mouth, kissing me so fiercely and rocking his hips against me. I thought I had died and gone to heaven.

This was really happening; it didn't get any closer than this. Chris drew back a little and positioned himself to glide his way inside me. He was teasing, gentle, soothing me for what was to come before he pushed, and just before he did, panic twisted in my stomach.

"Chris, wait," I said.

He froze. "What's wrong?"

I bit my lip, feeling awful for stopping right before, but better than after.

"Do you, um, do you have … protection?" I asked, my voice small. I inwardly cringed, hoping it wasn't a mood killer. My gaze lifted, expecting to see his face crease with disappointment.

Instead he backed away a little, which was almost worse. His brows lifted and his eyes, once cloudy and deep with need, blinked as if clearing the fog.

"Shit, Tam, I'm sorry, I didn't even think."

This was what I had been afraid of, the sudden burst of reality slamming home. I braced myself for more apologies, for mutterings that what we had done was a mistake and it wouldn't happen again.

I cursed myself for stopping him, but some things were just non-negotiable.

No part of him was touching me now. I wrapped my arms around myself, my body aching as the heights of the pleasure and heaven I had felt a mere moment before were ripped from me.

"Hey, Tam." His hand touched my cheek, forcing me to look at him. "It's all right, we just got carried away is all, but we stopped in time."

I closed my eyes, feeling the hot moisture pool behind my lids.

"Yeah, stopped before you did something you would live to

regret," I said, pushing away from the wall and moving to pass him.

"Whoa, wait a sec." His hand snaked around my wrist and he pulled me back. "This isn't over, not for me," he said seriously.

I stared up at him, my mind whirring in maddening circles, fearing to hope.

"What are you saying?" I whispered.

He pulled me closer, circling his arms around my waist. "What I'm saying is I want to go to the ends of the Earth with you."

He swept a wet tendril of hair away from my brow, cupping my face, before lowering his mouth against mine so tenderly I melted against him.

"And, furthermore, if we're going to do this, we have to do it right. In every way." His thumb brushed tenderly across the seam of my kiss-swollen lips.

My heart swelled; I was falling for what could be the most amazing person I had ever met. It was almost impossible to comprehend that I was once so intimidated by him, hiding under tables and dreading the hours spent by his side on this trip. I knew this tender side to him was not always front and present, that it was often overshadowed by the equally brooding, bossy, moody part of him. But I couldn't help but be completely and utterly in awe of all that was Chris. To me, he was bloody near-on perfect.

Chapter Forty-Five

I had never felt more alive.

Chris turned around as I stepped out of the water and grabbed for my bikini. I slipped into it lightning fast. I glanced anxiously toward Chris's back as he looked out over the ocean. My lips tilted up at the endearing gesture, considering the heat and passion of only moments before.

Securing the knot at the nape of my neck, I scooped up Chris's shorts.

"All done. Here!"

He turned in time to catch them.

"Lucky they didn't get swept away," I said.

"Well, that would have been awkward," he said, pulling them on under the waterline. "I don't see any fig leaves I could have used in their place."

"Oh, I don't know," I said, looking out at the dunes. "We could have gotten creative. Worst-case scenario we could have made you a nice mankini out of my bikini top." I laughed.

Chris grimaced, lifting himself out of the water. "I think I would have opted for a moonlight nudie run, for both our sakes."

I combed my fingers through the knotted tendrils of my hair. I may have been refreshed from the swim, but as the salty seawater dried on my skin it certainly didn't leave me feeling clean.

As if reading my very thoughts, Chris grabbed my hand. "Ready for that shower?"

My eyes narrowed; he was just teasing me, and a shower was an impossibly cruel taunt.

"You should never joke about such things," I said, looking at him sceptically.

"I wouldn't dare," he smirked and led me up the concrete steps. We reached the very top and stopped.

"See?" he said, tilting his head forward.

There it was – an outdoor beach shower. "Does it work?" I asked, trying not to dance on the balls of my feet.

"There's only one way to find out." Before his last words had left his mouth the race was on.

Not only did it work – and sure, it was cold, but I couldn't have cared less – but it was clean, fresh water that flowed over my salty body and I had Chris by my side, playfully nuzzling my neck and skimming my ribcage in tortuous, ticklish circles.

No one had ever made my heart pound so hard just by the look in their eye before. My body flooded with heat even after an ice-cold shower.

The second thing I wanted perhaps more than a clean shower was to get back to the van and fast.

Even walking back up the sandy dunes to the track seemed more manageable when Chris was holding my hand. I had to fight the urge to stop him in his tracks and kiss him like crazy, but he strode a long, determined path back to the van – so determined I struggled to keep up. As we made our way through the clearing, my heart rate spiked as I saw the panel van in the distance. We closed in and I instinctively moved to the back doors but Chris stopped me. Instead, he pulled me toward him and lifted me onto the bonnet of the car.

I squealed at the unexpectedness of it. The engine still felt warm underneath me as Chris pushed his body between my legs, cupping his hand behind my neck and drawing a deep, passionate kiss from me. My insides were on fire and adrenalin coursed through me at the thought that he was going to do me on the bonnet of his car.

Oh, how my life had changed.

His hands rested on either side of my hips, and he leaned forward and stole another kiss.

"Wait here," he said against my lips, before he drew away and walked to the back of the van. I pressed my fingers to my lips, and, still tasting the remnants of his salty kisses, I smiled. I hoped that he was searching for something in particular. So when he returned holding a … towel? I couldn't help but feel bitterly disappointed.

He threw it toward me, catching it before it engulfed my face.

"Thanks," I said, smiling weakly as I started to towel dry my hair. "What's that?" I eyed the folded square of black fabric in his hand.

"Oh, I thought you might want to do away with the flanny PJs tonight. I have a clean T-shirt." He handed it over to me. "It will swim on you, but it will be more comfortable."

This time my smile was genuine as my fingers traced the soft black material in my lap. Here I was, like a sex-crazed nympho thinking about nothing but wanting him to grab a condom, and his first thought was getting me into comfortable clothes, not pulling me out of them. Chris had even changed into a dry pair of board shorts.

I blanched at my wicked thoughts.

I towel dried the end of my hair in a daze, my bones weary from a long day as I pushed my wanton desires aside.

"Here." He laughed, taking the towel from me, and, draping it over my head, rubbed vigorously, to the point that I complained.

If he thought this was sexy …

"Ow-ow-ow!"

He pulled the towel away, breaking into a fit of laughter as he looked over my tousled hair, rubbed into the consistency of straw.

"Shut up," I said, glowering at him as I ran my fingers through the untamed mass.

Chris smiled so brilliantly I couldn't be mad for long. He grabbed for the T-shirt, flicked it out, and bunched it up to the neckline.

"Arms up," he announced.

I rolled my eyes. "You're actually enjoying this, aren't you?"

"Well, I don't fancy my chances of explaining to everyone how you managed to get pneumonia in the middle of summer," he mused.

I lifted my arms straight up, allowing him to drape the oversized T-shirt over my head, yanking it free with a forceful pull as I poked my arms through the sleeves.

Under the T-shirt, Chris's hands skimmed around my back as he pulled the strings to my bikini free. A thrill shot through me. I may have been covered by the T-shirt, but it didn't make what he was doing any less exciting. He moved up to the nape of my neck and gently tugged the cord with expert ease. The bikini fell away as he pulled the material free.

I watched as his Adam's apple bobbed in his throat, his hands skimming along the edges of my breasts and down my ribcage to the bikini strings at my hips. My breath caught in my throat. He stilled for a moment, carefully watching my face for my reaction, before he slowly started to slide my bikini bottoms off me. I leaned back on my hands, lifting my bottom so he could free them and slide them down my legs.

I had never felt sexier, perched up on the bonnet of a black car in nothing but an oversized black T-shirt, with Chris's hungry eyes on me.

I knew what was to come; I sensed it in the intense way we looked at one another, in the way our chests heaved, the way my body arched toward Chris at the slightest touch. Blame it on the summer holidays, the full moon or the moonlight swim. I didn't know exactly what was to blame but all I knew was my blood burned with need for him.

Regardless that in the light of day it could be a colossal mistake. I didn't care; all I cared about was the next instant he touched me or kissed me. I slid slowly off the bonnet.

He had made the most important first move tonight, so now it was my turn to make the last. I grabbed his hands and laced them with my fingers, pulling him toward the van. Stepping past the passenger door he stopped me dead in my tracks and my heart sank.

"Tam, hang on a sec." Chris let go of my hands and pulled open the passenger door. "Don't want to cover the mattress with sand," he said, tilting his head with a cheeky grin.

My eyes fell to our bare feet caked in wet sand. Relief flooded every part of my being as I dived into the front bucket seat and slid across.

Chris followed me in and closed the door.

Chapter Forty-Six

We were, once again, just two people in the front seat of a car.

Well, a little bit different than any way we might have occupied the front seat before.

I straddled Chris's lap, his fists gripping the material of the T-shirt at my hips. Our hot, delving kisses stole the ability to breathe from us both as we frantically clawed at one another. I ran a trail of kisses teasingly down his jaw line and neck to his collarbone. He groaned with approval and grabbed the backs of my knees, pulling me closer to him still. I gasped at the friction. Chris kissed me so passionately, murmuring words between his draw of breath as he tauntingly skimmed his hands under my T-shirt.

"Let's get in the back," he breathed into my mouth.

"What about the sand?"

"Fuck the fucking sand," he said, motioning for me to lift off him. We frantically manoeuvred our way over the back seat and crashed clumsily onto the soft mattress in a heap.

We couldn't help but laugh at ourselves; we had finally made it here, to the darkened, secluded van. I took the moment to mention the main issue.

"So, um, do you still have Ringer's … you know?" I asked,

feeling heat flood my already flushed face.

Chris sat up. "Shit, yeah, hang on a sec …" He stilled. "FUCK!"

I flinched. "What?" My eyes widened and I sat up.

Chris ran his hands through his hair in despair.

"How could I be so freaking stupid?" He threw himself back on the mattress.

"Chris? What the hell?" I shifted onto my knees, alarm rising in me more every second that passed.

He sighed deeply, hitching himself onto his elbows. "I put it in a really safe place," he deadpanned.

"H-how safe?" I asked, fearing to know the answer.

"I tucked it in one of the shoes you brought back last night."

My eyes widened, horror overriding my worry.

Toby's shoes? The shoes I had thrown against a tree in a fit of rage?

"Why would you do that?" I asked.

"Well, I didn't want it swimming around the back of the van, I wanted to hide it, so I just shoved it in there when I was packing up the van."

"You know, wallets are also handy places to stow such things," I said.

"Yeah. Well, I didn't think of that at the time, obviously."

I cupped my face with my hands before something dawned on me. "Wait a minute, you watched me take those shoes from you, knowing I was going to return them to their rightful owner, knowing full well that …"

"I swear, it completely slipped my mind. There is no way I would have let you. I just … I don't know. Got distracted." He sighed, before the lines in his face transformed into pain. "Whose shoes were they, anyway?"

"Toby's," I said.

Chris scoffed. "Well, he's going to get a nice surprise next time he tries them on."

Um, yeah. About that …

I chewed on my thumbnail. I looked at Chris eating himself

up over a foolish mistake. I could have kept it to myself, but thought better of it.

"He's going to get a bigger surprise than you think," I said, cringing at what I was going to say.

Chris's brows lowered. "What do you mean?"

"Well, they didn't exactly make it back to Toby," I confessed.

Chris lifted one brow. "Oh?"

"Before you get too excited, they're not here," I said quickly.

A bemused tilt formed in the corner of Chris's lips. "Where are they, then?"

I squirmed under his gaze. "They may or may not be up a tree, back in Evoka."

Chris blinked, as if he wasn't fully comprehending.

"Why are they up a tree?"

To tell Chris why meant explaining why I'd been so pissed at him and I really didn't want to have to revisit this morning's fight. Not tonight. I just wanted to forget; in these glorious moments in Chris's arms, I wanted all the worries and the weight of the world to melt away.

"A prank gone wrong, you might say."

"That's an understatement." Chris sighed, throwing himself back onto the mattress.

I lay down next to him and placed my head on his chest. "Is now when you tell me not to stress because you have one in your wallet, anyway?" I asked, hoping against hope.

Chris scoffed. "Well, to be honest, it was originally going to be an all-mates' fishing adventure; I didn't see the need to stock up."

I felt both disappointed and relieved. I lifted myself onto my side, staring down at him.

"What, no woman in every port?" I teased.

"What?" Chris asked, confusion etched on his face.

"Nothing," I said, settling down, resting my head back on Chris's bare chest. His heart pounded hard and fast against my temple; it was soothing, as was the familiar feeling of Chris folding his fingers through my hair.

I still didn't know whether to laugh or scream – against all the odds of trying to forget the disaster of this morning's run-in with Toby and Ellie, my actions had only led to completely backfire tonight.

Was this the universe's way of punishing me for being a coward and wanting to leave the trouble behind me, to avoid confrontation for as long as I could? Maybe it served me right – my fence-sitting ways in the past hadn't exactly gotten me far. If anything, the moment I stepped out of my comfort zone, look what happened: I was lying in Chris Henderson's arms, and I had never felt more alive.

I wanted to hold onto that, and I wanted to release the burden I carried with me. Maybe by talking to Chris about it he might be able to help. He had known Toby all his life, after all.

I lifted my head off his chest. "Chris?" I whispered, touching his shoulder.

I was met with silence and the sudden realisation that he was no longer stroking my hair. Instead, he lay there, sound asleep. His chest rose and fell slowly, his beautiful bow-shaped lips relaxed and no lines etched his brows in worry or stress. He looked so peaceful.

My heart ached for him – he had had no sleep last night after our awkward exchange. He had then had a long day's worth of driving, only to end it with a moonlight skinny dip with me.

I smiled at the memory of every kiss, every touch. I didn't want to wake him, especially not to tell him about Toby. I would let him get a good night's sleep, rest up for the last leg of the journey tomorrow. If anything, I had to fight the selfish urge to wake him up to assure me that no matter what, in the light of day there would be no weirdness or regret between us.

I had seen it so many times before – late night Saturday rendezvous usually led to awkward avoidance the next day. The one thing in our favour was that there had been no alcohol involved, but still Chris wasn't the most predictable creature I had ever met. I tilted my head, looking down at the sleeping, gorgeous Onslow

Boy. His features twisted into a familiar frown in his sleep. I didn't know what was racing through his mind to cause such a worrisome look, but I did what I had often thought of doing before brushing the insane moment away.

I leaned over him and gently kissed his forehead. I felt the puckered worry lines melt under my lips and I smiled, lifting myself slowly to admire my handiwork.

Chris shifted slightly and I froze, hoping he wouldn't wake. He pressed his lips together and a fleeting frown creased and disappeared as he sighed.

I moved now. Edging my way carefully to lie beside him.

"Tam?" his voice croaked.

"Yes?" I whispered.

"You got to put the pool cues back."

I bit my lip to stifle my giggles. Dreaming of work. No wonder he scowled in his sleep.

"Okay, I will," I assured him, lying down in the space beside him.

"Tam?" Chris called out.

I sighed. "Yes, Chris?"

"I love you." He turned onto his side leaving me stunned, silent and staring at his back.

Chapter Forty-Seven

You can never read too much into a dream.

How could I possibly? It was just a dream; he had no control over it, he had been dreaming of pool cues only seconds before, for Christ's sake. And if I believed that dreams had any weight to them, considering my reoccurring dream in which my teeth fell out, I was in serious trouble.

The night had left me frustrated, confused and in a bed full of sand for no reason. Sure I was clean and comfortable without my flannelette PJs, but the only problem now was that my thoughts plagued me, making sleep fitful.

I awoke with the sun streaming across my face, an unexpected intrusion considering the panel van's windows were blacked out. Shifting onto my side and shielding my eyes, I peeked through one squinted eye to spot a blurry silhouette standing at the open doors of the panel van.

"Morning," Chris beamed.

I sat up, stretching and groaning. I brushed my matted locks of hair to the side and cringed at its Brillo pad-like consistency. Suddenly I became very aware of my appearance.

Chris stood in the doorway, a warm, friendly smile spread across his lips as he leaned casually against the open door. He was dressed in navy shorts and white T with an open checked shirt over the top. He looked like he belonged in a David Jones catalogue, and here I was looking like a bag lady.

"Morning," I croaked.

"You hungry?"

I rubbed my stomach; it was hollow and begging for substance. "Famished," I said.

"Get dressed and we will hit the road." Chris stepped back in the sunlight and stretched his arms to the sky.

He seemed awfully chipper. It was a welcome sight to wake up to. I'd had a fitful sleep plagued with dreams of waking up with a note next to me, telling me he had hitchhiked back to Onslow – Happy New Year. So when I had woken to Chris's beautiful smile instead, butterflies fluttered happily in my stomach. Or maybe it was hunger? No, it was definitely butterflies, and it was nice.

By the time I got dressed into some cut-off denim shorts and a lime green singlet top, I had opted to throw my hair up into a messy bun style. Using my drink bottle I washed my face and brushed my teeth, staring off into the distance, admiring the sandy, scrubby surrounds and how different everything looked in the light of day.

What did look different, as in a hundred times better, was Chris Henderson. He whistled animatedly to the radio as he leaned over a map he had spread across the bonnet, the very bonnet he had slid my bikini bottoms off me on last night.

I blanched at the memory as my eyes wandered over the curve of pronounced muscle that flexed whenever Chris shifted, the same muscles I had explored only hours before with my hands and mouth. I shook my head, blinking away last night before I choked on my toothpaste. Now that would not be a good look.

I rinsed my mouth out, quickly spraying a zigzag line of Impulse body spray over me and dabbing on some strawberry Lip Smacker. I casually made my way around the front of the van, with a casual, no-big-deal attitude.

So we nearly had sex last night. That's what happens: people hook up and get on with it, people dream, people declare their love and then they wake up and start their day like normal. No big deal at all. Nope, nothing to write home about here; just a normal summer fling.

I stood by the side of the bonnet and leaned my elbows casually on its surface, hoping I didn't look too try-hard.

Chris's serious eyes flicked up to me with brief acknowledgement and then back to the map.

Hmm.

"I'm trying to see if there's a shorter route to Point Shank."

My heart pounded, worry licking at the edges of my overactive imagination.

"That keen to get rid of me, huh?" I teased, regretting the words as soon as they had fallen from my mouth, even more so when Chris's less-than-amused eyes flicked up to meet mine for a second before going straight back to the map.

He ignored me. "If we go this way it's about three hours." He traced his finger along a red line. "But if we go this way, we should be able to shave off about half an hour."

I nodded, looking at the map. It could have been a map of Berlin for all I knew. If I never reached Point Shank it really wouldn't have worried me; I would have forgone the seaside city famed for its New Year's Eve festival of bands and fireworks. I would sooner have stayed here, if we'd had the proper supplies like food, hair conditioner and condoms. This place would be paradise. But I knew we wouldn't stay.

I shrugged. "Which way is closest to food?"

That caused Chris's lips to tug into a crooked line. "This way." He pointed at the map.

I frowned. "The long way?"

Chris nodded.

Ha. What do you know, I was paying attention, I thought to myself proudly.

Chris folded up the map. "The long way it is."

"Oh, um, is that okay? I mean, we can go any way, it doesn't really matter. I can wait, I'm not that hungry. Seriously, go the shortcut if you want." I was babbling, I knew I was; it was a clear sign of my anxiety. It was like an out-of-body experience in that I could see myself and hear myself but I couldn't make myself stop.

Chris stared at me, amusement lining his face. He stepped forward and the subtle motion made me shut up instantly. Or it could have been the finger he placed on my lips.

My eyes narrowed but not because he had silenced me. I quite liked him touching my lips – it caused a familiar heat to flourish – but my eyes darted from his face up to his hair. I grabbed his wrist, drawing his hand away.

"Your hair's wet."

Chris ran his hand through his messy, damp hair. "Went for a morning dip. I didn't want to wake you."

Something inside me panged, annoyed at him for not waking me to freshen up with him before the last leg of the journey. The result had him looking like sex and sunshine, and I looked like sludge and death. So he had slept like a baby and had a morning dip. No wonder he was in such a jolly mood.

I crossed my arms, hoping I didn't appear as resentful as I felt; I didn't want to do an Amy and sulk for the rest of the trip.

"You talk in your sleep, you know." The words fell out of my big mouth.

Seriously, Tammy. Shut. Up.

Chris's brows rose in surprise. "Yeah? What did I say?"

I love you – I love you – I love …

I shrugged. "Just mumbling, mostly."

"Must have had something on my mind." He half laughed, moving around the car to put the map back into the glovebox. "You know what they say about dreams?"

I moved to the passenger door and opened it, listening with interest.

"No, what?" I asked.

"They say if you dream it, it won't come true."

I forced a smile on my face, trying to be pacified by Chris's words. I mean, great – so my teeth wouldn't fall out, but his words also hit a nerve in me.

Was this his way of covering himself? Maybe he remembered his dream last night and was just whacking a disclaimer on it, unsure of which part I had witnessed.

Either way, it wasn't the way I had wanted to leave our little paradise. There had really only been awkwardness on my end of things. Chris was so relaxed, with not even any acknowledgement over last night's heat between us; it was like it had never happened.

I didn't know how I felt about that. I had been dreading so much any potential 'talk' I might be faced with in the light of day, but now there was no recognition whatsoever, as though I had imagined the whole thing.

It made me feel a bit shitty. I know that's what happens with some boys – they hook up with a girl and then go about life again. I wasn't going to be a *Fatal Attraction*, bunny-boiling 'do you want to be my boyfriend?' psycho, but I had at least thought that the exchange between us last night had been real. Intense. I knew how he had made me feel and I knew he'd felt something too.

Or at least I thought I'd known.

Suddenly I was really relieved that we didn't have a condom, because if this was how I felt about him after just fooling around then I would have been a thousand times worse if we had slept together. It was a painful realisation. Things were different in the light of day, all right.

All I had to do was put on a brave face for the next three hours.

Crap!

"Why don't we take the short way?" I said.

Chris paused before sliding into the car. "Didn't you want something to eat?"

I looked out of the passenger window, trying to keep my emotions in check.

"It's okay; I'm not that hungry anymore."

Chapter Forty-Eight

The short way was both a blessing and a curse.

Although I had claimed to have lost my appetite, try telling my ravenous stomach that. I felt nauseated and was quiet throughout the trip. I didn't entirely know if it was because I was just hungry or because my insides were churning with anxiety and bitter disappointment. Considering I had dreaded our arrival at Point Shank only yesterday, now we couldn't get there soon enough even if it did mean having to face Toby and Ellie. I cared little now. I was over game players and the deception. Arriving at Point Shank meant that I would at least get a distraction and alternative company. As soon as possible I planned to give Chris some space and move into the 'singles' tent; I didn't want to be a needy nympho following him around.

Chris never asked why I was so quiet, which was more natural than anything. If there was one thing we had fallen into over the last three days it was the ability to have comfortable silences; it was one of the things I had liked most about us. Except now the silence hung in the air so thick you could carve it – for me, anyway. I was sure Chris was none the wiser over my whirring thoughts of inadequacy that only served to make me more miserable.

Over an hour into the journey we had managed to grab some

takeaway food and kept going toward Point Shank. Chris seemed anxious to keep up a quick pace and when we were a mere twenty minutes from Point Shank, Chris suddenly became fidgety and unsettled. He shifted in his seat, drummed the steering wheel and adjusted his side mirror several times. I had almost been tempted to tell him to settle down, but then the scenery changed and once again we were on the outskirts of civilisation, whirring past a mixture of shops, cafes and people. Finally we approached a sign that cemented where we were: 'Point Shank NYE Beach Bash' was scrawled across a giant banner, high above the main street. There was an air of excitement, a mass of people converging on a densely populated city to see in the New Year. We'd made it.

Having arrived early on New Year's Eve itself, it was a relief knowing that at least we would have time to unwind and settle in before the madness of tonight's festivities began.

Now for the first time I actually wished the others were here too. We had arrived early, so what would we do? Locate our campsite and sit in the van all day until the others caught up? My mind wickedly flashed to a way we could kill time, but I quickly stomped that out.

Yeah, that was not going to happen.

Considering we had spent a few nights in the solitude of quiet, bushy surrounds or coastal beach culs-de-sac, now we had hit Point Shank everything seemed … loud. And visually over-stimulating. There were shouts, 'woot's and screams from merry crowds of people lining the streets, enjoying their official last day of the twentieth century. We drove past a packed caravan park where tents were dotted side by side with barely a spare patch of grass in between. There were caravans, trailers, utes, boats and four-wheel drives cluttering every inch of the road; it took us every second of our free time to manoeuvre our way through the town.

My fantasies of Chris pulling off the main road and winding through side streets to take me to some undiscovered, secret location overlooking the ocean seemed less and less likely. My heart sank.

Maybe coming here was a bad idea?

I thought Chris would say as much, seeing as he was the one actually navigating through the chaos, but he didn't seem in the least bit fazed. If anything, he was excited. I then had visions of the boys wandering off tonight, partying into the New Year. What if Chris met some girl? What if he brought her back to the campsite – what then? Sleep toe to toe with Ellie?

I really had to shut my mind down.

"So, is the camping ground nearby?" I asked, hoping that the hill we were driving up was closing in on our destination. If nothing else, there would be facilities for a hot shower and a toilet that wasn't a bush. I was desperate for a real shower.

"Not exactly," Chris grimaced.

I straightened in my seat. "Oh?" I pressed, preparing myself for the bad news.

Only four more hours past Point Shank and we're there.

"We're not exactly 'in' a camping ground," said Chris.

"Sounds ominous."

"Oh, it is." Chris flashed me a bright, pearly smile that caused my traitorous heart to jump.

My hands became clammy – the possibility of no showers, no toilets, no privacy ran through my mind in a long line of hideous scenarios. This was originally an all-boys trip and roughing it to them was no big deal. And then my mind flashed back to the last conversation Chris had had with Sean before leaving the petrol station.

"All right, then, you know where we plan to meet up?" Sean had said.

"I know the place," Chris had replied.

"Remember?" Sean had then held a finger up to his lips and mimed 'not a word'.

Oh God. What kind of hellhole had they planned to take us to? Was this some form of punishment because we gatecrashed their road trip? Was it some kind of prank Sean wanted to play on Amy that we all had to suffer through? If I had dreaded arriving at Point Shank before, now I wanted to turn around and go back home without stopping.

"Okay, I'm scared," I admitted.

Chris laughed. "Oh relax, it's not that bad. It's just going to take some … adjusting to."

Oh God, it must *be bad.*

I gazed out toward a grassy embankment, divided by pavement then the sandy beach. By now I was all beached out; I was no longer bewitched by the beauty of it. If anything, I was filled with so much dread and anxiety, the blue water and golden sand just whizzed by in a blur. To think I could have painted my laundry by now and be helping Mum sell her clay vaginas at the market instead.

I had never thought that would be a more appealing option than road tripping with my friends.

My thoughts were jolted back to the present as Chris pulled off the road onto the side.

I sat patiently. He probably wanted to get something out of the back. I kept looking out of the window.

"What's wrong?" His voice snapped me away from the view.

"What?"

"You're disappointed?" he asked.

My eyes met his; was he asking about last night, or Point Shank? The last thing I wanted to do was be the whingy tag-along.

I swallowed, shaking my head. "No," I lied.

"Well, we're not far, so we can settle in and wait for the others," Chris sighed, tilting his head from side to side.

"Sounds like a plan." I tried to sound upbeat but I knew I was not pulling it off.

"God, my neck is killing me. I might get a massage," he said.

Was he asking me for a massage? Is that what he was hinting at?

"Where do you suppose I could pay for one?"

No, he wasn't asking me for one.

"I don't like your chances of finding anywhere on New Year's Eve," I said.

"Maybe, but I think any place with complimentary fluffy white robes and room service should be able to offer something. I don't know, someplace … well … like that." Chris pointed over the road. There was a massive, sprawling, sandstone-coloured resort, lined with palm trees and a giant waterfall feature illuminated with coloured lighting that read 'Point Shank Beach Resort'.

"You can't just walk in off the street and ask for a massage." I frowned.

"Why not?" Chris asked in all seriousness.

"Because you can't."

"Well, it's worth a try; we have some hours to kill. Don't you want a massage?" He pulled the van back out onto the road, indicating a turn into the expansive driveway.

"Not at the risk of getting laughed out of the reception."

"Don't be dramatic."

It was the equivalent to a slap in the face, and my blood boiled at his ignorance.

"The fact that you're a part owner of a hotel mean it's absolutely mind boggling that you don't get how wrong you are," I argued.

Chris defiantly steered into the driveway, the thrumming sounds of the V8 engine echoing as we drove under the resort's sweeping awning.

We so didn't belong here. I wanted to shrink into my seat.

"You are so embarrassing." I smiled politely at the doorman who tried not to look over our car with judgemental eyes.

Chris killed the engine. "How about this: if you're right and they turn me away, I'll give you a massage. But if they say 'Of course, Mr Henderson, welcome to Point Shank Beach Resort, please follow me to your masseur,' then you have to give me a massage on top of my massage." He held out his hand.

He thought he was so clever.

I straightened in my seat. "I am going to so look forward to that massage." I took his hand and yanked it with all my strength.

"Deal."

We both exited the car, offering each other knowing smirks. For someone who ran a business he really didn't have a clue. The doorman opened the door for us.

"Good afternoon," he smiled brightly.

Chris stopped next to him. "Tell me something…" His eyes lowered to the man's name badge. "Graham, do you offer massages here?"

Graham nodded animatedly. "Oh yes, sir, we have a very luxurious day spa."

Chris flashed me a bright white smile. "Excellent."

I rolled my eyes and followed Chris through the door that Graham held open for us.

The first thing that hit me was the chill of the powerful air conditioning, followed by the high, cathedral-style ceilings with luxurious chandeliers that cast a bright glow across the reception's polished surfaces and the reflective gloss of the marble tiles.

Chris and I stood in the middle of the massive reception area: me in my denim shorts, singlet and bird's nest-like hair; Chris in his white T and cargos. We definitely didn't belong here, although you wouldn't have thought it by all the warm smiles every passing member of staff gave us.

We were called up to the main desk, something I was both dreading and looking forward to.

"Welcome to Point Shank Beach Resort, how can I help?" An immaculately kept woman, hair slicked back in a shiny bun, with bright red lipstick, bright sparkling eyes and a figure to die for flashed a winning smile. She made me feel like a gutter rat as I self-consciously tucked a stray hair into place.

"I was just wondering, we have just arrived in Point Shank and we're looking for a place we could get a massage. We have been on the road for three days and had some time to kill and thought we might try our luck." Chris had spoken every word with a sexy grin across his face as he looked Wonder Woman directly in the eyes and pleaded his sad case.

I sighed, amazed at how easily he could turn on the charm

when he wanted. More importantly, I braced myself for the answer. The answer that I knew would come, and it did.

I saw it the second her head tilted and her high-wattage smile dimmed a little. "Oh, I'm sorry, sir, but the facilities are reserved for guests only."

Yes!

I grinned so broadly I almost wanted to break out into a dance, chanting, "I told you so, I told you so."

Chris's smile evaporated. He shifted uneasily as he glanced at my big, toothy grin with annoyance. Wonder Woman's eyes passed from Chris to me, probably thinking we were a pair of weirdos, but her professionalism never faltered, not once.

He cleared his throat. "I see."

"Is there anything else I can help you with today, sir? Maybe help yourself to some brochures on the local establishments."

"No, that's okay. Actually, um, there is something else you can help me with."

Chris pulled out his wallet from his back pocket, taking out a white square piece of paper and unfolding it.

Ugh, he was probably asking for directions to our site. I yawned, folding my arms, and admired the decadent display of flowers sitting on the marbled desk.

Chris slid the paper over. "We have a booking for a party of nine, under Sean Murphy."

WHAT?

I spun around so quickly I almost knocked over the massive flower arrangement.

"What did you just say?" I breathed.

Chris smiled, reached out, and swept a loose tendril of hair out of the way of my wild, shocked eyes.

"Welcome to Point Shank."

Chapter Forty-Nine

We followed the porter down a long, carpeted corridor. I half expected a camera crew to appear from behind a pot plant, announcing I was on candid camera. My eyes skimmed every angle of the luxury digs.

"Are you okay?" asked Chris as he walked by my side.

My mouth gaped as I tried to summon the words; I had been stunned into silence since Chris had booked us in. After his massage ruse I feared I would never believe another word he said.

"What are we doing here?" I laughed, my insides twisting with giddiness every step we took down the hall.

"We thought that seeing as you girls would be roughing it to get here the least we could do would be to end the trip with a bit of luxury. It was Sean's idea."

"Do the others know?"

"The boys do. We wanted it to be a surprise; I think it's been the most difficult secret to keep in the history of mankind."

Chris looked at the room key card he held in his hand. "Here's your room."

I danced on the balls of my feet as Chris tipped the porter to leave the luggage. Chris couldn't open the door quickly enough. He slid the key card into the slot and the magical green light flashed in unison with Chris's smile.

"You ready?"

"Open-open-open!" I clapped.

There is always that moment of wonder when you enter a spectacular room, and after three nights sleeping in the back of a panel van, the apartment I stepped into was as luxurious to me as the Taj Mahal. Glossy white tiles, sleek, modern and massive. I ran from room to room turning on lights, inspecting cupboards and announcing every discovery.

"There's a spa! This one's got an en suite ...Whoa, check out the kitchen!"

There were three bedrooms, two bathrooms, a huge open living space, a dining room and a sliding wall of glass that led out onto a balcony overlooking the ocean.

I pressed myself against the glass. "Oh my God, Chris!"

I turned to see him watching me with a glimmer of amusement as he set our bags down. "You approve?"

Did I approve? I had expected the pits of fiery hell, not a clean, crisp paradise.

"I *so* approve," I said, running over to him and throwing my arms around his neck.

I looked up into Chris's eyes. "It's a fantastic surprise."

Chris sobered as he studied the lines of my face; his eyes flicked to my mouth for such a brief second that I almost missed it. He still held me, his hand resting on my lower back. I so wanted to kiss him. My eyes strayed to his mouth, not caring if he caught the unmistakable moment of distraction. He had a beautiful mouth that did wicked things, and although last night had probably meant nothing more than just a bit of fun, I really wanted to do it again.

"I think you're forgetting one thing," he said, causing my eyes to snap back up to his.

"What's that?" I asked.

Chris leaned forward, his lips brushed against my ear and I felt my skin tingle.

"Running. Hot. Water."

Reclining in the huge, blistering hot corner spa with my hair completely caked in so much conditioner it was pure white, I channel flicked through my TV.

Yeah. There was totally a TV in the bathroom. I had changed it onto the music channel where Cindy Lauper was crooning 'Girls Just Wanna Have Fun'.

Yeah, they did!

I bit a chunk out of the strawberry that was wedged on the side of my champagne glass, like any classy chick would, and mused how very Julia Roberts this all was, à la *Pretty Woman.* Minus the whole being a paid escort thing, of course.

I had emerged from the bathroom wrapped in large white towels, one around me and one around my head.

"Chris?" I called down the hall. He'd said he would be back in five, that he was going to check out the others' apartments, but I had definitely been in the bathroom for longer than that and expected him to be in the lounge where the TV had been left blaring.

"Hello?" I looked around the apartment.

There was a notepad and pen left on the kitchen bench.

I spun it around, reading Chris's neat handwriting.

Check the main bedroom.

I read it over three times, every time my heart rate elevating and the same insecure girl clawing her way to the surface, turning me into a puddle of nerves. I took in a deep breath and made my way up the hall to the master bedroom, clasping my towel around me tightly before remembering the turban-esque wrap on top of my hair.

Shit! Not a good look.

I unwrapped it from my head and scurried back to the bathroom, throwing it onto the floor. I quickly wiped the foggy mirror and checked my complexion. I ran my brush through my hair before bending over and flicking it back and forth two to three times for that natural, tousled look.

"Okay," I sighed, looking at my reflection and giving myself a pep talk. "Let's go."

The walk down the hall was so incredibly long. The downlights lit the tiles that were cool underfoot. Of course, the main bedroom door was last. I stopped at the door and took a deep breath before I grabbed the gold handle, twisting and pushing it open.

I paused in the doorway, firstly confused until I switched the light on, illuminating the room and causing me to burst out into laughter. I cupped my hand over my mouth, trying to muffle the sound of hysterics as I edged closer to the bed, hardly believing what was laid out on the bed.

No, it wasn't Chris like I had hoped; instead lay a plush, fluffy white robe, the kind Chris had spoken about. I bit my lip, and shook my head. He was turning out to be quite the practical joker.

By the time Chris had returned, I was on the rather generous balcony in my fluffy robe, enjoying the ocean views. I heard him enter and smiled to myself, keeping my focus on the waves.

"Nice robe," he said as he settled in the seat beside me.

"What, this old thing?" I tugged at the neatly tied bow.

"Feel better?"

"Almost human."

"Well, enjoy the serenity while you can; the others are on their way. I just spoke to Sean on the phone."

I shifted upright in my seat. "How's Ringer?"

Chris smirked. "According to the staff at outpatients, he is a complete pain in the arse, so, yeah, sounds normal to me. He got eight stitches."

"Are they still coming?"

"Yeah, they're on their way, too, but they won't get here till later tonight."

"Well, we will have to make a big fuss over him when he arrives."

"Yeah, he'll hate every minute of that," Chris said with a laugh. "I hope you bagsed the best room?"

"Indeed I have: master bedroom with en suite." I beamed.

Chris grimaced. "Ellie won't like that."

And with that, all good humour evaporated. "Who's staying in this apartment?"

Chris watched me with interest. "You, Ellie, Toby and Tess, I think. Sean and Amy are sharing with Bel and Stan, and I'm shacked up with Ringer and Adam. Why?"

I'd had no idea that paradise could turn into hell in the span of two seconds, but it just had. Me, Ellie, Toby and Tess all sharing the same apartment? Now that's what you called a Love Shack.

Chris touched my knee. "Tam? What's wrong?"

I looked at him, his eyes narrowed in concern. How could I tell him? How could I complain when all the boys had done their adorable best to surprise us all? How could I be so ungrateful as to complain about my roomies? But how could I also expect myself to cohabitate with them, knowing what I knew?

I couldn't do it; I couldn't live with the very people I was aiming to confront, whose lives I was potentially going to destroy. I couldn't. Not even for just one night.

"Can I stay with you?" I blurted out. "Or can you stay here? Or I don't, I just want, or rather … stay, please?" I was pathetic, a rambling idiot and I half expected Chris's expression to reflect as such, but it didn't. Instead, his dark, broody stare narrowed in a steely gaze.

"Who do you want moved?" he asked, his words dripping with icy intent.

I broke from his gaze. "Ellie," I said lowly, looking down at my hands, almost ashamed I was asking without telling him why.

After a long, drawn-out moment, he said, "Okay."

Without another word or, like always, never even wanting to know the reason why, Chris got up from his chair and left me on the balcony, his footsteps disappearing down the hall before finally I heard the sound of the apartment door.

What must he think of me?

Chapter Fifty

I couldn't even bear to be wearing my robe anymore.

I felt like an utter coward, an ungrateful coward. I wanted to go and pound on Chris's door and blab everything. Tell him exactly why I had wanted to leave without the others, why I couldn't stand to be anywhere near Ellie, but that, above all, the one constant in this whole trip was the complete, unexpected joy of the past three days with him. The person I had nearly made love to last night; the one I still wanted to. And I didn't want to give him up.

I paced the up and down the hall, plagued by the actual problem of not knowing where the boys' apartment was. Of all the times to have the sudden compulsion to confess everything, it had to be the rare moment that Chris wasn't around.

I figured I could find out where he was at reception, so grabbed my key card. I marched for the front door and slammed right into Chris with a yelp. He grabbed my elbows to steady me and I clutched at my chest in surprise.

"I didn't hear you come in," I breathed out, my heart throbbing in my chest.

"You were kind of preoccupied," he said, throwing his key card on the bench.

"Chris, I have to tell you something." I wrung my hands anxiously together.

His gaze burned into me so intently I almost forgot what I was meant to be saying.

He shook his head slightly. "Don't."

I was the one now staring intently at him. "Don't what?"

"Don't tell me," he said.

"Well, you don't know what I have to tell you."

"Is it about you?" he asked.

"Well, no, not really."

"Is it about me?"

"No."

"Then I don't want to know."

Wow.

So much for the pep talk and making myself feel better. I had anticipated pouring my heart and soul out to him, and he would reassure me that no matter what, everything would be okay. There may have been some embracing and heavy pashing in my daydream, too.

But, instead, he had said, "I don't want to know."

I felt a bit gobsmacked, and, to be honest, a bit pissed off.

"Wow, thanks, great pep talk," I said, coolly brushing past him before stopping just before the hallway.

I turned back around to face him. "Do you trust Toby?"

Chris's gaze was so piercing, so intimidating I almost wished I had never asked.

"With my life."

He didn't even think about his answer. It was an honest one. Was the bro code blind to all things? I wasn't sure and I wouldn't find out – not from Chris, anyway.

Soon the others would be here and our time alone would come to an end as we were engulfed by the loud, excited reunion.

I would go back to being on the outer – more so than ever now, as I felt so uncomfortable and awkward around Ellie and Tess. Although things hadn't automatically been awkward from first thing this morning, things would be heading in that direction, and I didn't know how to claw my way back.

There was no better way of killing time than drawing the blinds and falling into the welcoming abyss of sleep, nestled on top of a queen-sized bed. The utter bliss of allowing my tense muscles to melt into the soft mattress was exactly what I needed. What I didn't need, however, was to be jolted awake by a loud scream and slammed into by a large flying weight that bounced up and down on the bed beside me.

"OH MY GOD, TAMMY!!!!"

Bounce-bounce-bounce.

Amy?

The light switch flicked on-off-on-off-on before another body sailed through the air and slammed onto the mattress, singing horribly out of tune.

Off the Florida Keys
There's a place called Kokomo
That's where you want to go
To get away from it all …

Sean.

"Get off!" I pushed them away but it was like pushing at two boulders.

Amy dropped on her side, laughing like a maniac; Sean still lay across my legs, pinning me to the mattress.

"Not bad, huh?" He smiled.

I shook my head. "You're a crafty devil, Sean Murphy."

"Indeed," he said, getting up off the bed. "My job here is done – you're awake." He dusted his hands and disappeared out of the door.

Amy lay next to me on her side, resting her head casually on her hand as she watched him go.

"God, I love that man," she said dreamily. "I have never felt more loved and so blessed than I do having him in my life."

It was a surprisingly candid and heartfelt admission from Amy – so touching to hear her say that.

I would have smiled had I not taken it upon myself at that very moment to burst into tears.

Amy sat up like she had received an electric shock. "Hey, hey – Tammy, what's wrong?" She pulled my hands away from my face.

I shook my head, trying to shrug her insistent hands away. I felt so stupid.

Amy scrambled off the bed and quickly shut the door, before moving to sit by my side.

"Hun, what's wrong?" she asked, brushing the hair away from my face as I hugged my pillow.

I didn't know how to answer that.

Nothing? Everything?

I really didn't know myself, which only made me even more miserable as the sobs hitched at the bottom of my throat.

Amy's chin wobbled. "Tammy, don't cry, please don't, it's going to be all right," she said soothingly, rubbing my back.

There was a knock on the door before it opened a crack and Toby stuck his head in. It only took him a second to realise that it really wasn't a good time.

"Oh, sorry, I didn't mean to ..." he stammered. "I just wanted to ask Tammy for my shoes." He grimaced, as if he really hated to ask.

It was the final nail in the coffin of my pity party as I wailed into my pillow, my shoulders convulsing. I'd completely lost it.

"I'll, um ... I'll come back later." Toby closed the door quickly.

Amy rubbed my back more urgently now, as she shushed me and spoke gentle, soothing words like a best friend should. She also gave up asking questions; instead, she did the one thing I needed. She moved quietly to turn off the light and gently crawled into the bed, shuffling into the space behind my back, sliding her arm around me securely.

"It's going to be okay," she whispered. "I'm here now."

The next time I awoke was less of a rude awakening. I woke

naturally and rubbed at my sore, swollen eyes before rolling onto my back, expecting to find Amy there. But she was gone. She had probably waited for her psychotic friend to cry herself to sleep, and crept out of the room wishing she had left me behind in Onslow.

I dragged myself out of bed, never having been more thankful for having my own en suite bathroom. I looked at my puffy, bloodshot eyes in the reflection and saw a stranger. I saw a girl so full of misery and self-pity it made my stomach turn. This was what Amy had found. She had no doubt been just as surprised as I had been when Sean pulled into the drive; she had no doubt, in true Amy style, raced up to my apartment to jump around and celebrate with me to share the excitement. Instead, she had found a crumpled mess, crying in her plush suite, offering no more explanation than cryptic sobs.

That wasn't fair. She must have been so worried.

Tonight was the night. It really was; it was the last night of 1999 before the clock ticked over to a new millennium. It would probably be the last time any of us would go on a trip like this together, and after I confronted the people I needed to, it would probably be the last time we were even in the same room together. Things would never be the same again. I just had to work out when to do it.

I either ruined their lives this year, or next year. Neither option was fantastic.

As I washed my face and stared at my sullen reflection in the mirror, I made up my mind.

One more night.

One more night of living the lie, one more night in which we were together, all friends, under the belief that life was grand and weren't we lucky. Yes, one more night to kiss it all goodbye. It was rather poetic really; as we would count down to a new beginning, a new millennium, everyone would be none the wiser that it was all about to end.

Maybe Chris could have been prepared if he hadn't drawn the ignorance-is-bliss card, the one that had made me so furious it probably explained my tears more than anything else.

I had put too much hope in Chris, hope that I could share the burden of Toby and Ellie's secret, that Chris would be there when I needed him most.

But he wasn't.

Before any of this I had been an intelligent, driven person who didn't define herself by anyone else, but during this trip I had become a lovesick mess, dependent on the whims of a sullen, stubborn man. That intelligent, independent woman was still in me, I knew she was, but the person I saw now was more like the insecure, frizzy-haired, invisible girl from long ago.

I don't think so.

I squared my shoulders, delved into my make-up bag and applied some bronzer, lip balm and a touch of mascara – not even waterproof mascara. Now I really *couldn't* shed any more tears.

I ran a brush through my long, light golden brown hair and swept it over one shoulder.

That was better. I felt better by simply looking less pitiful. I hoped that I looked less like I had in the foetal position in a blubbering mess and more like a diva ready to count down to the year 2000. Okay, so I would never be a diva, but at the very least my mind's position for the night was to party like it was 1999.

Chapter Fifty-One

I made my way into the living room and conversation immediately came to a halt.

Awkward.

Ellie, Amy and Tess were all lounging around on the couches with champagne flutes in hand. The boys were nowhere to be seen.

"Hey, Tim-Tam." Ellie jumped up, bouncing her way over to me, embracing me with a hug. I stiffened against her hug. This pretending everything was fine for the night was going to be really hard.

"Hey." I smiled, hoping it seemed real.

"Can you believe this place?" She beamed.

"What I can't believe is that Adam kept a secret," Tess said, moving past Ellie and hugging me.

"Are you okay?" She squeezed me tight.

"Yeah, fine."

Okay, this was going to be really, really *hard.*

"True," laughed Ellie as she topped up her champagne glass. "He is a shocker for keeping secrets."

Unlike you.

"Where are the boys?" I asked as Amy passed me a glass of champagne.

"Probably bonding in the bar," said Tess, "but I think we will allow that." She winked.

"Hells yeah, they can do whatever they like," Ellie said. "They've earned enough brownie points for the next millennium. Cheers, ladies, here's to this year and the next." Ellie held up her flute.

"Cheers!"

We all clinked our glasses together, followed by me sculling mine and holding my flute out for more, much to the amazement of the others.

"Go, Tammy!" laughed Tess.

Yep, everyone was buying it. Good. I sculled my next glass and glanced at Amy mid-gulp; she looked less than happy about my party-girl attitude.

After downing the last of the champagne from my glass, I clinked it down on the kitchen bench with a gasp of satisfaction.

"Let's order room service!"

Come seven o'clock and four empty plates of chocolate mud cake, we decided to think about tonight's wardrobe.

"Oh my God, I almost forgot," said Tess as she jumped out of her chair and ran down the hall.

I looked around at the others. They shrugged and shook their heads, obviously none the wiser, either. I heard the rustling of a plastic bag long before Tess reappeared with something behind her back.

"Bell gave this to me before she left Evoka, just in case she didn't make it here." Tess smiled at me. "Close your eyes."

"Um, okay …" I said, obeying.

"Hold out your hands."

I did as she asked, waiting anxiously as she gently placed a plastic bag onto my waiting hands. They dipped slightly under the delicate weight.

"Okay. Open them." Tess clapped.

I opened my eyes to find, yep, a white plastic bag. I peered inside.

"You have got to be kidding me."

"What? What is it?" Amy sidled up next to me.

I shook my head. "It's official, I am completely in love with Bell," I said laughing, as I turfed the bag upside down and a bundle of fabric spilled onto the floor.

The dress from Evoka Springs.

"Oooh, pretty. What is that?" Tess asked.

"I tried this on at the hippy shop in Evoka. I really liked it but I put it back on the rack," I said, rubbing the soft, layered fabric between my fingers.

Ellie's eyes lit up. "That is so what you're wearing tonight."

I stood and held the long skirt to my hips, musing about how I didn't buy it because I didn't want to stand out. I was afraid about what others might think, but so much had changed in two short days and now I wanted to wear it more than ever.

"I feel a fashion parade coming on," announced Amy.

"Quick! Before the boys get back," said Tess.

"Crap! Wait for me – I'll have to grab my stuff from my room," said Amy as she dodged past a coffee table.

"Me too." Ellie followed her out of the room.

Tess stopped mid-step into her room, confusion lining her face. "Ellie, where are you crashing tonight?"

"Ugh! I've been checked into the honeymoon suite with Sean, Amy, Stan and Bell. As if that's not going to be awkward," said Ellie, rolling her eyes.

"Hey, we're not that bad," Amy said, glowering, by the front door.

"As long as you don't keep me awake with your kissy-kissy noises all night," Ellie said as she followed her out of the door. It swung shut with a heavy bang behind them.

So it seemed Chris had made arrangements for Ellie to be placed in their apartment before they had arrived. It had been the last conversation we had had. I cringed at how pathetic I had been, how needy, how pitiful I was when I had asked him to stay. But I didn't see him coming to sleep in the now spare room. As far as I knew he was still sharing an apartment with Adam and Ringer tonight. I was grateful that he had organised it, yet it was still a rather anticlimactic ending to what had been a trip full of surprises.

Since the boys were catching up in the bar, us girls swanned about getting ready. It wasn't a completely awful situation, aside from being stuck between Tess and Ellie and not knowing where to look.

"The honeymoon suite? Poor Ellie." Tess pouted as we went to the main bathroom with our arms full of make-up and hair product.

Yeah, poor Ellie, I thought. If only Tess knew.

It didn't take Amy and Ellie long before they were knocking on the door to be let back in. I opened the door and they walked in with clothes draped over their shoulders and make-up bags in hand, arguing over the gripping subject of whether to wear their hair up or down.

"Well, I'm going for down," declared Ellie as she padded her way to share the bathroom with Tess. I watched her and wondered how she could even sleep at night, how she could be so casual about betraying her best friend and lying to her face.

"You okay?" Amy touched my hand, breaking me from my death stare.

"Oh, yeah, fine." I tried for an airy shrug-off, but Amy was not buying it for a second.

"Well, you weren't quite fine an hour ago."

"I think I was just overtired," I said, avoiding eye contact.

"Oh, well, if that's all it was I kind of feel bad about abusing Chris now."

My eyes snapped up to meet hers. "What?"

"Well, what was I meant to do? You weren't talking and there was only one person who could have made you so upset and that was my idiot cousin. So I may or may not have ripped him a new one."

"You know, when you say I may or may not have, it usually means you did."

"Well, yeah, I totally did." She grimaced.

"Ammmyyyy," I groaned and thumped the back of my head against the hall wall. "He would have had no idea what you were talking about."

"I don't know about that. When I told him how upset you were, he seemed really concerned; it took all my strength to stop him from marching to your room and kicking the door down to see if you were all right."

I inwardly cringed. *Why? Why did she have to tell him about my meltdown? He probably thought I was some oversensitive clingy girl, flipping through bridal magazines and picking out names for our children.*

"Yeah, well, I don't see him breaking down the door to check on me now," I said, my heart sinking a little.

"After the tongue-lashing I gave him, don't be surprised if he gives you some space tonight."

"Ta-DA!" Ellie jumped into the room wearing her tight, electric blue '80s dress with shoulder pads that would make Joan Collins envious. Ellie sashayed her best runway walk down the hall.

"What do you think?" she asked as she cocked her hip, did the three-second pouty stare off into the make-believe crowd before turning and criss-crossing her legs as she swayed her hips back down the hall.

"I thought you were going to take the shoulder pads out," said Amy.

Ellie peered at her shoulder. "They are ludicrously huge, aren't they? But I don't know, they are kind of growing on me."

"Well, be prepared for Adam to give you shit about them for the entire night, then," Amy warned.

"What else is new?" Ellie said, rolling her eyes.

A knock sounded on the door and Ellie froze mid-stride, her eyes bugging out. "Wait, don't let them in," she squealed and ran to hide in the bathroom as best she could in her skin-tight dress.

A part of me wanted to follow her and hide in the bathroom

too, my heart slamming violently against the wall of my chest. I knew Amy had meant well but she had turned an already awkward situation with Chris into … Well … I guessed I would find out.

As Amy headed for the door, I straightened and lifted my chin.

Remember, Tammy: positive!

Amy squinted through the spy hole before she looked at me with surprise.

"It's Chris and Toby."

Holy shit!

"Wait-wait-wait, don't open the door," I whispered to Amy as I quick-stepped down the hall.

"Where are you going?" laughed Amy.

"I'm getting ready. No! I'm asleep. No! I'm in the shower … No-no, I'm, I'm …"

Amy wound her hands in a circle as if to say spit it out. A fist pounded on the door again, making me jump.

"Just go." Amy ushered me away. "I'll say you're on the phone, or trapped under a vending machine or something."

I was going to argue but Amy was already opening the door. I dived into my room and slammed the door behind me, pressing my back against it, trying to still my breath.

Who was avoiding who now?

Chapter Fifty-Two

I was a prisoner.

Sitting on the edge of my bed with my hands neatly clasped in my lap, I heard voices and laughter in the living room. Ellie, Amy and Tess were being sociable; I was the only weirdo who refused to come out and say hello.

I should have gone out and said hello; I was being rude and weird. Regardless of what Amy had said I should have just gone out and pretended everything was okay.

I stood and wiped my clammy hands on my skirt, took in a deep breath. I rested my hand on the gold door handle.

Everything was clearly not okay.

The room would be filled with Toby, Tess, Ellie and Chris, and Amy would burn her speculative gaze into my temple.

And what if Toby was here to pick up his shoes? Just as I was about to back away from the door, the voices in the other room became louder, making their way up toward the hall again. I dared not move (okay, I moved enough to press my ear up against the door).

This is what I had resorted to.

"Well, come down when you're ready, we'll just be in the bar," I heard Chris say.

"Of course you will," scoffed Amy.

Silence.

"She still on the phone?" asked Chris.

"Uh, yeah, must be," Amy said.

Silence.

"Okay! Well, see ya down there," Amy's voice went up a few stress-induced octaves; I had visions of her pushing them out of the door, which was probably what must have happened because when I heard the click of the door shutting my shoulders sagged with relief.

I blew out a long breath and ripped the door open.

"Thank God! I thought they would never lea—"

I froze in the doorway, my eyes locking with Chris's as he leaned on the opposite wall, arms folded across his chest.

Busted.

He cocked his brow with interest. "You were saying?"

My mouth gaped and I looked to Amy for an explanation. She stared at the floor, walls, the ceiling – anywhere but at me.

"I'm so sorry," she mouthed.

Betrayal was a bitter pill to swallow. Still, I didn't have to wonder too hard to guess how it had come about. Chris would have tilted his head for Toby to go out of the door then looked at Amy and pressed his finger against his lips as he motioned for her to shut the door. Then he leaned against the wall opposite my door. I didn't even give him time to settle in and get comfy as it had taken me all of 1.5 seconds to come bursting out.

My brows knitted together as I stared, not at Amy, but locked my eyes firmly on Chris whose own burning gaze darkened as the defiant staring competition began.

Amy shuffled awkwardly next to Chris. "Um, I'll give you two a minute."

I could feel her wanting to grab my attention, for me to give her a nod of forgiveness, but I couldn't break eye contact from Chris; I didn't even so much as bat an eyelid.

"All righty, then," she breathed as she slowly backed away. "I'll just leave you two to it, then."

So he was here and he was pissed off. I could tell that Chris Henderson, a man of few words, was itching to say something. It was as if I could hear the cogs of speculation turning inside his head.

Well, let him speculate. He could stew about it and wonder why I was avoiding him as long as he wanted; it was probably the very question that was dancing on the tip of his tongue.

Just as I was about to speak, Chris pushed himself off the wall and strode over to me.

He grabbed my upper arm and pulled me through the doorway of the bedroom and kicked the door shut behind us. I was barely able to gather my thoughts as Chris pressed me against the back of the door and claimed my mouth in a hot, mind-bending kiss. His lips were demanding, firm, slow, coaxing mine to open for him. I was unable to move, enticingly ensnared by him as his scorching kiss robbed me of all thought, all breath.

He broke away, breathing hard as he stared down at me and gently swept a lock of hair off my brow.

His mouth curved in triumph. "Snap out of it, Maskala." His voice was raw, disjointed, but it was still filled with cockiness as he reached for the door handle. I stumbled aside, my legs like jelly. I touched my lips, staring after him as he made his way to the front door and left without a backward glance.

What the hell was that?

Amy's eyes narrowed with worry as soon as they had locked onto me when I entered the kitchen.

She stopped mid-pour of juice into her glass. "Are you mad?" she asked.

Was I mad?

I had just had the most intensely hot pash of my life, a mind-blowing moment that had ended way too soon. My mind was still in a fog, my thoughts fragmented into a million different hazy pieces. Mad? I was *so* not mad.

I pulled out a kitchen stool on the opposite side of the breakfast bar, trying to keep myself from smiling dreamily.

"Tammy Maskala, you have to spill. Now."

My eyes blinked in Amy's direction. "Sorry?"

Amy's lips quivered. "What is going on with you these days? I'm your best friend and I feel like I don't know about anything in your life anymore."

I wanted to deny it, to tell Amy she was exaggerating, but I knew she was right. Of course she was – I had been more guarded than ever these last couple of days and I couldn't explain to her why.

If Amy was truly my best friend, I would tell her the things that plagued my thoughts. The complexities in my so-called love life, the burden of Toby and Ellie's secret – I would, I *should* tell her about it all. But I didn't want to; I wanted to keep it locked away and not talk about the things that worried me.

Then why had I wanted to tell Chris? Ha! That had worked out so well.

"I'm sorry, I just don't know where my head's at lately," I lied.

Amy reached out and touched my hand. "Well, tell me where it's at and I might be able to help."

I laughed. "I wouldn't even know where to begin."

Amy walked around the breakfast bar and propped herself on the stool beside me. "How about we start with Chris?"

She leaned on the counter, holding her chin in her hand as if settling in for the long haul.

So I did it – I unpacked all my emotions and all my frustrations and, to my surprise, something I had never voiced before, not even to myself.

"I like Chris," I said. "I really, really like Chris."

Amy rolled her eyes. "Tell me something I don't know."

That was a surprise. To me, voicing that very thing was an admission of epic proportions. I had kind of expected more shock, more excitement, maybe. But it *was* Amy I was talking to.

I decided to disclose only the things that affected me directly, and tried to ignore the echoed laughter from the spare bathroom as Tess helped Ellie to straighten her hair. I really tried to ignore it.

"So, what are you going to do about loving Chris Henderson?" Amy grinned as she sipped on her drink, a mischievous glint in her eye.

I sighed and shook my head.

Loving Chris Henderson would be wrong. I mean, what was there about him to love? He was moody, bossy, a control freak, and that was on a good day. But there was one achingly obvious fact that haunted my every thought, every minute of every day …

The man sure could kiss.

Chapter Fifty-Three

Apparently I had to cut the shit and take control.

"I'm serious, Tammy, tonight's the night. You have to seize the moment, tell Chris how you feel and just lay it all on the line. He likes you back, I know he does."

From the moment I had finally confessed I liked Chris, Amy had nearly drowned me in these speeches. I think she was quite liking being able to do the 'best friend' advice thing.

"Ow! Amy, watch it." I tilted my head to the side, wincing as she jabbed a bobby pin into my skull.

"Sorry. Anyway, seriously. Men are not complicated." She reached for another pin from her make-up bag.

"We *are* talking about Chris," I said. "I think he invented complicated."

"There!" Amy stood back and admired her handiwork. "What do you think?"

I looked at my reflection, smiling at the unfamiliarity of my long hair cascading down my shoulders in tousled waves. She had pinned back the longer wisps of my fringe and dotted my hair with pins that shone with diamantes. I tilted my head from side to side, looking at it from every angle.

"I love it!"

Amy beamed. "You're going to look so hot!"

"All right, who's next?" asked Ellie as she walked into the bathroom. She slammed her giant make-up case down on the counter.

"Do Tammy. I have to go make sure my outfit doesn't smell like mothballs." Amy skipped out of the bathroom.

"Oh, it's okay," I said, "you don't have to do my make-up." I started to get up from the edge of the bath.

"Don't be silly," Ellie said, pushing me back down, "it's what I do. Now, first we're going to cleanse and tone."

I bit my lip, feeling increasingly uncomfortable whenever I was around Ellie. I gritted my teeth as she worked with expert hands to clean and swab my face.

"You have the most beautiful skin. Must be all the water you drink."

Every sentence was said more to herself than to me, because I didn't respond.

At the end, when she was gently applying the finishing glossy layer to my lips, she said, "Pout, like this." She pulled her lips inward as an example of what she wanted me to do. "That's it." She gently slid the wand over my lips, before stepping back and tilting her head with a brilliant smile. "My finest work yet. Of course, it helps when I'm working with someone as gorgeous as you." She winked.

I wanted to hate Ellie, to openly scoff and scowl at all her words and flinch against every touch, but it was impossible. No matter what higher moral ground I chose to stomp on, one thing was clear: I couldn't hate her, and it utterly killed me.

"Take a look," she said with pride, motioning me toward the mirror.

I stood, expecting to see hooker-red lipstick and overly blushed cheekbones. Instead, to my utmost surprise, the make-up Ellie had used was all bronzes and natural tones. I leaned in closer to inspect the flawless job of glossy golden shades that highlighted my eyes and brought out the contours of my face. I looked amazing.

Damn her, she even did fantastic make-up.

Ellie squeezed my shoulders. "Chris's jaw is going to hit the floor when he sees you tonight." She beamed.

My eyes locked with hers in the reflection, narrowing in confusion.

She shrugged. "Oh please, everyone knows."

I turned to face her. "Everyone knows what?"

"Well, there is obviously something going on between you two. I think it's great." She smiled brightly.

Under normal circumstances I probably would have giggled and confided in her about what had happened these last few days. But, try as I might, even though I enjoyed her company, was entertained by her careless charm and, yes, her ability to apply flawless make-up, resentment still churned in the pit of my stomach and although I had promised myself just *one more night* of carefree, normality and fun, I couldn't stop myself from what I was about to do.

"I'm on to you, you know," I said coolly, causing Ellie's big blue eyes to lock onto mine, the sparkle fading.

"What?" she breathed out, as if the mere weight of my words had knocked the wind out of her.

"Just do me a favour, okay? Just stop acting like everything is okay, because it's insulting."

Ellie gaped; she stammered trying to find some words, but whatever it was she wanted to say, I didn't want to hear it.

"Thanks for the make-up," I said emotionlessly. I walked out of the bathroom, my hands balling into fists at my sides, trying to disguise the tremor. It was a step forward. A step toward the confrontation that had to happen, that would change everything. I felt sick.

What had I done?

Well, one thing was for sure, I didn't have to worry about feeling awkward around Ellie anymore, because she avoided me like the plague. She had come out of the bathroom all flushed, walked a direct line to the spare room and closed the door.

"Hurry up, Ellie, we're heading down soon," called Amy before fixing her gaze onto me.

"Bloody hell, Tammy, get dressed already!" She motioned me back into the bedroom.

"Okay, okay, I'm going." I walked up the long hall, trying to cut off my mind.

Stay out of it, Tammy, you already said too much, too soon. Just enjoy the night and forget. Forget about it all. Stress less!

Ha! Stress less. My mum's advice worked through my mind like a constant drill into my brain. I shut the bedroom door and checked my phone on the charger. Several missed calls and messages appeared on my screen. I smiled as I dialled the number for home.

It rang out. I closed my eyes, hot tears burning under my lids.

Crap! Don't cry, Tammy. Don't. Cry. Not now. You can't afford to screw up your make-up.

I hadn't realised how much I was actually relying on hearing my mum's voice. I had sent her a text to say that we had arrived safely, but I was yet to talk to her. I really wanted to before the New Year began. The line clicked over to the answering machine and I listened to my mum ramble on with a five-minute spiel about what to do in the event that she or Dad weren't available. I had begged her for years to change it.

"Hey, Mum, just wanted to give you a call and wish you and Dad Happy New Year. I miss you heaps and I'm having a really good time." I tried to sound convincing, but wasn't sure I had pulled it off. "Anyway, I'll see you when I get home. Try not to party too hard, okay? Love you heaps, bye."

I sighed and pressed the phone to my forehead; I really needed my mum's upbeat words to soothe me, to tell me to 'stress less'. If my apparent mantra was to be positive, hers was not to stress. And in order to do the latter I had to be the former.

I slapped my hand defiantly on my thighs.

"Let's do this," I said aloud to myself. Standing and walking a proud, determined line to the wardrobe, I laid my outfit out on the bed.

No matter what happened tonight, or was going to happen tomorrow, I was going to make the most of what was left of 1999.

Like Amy had said, I was going to cut the shit and take control.

I was going to let Chris know how I felt.

Chapter Fifty-Four

It could have been the dress.

Or it could have been the champagne? Heck, it could very well have been the decision to shut off that crucial part of my brain that plagued me with worry. Whatever it was, I had never felt sexier and more bad ass than I did right now.

I had even decided to act natural around Ellie, leading the way for her to do so as well. It was almost as if we hadn't even had the conversation in the bathroom. But of course, we had, so although we faked it pretty well, I knew tonight we wouldn't be dragging each other onto the dance floor in the name of girl power.

As the four of us stood in the elevator, we each fidgeted with our foreign attire in the reflection of the elevator mirrors.

"Seriously, Tammy, Chris is going to freak out when he sees you," laughed Amy.

My normal response would have been to repel any such notion, but as the glasses of champagne I'd sculled in the suite made the edges of my mind blur, I admired my shimmery white and gold skirt that fell low on my hips and the midriff top that hugged into a V falling short of my belly button. My skin was a deep brown, in stark contrast to the white of the fabric, and my hair pooled into a cascade of soft, loose curls to the middle of my back. I felt beautiful and exotic and for me that meant more than what anyone else might think. For the first time, I actually embraced the thought of dressing up, of socialising. Maybe the New Year would continue for this new Tammy. As long as the alcohol wasn't the sole cause for my new-found confidence, that is, because that could be a problem.

The elevator came to an abrupt, stomach-plunging halt on the ground floor, and when the doors slid open we quickly moved from the claustrophobic space.

The four of us certainly were a motley crew. Ellie, with her electric blue,'80s figure-hugging dress (minus the shoulder pads), had opted to wear her long blonde hair sleek and glossy. To be honest, she needed little else to make a statement; my automatic reaction had been to tell her how great she looked, but I thought against it.

Tess looked beautiful in a powder blue baby doll dress; it looked like it was specially made for her and was by far the least outlandish of all our attires. Amy might have thought my outfit was show-stopping, but Tess would always be the one to turn heads, even if she was dressed in a paper bag.

Amy pulled off black and animal print like no other, and although she had fully intended it to be a bit of a laugh, she looked hot all the same.

"Sex on legs, coming through," I announced as Amy rocked a seriously lethal pair of black stilettos.

"Shut up, Maskala." She looked back at me with a smirk.

We'd aimed to stick out from the crowd, but compared to a lot of others moving around the hotel, we looked disturbingly normal.

I watched as we passed a group of guys wearing coconut shell bras and grass skirts.

We walked out of the reception area and wove our way through the curved garden path, flickering with shadows from tiki torches along its sides. We heard the distant screams and splashes of late night swimmers who still lounged and hung out by the pool bar.

"Where are we going?" Tess asked as we followed Amy further and further into the depths of the resort and its immaculately kept garden.

"The bar's down near the second pool," Amy called back, as she stepped carefully along the stone path. I, myself, gloried in the atmosphere of the summer's evening. It was definitely a lot cooler along the coast than it was at home. I ran my hands along the tops of the foliage that ran along the edges of the path; I didn't have to worry about heels with my beaded, casual sandals and I felt free and fabulous in my sexy attire. I certainly could never have worn this to the Onslow. But none of that mattered here. We passed another group of guys on the path, all wearing sombreros and Hawaiian shirts. They stood to the side and let us pass, bowing graciously.

"Ladies."

We smiled politely and ignored the wolf whistles and invitations to party with them, and followed the distant music that flowed out from the bar.

Soon we saw the glow of the bar up ahead. Double doors led into a darkened building, with only the pulsing lights of a music station lighting the space in neon flashes. It was no darker than Villa Co-Co had been, but the Point Shank Beach Resort bar was clean, open, airy and far more tropical than a couple of potted palms. If anything, this place should have been called Villa Co-Co, but instead the neon sign by the entrance door read 'Hibiscus Nightclub'.

A very handsome staff member waited by the door with a tray of complimentary cocktails and a glow-in-the-dark wristband each (probably tagging us so we didn't double dip on free cocktails, but nevertheless all given with an inviting smile).

Tess was the last to take a cocktail from his tray – it matched the electric blue of Ellie's dress.

Tess sipped it, looking around in wide-eyed wonder. "This is what heaven must be like." She grinned.

I had thought finding the boys was going to be as easy as

walking into a bar – there they'd be, propped up against it – but it seems that there were a few more bodies to look through than anticipated. Apparently, the entire guest list at the resort had converged at the bar for pre-celebration cocktails. We carefully pushed our way through the crowd, ensuring as best we could that we didn't spill our drinks – the last thing I needed was a blue streak down my front.

"Do you see them?" shouted Ellie above the music.

I shook my head. "Amy, are you sure this is the right bar?"

"This is the only one here," she said. "That I know of." She shrugged while involuntarily swaying to the beat of the music.

"So much for a grand entrance," laughed Tess.

"Well, let them find us," I said and in that moment it was like a light bulb lit above all of our heads.

"Yeah, let them come to us," agreed Amy, finishing the last of her cocktail.

I followed suit, cringing against the pure alcohol at the bottom of my glass before I slammed it down triumphantly on a nearby table. I pointed to the dance floor.

"Ladies, floor, dance, now," I declared.

Unlike what dominated the jukebox at the Onslow with the usual 'Smells Like Teen Spirit' or the odd Cold Chisel number, we gloriously revelled in the catchy little number of 'Rock the Boat' by Hues Corporation.

We were so lost in the glorious throes of the music, all trying to outdance each other with shimmies and other questionable dance moves, we had completely forgotten about the boys. But then out of nowhere a hand scooped around Amy's waist and whizzed her around in a screaming flurry.

Sean.

How we didn't see him coming, I will never know. His six-foot-three frame stood out above the crowd even more than usual as he was dressed in a sleek, single-breasted black suit with a white shirt and thin black tie. I know I joked before about sex on legs, but, seriously, Sean was raw, and dangerously handsome tonight.

Amy seemed to agree; I could see it in the way her eyes lit up, despite how she laid into him with a slap to the upper arm.

"Don't do that, I'm full of blue stuff," she cringed, rubbing her stomach and sticking out her blue tongue at him. "I'm pretty sure we just drank lighter fuel."

Sean ignored her protests, and instead pulled her to him and captured her mouth in a searing kiss that even made my own heart rate spike. I tore my eyes away from them and darted around, seeing if I could spot any of the other Onslow Boys in the crowd, my heart pounding so loudly I was sure everyone would hear it above the music.

Amy drew away from Sean, her eyes smoky and dreamy as she looked up at him. "Hi," she said, smiling coyly.

"Hi." He grinned down at her.

I pushed Sean in the arm. "Where did you come from?"

And more importantly, where were the others?

Sean looked at me as if noticing me for the first time. "Whoa, Tammy?" He looked me over as if he was seeing a stranger.

A pang of insecurity rushed passed my alcohol-induced buzz and clawed its way to the surface.

I was all but ready to sidestep away and change my attire when Amy leaned into Sean, grinning widely. "Do you think a certain someone will approve?" she asked him.

Sean broke out into a knowing grin. "Oh, I think a certain someone is going to fall off his stool."

"Excellent!" said Amy. "That is exactly the reaction we were going for."

She winked at me. I really didn't want to talk about this with Sean, even if it did have cryptic undertones. His attention casually flicked from me to the others, his eyes narrowing at all our revealing outfits.

"I think I'm going to need a shotgun tonight," he mused.

"We can take care of ourselves, Murph. Where are the others?" asked Tess.

Sean smiled. "Bar. It's this way." He pointed to a corridor

leading off the main club room. He offered Amy the crook of his arm before leading her off the dance floor. "Come on, ladies, stick with me and I'll make you stars."

One more of those blue things. That's what I needed, a pure hit of top-shelf alcohol to still my nerves. I had excused myself from the group, but hadn't exactly announced that I was grabbing a drink from the bar across the room. They would have wondered why I didn't grab a drink at the bar that we were headed to, where the rest of the Onslow Boys were.

Where Chris was.

Oh God.

I took a deep gulp of the cocktail that the bartender slid my way and squeezed my eyes shut with a shudder at the sour aftertaste.

Okay, down this and face the music. Make the entrance you wanted.

Considering the last exchange Chris and I had had, I really should have felt more at ease. I remembered the way he had stalked toward me, pulled me into the room and pushed me against the door. Heat rushed inside me just thinking about it, or was it the alcohol? No, it was definitely Chris.

I downed the last of my hundred percent alcoholic cocktail and made a determined line towards the corridor Sean and the girls had disappeared down. It was a long, subtly lit corridor.

Crap, I thought, *maybe I should have gone with them*, as the remnants of the last cocktail took effect. I steadied myself against the wall, hoping by doing so it would stop the room from spinning. I needed to focus.

As I fixed my eyes on the brighter glow of the bar at the end of the stuffy, dark hall, my gaze zeroed in on my target: oblivious to my watching him, Chris appeared out of the end room and darted down an adjacent walkway.

He was dressed like Sean, in a dark dress suit that even with the briefest glimpse had my stomach twisting and caused my breath to catch in my throat. I didn't need any grand entrance, or any longing looks across a crowded room; all I needed was him. My foggy mind cleared with intent as I moved down the hall quickly, my skirt swooshing around my legs. I dodged the sea of bodies and turned down the same side walkway Chris had.

There he was, leaning casually near the end of the hall, his back turned to me as he thumbed through his mobile phone.

I smiled to myself as I closed the distance between us. He had taken great pleasure in taking me by surprise today, robbing me of all my thoughts, all my breath, all my momentary anger and frustration. Now it was time to return the favour, and what's more, I wanted to do it now, before nerves and doubt rose within me and convinced me that 'Tammy Maskala did not wear provocative dresses, Tammy Maskala didn't swirl cocktails, Tammy Maskala didn't attack unsuspecting men in darkened hallways.'

Because, despite the niggling voice of doubt, tonight I wholeheartedly embraced all those things.

I shut down that voice inside my head and strode toward Chris. I pushed him against the wall with such force that he dropped his phone, but I didn't care. My mouth claimed his with such a deep-seeded need that I grabbed the lapels of his jacket and drew him closer toward me. At first his entire body was rigid in shock as I slammed him against the wall, but his hands eventually lowered to rest on my back as he gave in to my mouth, kissing me in return and moaning his approval as my tongue slipped into his mouth, tasting the remnants of beer and the tang of toothpaste. His fingers dug into my bare lower back; it caused me to gasp his name on his lips.

"Chris."

I felt him freeze, his hand stilling on my back, almost as if he was afraid that if he touched me I would break.

He swallowed deeply. "Well, this is awkward."

Chapter Fifty-Five

"Tammy, it's me … Adam."

I flinched away so quickly, backed away so fast I slammed into the opposite wall. My hands clasped my mouth and my eyes widened with horror.

Oh my God, oh my God, oh my God.

My eyes focused on what was most certainly and definitely not Chris. *Adam* stood across from me, his hands held up as if begging for a truce.

"Tammy, it's all right, it's just a mistake." He tried to smile in good humour.

All I could manage was to shake my head repeatedly. How could I have not known? How could I have attacked the wrong person? The wrong *brother!*

I cupped my flaming cheeks as all words failed me. This was why you don't dress like a ho, this was why you don't drink like a ho, and most certainly why you don't act like a ho.

I moaned in embarrassed despair and slid down the wall.

Ho-ho-ho!

Hot tears of shame pooled behind my lids and I buried my face in my hands. I couldn't even bring myself to look at Adam.

"Hey, hey, hey. Tam, it's all right." Adam knelt before me.

"Come on, look at me." He tried to prise my hands away from my face but I didn't make it easy for him. He eventually won out.

"Tammy, come on. This is getting insulting. I'm not that bad a kisser," Adam joked, which only made my tears fall.

He rubbed my upper arms. "Hey, come on, I know you like Chris; this didn't even happen, it's forgotten already."

I forced myself to look up at him. "I am so, *so* sorry, Adam, I thought that … that …"

"I know. It's all right," he said, wiping my tears away. "As far as mistakes go, this was right up there with some of the best of my lifetime."

I scoffed, shaking my head.

"I'm serious," he smirked. "At least in my top five."

"I am so embarrassed. And just so you know, I don't do things like this. I don't dress like a gypsy, scull cocktails, and attack random men in corridors. I just want to make that clear."

"Well, thanks for clearing that up; I really was thinking all those things." His mouth pinched upward in the corner.

"And these bloody corridors are really badly lit," I added.

"Really bad," Adam agreed.

"I mean, it's like an OH&S issue."

"I'm writing a letter to management first thing in the morning," Adam teased.

He did actually help me feel better.

He sat beside me, leaned against the wall and let out a sigh.

"You know what happens in the '90s stays in the '90s," Adam said, looking at his watch. "And as it goes we only have an hour and twenty-five minutes of guilt to live with before the stroke of midnight washes all our sins away."

"Really?"

"Truly."

Adam climbed back to his feet and held out his hand to pull me up. I looked at his hand and then up to him.

"So you're not mad at me?" I asked.

Adam burst out laughing. "Um, *no*. It would take more than

being attacked by a beautiful girl's face to tick me off. I am most certainly not mad at you." He grinned down at me.

I slid my hand into his and he pulled me to my feet.

"Well, of all the people to have accidentally kissed, I'm relieved it was you." I cringed with embarrassment.

"Think of it as an early New Year's Eve kiss." He bumped my chin with his fist. "Because I totally kiss girls like that at the stroke of midnight."

I smiled. "Do you think you could do me a favour?"

Adam's brows rose in surprise. "Sure."

"Do you think you could escort me to this bloody bar before I disgrace myself any further?"

Adam's mouth pulled into a crooked smile. "As long as you promise to keep your hands to yourself."

I laughed. "I can only try."

By now, I wanted to blend into the wall, to slink into the crowd and hover around the group, unnoticed and unannounced.

No such luck.

Adam pointed across the room to a fully occupied table, where everyone sat, present and accounted for, including Ringer, Stan and Bell.

Amy was the first to see us and she waved animatedly. Everyone turned to look.

"Shit, I'll be right back," said Adam.

My panicked eyes darted to his. "Where are you going?"

He leaned towards me, whispering near my temple. "I have your make-up on my jacket."

I looked at his suit jacket and, sure enough, a light sheen of unmistakable glittery dust was smudged there from our heated embrace.

"Oh God." I swallowed.

"Yeah, I'll take care of it," he said. "Be right back. See you at the table." And just like that, Adam disappeared through the crowd toward the men's room. I wrung my hands anxiously, drew in a deep breath and walked across the room toward the table of our friends. Of course, I didn't think myself so special that I would be the centre of attention as I crossed the floor, but I was very aware of a particular pair of eyes that watched my approach. Chris leaned his elbows casually on the tabletop, talking and listening to Ringer, but his eyes flicked towards me, studying every step I took until I came and stood right next to the table.

"Here she is!" announced Sean. "We thought we had lost you."

Ringer turned in his seat and his eyes widened. "Holy shit, Maskala. What the fuck are you wearing?"

Stan whacked him across the back of the head but it did little to snap him out of his wide-eyed gawk.

"I see they didn't stitch your mouth up," I mused.

"Ha! We should be so lucky," said Sean.

Bell leapt up from her chair. "Here, sit here, Tammy, I'll grab an extra chair." Her smile was not lost on me as Bell quickly vacated her seat next to Chris.

Subtle.

Bell skimmed past and whispered in my ear, "You look hot!"

"Thanks to you, I do." I hugged her.

"Thought you might like it." She winked, moving to steal a chair from another table.

I sat in Bell's vacant seat next to Chris, who made no move from his casual lean on the table as his eyes fixed intently on me, much like they had when he had kissed me.

"What took you so long?" he asked.

I could have looked away, let the pangs of regret for my colossal mistake moments before flood my face with crimson, but instead I was drawn so deeply into the depths of his warm brown eyes. I stared back at him, without apology; it was like we were the only two people in existence and I leaned my elbows onto the table in mirror image of him.

"I was looking for you," I said, so only he could hear.

I felt the press of his knee against mine and it made my heart pound faster. Such a simple touch.

"Well, you found me." He smiled.

"I did," I said, pressing my leg back against his, feeling the heat of him burn through the silky fabric of my skirt.

He broke away from my eyes, fighting not to smile as he glanced at the tabletop and back up at me with a shake of his head.

"What?" I asked with a confused frown.

He leaned in closer, and whispered in my ear. "You have no idea what you do to me." He drew away, his eyes locking with mine.

"W-what do I do?" I breathed out, mesmerised by the varying colours of brown framed by his inky lashes.

He bit his lip, pushing himself back in his seat.

"Remind me to tell you later," he said, a glimmer of amusement in his eyes. "Don't forget."

I shook my head. "Don't worry, I won't."

Chapter Fifty-Six

"So tell me again …"

"Why have we travelled all this way to sit around a table and look at one another?" asked Ringer.

"Well, you see, we have this friend and he can't walk long distances, or be on uneven ground or basically throw himself into the full-fledged party scene," said Chris.

"What, this old thing?" Ringer pointed to his elevated, bandaged foot with his walking crutch. "It's just a scratch," he scoffed.

"Oh puh-lease, we've had to listen to you bitching for the last two days," said Bell.

"Yeah, 'I'm too hot, I'm too cold, I'm thirsty, I'm hungry, my foot's ouchy,'" mocked Stan.

Ringer grinned with an evil glint in his eyes. "Well, it sounds bad when you say it all together."

"It *was* bad," said Bell.

"So this is it, is it? I'm stuck in here for this monumental moment in history because I'm an invalid? Great – it'll be remembered as that time when Ringer completely ruined our New Year's Eve. I might as well have gone home," sulked Ringer.

"Mate, you know New Year's Eve is the most overrated night

of the year, right? It's been a good trip. It doesn't matter where we are or what we do tonight as long as we're in good company," said Sean.

"That's beautiful, Sean, you should really put that on a bumper sticker." Adam arrived at the table, his jacket a little damp, and pulled up a chair. "So we're all frocked up and nowhere to go," he said.

"Don't you start," warned Chris.

"We do look like the Blues Brothers," added Toby as he adjusted his tie.

"Well, I think you look beautiful," Amy said, slinging her arm over Toby's shoulder. "I love seeing my boys suited up, it doesn't happen often enough."

"Maybe we should turn the Onslow into black tie?" mused Chris. "Just for Amy."

"That'll be the day," laughed Sean.

"I'm just saying, there is a massive music festival happening down the road, on the beach, that every man and his dog is at, spending everything in their wallets and having the time of their lives, and you're all here babysitting me," Ringer piped up.

"Ringer, we're not leaving you so just forget it," said Ellie.

"Well, don't think for a second that I wouldn't ditch you lot if the stitch was on another foot," Ringer said, folding his arms across his chest.

"I know you wouldn't, so just drop it, tough man," said Ellie.

Ringer sighed, admitting defeat. "You're all insufferable."

Chris leaned over to me. "Did you want a drink?"

"Uh, no. I think I'll wait, I've had quite an array already."

Chris pulled back and lifted his brow. "I thought I tasted champagne today." His mouth curved.

I blushed at the memory as Chris smugly lifted his stubby to his mouth and sipped.

"There is one line I draw in the sand, though," said Ringer.

Everyone sighed, wishing that Ringer would just accept that we weren't leaving him.

"And what's that?" asked Toby with little enthusiasm.

Ringer shifted awkwardly to stand, gathering his crutch under his arms. "We may be prisoners of my ill-fortuned circumstance ..." he said, looking over the entire table. Ringer grabbed his glass and lifted it upwards. "But by God, there will be dancing."

We abandoned our table and, in the spirit of Ringer, rallied down the same ill-fated corridor I had been in not long ago.

"Keep your eyes on the time, guys; we'll meet back at reception at ten to," Sean said, grabbing Amy's hand.

I wished Chris would reach for my hand, would guide me down the hall and wrap his arms around me. Instead, we walked side by side next to Stan and Bell.

"What's at ten to?" asked Stan.

Chris shrugged. "Who knows? Some scheme, knowing Sean."

"Well, I must say, I am a fan of his scheming ways. Did you nearly have a heart attack when you pulled up at this place, Tammy?" asked Bell.

My gaze flicked to Chris, who watched me expectantly, as if he really wanted to know the answer too.

"Indeed I did." My mouth twitched.

Stan and Bell led the way down the corridor, dodging bodies loitering in the hall. I kept my gaze forward, trying not to be swept away by less-than-savoury memories of what I had done with Adam.

Chris leaned in towards me.

"Don't think I've forgotten that you owe me a massage."

I blinked, my mind snapping from my daydreams. "Sorry?"

Chris smiled. "You lost the bet, remember?"

I gaped at him. "No, I didn't; you tricked me."

Chris rubbed the back of his neck. "A bet's a bet."

"You're unbelievable," I scoffed.

"Why, thank you," he laughed.

"It's not a compliment."

Chris smiled at my curt response as we entered the main room of the club. He guided me to the side of the dance floor, out of the way of the flow of traffic.

"I guess I kind of tricked you today when you thought I'd left the apartment." He looked down on me.

"You did," I said, hypnotised by the disco lights dancing across his face.

"Are you sorry I did?"

"No."

"Are you sorry I kissed you?"

I shook my head. "No." I reached out and traced my fingers down the strip of his thin black tie. He looked so beautiful in his suit. I had never seen him suited up before; he was born to wear it. He stepped closer to me as if encouraging me to touch him.

A smile tugged at the edges of my mouth as my eyes lifted to his. "You look really nice tonight," I said.

Chris broke into a brilliant white smile, his teeth glowing in the disco lighting.

He looked away and I followed his gaze to the others on the dance floor, to the familiar scene of Sean spinning Amy around like a rag doll and Adam and Ellie tearing up the floor in the most disturbing uncoordinated way.

"Dance with me?"

Chris hadn't looked away from our friends. I watched his profile, thinking I had imagined what he had just said. I had to have. In all the times I had been to the Onslow, I knew one thing for sure. *Chris Henderson most certainly did not dance.*

He broke his eyes away from the revellers and looked at me expectantly. "Well?"

"Are you serious?" I asked.

"I'd never joke about such a thing." He grabbed my hand and led me onto the dance floor.

Chapter Fifty-Seven

Oh, to hell with it, you only live once.

"One beer and one of those horrendously toxic blue cocktails!" I shouted above the pounding of the music.

I felt a body squeeze in next to me. "Make that two beers, and two cocktails, please." Tess waved a fifty at the bartender.

"Having fun?" She leaned into me so I could hear her.

I nodded. "I am. I can't believe I nearly didn't come."

"What? And miss out on hanging with us? Surely not." She elbowed me playfully.

"It feels so weird, I feel like I've hardly spoken to you these past few days."

"Yeah, well, I haven't exactly been the best company lately. I feel actually really bad, I feel like we've dragged the group down," admitted Tess.

"Come on, now you're starting to sound like Ringer," I said.

Tess smiled, but it didn't quite reach her eyes. The most natural thing would be for a friend to ask how things were between her and Toby, to be supportive. But I had been avoiding them ever since Evoka, or otherwise too wrapped up in Chris to fully notice what was happening between them. I looked into Tess's sad eyes. I was such a bad friend.

"Are you okay?" I asked as the barman slid the drinks in front of us. "Put your money away, I got this," I said, handing over a fifty dollar note.

"Thanks," Tess said, reaching for her cocktail like it was a lifeline.

"If it wasn't bad enough that Toby has been running hot and cold this entire trip, now I have to try to deal with Ellie."

I choked mid-sip of my cocktail, working myself into a violent coughing fit.

Oh God.

"Ellie? What about Ellie?" I rasped.

"You haven't noticed? She's not herself tonight, is she? I think she had been crying before but she won't tell me anything."

Oh God, please put two and two together, I thought, *if not now then soon.* I knew I was being selfish, but if she worked it out herself then I wouldn't have to get in the middle of it.

I was by far the worst friend ever – sitting on vital information for Tess, just so I could enjoy myself. I should have come out with it the second I had left the bushes in Evoka; instead of marching in the opposite direction I should have ploughed through those bushes and confronted Toby and Ellie there and then. How different the trip would have been. We probably would have all turned around and gone back to Onslow straight away.

"Do you think you could speak to Ellie? Try to find out why she's upset?" asked Tess.

If anything, the thought of finding it hard to dislike Ellie wasn't a problem anymore; in fact, looking into Tess's troubled eyes made it all the easier.

"Sure," I lied.

"Thanks, Tammy, you're the best."

If only she knew the truth.

"It's not ten to yet, why are we heading back?" called out Adam, trailing behind the group as we headed back up the garden path to the reception lobby.

"Because, as a whole, our time-keeping skills leave a lot to be desired," said Sean.

"Still doesn't explain why we're meeting at reception, anyway," said Stan.

Sean sighed. "Oh ye of little faith, trust me; I have something worked out."

"Amy?" Stan asked.

"Hey, don't look at me, I haven't a clue what Captain Cryptic is up to," she laughed.

Sean, as usual, loved every minute of our confusion.

I leaned into Chris. "Do you know?"

He curved his brow at me. "He's my business partner, he's under contract to tell me everything."

"So do you?" I pressed.

Chris shrugged. "I haven't a bloody clue."

The main foyer was deserted (as would be expected in the lead-up to the most hyped-up occasion of this century). I kind of felt sorry for the lone staff member that had drawn the short straw and had to work tonight of all nights.

Sean walked over to the desk, leaned against it and talked in hushed tones to the cheery fellow behind it. The man nodded at everything Sean said, checked the computer, and nodded some more.

"What on earth is he up to?" Bell said as we all looked on, wondering the same thing.

Sean walked back over to the group, his brows drawn in a no-nonsense, serious frown.

"Right, you have ten minutes to use the little girls' and little boys' rooms, or whatever you need before we meet back here."

"Do I have time to go grab my camera?" asked Tess.

"As long as it doesn't take any longer than ten minutes," Sean said. "Shall we all sync our watches?"

"Oh, for God's sake, Sean. Back here in ten, everyone." Amy rolled her eyes and dragged him to the elevator.

Everyone moved quickly, all in opposite directions – some slid to the elevators to go up to their rooms; others headed for the reception toilets. I thought myself particularly crafty as I headed for the poolside Ladies' room, knowing I would be able to be in and out more quickly. By now, the pool was long abandoned and all the sun-lounge mattresses had been hooked over the backs of the chairs to dry out for the night.

I hurried into the Ladies' room I was almost blinded by the bright fluorescent lighting that reflected off the gold tap fittings and black and gold marbled countertops.

As I finished my business, I made sure I didn't commit the ultimate disaster: I checked for toilet paper stuck on my shoe, or, worse, my skirt tucked into my undies. I unlatched the cubicle and froze in surprise.

Ellie stood by the basin, nervously wringing her hands together. "Hi, Tammy. Can we talk?"

I made a direct line to the sink, pumped the hand-soap dispenser and turned the elaborate gold tap.

"What could you possibly say in seven minutes that I would want to hear?" I said coldly, deliberately avoiding her eyes.

"Do you think Tess will be mad?" Ellie's voice was sad, almost inaudible.

I slammed the tap off. "Oh my God, Ellie! You think?" I yelled, my voice echoing off the tiles.

Tears welled in Ellie's eyes. "You can't help who you love," she said, her chin trembling.

"The thing is, Ellie, sometimes there has to be a line drawn, and you know what that line is for? So you don't fucking cross it." I was so angry, so absolutely enraged that I had been put in this position, to be sought out by her and just before we all had to meet back.

Ellie was crying and my face flushed crimson.

I breathed deeply. "Do you love him?" I asked, not knowing entirely why I did.

Ellie's big blue eyes lifted to mine in surprise. "I think I've always loved him," she said.

"Does he … Does he love you?"

Ellie thought for a moment. "I don't know. As a friend, yes, but I don't know about … more."

"I hope it's worth risking everything for," I said. "Risking your friendship with Tess, your friendship with everyone for." I moved toward the door.

Ellie reached out to stop me.

"Please don't say anything, I don't want anyone to know," she said, her eyes pleading.

The hairs on the back of my neck rose and my blood chilled in a way that almost scared me as I pulled away from Ellie's grasp.

"I have been tortured long enough by your secret; if you don't tell Tess about you and Toby, then I will. Don't think for a second I won't."

I pushed past her, ripping the door open and storming into the night. I was so angry, angry to the point that hot tears burned in my eyes.

Perfect.

"Tammy, wait!" Ellie's panicked call followed me, causing me to walk faster. I had had enough of talking. I didn't know what Sean had planned, but I didn't really care. I just wanted this year to end and, like Adam said, have all the sins of the '90s washed away forever. Ha! We should be so lucky, because little did everyone know that it was only the beginning, the beginning of a bigger nightmare that would tear us all apart, and the worst of all?

It was up to me to do it.

Chapter Fifty-Eight

I stormed back to reception.

My sole intent was to make it to the elevator without being spotted, only to be stopped dead in my tracks as a hand snaked around my arm, making me yelp.

Chris.

"Where do you think you're going? We've only got five minutes ... What's wrong?" Chris's brows narrowed.

Before I could answer, Ellie ran into the reception and skidded to a halt upon seeing me and Chris. Her eyes were all bloodshot and her mascara had smudged a path down her cheeks.

The three of us stared at one another, frozen and silent. To speak was to confess, and now was not the time. No time was the time. I was about to ask Chris to take me away from this place, to just get in his van and drive until it was the New Year and all the hype, all the expectation was over with. I knew he would, too. I knew that, without question, he would take me away and that was what I loved about him most.

Sean broke the silence, his cheerful upbeat voice echoing through the large space as he re-entered the room with Amy in tow.

"Look out!" Sean paused and looked at each of us, one at a time. The scene before him must have been comical. Chris separating two tear-stained, dishevelled chicks.

Sean's eyes narrowed on Chris. "What the hell have you done?"

"Me? I haven't done anything," Chris said incredulously.

"Well, you have thirty seconds to sort it out." Sean jangled a set of keys in his hand.

The elevator door dinged and slid open.

"Finally!" Sean walked away, leaving only Amy's uncertain gaze fixed on us.

"Um, can this wait?" she asked.

"No!"

"Yes!"

Ellie and I spoke at exactly the same time.

I turned to Chris, my rock, my saviour, my …

"You heard the man – sort it out."

My traitor!

Chris brushed a strand of hair behind my ear as he leant down to brush his lips against my temple. "Sort it out," he whispered.

Pulling away, he winked before abandoning me to join the others near the elevators.

I slowly turned to meet Ellie, her hands fisted at her side. Her angry eyes flicked briefly from me to the others. She grabbed my hand and dragged me into the alcove of the nearby Internet kiosk, away from prying eyes.

"Who were you talking about just now?" she asked, her eyes wild, her voice demanding.

I couldn't believe this girl. "Oh, please, who do you think I'm talking about?"

Ellie looked at me incredulously. "Well, Adam, of course, who else could you possibly …"

The penny dropped as she slowly gained her composure; I saw it in her eyes – her big, blue, horrified eyes.

"You thought I was talking about Toby?" she gasped.

Oh God, this was awkward.

"How could you even think that I could do that? Tess is my

best friend. Toby is like a brother to me!"

I wanted to crawl into a hole.

"Ellie …"

"Like you said, there are lines you don't cross. To think that you even thought for a second that that was one I would have …"

"Ellie …"

"Oh my God, who have you told? Does anyone else think that?" Ellie cupped her cheeks in horror.

"No! No one," I said, shaking my head. "I haven't told anyone, I swear."

"But why did *you* think that? Did I do something? Say something?" I could see Ellie's mind racing at a hundred kilometres an hour.

I had nowhere to look but at Ellie; I owed it to her not to look away. What could I say? By what they were saying, by how they were acting, I naturally thought they were having an affair?

Oh God, even repeating it inside my head, it sounded really, really lame. And worse – not only had I gotten it wrong, but I had gotten it so very, *very* wrong.

I had ruined the trip for myself, almost ruined it for everyone, based on nothing but a misunderstanding. And now, hurt and tears were in Ellie's eyes, whose crime had been nothing more than having feelings for her best friend. Was it midnight yet? I wanted the Y2K bug to make the planet burst into a ball of fire or whatever was predicted already and end us all.

It was the only thing that could save me from the shame that made my insides hurt.

I stepped forward and grabbed Ellie's shoulders.

"You did nothing wrong, it's just me and my stupid over-analytical imagination." I let go of her shoulders and grabbed her hands. "Ellie, I am so, so sorry. Please forget everything I've said. I guess I was just trying too hard to figure out what was happening between Toby and Tess and you know what?"

"What?" Ellie sniffed.

"It's none of my bloody business; it's none of *any* of our

business. Yeah, it's human nature to worry about them, but it's out of my hands. It's something that they have to sort out on their own. I'm just sorry I didn't realise that before. Then I wouldn't have gotten into this mess."

"I guess it was only natural to assume Ellie 'the whore' was the reason," she scoffed sadly.

My shoulders sagged. "Ellie, you are not a whore, you are a good friend – a great friend. If you weren't you wouldn't care about liking Adam and how it might affect your friendship with Tess." Ellie's eyes flicked up to mine, as if something I had said resonated with her.

"Why would Tess be mad if you liked Adam, anyway?" I asked.

Ellie opened her mouth to speak but then thought better of it. I guess I couldn't blame her for feeling guarded around me. When she actually did speak, her words surprised me somewhat.

"Me, Tess and Adam have been friends all our lives. Best friends. Our bond is something that can't be explained and it's so incredibly precious to me I don't know if it's worth risking."

"Well," I said thoughtfully, "I know I'm the last person on the planet that you should probably take advice from right now, but someone showed me that sometimes if you step out of your comfort zone you can experience some pretty amazing things."

"That someone sounds like a very wise person," Ellie mused.

"He is."

Ellie sighed. "Truth is, I don't know the answer right now, and it's not a decision I'll make lightly."

"Well, that's smart too. Even if you don't know now, in time you will and if there is something else that I've learned, it's that best friends are there to listen to you. Don't shut Tess out."

Silence fell between us.

"Ellie, I'm really sorry." I swallowed hard.

She smiled. "You know, you actually scared the hell out of me. You were *so* mad."

I cringed.

"Tammy, I know you don't always feel a part of things with us, but for what it's worth, whether you like it or not you're one of us. You just proved it."

Tears blurred my vision. "I wish I'd proved it in some other way."

"You have; you proved it in the way you care about Tess and Toby, about wanting to do the right thing, by the way you love Chris."

My eyes snapped up to see Ellie's knowing smile.

She nudged me with her hip. "We all know," she said. "How about we just find comfort in the truth and move on?"

It was like music to my ears. Before I could tell her that I wholeheartedly agreed, footsteps sounded up the passage and screeched to an abrupt halt.

Adam.

His brows rose in surprise as he parted his suit jacket and plunged his hands into both pockets of his slacks.

"Sean says if you're not there for countdown he is going to haunt you for the next millennium."

"We're coming," said Ellie. "Just had some gossip to catch up on." Ellie looked at me, her mouth tilting into a crooked line.

Adam's eyes shifted to me uncomfortably and I knew he had just gotten the completely wrong idea. Why the heck would I tell Ellie about my mistaken kiss?

"We were just speculating what Sean was up to, is all," I said. "Any clues?"

"None, but if you hurry up I think we're about to find out."

Chapter Fifty-Nine

"All right, we're all here?" called Sean.

"Yes," we all groaned, completely over the build-up to the big mystery surprise.

Sean pressed the button for the elevator and the doors instantly glided open.

He checked his watch. "This is it, people, the final countdown."

We all piled in, cramming ourselves into the small box like sardines.

Tess earned herself a whack to her temple by one of Ringer's crutches as he hopped inelegantly into the confined space. Amy screamed with pain as Sean accidently stood on her foot, and I was wedged up against Chris's chest. Admittedly, it wouldn't have been the worst place to be if Toby hadn't elbowed me in the spine.

"Shit, sorry, Tam."

I managed to smile through the pain, and thought, *Well, at least I could look Toby in the eye now.*

I felt Chris's hand splay over my bare back, rubbing soothing circles along my skin. Considering he was laughing and joking with Stan next to him, seemingly oblivious to his hand's actions, I wondered if it was as natural for him to touch me as it seemed.

"Where to from here?" Stan asked, his hand hovering over the floor panel.

Sean broke into a brilliant smile.

"The only way is up, Stanley."

Amidst the chatter and the stomach-plummeting jolt that catapulted us upward, I felt the gentle brush of Chris's lips against my brow, a stolen moment between us in the crowded space. I clasped the lapels of his jacket and breathed him in.

With eleven of us trapped in a confined space, you would think that the elevator door couldn't have opened soon enough, but as we piled out of the crammed, mirrored prison, the reality of breaking away from Chris was not a welcome thought … until we stepped out to the foyer. Our mouths gaped open, an unusual silence sweeping over us.

"Oh no, you d'int!" screamed Ringer like a diva.

Before us was a wall of glass, and beyond that wall was a glittering, candlelit terrace with rooftop pool. A long table lined with ice and champagne was the first thing to greet us as we all merged forward, Sean opening the door with pride.

"Best seats in Point Shank," he said.

Chris slapped Sean on the shoulder. "You did good, mate, you did good."

"Why get sand in our shoes when we can hear and see all from up here?" Sean swept his arm out like an emperor addressing his subjects.

"I wonder what the poor people are doing tonight?" joked Adam. He busied himself plunging a strawberry into his mouth from one of the fruit platters.

The breeze whooshed through the folds of my skirt, my hair flailing around as I walked along the terrace, past the pool, to look out over the balcony. The very strip that we had driven along earlier that day was now in darkness, highlighted only by an orange glow of high-powered street lights. Distant screams and laughter carried on the wind, the music from the festival clear and crisp to our ears. For long moments none of us said a word, we just listened and flashed cheesy, happy grins at one another. All those people below didn't have a clue how good we had it up here.

I spun around and clutched my hair at the nape of my neck to prevent it from blowing in my eyes and robbing my vision.

"Sean, I am officially the president of your fan club," I said.

"I'll be the vice president," added Ellie.

Sean pulled up a seat at the far end of the balcony, nursing a Crown Lager and casually crossing his long legs at his ankles.

"I would prefer to call you my groupies," he said, flashing a boyish grin before taking a deep swig.

What made this whole feat even more impressive was Sean's fear of heights. Noting his position, wedged up near the entrance, away from the edge – obviously nothing much had changed.

It only made this decadent surprise even more selfless.

"I think I'm actually glad Ringer injured himself," said Stan, looking down at all the insect-sized people on the footpath.

"Yeah, come to think of it, I don't fancy stumbling drunk along the beach, stepping in vomit and waking up with sand in my bum crack," said Adam.

Chris eyed his brother with interest. "I don't know what you get up to on the beach, but—"

"You know what I mean," snapped Adam.

Chris's brows rose. "Do I?"

Adam ignored him. "This is heaps better."

"What time is it?" I interrupted.

"Time to get moving …" said Stan.

"See!" said Sean. "That's why I wanted to get here early; otherwise we would have missed the bloody countdown."

Amy chucked a wedge of pineapple in her mouth, wincing at the sour aftertaste as she casually slid into Sean's lap. He welcomed her without a moment of hesitation, circling his arms around her.

"How long do we have this place for?" she asked, straightening Sean's tie.

"As long as we want. It's not exactly a space they hire out but I can be very persuasive." Sean pressed his forehead against Amy's, a devilish tic in the corner of his mouth making her blush.

The only person who didn't seem overly impressed or

interested in our surprise five-star venue was Toby.

He leaned on the balcony railing, looking out onto the stretch of black ocean across the street.

His sombre mood didn't go unnoticed. Tess tore her eyes away from his back and locked with my gaze. She looked so defeated, so tired, to the point that there were no more tears to shed. She just shook her head and turned away, finding salvation in a fresh glass of champagne. Although I had been more than relieved that Ellie had nothing to do with the wedge growing between Toby and Tess, it still did little to stop my heart from aching for them. I felt the press of Chris next to me as he leaned against the railing beside me.

"You and Ellie all good?" he asked, mid-sip of his stubby, as if trying to disguise his words.

I nodded. "All good."

"I don't have to switch her back to your apartment now, do I?"

"No, I think she is pretty settled in the honeymoon suite," I said.

We looked across at Amy and Sean, making out like two teenagers at a Blue Light disco. I felt a moment of sympathy for Ellie and the company she was keeping. It was a stark contrast between Amy and Sean to the likes of Toby and Tess, and for a moment I found it hard to believe that out of the couples, Chris and I were the least complicated.

Not that we were a couple or anything. Actually, I didn't exactly know what we were. Friends with benefits? We weren't exactly friends and benefits would imply more than second base …

Even on the brink of a new century I realised that I knew just as little now about him as I had at the beginning of the trip.

I studied his stormy profile, marvelling at the strong, chiselled lines of his insanely kissable lips and the faint workings of a permanent wrinkle on his brow from too much frowning.

As if sensing me staring, Chris tilted his head toward me and drew his beer away from his mouth.

He didn't smile, or say a word, he just looked into my eyes and it was in that moment I knew something had changed. Before the trip I would have turned away, quickly broken from his darkened, intimidating eyes. But now, I stared straight back, lost in the depths of them, never wanting to turn away. I wanted to live there.

That was the difference.

However wonderful it was, poolside, on top of a resort about to be showered in a cascade of colours from the New Year fireworks, there was only one thing I wanted, and my eyes spoke as much as they flicked to Chris's mouth: a silent invitation, a whispered promise. I met his eyes once more. I may not have spoken, but he understood every word. Chris turned to me, shielding me from the frantic winds that made my skin form into gooseflesh.

He stared thoughtfully at me for a moment.

"Come here," he said softly, darkly, a promise of something greater to come.

It made me afraid of what might happen if I didn't. I breathed in deeply, feeling an invisible pull between us as I drew nearer. Chris slid his hand along my belly, skimming around to dance along my spine. This was it, this was what I wanted; this was what I had been waiting for. Just as I saw Chris swallow in anticipation, the moment was shattered.

Tess screamed.

Chapter Sixty

All it took was one moment.

Time slowed as people down in the club and on the distant shore started counting down to the new century, new beginning.

They danced, cheered, laughed – surrounded themselves with the warm, glittering night as they rang in the New Year with hopes and dreams for the future. That's what we had all wanted; whether secretly or publicly, we hoped for our lives to change in some way from this night on.

But we'd never thought it would change like this.

Tess's eyes were wide, fixed ahead of her. She stood frozen, cupping her mouth, small whimpers escaping unheard on the breeze. The wind carried the joyful cries of "Happy New Year!" on invisible wings, but up here on the balcony we were silent.

A dull ache sliced my abdomen and my breath caught in my throat. I only remembered to breathe when I felt Chris's fingers lace with mine so tightly I felt he may break me.

An explosion of colour filled the night sky; popping and spiralling in rampant surges, the fireworks cast a magical backdrop against our open-air retreat.

Tess's soft whimpers washed over us; I wanted to go to her, to console her in some way, but I didn't need to. Her gaze dropped to the tiled floor, her watery eyes shiny with hot tears as she shook her head, barely believing the promise before her that would change her life forever:

Toby bending on one knee.

He curled his fingers around Tess's trembling hand, his warm brown eyes fixed on her intently.

"I know you've seen nothing but the worst of me since we left Onslow. But you know me. You know more than anyone that I am never one to love for the sake of being in love, but I love because of you. You make the ordinary man in me feel extraordinary and I want to go on loving and discovering with you for the rest of my days."

Toby delved a shaky hand into the inner pocket of his jacket. He turned the black box and opened it toward Tess, a nervous lilt to the curve of his mouth.

"Please say yes."

In that moment I couldn't feel anything but the squeeze of Chris's hand as I held my breath, watching, waiting.

Tess moved to kneel in front of Toby, wrapping her arms around his neck, the sheen of tears overflowing to trail a path down her face. She looked at him, really looked at him and swept her hand along his jaw line, her thumb grazing his lips.

She shook her head. "As if there could be any other answer."

At 12:01 a.m. on the first of January, year 2000, on top of a resort terrace in the coastal town of Point Shank, a group of friends converged on two people: a screaming, crying heap.

We broke the mould that night. We didn't scream "Happy New Year" or vomit up our drinks and get sand in our butt cracks; no, we did so much more.

Us girls cried and pawed at Tess's diamond engagement ring that by far out-blinged every firework in the sky. The boys engulfed Toby with macho congratulatory hugs and ruffles of hair, but none quite as touching as when Sean and Toby embraced, thumping one another in bone-jarring thuds on the back. Toby drew away and nodded his silent thanks. It made me suspect that Sean was the only one who had known Toby's intentions throughout the trip. Thinking about it, he'd probably masterminded the private rooftop terrace space for the perfect backdrop and romantic beginning for his best mate's proposal, let alone everyone else's enjoyment.

I took a moment to break away from the pack and walked over to Sean.

Standing on the very tips of my toes, I kissed him on the cheek. "You are an amazing man, Sean Murphy." I smiled.

Sean's brows rose in surprise. "Now, Tam, I know you have always been desperately in love with me, but you're just going to have to learn to control your urges."

I rolled my eyes. "You're unbelievable."

"What? Did you honestly think I would turn over a new leaf in the year 2000?"

I shook my head. "Don't you dare go changing, Sean Murphy – not one bit."

Sean broke into a wicked grin. "Happy New Year, Tam," he said, bending down to kiss my forehead, before ruffling my hair and walking away.

Well, maybe some things he could *change.*

I wiped the tendrils of hair out of my eyes and spotted Ellie watching Toby and Tess completely lost in each other.

Ellie wiped away what little eye make-up she had left. Her nose was red and her eyes bloodshot from the tears of joy that poured as she witnessed her best friend's proposal.

I stood beside her. "You knew, didn't you?" I mused.

Ellie sniffed and nodded. "Since Evoka. It nearly killed me keeping it under wraps."

I fought the urge to laugh. I had been so wrong, so wrong about everything. I remembered how Ellie had threatened Toby, told him that his weird behaviour was stressing Tess out, how emotional she was because of it.

It was all so clear now. I had thought it to be something so sinister, but it was nothing more than Ellie being a true friend, pacifying a stressed-out fiancé-to-be.

Poor Toby.

I brushed past the bodies flanking the now beaming happy couple. I worked my way in a direct line through to Toby and threw my arms around him. He stiffened in surprise before his arms rested around me.

"I am so sorry about your shoes."

Toby laughed. "Uh-oh, that sounds ominous."

I broke away, fighting the urge to let the tears flow; emotion I hoped would pass for happiness for them instead of the raging guilt that bubbled up within me.

How could I explain that they were up a tree in Evoka? With a condom inside?

"You see …" I started.

"They're gone, aren't they?" Toby said. "It's all right, they weren't my favourite pair," he said.

Mercifully I was saved from admitting it by Adam's grand announcement.

"HAPPY NEW YEAR!" he screamed. He ran, fully clothed, and cannonballed into the pool, splashing water over all of us.

"Adam! Don't be a bloody dickhead!" screamed Amy, shucking the excess water from her arms before she recognised the devious glint in Chris's and Sean's eyes.

"Don't. You. Dare," she warned.

"Whatever do you mean?" said Chris as he innocently set his beer on the table.

"I think she's accusing us of something," said Sean as he began to inch around in the opposite direction.

Amy backed away. "I mean it, you two. Your lives will not be worth living." Amy broke into a run.

But she, of all people, should have known: you can't outrun an Onslow Boy, let alone two … Something I found out the hard way a minute later.

I gathered up the saturated layers of my skirt, waited for a moment of distraction and crept slowly through the open glass doors of the terrace, dripping a trail of evidence to the elevators. I pressed frantically on the down button, urging it on with silent prayers.

Come on, come on, come on …

The red digital readout ticked agonisingly slowly up toward the rooftop terrace. Even though I was alone, I hugged my arms around myself, masking the mortifying transparency of my top that evidently wasn't meant to be swum in.

I looked over my drenched state with great annoyance, hoping that the new dress wasn't ruined. It had been fun, though. Aside from Ringer, we had all gone in, clothes and all, a line of dripping wet Onslow Boys in their suits; it looked like we were shooting a music video for a new boy band.

It was actually very hot. Not so hot when Bell pulled me aside and pointed out my little wardrobe malfunction that would have given the video an R rating, however.

As if I had conjured her up with my mind, I heard Bell's voice.

"Hey, wait for us," she whispered, dragging Stan behind her.

I inwardly cringed. I had planned for a crafty exit, but the more of us that left at once would definitely arouse suspicion in the others.

'Shhh," Bell pressed her fingers to her lips. "We're on a mission."

"Oh?" I whispered.

Stan held up a room card with a smile.

Oh God, I hope they weren't referring to a sexual mission.

"Sean organised so Tess and Toby can have a room of their own," beamed Bell. "Kind of like a pre-Honeymoon Suite, I suppose."

Stan nodded. "We have to sneak in to grab their gear and relocate them."

The elevator door dinged and opened. The three of us dived inside, leaving behind three puddles on the tiles as evidence.

We thought ourselves quite the escape artistes as the doors drew slowly closed. We thought we had made a stealthy getaway until we heard footsteps closing in, followed by the screeching of sliding footwear on the tiled floor and an arm that plunged through the nearly-but-not-quite-closed elevator doors. Flinching backward as the doors opened again, a figure squeezed through the opening.

Chris.

Chapter Sixty-One

I made a last sweep around the bathroom before returning back into the hall.

Chris stood in the doorway to keep the door wedged open while Stan and Bell lugged all of Tess and Toby's gear out of the spare room.

"I think that's everything," I said, standing at the front door with Chris.

"Cool," whispered Stan, although I'm not sure why he whispered; we were three floors below the others.

"Now we're going to go and put a trail of rose petals in their new room," said Bell.

"And they have no idea?" asked Chris.

"They haven't a clue," beamed Bell. "We just casually walk back up and hand them the new card and point them that way."

"Yeah, well, remember, you never saw me," said Chris.

'Or me!" I added quickly.

"See who? I don't see anyone, do you, Bell?"

"Not a soul," she said, her knowing eyes shifting between the two of us. "Well, goodnight."

"Night," Chris and I said at the exact same time, not without seeing the subtle wink that Stan threw Chris.

We watched them bundle the luggage into the elevator on their mission. I thought maybe I would feel the sag of relief hit me once the doors had closed and the elevator whirred into life. But I didn't. Instead, I felt the weighty stare of Chris's eyes burning into my profile. I turned, my arms still wrapped around me.

Chris leaned casually against the doorjamb, leaving a damp mark on the wallpaper. His hair was all shaggy and dishevelled and oh-so sexy.

"Are you cold?" he asked, his eyes roaming in speculation over my self-embracing arms.

"No," I said quickly.

Chris nodded, as if accepting my answer without too much thought. He pushed off from the doorjamb, uncrossed his arms and plunged his hands into his pockets.

"Okay, well, goodnight," he said, starting for the hall.

Seriously? Goodnight?

No "Happy New Year", no New Year kiss … Nothing? I didn't get a chance to let the disappointment override me.

I was too busy being fucking pissed off. I knew he hadn't promised me anything, that there was no admission of undying love. But seriously? The knee touching, the hand holding, the slow dancing, the moment we were going to kiss on the terrace? Was I just a boredom killer to him? Was I just a way to pass the time?

No, I wasn't upset; no tears were going to fall from these eyes. I was far too busy glaring incredulously at his back. Chris sauntered a few steps up the hall before he paused and turned back around. I altered my gaze – I didn't want to give him the satisfaction of thinking I cared one way or another if he stayed or walked off the edge of a balcony.

His eyes met mine, a line of amusement curving the corner of his mouth.

"You know, this is the part where you stop me, and ask me to stay."

My mouth gaped, my hands falling to my sides. "And why on earth would I do that?"

Chris shrugged, a casual, one-shouldered shrug like he always did. "Oh, I don't know," he said as he slowly stalked his way back in my direction, trailing his hand along the hall wall. "That's a hell of a big apartment for just one person."

Chris's words suddenly dawned on me. No Ellie, no Toby and no Tess … Just me.

I lifted my chin. "Well, I asked you to stay before."

Chris's brows lowered in confusion. "What? When you asked me to move Ellie?"

I nodded.

Chris was right in front of me now, so close I could feel the warmth of his breath on my face.

"It wouldn't have worked," he said, his voice low.

"Why?"

"Because if I'm going to stay," he said, trailing his finger lightly over my collarbone. "I can't promise that I can keep you quiet." His eyes lifted to mine: dark, smouldering and full of promise. Heat flooded my cheeks as his words hung heavy between us.

My chest heaved as I fought to control my breath, the breath he robbed from me by one look, one touch, one hotter-than-hell insinuation. His eyes dipped lower, roaming over my translucent dress, the wet white clothing I had all but forgotten to shield. What's more, with the way Chris looked at me, the way his eyes burned for me … I really didn't want to. Let him look, let him see, because, as far as I was concerned, tonight I belonged to him.

Chapter Sixty-Two

The apartment door slammed.

A second later, Chris's back thudded against it so fiercely I swear I heard the air escape from his lungs.

Payback, I thought, as I claimed his mouth, working to frantically peel the wet black suit jacket off his shoulders. There was nothing nice or sensual about the way we kissed, the way we clawed at one another's clothing. I worked on pulling and stretching his tie apart as his fingers dug into my hips, skimming over the sheer fabric of what he murmured into my mouth as an "infuriating skirt". I smiled against his lips, revelling in his torture.

Chris edged me backward until I thudded against the opposite door.

"If you tell me you don't have a condom, I swear …" I breathed, before kissing him deeply. He broke the kiss. "If I didn't I would drive straight to Evoka and climb a fucking tree if I had to."

My heart leapt: the way he kissed me so passionately, the way his breath caught when I ran my mouth down his jaw line.

My fingers clawed a slow, taunting trail up over his muscular stomach. He flinched away.

I giggled. "You *are* ticklish."

Chris grabbed me by the wrists and pinned them above my head.

"Best get you out of these wet clothes, Miss Maskala." He nuzzled the words into my neck, causing me to squirm at my own sensitive skin.

He let go of my hands so he could reach for the handle that led into the bathroom. Edging into the space, he flicked the light on, exposing us and snapping me completely out of my sexy mood.

I clasped my arms around my top again.

"What's wrong?" Chris asked.

"What?" I said nervously. "Nothing, I …"

Chris paused. "You have no idea how beautiful you are, do you?"

I tilted my head incredulously. Even I could take a guess that under the harsh bathroom lighting with chlorine-filled hair I looked like a drowned rat. Unlike Chris with his crazy-cool, casual, messed hair and white dress shirt and black slacks that fitted him to perfection.

He moved toward me.

I drew my arms tighter around myself.

He leaned past me and turned the shower on. My eyes widened in surprise and he smiled.

"This will be our third shower together," he mused.

It was an interesting thought; I hadn't even showered once with my ex-boyfriend, and in the space of four days I'd had three showers with Chris?

A hazy steam slowly rose, misting the air. He never took his eyes from me as he undid his cufflinks, first one sleeve, then the other. How could something so simple be so damn sexy?

He then worked down in a slow, confident line, undoing his shirt buttons, until I stopped him.

His face was stony; he probably suspected I had changed my mind. Instead, I took over. One by one, I popped the buttons free with trembling fingers, before finally peeling the fabric apart and pushing it back over his shoulders. It was like unwrapping a present: a beautiful, tanned, flawless present – the one I had been waiting so long for and now had the chance to play with. I smiled at my analogy. My hands lowered to work Chris's belt buckle, but this time his hands stopped me. Instead, his fingers gathered at the base of my midriff top and he slowly peeled it upwards, exposing me so completely to his heat-filled eyes. He pulled it up and over my head and let it fall to the floor. I shut my eyes as his hands trailed a maddening path over my stomach, upwards to cup my breasts as he stole a heated kiss. He slowly led my hands down to his belt buckle again.

He broke away from my mouth. Nuzzling and pressing his lips to my temple, he whispered, "It's going to be so good."

I never doubted it for a second, and all of a sudden I also found my skirt infuriating and it simply had to go as soon as I edged his own infuriating pants down. I only got as far as unzipping his slacks before Chris had his own ideas of bunching and gathering my skirt far enough to slide up my thighs, lifting the barrier between us. He edged me towards the vanity and, without hesitation, propped me on top of it, sweeping off a line of toiletry products that clattered to the tiled floor. A thrill shot through me just like it had when he had lifted me onto the bonnet of the car, and just like he had that night, Chris worked on hooking my knickers around his fingers and edging them over my thighs and down my legs with expert ease.

"You're very good at that," I mused.

"I'm good at lots of things," he said, curving his fingers around the backs of my knees and pulling me closer to him. His words whispered against my mouth as his hand made a slow burning trail along my skin, sliding over my inner thigh and dipping between my legs. Chris was there to catch my gasp as he kissed me and showed me how good he was, how utterly mind-bendingly good he was and how wickedly wonderful and clever his hands were as he pushed me to the edge of madness. My cry rang out and echoed against the tiled room, the steam dampening our skin as I tried my best to keep from falling off the vanity in my boneless, sated state.

It took a hot, chaste kiss to bring me back around as I met the smug glint in his eyes.

"Ready to wash your sins away?"

My body ached.

Don't get me wrong, it ached in the most delicious way. Lying entwined in 1000 count thread sheets on a queen-sized, feather-top mattress. Having sinned, as Chris called it, in every spot in the hotel room possible, we went to the imaginative lengths that a giant apartment to ourselves could offer. It was the perfect ending to a perfect New Year's Eve.

Ellie wasn't a home wrecker.

Toby loved Tess beyond imagination.

Sean had successfully pulled off a New Year's Eve bash that would go down in the history books. And Chris: well, Chris took me to places and pushed me beyond anything I could ever imagine possible.

I stretched, wincing against my aching body, but absolutely sated in other ways where my muscles were so relaxed I felt like I had woken from a hundred-year sleep. I thought about rolling over, thinking I would find an empty space, maybe a note saying 'Thanks'. Maybe I would hear a million excuses and be given the whole, 'Uh, yeah, I'm not looking for a girlfriend right now' speech. Or worse, palpable awkwardness followed by 'It was a mistake and must never happen again.'

Who'd ever have thought that rolling over could be so terrifying?

As I slowly, tentatively rolled over, blinking against the sunlight, something took me by surprise.

Chris was sitting up in bed, reading a newspaper. I lay on my stomach, looking up at him, transfixed by the familiar crease between his brows as he concentrated. So deep was his concentration that I doubted he even realised I was awake.

And then he cleared his throat.

"Man injured in Point Shank prank … Music Festival reaches

record numbers … Coastal earthquake as woman endures multiple orgasms?"

"Oh, stop it!" I sat bolt upright, pulling the paper out of his hands, my cheeks flaming.

"That's not what you said last night." Chris smiled, broad and cheeky as he folded his hands behind his head.

All I could manage was an incredulous shake of my head. "You're unbelievable."

Chris winked. "You know it."

I scoffed and reached out to whack him across the arm, but he was too fast. He grabbed my wrist and then the other. I squirmed and squealed as he wrestled me to the mattress, overpowering me with his strength. The hard lines of his heated bare skin pressed up against me.

My breath quickened as Chris stared down at me, his own chest rising and falling heavily.

Relief flooded me as I looked into his eyes; they were the same eyes, looking at me the same way they always had. Chris was not a mystery anymore.

"You forgot to remind me."

Chris's words snapped me from my daydream.

"Last night when you were at the table, you asked me 'What?', and I said I would tell you later."

I vaguely remembered. "Well, I'm reminding you now."

Chris loosened his grip, his body visibly melting against mine.

"But, if it's to tell me you thought I looked nice …" I warned.

Chris laughed. "No, nice wasn't the word that popped into my mind."

"Good." I nodded.

All humour disappeared from Chris's face as his eyes ticked over mine.

"When you walked into the room I was terrified."

Terrified? Um, okay … Bring back nice.

"I was terrified because seeing you across the room cemented everything I was afraid to admit. I connected the moment I started falling for you and when you came and sat beside me I knew. I remembered. I loved you from the moment I pulled you into my wardrobe, even more so when I accidentally kneed you in the face at the Bake House, and I was well and truly gone by the time you mocked my black panel van." He smiled.

I felt the pressure inside my chest, my heart wanting to leap out to give all of myself to him. My eyes fixed on Chris as he gently traced a line with his finger along my bottom lip.

"So if you don't mind, I want to take you home." He slid his hand under the sheet across my stomach. "There'll be a few stops along the way ..." His fingers dug into my hip, before sliding upwards.

I arched against him. "What did you have in mind?" I breathed.

"I want to finish what we started in the ocean, eat seafood at The Love Shack, run a tab in Sean's name at Villa Co-Co."

I burst out laughing. "Sounds divine."

"And then last, but not least ..." Chris smiled wickedly. "We'd better find Toby's shoes."

Epilogue

I found one shoe.

And there was no condom inside it. Aside from the very important, yet unsuccessful, task of Converse recovery, we took our time travelling back to Onslow, winding our way through the terrain we had already explored. It seemed to take less time to return; admittedly, we did find better ways to occupy ourselves. We had kept a pretty tight line travelling with the others home, except for our secret place with the ocean pool – that was our place – and as planned we left a day early from Point Shank to experience it in the way it was intended.

It wasn't until I was on my lone shoe hunt camped up at Evoka Springs for the night that it actually occurred to me that I hadn't suffered from a migraine since way before Calhoon on day one. I walked down the track, swinging the single navy Converse around, smiling at the realisation. I can't say that I was miraculously cured, but I certainly felt different; I hadn't even had the need to remind myself to be positive.

I just was.

After disposing of the evidence of Toby's shoe in the back of the van, I wound my way back down toward the main campsite. Bell, Amy and the boys had gone fishing for a few hours so I decided to join Ellie, Tess, Ringer and Adam sitting in shade at the folded-out camping table.

"I can't believe we are going back to Villa Co-Co," Ellie said, wrinkling her nose in disdain as she feasted on a bag of Burger Rings.

"Oh, come on," said Ringer, stealing a ring from her packet. "You saw the sign, it's Ladies' Night." Ringer raised his brows as if we should have been ecstatic.

Ellie turned, narrowing her gaze. "Now tell the truth, Adam, tell us the real reason you want to go there."

Adam straightened in his seat. "I don't know what you are talking about." He reached for a Burger Ring but Ellie slapped his hand away.

"Oh, nothing about a certain something it said on the sign under 'Ladies' Night'?" said Tess.

Adam picked an invisible hair off his shoulder. "Still no idea. You girls are crazy."

"What's this?" I asked sitting down next to him.

Ellie rolled her eyes. "It's karaoke night at Villa Co-Co."

"Wow!" I laughed.

Adam stretched his arms to the sky. "Wow indeed, ladies, wow indeed. Hope you're prepared, that's all I'm saying." He stood up with a cheeky wink and the three of us staring after him.

"Ladies' Night means cheap booze, right?" asked Ringer.

Tess sighed. "Yep!"

"Well, thank God for that."

"Trust me," said Ellie, "if Adam's singing karaoke we're going to need it."

We watched with a mixture of horror and respect as a short, pierced man with a stringy goatee and cowboy hat belted out a well-tuned, passionate version of Bon Jovi's 'Dead or Alive'.

Stan leaned across the table and tapped Adam on the shoulder. "Mate, I think they take their karaoke pretty seriously in Evoka."

"As do I, Stan, old boy. As. Do. I." Adam's eyes scanned the room, assessing the competition.

Chris shifted uncomfortably in his seat, dreading the night more than anyone. Adam and Amy often tried to twist Chris's arm to host a karaoke night at the Onslow, to which his consistent response was always a resounding, "I would sooner poke myself in the eye with a sharp stick."

So it didn't seem likely.

Tess nudged Ellie. "Remember when you and Adam entered the talent show in Year Seven?"

Ellie cut Tess a dark look, but it was too late; Adam swivelled around in his seat.

"The year was 1991," he began. "The competition was fierce …"

Ellie cringed and slipped down in her seat, obviously wishing the ground would open up.

"We practised every night after school; Onslow High didn't know what hit them." Adam's eyes looked far away as if remembering a fine moment in history.

"What did you sing?" asked Sean with interest.

"Adam …" Ellie warned. "Don't."

I could tell Adam danced on the edge, you could see it in his eyes as he looked at Ellie, battling between loyalty to her and his utter desperation to tell a good story.

He shrugged. "I'm afraid I cannot say."

By now, everyone had edged forward on their seats, leaning elbows on the tabletop, waiting to hear what had been so mortifying about a Year Seven talent show. We all sagged in disappointment.

Ellie sighed and mouthed "Thank you" to Adam. He took his beer in hand and gave her a casual wink mid-sip.

Our attention focused back onto the stage as the residential Madame of Villa Co-Co stood front and centre. She wore a lime green kaftan with matching acrylic nails and blue eye shadow. It really brought out the bleached yellow in her cropped spike hairdo. The Pineapple was in fine form tonight.

"Now, ladies and gentlemen, we have a very welcome guest that has travelled all the way from Onslow to be here with us tonight. Please put your hands together and welcome to the stage …" She looked at her card. "Aaron Henderson!"

It didn't take much for us to break into hysterics. The boys clapped and cat-called, "Go, Aaron!"

As Adam got up from his chair, he confidently strode towards the stage and took the mic.

"Ah, yeah, it's Adam." He smiled coyly toward our table. Bell near on deafened me by putting her fingers in her mouth and whistling.

I never could do that.

Adam cleared his throat. "All right, um, there's been a bit of a change of plans. I'm feeling a bit nostalgic tonight so I thought I might take a trip down memory lane."

"Hello?" said Sean, leaning forward in his chair.

"But I'm going to need your help, because ya see, I can't do it on my own, and there is only one person in this room that can complete this duet …"

"Oh God!" Ellie stared towards the stage, her eyes wide with horror.

"And that person is Ellie Parker." Adam pointed, directing the spotlight to her.

"Ellie! Ellie! Ellie!" Adam chanted into the microphone, encouraging the entire room to join the chorus, none louder than our own table. Toby placed his beer down before grabbing Ellie's hand and pulling her out of her seat toward the stage.

"Traitors! The lot of you." She glowered back at us. It only led us into further hysterics, watching her take each furious step up to the stage where Adam waited, grinning from ear to ear as he handed her a microphone.

"I hate you so hard right now," she said to him.

Adam's smile just got bigger.

"They fight like a bloody married couple," said Ringer.

"They'll get married one day – no one else would put up with them," joked Chris.

"Don't be awful," said Tess.

"All right, now you have to cut us some slack," Adam said. "It's been a while."

It was a pretty high-tech set-up as far as outback pub karaoke went. There was a screen at the foot of the stage for the singers and one mounted on the wall for the crowd to sing along if they so desired.

The music started up just in time for the song title to flash across the screen:

'Islands in the Stream', Kenny Rogers and Dolly Parton.

"No way!" laughed Sean.

"Ugh, I remember it now – hours and hours they practised in his bedroom." Chris grimaced.

"I love it!" I clapped in excitement.

"Better save your enthusiasm until it's over," said Ringer.

Confidently, Adam took the lead with Kenny's lyrics, and he was good – *really* good. We were all stunned into silence. Then Ellie kicked in with Dolly's part and we were all smiling and eyeing each other with surprise. They were kind of … excellent?

"I am beginning to wonder if my little brother really joined the army or if he's been touring the professional karaoke circuits." Chris looked on with a mixture of horror and pride.

By the chorus you could hardly believe that Ellie had protested in the first place. Eye contact, a bit of heart clutching, it was a well-rounded performance that had us all up on our feet singing along, cheering for Ellie and Aaron. He would never live that down.

As the duet faded to a close and the screen went black, the crowd went wild. Adam took Ellie's hand and they bowed. It was an unlikely end to our road trip, a trip that was originally supposed to be girl-free and full of fish, camping, talking sport and drinking beer. Instead, it had ended up so much more and I hoped everyone had enjoyed it as much as I had. I looked over at Chris, marvelling in his laughter, the way he was so completely relaxed and happy. He banged the side of his stubby with the edge of his car key.

"All right, on that rather disturbingly impressive note, I propose a toast." He centred his beer in the middle of the table and everyone followed suit in a multitude of clinks.

"To the new millennium," he said.

"To the new millennium!"

With no takers on stage for karaoke, music started up and we all cheered and headed to the dance floor as Meat Loaf's 'Paradise by the Dashboard Lights' played.

Not one of us opted out of busting a move; even Ringer twisted as best he could on crutches. Who would have guessed that in a dank, dodgy little bar we could find so much entertainment? It wasn't a place you'd want to be involved in an after-hours lock-in or anything, but come closing time, knowing this was our last night away from home, we sang and fist-pumped the air until our voices were hoarse. We belted out the final request of 'Just Like Jesse James' like it was our own personal theme song. I don't know if it was the beer, the music, the atmosphere or – hell, it might have been Villa Co-Co magic – but what happened next was a serious game changer. In the middle of the dance floor, Chris turned me into a spin and pulled me into him like he had done a dozen times before, except this time he held me there. His eyes fixed on mine so intently my smile slowly fell from my face. And for the first time Chris leaned forward and in front of his mates – *our mates* – he kissed me, *really* kissed me. Cupping my face, Chris kissed me with no mind of who saw or what whistles and cheers and taunts came from around us (and there were plenty of those). Chris Henderson kissed a girl for all to see and my heart swelled with absolute tenderness and joy, because that girl was me.

Can't wait to read more about the Onslow Boys?

Be sure to catch the exciting spin-off to C.J Duggan's Summer Series…

Forever Summer
'Adam & Ellie's Story'

By C.J Duggan.

2014

You see there's this boy.
He makes me smile, forces me to listen, serenades me out of tune and keeps me sane, all the while driving me insane. He's really talented like that. But for the first time in since, well, forever, things are about to change. The question is, how much am I willing to lose in order to potentially have it all?

Add to Goodreads

Coming May 2014

Someone Like You

By C.J. Duggan

'Sometimes, life breaks your heart.'

The idea was simple enough. Lock myself away for the summer, devour copious amounts of chocolate, and listen to 80s power ballads, all the while mastering a list that would help me completely reinvent myself to my friends back home.

Welcome to Operation Summer Fun: Get drunk, party hard, and lose my virginity!

But when the sound of piercing power tools drowned out my power ballads, my chocolate stash was devoured by tradies, and just when things couldn't get any worse and all hope was lost…

there was Rex Shervington.

Eighteen-year old Lola Kudrow has always followed the rules. But when her world is shattered by the ultimate betrayal, she flees the small town gossip and seeks refuge at her sister's house in the city.

With only a few weeks to reinvent herself before the dreaded Valedictory ball, her plan is clear: *It's time to break some rules.*

The one thing that definitely isn't a part of her plan is living on a building site, especially sharing it with the likes of Rex, the snarky, gorgeous builder who sleeps on the lounge room couch. The very same builder who accidently discovers her mortifying list of rules to be broken.

Operation Summer Fun is in full swing, and what could be more fun than a willing accomplice? Not much. Rex Shirvington is definitely no stranger to breaking the rules. And in the course of a few hot summer nights, he's going to help Lola break them *all.*

Acknowledgements

Writing is a very solitary endeavor, but it is the people by my side that make it so utterly rewarding.

Much love to my amazing husband Mick, for continuously reminding me to eat, drink and sleep. For being the beautiful part of my reality and supporting me in all I do, I know it's not easy but I wouldn't want to share it with anyone else.

I am blessed with such a talented hard working team, these ladies always go above and beyond for me. A special thanks to: Sascha Craig, Sarah Billington, Anita Saunders and Keary Taylor.

Many thanks to my formatters Karen Phillips, Emily Mah Tippets; my proofreaders Lori Hereford and Frankie Rose.

Always grateful for the love and support of my friends and family, especially Mum, Kevin, Dad, Daniel and Leanne.

My fellow Authors for their inspiration, support and friendship: Frankie Rose, Jessica Roscoe, Lilliana Anderson, Keary Taylor, Pepper Winters. I adore you ladies and would be truly lost without our daily chats.

To my fierce 'Team Duggan' warriors, for your unwavering support and enthusiasm. For always spreading the word and fighting the good fight to help put the Summer Series out there for the masses. I feel incredibly privileged to have each and every one of you on my team and in my life, thank-you.

A special thank you to Jessica Rt from the Three Bookateer's. For being the most lovely, helpful PA any author ever could hope for. I cannot thank you enough for your support and guidance.

To all the bloggers, reviewers, readers who have enjoyed and shared the Summer Series. For taking something away from the story, for loving and embracing the characters. In a world that is often dark enough, it has been an absolute pleasure injecting it with a bit of sunshine.

I am not sad that this story is over, because I will be taking you all back to Onslow very soon. And as for what is to come? … It's only the beginning.

About the Author

C.J Duggan is a Number One Best Selling Australian Author who lives with her husband in a rural border town of New South Wales, Australia. When she isn't writing books about swoony boys and 90's pop culture you will find her renovating her hundred-year-old Victorian homestead or annoying her local travel agent for a quote to escape the chaos.

That One Summer is Book Three in her Mature Young Adult Romance Series.

For more on C.J and 'The Summer Series', visit www.cjdugganbooks.com

NO LONGER PROPERTY OF
PUBLIC LIBRARIES OF SAGINAW

Made in the USA
Lexington, KY
19 January 2015